JUST INTENT

BY

J.J.KAMINSKI

ISBN (Paperback) 978-1-8380626-5-1

For more about the author, a background to this story, and details of new editions, visit:

www.jjknovels.com

Cover design and illustrations by JClassix.

Previous Titles

HONOURED MEMORIES

DUTY BOUND

Coming Early 2022

COLD DECEIT

MAP OF THE MEDITERRANEAN REGION

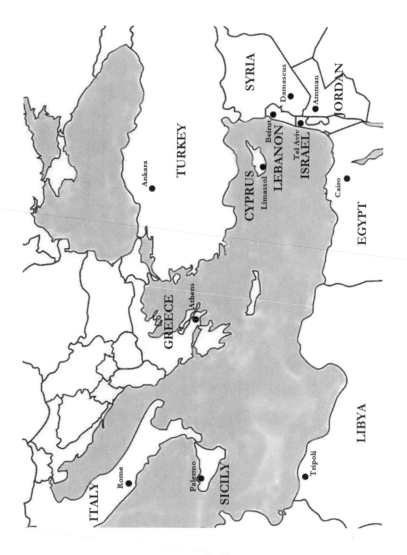

1   July 22nd, 1973

Kfar Remen, Lebanon

It was the fourth day of the stakeout, and still no sign of activity from the target of their surveillance – a large, two-storey house in the sparsely-populated, eastern outskirts of *Kfar Remen*, a city in the *Nabatieh Governate*, in southern Lebanon. Ray stepped back from the tripod-mounted binoculars and, interlocking his fingers, raised his arms above his head, stretched, and eased the tension in his lower back. He massaged the back of his neck, then glanced at his watch – 6:46 pm.

"Less than an hour before dark," he muttered, unconsciously stroking the week's growth on his chin.

"I'll take a turn," Simeon said, handing him a metal mug of sweet milky coffee.

The team were set up on the second floor of an abandoned metal fabrication shop – a large, corrugated metal building some three hundred metres from their mark and on the other side of a shallow, overgrown gully. A few pieces of rusting equipment and a lingering odour of oil and grease – still permeating throughout the disused building – was the only residue of a productive past. Ray wandered over to a make-shift table and sat on a metal folding chair next to Avi and frowned but said nothing. Avi smiled reassuringly.

[1]

"Do not worry, my friend. Our intel is solid. We just have to be patient." He was right, of course. They had no idea how long they would have to wait, and his intelligence was more often reliable than not. Ray nodded in silent acquiescence, then took a sip of the hot brew, and stretched out his legs.

Avi was muscular build with a chiselled face, buzz cut, a perpetual heavy stubble and stood two inches shorter than Ray's six-foot-one-inch frame. An expressive yet calm and steadfast individual in his late thirties, he was also the leader of a specialist unit of highly-skilled ex-members of the *Israeli Defence Force* (IDF) and trained in undercover operations. What made the team members particularly unique was their native language Arabic, enabling them to operate deep in Arab-held and occupied territories.

Ray's association with the contingent dated back to late 1970 when they worked together to track down and uncover a contract killer and a mysterious organisation, *Alhalu* (the *Solution*). During a previous incursion into Lebanon – while chasing a suspect – Ray had saved Avi's life. Since then, they had become firm friends and remained in touch – albeit infrequently.

"All quiet outside," reported Gila – one of the two female members of the group – as she came towards them across the metal walkway carrying her Israeli manufactured *Galil Short Automatic Rifle (SAR)* loosely by her side. A classic, dark-haired Jewish beauty whose looks belied her fighting prowess. "Any coffee left?"

She brushed her hair off her brow, then took a mug from Avi and sat on an old, worn-out leather settee, placing her weapon by her side. She gave Ray a dazzling smile with her stark-black, almond-shaped eyes under thick lashes as she cradled her drink. He grinned back and arched his eyebrows at the sudden snoring from Dalfon, who had been on the early-morning shift and was still asleep on a canvas camp bed.

"That man can sleep anywhere!" she chuckled.

"What time is it?" an awoken and drowsy Rani asked from the neighbouring bed.

"Just past seven," replied Avi leaning over to pour out another coffee for the fifth member who had shared the watch with Dalfon. Rani swung his legs off the bed and yawned, rubbed the sleep from his eyes, then ran his hands through his hair. He got up, stretched his tall frame, walked over to Avi, took the drink, and sat beside Gila.

Terach – the sixth and last member of their mission – came up the stairs from where the team's canvas-covered truck was parked in a loading bay at the back of the building.

"Did I hear coffee mentioned?"

"Okay?" Avi referred to their vehicle. The truck was Terach's responsibility. He checked it regularly to ensure it would fire up and be ready when needed. They would need to move fast when the time came.

"Yeah, no problem." He reached for the coffee pot. "Great!" he exclaimed on finding it empty.

"We have activity!" Simeon suddenly urged from the window.

Ray and Avi sprang off their chairs. Ray grabbed a pair of binoculars off the table and darted to the window. Simeon stepped back, allowing Avi to view through the tripod-mounted field glasses. They watched as three vehicles pulled up outside the house – a dark-blue Mercedes-Benz followed by two dusty, sand-coloured Toyota Land Cruisers. Ray counted nine men armed with *Kalashnikov* assault rifles exit the four-wheeled cars and spread out around the vehicles – alert and looking in all directions. Four entered the premises leaving the others outside.

[3]

Ray and Avi continued watching. A short time later, one returned to the vehicles and walked over to the Mercedes. He leant down to the front window and appeared to speak to an occupant. The nearside back door opened, and another armed individual stepped out. He walked around the car and stood back as a hooded figure was pulled roughly out from the vehicle on the opposite side of their vision. Bundled between two of the captors, the man was hurried through the gate and into the building.

"I think we can safely assume that's *our man*," said a somewhat relieved Avi standing up and rubbing his hand over his face. He had set a lot of store in the intelligence, and had it failed to materialise, not only would there be eggs on faces, but valuable time would have been wasted. Time that was running out each passing day.

Their *man* was *Ariel Brachfield*, the oldest of two children of *Ezra Brachfield*, a billionaire newspaper baron – a close associate of the British Government, and particularly the Israelis. A business magnate who also invested heavily in Israel in publishing, textiles, and agricultural products. The twenty-two-year-old son was taken three months earlier while on holiday in Cyprus. The abduction was believed to have been carried out by a splinter group of the *Palestine Liberation Organisation (PLO)*. The group demanded five million U.S. Dollars and the release of six of its faction – currently reluctant guests of the Israeli Government.

The father was more than prepared to pay the ransom. However, the Israeli Government was unwilling to free the six individuals behind the bombing of a bus in Israel's most populous city, *Tel Aviv* – killing twenty of its citizens and injuring scores more. The Israelis were concerned about the possible political fallout should they have been seen to have even considered the demand or agreed.

[4]

Their procrastinations frustrated the media baron, and in desperation, he turned to the conservative British Government to add diplomatic pressure on the Israelis. Concerned with a growing threat from the country's Liberal Party and several upcoming by-elections, alienating Brachfield and losing support from his media network was too risky to contemplate. So, the British approached the Israeli government, hoping to secure a diplomatic solution. The Israelis, however, remained steadfast in their inflexibility.

"My dear, Prime Minister," the Israeli Prime Minister had stressed during an early telephone conversation with the British counterpart. "Do you really believe that the young man's life – tragic as it may be – can be evenly weighed against the lives of the twenty mutilated bodies we salvaged during that horrific episode? And what of the others who survived and are still dealing with their injuries?" It was a standpoint that could not be denied, turning the scales against the British Conservative Party's political aspirations. Another course of action had to be considered.

After careful deliberations, suggestions and counter-proposals, both governments eventually agreed that extraction was the only way to resolve the matter. Brachfield was naturally against the idea, worried that his son would be placed in greater danger – even offering to increase the ransom. He was finally made to see that a rescue was the only viable option. Who was to say that once the money was paid, the captors wouldn't continue to hold onto him and further their demands or, worse, kill him anyway? The threat was always present.

Having agreed on the course of action, the Israeli Government continued to play along and made as if they were playing hardball – stalling. The news media, unbeknown of the charade's real reasons, continued to report on fake progress. Meanwhile, the people tasked with the extraction were Avi Gershen's team.

Ezra Brachfield was a British citizen, and accordingly, *the powers that be* on the Brit's side believed that a British involvement should be included. After all, it was reasoned, should the operation turn out a success, valuable political points would be there for the taking. The Conservative Government would be able to claim some of the credit. A stand against acts of terrorism would go down well with the electorate – a threat the British public was only too aware with the ever-increasing violence perpetrated by the Provisional Irish Republican Army. The timing couldn't be more opportune, especially when the Conservative Party would soon be contesting several by-elections. On the other side, a handful of Israeli sceptics reasoned that should the operation fail – God forbid – it would be best to share the blame and potential backlash. Both sides could gain – whatever the outcome.

Fielding a British team, however, was not feasible. And so it was that Captain Ray Kazan – a decorated officer of British Military Intelligence and who had recently completed a two-year stint fighting the guerrilla insurgency in Oman – was appointed to join the group. An experienced soldier and operative with tactical experience, Ray also spoke fluent Arabic. His knowledge and prior dealings in the region and Avi's team made him the obvious candidate. He had joined the operation the previous month. The team's initial task was to locate the kidnappers' whereabouts and their captive, so an extensive network of informants was put to work. Brachfield's unconditional provision of two-hundred-thousand U.S. dollars greased the wheels, and soon information was quietly flowing to their side.

"Like weeds coming up out of the ground!" Avi had remarked.

The team soon realised that the kidnappers were constantly swapping venues making it difficult to pinpoint the exact place and, therefore, to stage a rescue. Their break came seven days earlier with what was considered to be the most reliable intelligence of a location to which the group was to move to next. No specific date was given when the move would occur other than *in the next few days*.

They were already geared up and prepared to mobilise at a moment's notice and were set up within eight hours. One lucky informant would soon receive a handsome reward should the information bear out!

"The Merc is leaving," Ray said, still glued to the binoculars. "It looks like we'll have ten to contend with."

"Enough to go around!" Avi gave Ray a cocky wink.

They stepped away from the window as darkness began to close in.

"Screen up, Dalfon," instructed Avi, seeing him awake and rise off the bed.

They waited by the table while Dalfon hung a large sheet over a make-shift frame behind Simeon – who had again taken up surveillance at the tripod – before lighting two kerosene lamps. The screening would avoid illuminating the window and alert their presence. Avi unrolled a sheet of paper and placed each of the two lamps on the top corners, casting a light over the building's two-floor hand-drawn plan.

Ray and Avi had climbed the perimeter wall at the rear of the property the first night of the surveillance, managing to get inside through a back window. Outfitted with the latest USA produced *AN/PVS-5 Night Vision Goggles,* they were accurately able to recreate the floorplan without switching on the house lights. The third-quarter moon's luminescence aided the equipment's built-in infrared, light source significantly adding to their view of the darkened premises. Ray was taken with the spooky-looking contraptions' with the two protruding tubes.

"Ray and I believe they will most likely keep him in one of the upstairs rooms at the back of the building," said Avi, pointing out the two rooms on the plan the two had considered during their recce.

"Makes sense," agreed Gila looking over Ray's shoulder.

"We have ten to contend with unless more people join them before the night's out," Ray said. "Anything new, Simeon?"

"Looks like just the one outside the gate at the moment," Simeon answered from the other side of the screen.

"We can safely assume they were not expecting anyone to be lying in wait for them when they arrived, and I very much doubt that they are too concerned at the moment..., certainly for the immediate period. It would make sense for us to go in during their most vulnerable point... sometime in the early morning," Ray added. "Assuming they have smarts," he continued, "they will most probably take four six-hour shifts considering their small number."

He checked his watch – 8:12 pm.

"I'm assuming they will change over sometime between midnight and two in the morning."

"We'll go in then one hour after their second change," Avi cut in. "The one-hour delay should ensure the first guys have settled in for the night. We all know how tiring keeping watch can be."

"I'll put on the coffee," Terach offered and picked up the pot. "As you guys didn't leave me any!" he added, giving the others a sour look. They spent the next hour planning the extraction until everyone was fully clued to their roles.

"Remember, we go in hard and leave no trace of being here. No witnesses!" Avi stressed, touching the forehead with his forefinger.

"Avi. A quiet word?" Ray led away from the others towards the stairs.

Avi leant back against the loading dock, safety railing next to the truck and removed a packet of *Marlboro Gold* cigarettes from his shirt pocket. He opened the flip-top and impulsively offered one of the contents to Ray.

"Sorry! Forgot you don't smoke," he said apologetically and pulled one out for himself, then replaced the packet and lit up the cigarette with a butane lighter. Ray waited patiently for Avi to finish. He drew in deeply, then exhaled a thick-blue cloud of smoke towards the corrugated roofing.

"Something's been on your mind," he said. A statement rather than a question, then inhaled again.

"I'm intrigued. Why wouldn't you want to question these characters first? Surely the intelligence could be worth something?" Ray said.

"Come on, Ray! Let's not forget we're taking a huge risk being here, and the longer we stay, the riskier it gets. This part of the country is crawling with our enemies who would delight in burning us – given a chance. Cross-border violence has increased beyond reason since the PLO leadership and its *Fatah* brigade's expulsion from Jordan. It's also getting a lot tougher getting in and out of the country. Right now, we're invisible – we don't exist. As soon as we go in for the extraction, we'll have shown ourselves – be exposed… vulnerable. Once we've got the kid, we still need to travel some fifty kilometres to our pick-up point. The chopper will also take around thirty minutes to reach us, leaving us unprotected for even longer. We can't afford to betray our presence. You know that as well as I do!"

Avi broke off as he drew heavily on his cigarette.

"Look, Ray… the last thing we want is to drag along

an unwilling prisoner who may or may not have valuable intel. Our priority is junior's safe return. Once we go in, we can't afford to leave any of those pricks alive." Avi paused again briefly. "I have my orders, Ray. We are to secure the kid, eliminate the kidnappers and get the hell out of here. That's all!"

"I understand all that, Avi… But aren't you just a little curious?" Ray understood only too well the precarious position the team was in. Ray crossed his arms and fixed his gaze on his friend. He tilted his body closer.

"One thing has puzzled me from the start of this affair. We both know it takes a lot of planning and logistics to abduct someone as neatly as this kid was taken. We're also talking about Cyprus… an island nation some three-hundred kilometres across open water from the Lebanon mainland. We know this was no random action, Avi!"

"I think we can safely assume that… So what are you suggesting?"

"You've been involved in this from the start. What do you think?"

Avi shook his head.

"Okay. I can't say I haven't considered it. It does smell like whoever's behind the kidnapping must have known the kid's plans well beforehand. However, that's not our concern. I repeat, our job is to extract him and leave no one behind to talk about it. I'm sorry, Ray, but my official involvement ends there."

Avi threw down the half-smoked cigarette and stubbed it out with his boot. He was about to leave when Ray placed a restraining hand on his arm. Avi resumed his position against the railing. He had sensed that something had been troubling Ray since before they had set up their surveillance.

"I know you got a few leads directly from your informants… but have you truly considered the origin of this particular titbit... accurate as it may well turn out to be?"

"Come on, Ray, you know the two-hundred-thou' Brachfield put up would yield results, and this info' came from an undisputed source. And why question it now? It appears that it was correct."

"Let me put it another way... How many leads did you dig up, and of those, how many did you believe or find had any possibility of turning up trumps...? The remotest chance?"

"Okay. I admit... less than a handful was feasible."

"So, from where did this beautiful bit of insight come? And why would you have believed it to be worth the effort?" Ray stepped over and propped himself against the railing alongside Avi and exhaled deeply. "What troubles me, Avi," Ray continued, "is that we may be getting played again. It just seems all too bloody convenient! Too coincidental!"

"God, you're getting to be a cynical bugger!" scoffed Avi.

"It's working with you doubtful characters," he chuckled. "So, old friend... are you going to confide in me?"

"Where are you expecting this to lead you, Ray?"

"In truth... I don't know. But I'm beginning to get the same feeling I had when I was chasing down Nadeem Asghar in '70."

"Our Asghar! The killer behind the Paris murders?"

"Yes! Being led along but always one step behind. This time it would be good to be running parallel... at worst."

Avi didn't immediately respond.

"The information came from Feuerman," he offered eventually and removed the packet of *Marlboros* once again. He lit another cigarette.

"Shaul Feuerman?"

"Yes."

"But he's *Shin Bet,* isn't he?"

"Yes."

"Why would the Assistant Director of your *Internal Security* be involved with this operation... I thought its function was restricted to Israeli-occupied territories?"

"True. But the word is that *Mossad* were reluctant to get involved, arguing that it was not within their sphere of responsibility. It also involves a non-Israeli citizen, and they're stretched as it is. You know how particular that bunch of *prima donnas* can be! Anyway, I believe he volunteered for the assignment. So the PM tasked him with the job."

"Didn't you find that a little strange?"

Avi inhaled and blew out a plume of smoke before answering.

"No, why...? Should I have been? It's not that my unit hasn't worked with the *Shin Bet* before."

"You're reporting directly to him for this operation?"

"Yes. As I said, nothing unusual about that." He drew in another lung full of tobacco smoke.

"Come on, Avi, who would volunteer to get involved in something like this? If the operation were to go *tits up*, it could end careers. I'm not a politician, but I wouldn't want to touch this with a barge pole if I were... What can you tell me about Feuerman? Is he well-connected – capable?"

"As I said, I've had the occasional dealing with him. In truth, he always appeared to be an ambitious, climbing-ladder sort... Has a bit of an ego as well. Not quite the rough and ready type. Certainly never came across as someone who could operate at the sharp end."

"He certainly sounds every inch the politician."

"I don't see why you're getting so concerned about it. Let's get the kid and deliver him to *Pops* safe and sound."

[12]

"You may be right… Perhaps I am being a little too sensitive, or maybe it's merely my imagination overreacting." Ray pushed off the railing and turned to face Avi. "So, in truth, you dug up nothing, yet Feuerman comes up with the only information that's looking to pay off." Avi was about to draw on the cigarette, then hesitated. Ray continued to press him. "You're the one who's always asking questions of those in authority – wanting to know the reasons behind judgements, rules. Even flouting those rules if they don't appeal to you."

Avi remained quietly in thought for a moment, as if he was recalling something – a detail.

"Now you mention it… he appeared very cagey when I questioned his source. Sort of dismissed it with a speech about working together, collaborating, pooling resources…, that sort of thing. I was too wrapped up with the organising and preparedness to have given it any further thought."

"Has anyone else discussed this with you… other than he?"

"No, no… Not even my team was told anything. The first they knew was just before we set out… As were you."

"Was anyone else present when he gave you the info?"

"Just me and him. I was called to his office and given the details personally by him…, which I had to commit to memory. You know how it is. Nothing written… Anyway, what are you driving at?"

"Did he give you specific orders to liquidate the captors… or is it a decision you've made?"

Again Avi paused for a while. He smiled conspiratorially before responding.

"Okay. We won't be able to hang around, but we'll see what we can learn… Before we take down the bastards!"

2   July 23rd, 1973

Kfar Remen, Lebanon

From the moment he was forcibly seized and a hood thrust over his head, immersing him in darkness, Ariel Brachfield's world changed to one of solitary confinement and desperate hope. He and Michael, his holiday companion, were walking to a disco – two blocks from the hotel – following up on a promise from two scantily-clad German *chicks* they had sweet-talked on the beach that afternoon. They had just rounded the corner and out of sight of the hotel when a dark-coloured van screeched to a halt beside them. The abduction was sudden and over in an instant, leaving his friend frozen to the spot and in a state of shock.

Ariel tried to resist and struggle but was immediately rewarded with a hard blow to the side of the head for his effort. He couldn't recall how long he had bounced about on the hard, metal floor of the vehicle before being bundled aboard a boat and locked in a cabin below deck in what he soon was to discover was a fishing vessel. Given a bucket, he was penned up for the duration of the trip. A bowl of fish or chicken with rice was provided twice a day together with a mug of tepid water. By the end of the second day, the awful stench of fish and his bodily waste filled the stuffy air of the cramped space, permeating his nostrils. He promised himself that once he was freed, he wouldn't touch seafood again. That night, and back hooded, he was taken ashore. After another uncomfortable journey, he ended up in a poorly lit room on the first floor of an old, dilapidated building.

Ariel had no idea who had taken him. His captors rarely spoke to him other than curt instructions in broken English from the group leader. Kidnap for a ransom was the only logical conclusion. His father was extremely wealthy and would – he was sure – meet whatever sum was demanded to ensure an early release. He would just have to be patient and tolerate his nightmarish conditions.

From the little he knew of the Mediterranean region, he concluded from the length of the sea trip and his captors' language – he determined was Arabic – that he must be somewhere between Lebanon and Syria. He had lost all track of time. His *Rolex Submariner* watch – a two-thousand Dollar gift from his father on his twenty-first birthday – had been *confiscated* on the first day along with his cash and gold money clip. He was granted three toilet breaks and fed twice a day. One of the bathroom respites allowed him to wash, shave and clean his teeth. Meals were limited to either chicken or fatty mutton with rice and a small, plastic bottle of mineral water. It was sweltering and humid. The water and a creaking ceiling fan yielded token relief.

Hours crept into days, days dragged into weeks, and the weeks crawled into months. Often moved from one location to another and never knowing where, Ariel became increasingly troubled. No one said, and no one showed him any consideration. He was always kept in the dark – never allowed a light at night. Over time sleep came less easily, and hopes of release slowly started to fade.

A few weeks into his captivity, four scowling and sneering abductors burst into his room. Without a word, they manhandled him onto his knees and, gripping his outstretched arms tightly behind him, painfully held him in position. The leader entered shortly after wearing his permanent, angry stare and placed a pistol barrel against Ariel's trembling forehead. Ariel screwed his eyes tightly shut and breathed heavily as fear gripped his body. The captor held back for a few agonising seconds before pulling the trigger. The resultant *click* resounded through Ariel's head like a hammer blow. He was left shaking, tearful and with soiled trousers. A while later, he was given a change of clothes.

That night, sitting on the floor in the corner of the cell, hugging his knees tightly, he continually played through the horrific ordeal. Something had triggered the cruel, mock execution. He concluded that they must have conducted the awful exercise out of frustration. Maybe it had to do with negotiations for his release – or at least that's what he hoped. Maybe his captors were asking for too much. Maybe his father was still in the process of raising the money. Maybe… maybe. So many maybes! Thankfully, the incident was never repeated.

Ariel awoke with a start from another troubled sleep. The slightest sound put him on edge – always fearing the worst. He sat unmoving for several tense moments – listening, straining to hear. Muted voices and muffled movements were coming from the other side of the locked door. It was pitch-black, but he sensed it was still early morning.

Are they going to move me yet again? Please, God, no!

He heard the key turn in the lock and swung his legs apprehensively off the bed just as the door was pushed open. A moment later, the ceiling lamp illuminated the room. He blinked his eyes, adjusting to the sudden light, then opened them to see a tall, fair-haired man standing in the doorway. He inhaled sharply, then let out a gasp.

◆◆◆◆

Earlier: The interior of the building was in darkness. The only light source came from a lamp above the front door illuminating the courtyard. Under Simeon's watchful eye, Ray, Avi, and Dalfon were waiting alongside the property's right-hand side perimeter wall. The clear night sky and a third-quarter moon gave the unit's sniper enough light to clearly make out the two forms standing lethargically on either side of the entrance gate. He smiled to himself as he panned the binoculars away from the gate to Avi.

"Graveyard shift! Must have drawn the short straw," he muttered under his breath.

Rani had made his way to the back of the building and positioned himself, ready to take out anyone looking to get out the back door and over the wall. No one was to escape and live to tell what was to happen. The four had taken a wide berth in their approach to the house, mindful that the night's denser and cooler air carried sound further and was more pronounced. Meanwhile, Gila had silently made her way through the foliage along the shallow defile to a spot covering the front of the building. She lay on her stomach with her *Galil Rifle* cocked and aimed at the two parked vehicles. The team had earlier cleared any evidence of its presence back at the factory. Terach was stationed in the truck, ready to be given the *go-ahead* over the walkie-talkie.

Avi glanced at the luminous dial on his watch – 1:12 am. Time to move. He half-turned his head towards Ray, nodded a silent green light, and raised his right arm, signalling Simeon.

Simeon placed the binoculars on the window ledge and picked up his *L42A1* sniper rifle – a conversion of the famed *303 British Lee-Enfield*. He quietly rested the heavy,

[17]

hammer-forged barrel on the window frame through a broken section of glass, giving him an unobstructed line of fire. Pressing the rifle butt in the crease of his right shoulder, he rested his cheek on the *cheekpiece*, bringing his right eye level with the metallic scope. The sight had been adjusted earlier to the correct distance well within the weapon's effective range. A highly-trained and skilled sniper, Simeon did not need to account for the usual external factors that can affect the bullet's flight path over a greater span, such as wind, humidity, temperature, and air density.

He took in a deep breath and took careful aim, then slowly exhaled and squeezed the trigger. The weapon's *7.62 mm* round exploded out of the suppressed barrel and, in less than a blink of an eye, punched through the sentry's throat and embedded itself in the concrete wall behind. The man to the right of the gate was thrown back and slid down against the wall.

Startled by the sudden commotion and momentarily confused, the second guard turned towards his fallen colleague. Simeon kept his eye on the scope and panned left as he calmly and quickly worked the bolt again, putting another round into the chamber. He aimed again and depressed the hammer igniting the gunpowder in the cartridge. He ignored the recoil as the bullet travelling at a velocity of over two-and-a-half-thousand feet per second slammed into the second man's chest, pitching him against the wall, then sending him head-first to the ground.

The three were on the two guards in a silent instant. Avi immediately placed his index and middle finger on the carotid artery of the first man's neck to the side of the windpipe. Ray did the same to the second guard. Both had been killed outright. Avi looked briefly towards the gully in Gila's direction before quietly pulling down on the

[18]

gate's handle. He carefully pushed the gate open wide. The three released the safety catches on their cocked and silenced pistols, then soundlessly entered the tiled courtyard. They paused briefly, listening for any giveaway sounds, then just as soundlessly crossed over to the front door. Leaving the gate open, they left a watchful Gila with direct sight into the lit enclosure.

Avi placed his ear against the heavy wooden door and strained to hear for movement on the other side. He made a thumbs up with his left hand, then placed his hand on the lever. Taking a deep breath, he slowly pressed down and pushed the door inwards, inch by inch. Quietly releasing the handle, Avi stepped into the open lounge with Ray and Dalfon immediately behind him. They were greeted by loud snoring in the middle of the room.

Avi and Ray had decided not to use the night-vision goggles. If they were exposed to sudden light, the *blooming-out* effect would have rendered them blind and defenceless for a few dangerous moments. It was too risky. They would have to rely on their natural eyesight.

Ray recalled that the staircase was a few steps ahead of him and to their left. He closed his eyes tight for a few seconds before re-opening them – a trick he used to adjust his eyes to the dark. Human eyes take time to reach optimal sensitivity in low-light surroundings. The quarter moon's glare had filtered through the various cracks and openings in the building resulting in partial darkness. However, a total absence of light is a rare condition – even at night. Ray had become accustomed to operating in the dark during the two-year stint fighting communist guerrillas in the Dhofar mountains on the Oman/South Yemen border – acquiring exceptional night vision. Ray gently tapped Avi on the shoulder. As they both made their way to the staircase, they caught the *phut, phut* sound of Dalfon's pistol. The snoring came to an abrupt end.

[19]

Thankfully the stairs were made of stone – no creaking of dry timber treads contracting during the coolness of the night. They silently made their way to the second floor. Ray hesitated before stepping onto the spacious landing and looked around at the five doors. The one to his left and at the back of the building was where they assumed the kidnapped Brachfield would be held. It was closed – probably locked. The central one opposite led into a toilet and shower. It was also closed – no surprise there. The other three were ajar and in the dark, except for the one to the right of the shower room, which was radiating a soft light. The only sound they heard was snoring and muffled murmuring – the sort of mumbling that goes with heavy sleep.

Ray turned to Avi and motioned for him to remain, then stepped over to the closed door and tried the handle. It was secured. He stepped back, tapped his chest and indicated that he would take the lit bedroom. Avi nodded in return and pointed out the left door for Dalfon. The three immediately went about their business.

With his weapon at the ready, Ray gently pushed the door open to reveal a solitary figure lying on a metal-framed bed facing away from him – a blanket pulled up to his neck. Ray looked briefly over his shoulder, catching muted sounds of Avi and Dalfon's guns, then stepped into the room. He tapped the sleeper with the pistol sharply on the shoulder. The man stirred and gave a throaty grunt of irritation, then reluctantly rolled over and turned his head around to face the person who had disturbed his sleep. He let out a soft gasp as he stared wide-eyed into the barrel of Ray's *Browning Hi-Power* pistol.

"Up you get!" Ray ordered in Arabic.

It took the man a few seconds to realise what was happening. His expression changed from surprise to anger. He glanced at a Kalashnikov rifle leaning against the wall next to the bedside table with the lamp, then back at Ray. His eyes betrayed defiance.

"Uh, uh!" Ray whipped the man across the side of his head with the pistol barrel, immediately drawing blood. The man recoiled from the blow – his resistance quelled. Just then, Avi walked in.

"I'm assuming this chap's in charge," Ray said.

"Okay. The others are taken care of… now, let's see if we can get this asshole to talk," he said. "Why don't you see to the kid and leave this shit to me?"

"Where's the key?" Ray urged. The man's face had turned ashen. He raised his arms nervously, his palms outwards in surrender, then reached into his righthand trouser pocket and extracted a key. Ray took it and left the room, leaving Avi alone with the abductor. After all, it was his domain, and he had an in-depth understanding of the Arab mind. Avi was better equipped to carry out the *interview*.

Dalfon was on the walkie-talkie informing Terach when Ray walked across to the captive's room. Ray unlocked the door and switched on the light. Ariel Brachfield was sitting nervously on the edge of his bed, staring in disbelief at his rescuer.

"Don't be alarmed! My name's Kazan, Ray Kazan. We've come to take you home," Ray said, smiling encouragingly from inside the doorway. "Come! We don't have much time!" he urged.

Neither spoke as they made their way carefully down the staircase – Ray leading the way with Ariel's apprehensive hand on his shoulder. The house lights were deliberately left off. They would leave the place as they found it – in the dark. A shrill cry erupted from above, briefly pausing their descent. Ray smiled in wry amusement. Avi had just raised the interview an extra notch! He had no qualms with Avi's methods. They got what they deserved. Gila, Rani and Dalfon were waiting outside the building. They didn't have to wait long before Avi joined him.

"I have a name!" Avi declared with a conspiratorial grin.

3   July 27th, 1973

London, England

The last time Ray had been in Somerset House –
located in The Strand, in west-central London – was
in September 1970. Shortly after that visit, he had
embarked on an assignment to Jordan that was to change
his life dramatically.

He was running late. He had underestimated the ever-
growing London traffic. It also took him a while to park
his car. Before entering the expansive central courtyard
overlooking the River Thames, Ray paused briefly to
marvel at the majestic Neoclassical building. He glanced
at his watch, then hurried across to the main pillared
entrance. Three uniformed personnel were operating the
reception desk.

"Yes, I have you listed, Captain Kazan," confirmed
one of the men running his index finger down a list
attached to a clipboard. "The suite's on the first floor, Sir.
Would you like for me to take you up?" one of the other
staff offered as Ray was signing in.

"No need, thank you. I can find my way," Ray said,
looking towards the grand, spiral staircase. As he climbed
the stairs, he looked around at the splendour of the
building with its unapologetic show of grandeur. At the
top of the stairs, he continued down a long carpeted

hallway until he arrived at a door marked *Suite N12A*. He knocked and immediately entered.

"Captain Kazan. I believe...?"

"Good afternoon, Captain. It's nice to see you again."

A smartly dressed, middle-aged woman interjected politely, got up from behind her desk, then immediately crossed the floor to an inner door. She knocked, opened the door, announced Ray, and then, stepping aside, allowed him to go through.

Ray was greeted by a man elegantly dressed in a pin-striped, double-breasted *Saville Row* suit and sporting an Oxford tie under a white, starched collar. The man in his late-fifties exuded power, authority and *old money*. Sir Foster Braithwaite, Minister for Domestic and Foreign Intelligence Services – knighted in the latest New Year's Honour's List for his services to the crown – stepped forward.

"My apologies, Sir. I underestimated the traffic," Ray said as he took the hand of the aristocratic gentleman.

"No apologies necessary, Captain," he replied, smiling warmly. "Introductions first... Of course, you are already more than acquainted with Colonel Madison and Toby Gilmore."

John Madison of British Army Intelligence, Ray's commanding officer before his two-year secondment to the Sultanate of Oman's army, stood in acknowledgement.

"Nice to see you again, Ray." In his mid-forties, he always reminded Ray of the British actor, David Niven, not just in looks and his neatly trimmed moustache, but also his relaxed and charming manner. "Incidentally, I read Brigadier Thomas's report. You are to be congratulated. You did a fine job over there."

"Thank you, Sir."

"We must catch up," he added before resuming his

. seat on one of two facing burgundy leather Chesterfield sofas.

"Afternoon, Ray!" greeted Toby Gilmore, the bespectacled man in his late-forties leaning against a large desk in front of two tall arched windows – a senior member of MI6 (Military Intelligence, Section 6 or better known as the foreign intelligence service of the Government of the United Kingdom).

"Toby!" Ray nodded in response at the man he had worked with during his Jordan assignment and most recently with the kidnapping of Ariel Brachfield.

"And this gentleman... is, Mr Benjamin Rutan... of the U.S. Central Intelligence Agency." Ray shot the Minister a questioning look before taking the hand of the American.

"Ben, please," responded the man clasping Ray's hand firmly. "Delighted to make your acquaintance," he said and sat on the sofa opposite the Colonel. The Minister noted Ray's bemused expression but didn't expand further on the CIA presence.

"Now that the introductions are out of the way, can I offer you a drink, Captain? As you can see, we've already started."

"Thank you, Sir," Ray took a seat next to his senior officer.

"I can only offer a rather excellent single malt scotch or a sherry – medium or dry."

"A Scotch would be fine," he replied, although he was more partial to vodka – a habit he had picked up from his father since before he came of legal drinking age.

Ray had tried a wide range of the various draught beers available at all English pubs, but unlike most of his peers, had not acquired the taste, preferring a vodka or a glass of wine – either red or white depending on his mood. His favourite was a Baczewski Monopolowa – commonly just referred to as the Baczewski. A legendary, Polish vodka and one of the few distilled from potatoes – a smooth and distinctive taste that evoked a warm feeling at the back of the throat. The Minister walked over to a sideboard and busied himself with a crystal decanter.

"As I recall, Captain, you take your whisky neat."

"Thank you," replied Ray, as he gave a cursory glance at the impressively large painting of a 19th-century sail ship riding a rough sea with sails fully-blown hanging above the sideboard – he recalled from his previous visit, then looked over at Toby. The MI6 man gave nothing away as he absent-mindedly rotated a tumbler in his hands. Ray turned his attention to the American. The CIA man returned his look with a polite smile – observing Ray with a level gaze. His presence spelt more intrigue. Ray sensed an unspoken understanding among the four that the Minister would be the one to open up the conversation and reveal the reason for his being summoned.

What revelation am I about to be hit with this time?

Foster Braithwaite handed Ray his drink, then sat next to the American facing Ray. He picked up a glass off the coffee table and, crossing his legs, leant back on the sofa.

"Now," mused the Minister, "where to begin?" He took a sip of his whisky and cleared his throat. "Firstly, congratulations are in order for the rescue of the Brachfield boy. By all accounts, it was a well-executed operation."

"I can't take the credit, Minister. I was merely invited along for the ride," said Ray.

"That's as may be, Captain, but the word from our Israeli friends is you conducted yourself with professionalism – a valuable contribution and a credit to our collaboration." He smiled broadly. "No need to sell short your participation." Ray nodded slightly with a light smile accepting the Minister's *pat-on-the-back*. The

[26]

extraction went well, and Avi had managed to prize a name from the lead kidnapper.

"I read through the debrief earlier today," he announced. "Toby has assured me of the thoroughness and completeness of your report. However..., I'm intrigued," he paused – his blue eyes widening as he leaned forward. "You appeared to have a concern with the source of the information that led to the exact whereabouts of Ariel Brachfield's location..., leading to the successful extraction." Ray hesitated momentarily.

Where was this leading?

He looked briefly at each of the other three in turn and cleared his throat.

"It was too convenient! Too easy! Information like that doesn't just fall into one's lap. I feel..., felt there was more to this kidnapping than met the eye," replied Ray coolly.

"The thing is, Ray, while you were sunning yourself in the mountains of Oman," Toby quipped, joining in the conversation, "we've been hearing..., learning more of this organisation. The one you seemingly encountered indirectly while in Jordan in '70. The same one Asghar mentioned to you before he died. This *Alhalu*. Nothing concrete, unfortunately... Breadcrumbs, here and there."

"I don't understand, Toby. Are you saying you believe it... they were behind the kidnapping?"

"We don't know. Like you, we have little to go on. Having read between the lines of your report, you looked to be pointing a finger at this Feuerman character?"

Ray looked blankly at the MI6 officer for a moment, then at the Minister. He had nothing concrete to share other than a hunch – a gut feeling. He had pushed Avi, and now Avi had a lead. It was up to the *powers that be* if it were to be pursued. He was no longer involved. Ariel Brachfield was back with his family – job completed. And Ray was seriously considering returning for a second two-year stint fighting the Dhofari rebels. He was missing the action.

"We would be interested to hear your reasoning, Captain," pressed the Minister. Ray hesitated momentarily.

"It was just a notion…a hunch, a sneaking suspicion that something wasn't right. A couple of points didn't seem to add up," Ray started. "First – as I mentioned earlier – it was the lucky tip-off… Too convenient! The other was the direct order to eliminate the kidnappers, no questions asked, no intelligence sought. It was only when I pressed Avi Gershen, the team leader, that he divulged the source of both. However, I wasn't suggesting anything beyond that. I hadn't heard a reference to the name, Alhalu since ending my assignment in Jordan, late 1970. The last time and most recently was from Asghar in Oman three months ago… and he was referring to the same time frame."

"Shaul Feuerman?" Colonel Madison intervened for the first time in the discussion, ignoring Ray's dismissal of the mysterious entity that appeared to be on their minds.

"He's the Assistant Director of Internal Security, whose function, I should add, is restricted to Israeli-occupied territories. There was no way the Brachfield boy would have been held in Israel. It wouldn't have made sense. So, why would the *Shin Bet* have become involved? Even stranger was that Feuerman had volunteered to head the operation. I found that all too… expedient."

"You're suggesting that he would have been in a perfect position to control events and cover tracks if tracks were indeed needed to be covered," said Toby Gilmore.

"It certainly appeared that way. I was accused of being overly cynical," chuckled Ray recalling Avi's comment.

"Captain Kazan, Ray. Would you be good enough to

take us back to your assignment in September 1970 and rebuild the history? The recap would be useful and perhaps cast new light and also give Agent Rutan an insight," said the Minister fixing an intent look at him.

Ray shrugged his shoulders and, uncrossing his legs, leaned forward and put his untouched drink on the coffee table.

"As you directed, I was sent to Jordan in September 1970 to investigate the murders of both Professor Malouf and Peter Hamilton at the Paris Ritz Hotel. I was assisted by Lieutenant El Kordy of the Jordanian Army. You may recall, Toby, at the time other interests were at play, confusing progress and misleading our suppositions."

"You're referring to the Jordanian General?" cut in Sir Foster Braithwaite.

"Yes, Major-General Abdulkareem. He was the man who shot himself in front of Brigadier-General El Kordy, Lieutenant El Kordy and me when he was confronted with complicity in the murders. He alluded to an association but wouldn't reveal the name..., fearing for his family."

"El Kordy...? Both with the same family name?" the Minister cut in again.

"The Lieutenant and I were at Sandhurst and graduated together... We're... close friends. The General is his uncle."

"I see," said the Minister and nodded for Ray to carry on.

"We subsequently deduced the General directed a subordinate of his, Captain Rahal, to kill the Professor and to secure King Hussein's letter to Golda Meir." Ray took a sip of the whisky before continuing. Details of his engagement three years earlier – all but forgotten – were flooding back to him.

"We believed the General or whoever he was in league

[29]

with was also behind an ambush that killed Lieutenant-Colonel Almasi. We were escorting the Colonel to Military Intelligence at the time of the attack. We were of the belief he was going to confess his involvement or at least provide damning information. It was another frustrating incident that took us to yet another impasse."

"Intrigue upon intrigue!" declared Foster Braithwaite.

"It was certainly that," chimed in Toby Gilmore.

"We shouldn't forget that Ray was caught up in the ambush, and if not for his and Lieutenant El Kordy's quick reactions, would themselves have been killed. They managed to take out all of the attackers." Ray smiled warmly at the Colonel's intervention. He noted that all the while, the CIA agent sat silently listening intently to his account.

"Unfortunately, none of them survived, so we were unable to question them as to who was actually behind the attack. A short while later a Captain Abboud of Army Records was suspiciously killed in a car accident. Again by a person or persons unknown. However, we concluded that he was indirectly involved – an incidental casualty" Ray smiled at the CIA man and added. "Collateral damage…, like you, Americans like to phrase it!"

"I need a top-up before you continue with your account, Captain," said the Minister turning to Toby Gilmore. "Would you do the honours, Toby?"

The MI6 officer refilled the others' glasses, then leaned against the desk. Ray declined. The Minister urged Ray to continue with his account.

"Captain Rahal was found dead in a hotel room in Irbid, Jordan, a couple of days later. The MO was the same, and the bullets also matched those that killed Hamilton, the Under-Secretary. That was when we could conclude Nadeem Asghar's existence, the killer of both men. Although at the time we didn't know who he was, other than we assumed he was working for the same people with whom General Abdulkareem was conspiring."

"Ray eventually tracked down the man's identity in Paris," added Toby Gilmore, reminding the Minister, who nodded his recollection.

"That was only possible following information Avi Gershen's team obtained. The *Mossad* agency was able to come up with a rough profile. Anyway, following a *tip-off*, we cornered him in a hotel in Tyre. We almost had him. I chased him over the rooftops. However, he managed to escape even with a damaged ankle."

"You sound as though you admired the man," said the Minister. His comment wasn't accusatory.

"He could have easily killed me at one point but chose not to. Anyhow, that was the only and last time I set my eyes on him until four months ago when he happened to turn up in Oman and appeared in my rifle scope..."

◆ ◆ ◆ ◆

Four-and-a-half months earlier.
Dhofar Mountains (Jebel), Southern Oman.
Ray raised the rifle, placed his left elbow on his left knee, rested his cheek on the *cheekpiece* bringing his right eye in line with the scope, and slowly adjusted the sight to five-hundred. He had a relatively wide field of fire from his site and a stable shooting position. Slowly and with little movement of his body, he rotated the bolt-handle anti-clockwise and drew it towards him – releasing one of the ten rounds into the chamber. Just as deliberately, he pushed the bolt forward, turning it clockwise into a locked position. He was ready for a kill.

An eerie silence loomed over the steep escarpment sloping towards the boulder-strewn ravine below as the thirteen men of *Badger* Command remained hidden and deathly still – lying in wait. A solitary spectator aided by rising thermals circled high above the Dhofar Mountains with outspread wings – scanning the ground, watching – hopeful for carrion. Ray focused in on the guerrillas' point-man leading a heavily-laden camel, then slowly panned the rifle in pace with the man's progress towards the planned kill zone.

He pressed the rifle in the crease of his right shoulder and lowered the sight aiming at *centre mass* – the largest part of the target's body. He took in a deep breath, then, without delay, slowly exhaled and squeezed the trigger. The bullet slammed into the man's chest, threw him backwards, and sent him sprawling to the ground.

The resounding *takka-takka* of the GPMG – manned by Sergeant Hunar Singh – and barking sounds of the team's rifles immediately sprang to life, throwing the guerrilla's supply column into complete disarray. Maintaining his view on the ensuing panicked commotion, Ray calmly worked the bolt placing another round into the chamber. His second shot caught another unsuspecting and bewildered enemy in the throat, ceasing his scramble for cover.

He was calmly looking through the scope for his next target when he caught sight of a figure that stood out from the rest of the ragtag *adoo* (enemy). The man had taken refuge behind a fallen camel and was shouting and signalling his desperate comrades. His height, demeanour, and clothing suggested he was someone of import – more than likely, the group's leader. Ray decided to concentrate his targeting on the man. A leaderless unit quickly becomes disorganised and ineffective. He trained his rifle at the rebel's position when the man suddenly burst out from behind the dead animal and dashed across to a rocky outcrop to Ray's left. Ray followed him and fired just as

[32]

the man threw himself behind a large boulder. The bullet ricocheted off the stone surface, missing him by a margin. Ray kept his eye on the scope as he worked the bolt again, putting another round into the chamber. He was focusing on his objective when the distinctive roar of a jet-powered plane shooting overhead heralded the arrival of a *BAC167 Strikemaster*, closely followed by a second attack aircraft. He was momentarily distracted as the two planes rose and looped back, discharging two air-to-ground rockets each at the insurgents' position.

Turning his attention back to his target, Ray traversed the rifle to the man's location. The aircraft's sudden appearance and the resultant explosions brought the man out for a brief moment from behind the boulder – enough time for Ray to take aim in an instant… and fire. He saw the man lurch to the side and drop behind the cover. Ray wasn't sure if his bullet had found its mark.

The two jets swept over the target area for a final run indiscriminately spraying *7.62mm* rounds from their machine guns, then gave a *goodbye wing-wave* and flew off southwards. Ray rested the weapon against the inside of his knee and scanned the devastation below through his binoculars. Sergeant Singh, meanwhile, had ceased firing along with the rest of the team. The surviving insurgents had already fled the destruction and were nowhere to be seen. Ray stood up and cautiously looked around.

"Sergeant Major!"

"Sir?" acknowledged the *Sikh* Sergeant.

"Move further down and pick a spot to cover us while we conduct a sweep."

Once the Sergeant had set up the machine-gun, Ray and his team's remainder made their way down and moved abreast slowly through the carnage. The rebels had suffered eighteen dead, with three severely wounded. Private Murshidi stopped at one of the mules tossing its head and attempting to stand, then put it out of its misery with a bullet between the eyes. All six camels and eight mules had been killed.

"Corporal Khan." The burly figure of one of the Pakistani soldiers immediately approached Ray.

"Captain Sahib?"

"Take this," he said, unshouldering the Lee-Enfield sniper rifle, then passed it to the soldier. "Pull the dead over to the side. They'll be recovered once we've left. And tend to the three wounded. See what you can do. Salvage whatever ammunition we can use and carry, then smash the remaining weapons against the rocks and pile them…, then blow the lot up."

"Yes, Sir!" He set about instructing the men.

Free from carrying the weighty rifle, Ray walked over to where he had seen the man fall. He peered earnestly around the boulder. Nothing!

"Did I miss him?" he muttered under his breath.

He moved around the stone and noticed a smear of red on the rock face. A line of spattered blood on the ground led away from the spot. It was apparent the man was wounded and was attempting to get away. The possibility that he was still alive could be an intelligence bonus. Ray cocked his Kalashnikov and set off warily in pursuit of the wounded insurgent.

He made his way slowly up a gradual incline through the craggy terrain, alert to the possibility of coming face-to-face, and without warning, with an armed and desperate enemy. He had covered quite a distance when a tremendous explosion, immediately followed by two more, stopped him in his tracks. He glanced over his right shoulder with a rueful grin. His team was destroying the weapons and ammunition, denying more deadly supplies for the rebel forces. Collecting himself, Ray continued to follow the trail of dark-red blotches further up the slope

[34]

when he spotted a cave opening. He paused and looked around before edging closer to the entrance. He held his breath and squinted into the semi-darkness. His quarry was inside the hollow, sitting with his back against the wall – his head slumped on his chest.

The sudden sound of crunching stone under Ray's feet alerted the man. He lifted his head and placed his hand on the weapon laid across his lap.

"Ah, ah! I wouldn't do that if I were you!" Ray spoke in Arabic. A crooked smile broke across the man's face as he removed his hand – a smile of submission. He looked up at Ray and nodded – his breathing rapid and shallow.

"Was it... you?" he asked.

"Me... what?" said Ray as he squatted in front of him and removed the man's gun, then tossed it to the side.

"You... shot me?"

"I need to staunch the bleeding," Ray said as he lay down the Kalashnikov, then started to unwind the *shemaagh* (large square cloth) from around his head.

"It's... too late for that," laboured the man.

Ray ignored him and folded the green cloth into a pad, then, leaning forward, applied it to the man's blood-soaked abdomen.

"Press gently on this."

The man's face twisted into a grimace as he reluctantly placed a shaky hand onto the make-shift compress.

"Thank you..." He spoke in English.

Ray bore the man no grudge. They were no different. Both were fighting a cause, and who was to say either was more righteous or just than the other. Who could truly assume the higher moral ground? They were mere pawns in a game of political chess played by power-driven politicians. Puppets whose strings were pulled by men who lacked the moral courage to do the dirty things they expected of others.

For his part, Ray was a professional soldier who was dispassionately prepared to take an enemy's life. Yet, when confronted with his action's helpless and defenceless result, compassion for his fellow man took over. He looked closely into the rebel's eyes. Even in the diminished light, he could sense an intellect and intelligence. Recognition suddenly dawned on him. The full-grown beard had disguised the younger, clean-shaven face in the photograph.

"Nadeem... Nadeem Asghar!" he blurted out.

"Do I know you," he struggled – naked anguish in his voice.

"I chased you... over the rooftops in Tyre."

"Hmm," he managed a smile. "Ah, yes... I remember."

Ray stepped back and sat on a small rock facing him. Perhaps now Ray would get the answer to questions that had been nagging him since that day. And maybe finally identify the person who had killed the Under-Secretary.

"Why didn't you shoot...? You had the chance."

"I don't know..." He gasped and coughed up vital fluid. Blood was beginning to clog up his airways. "It seemed... the right thing to do. It didn't feel right to kill you," he managed between shallow breaths.

His struggle to evade capture had added to his trauma, causing further damage to the internal organs inflicted by Ray's bullet. Ray waited patiently. There was nothing more he could do. A gut wound was a slow and agonising death.

"Was it you... who killed Hamilton? In the Paris Ritz?"

"There would... be no point... in denying it now," responded Asghar.

"Who employed you? Who was behind the decision to kill him?" It was a question that continued to burn at Ray.

"You... you have to understand... I was paid to do a

[36]

job. Who... who paid me was of little interest..." He winced and clutched his side as a wave of pain shot through him. "Although...I confess... I thought it was for the PLO."

"If it wasn't the PLO, then who was it?" Ray pressed.

"Alhalu. Then... they tried to have me killed... I was a loose end. You were to have been my executioner."

"Who the hell is this, Alhalu?"

"I know... no more than you seem to know. I... I had to protect myself." Nadeem raised his head wearily and gazed intently into Ray's eyes. "We are no different... you and me... We both kill."

"Maybe so," replied Ray, "but I'm no killer."

"Because you kill from... behind a uniform?" Nadeem suddenly bent forward, coughing and spluttering up thick, bloodstained fluid. He was in great pain and dying fast.

"I visited your parents' graves," said Ray diverting the subject by way of consoling the dying man.

"Yes. I was there... behind the tree... I saw you pay your respects. I thank you for... for that."

The sudden loud thrumming of rotor blades, sounding past their location, distracted Ray. He got up to leave.

"Wait!" Nadeem's breathing had become more laboured. He swallowed hard before continuing. "If you revisit... the graves... look... look under the flowers," he managed. Ray pondered the cryptic comment momentarily before hurrying outside to alert his team.

He returned a short while later. Nadeem Asghar was leaning with his head against the wall – his lips were holding a faint smile. Ray gazed down at the enigmatic killer, then leant over and gently closed his eyelids. He noticed a silver chain dangling through the fingers of the dead man's left hand, clutching something to his chest. Carefully prising open the hand, Ray removed a silver medallion. He recognised Saint Joseph's figure – the patron saint of justice – and smiled to himself at the irony. The inscription on the back read:

With lots of love, Henri and Gabrielle.

◆ ◆ ◆ ◆

"It was simply a pure stroke of luck... a fluke! What could be the odds? We had chased him without success. He was a shadow – always one step ahead. The only explanation had to point to inside knowledge... Then, as chance would have it, I unknowingly shot him two years later."

"A fascinating turn of events," interrupted the Minister, "and one that has possibly shed some light on this enigma... this Alhalu... Please continue."

"Until he mentioned the name, we only had an inkling of its involvement but no direct evidence. He himself had become a target – a loose end as he referred to it. Whoever was behind the affair was also covering tracks, which might suggest we were getting closer or had gotten too close to a tangible connection."

"Enter, Deputy Prime Minister, Malik Nazari, stage left," offered Toby.

"We believed so. Two days after Asghar managed to evade capture, Baqar..., that is, Lieutenant El Kordy, and I were called to a murder scene. It turned out to be Jordan's ex-DPM's home. Both security men and the DPM were shot with Asghar's particular *modus operandi*. A bullet to the chest followed by a fatal headshot. The safe was opened and had been cleaned out."

"The King's letter?"

"Asghar didn't say, but as you know, I recently recovered
it from a box buried between his adopted parents' graves. The only logical explanation was that Asghar had taken the letter from the safe. It also implied that Malik Nazari

[38]

and General Abdulkareem were in bed together – so to speak. We have to assume they were participants of a well-connected group."

"The King's letter?" the CIA agent queried.

"It wasn't mentioned in the report you, that is the CIA received, but there's no harm in divulging the importance of it now… Now that it's been returned and untouched," the Minister responded. "In brief, it was a personal plea from the King to the Israeli Prime Minister requesting they abstain from attacking the PLO during the Jordan Army's campaign against the organisation during September 1970. The conflict referred to as *Black September*. We believe the acquisition of the letter was the motive behind the murders. Had it fallen into the wrong hands, it would have resulted in a diplomatic disaster for the Jordan government with the very real possibility of the fall of the Hashemite reign."

"And you believe this Alhalu mob was involved?"

"Conceivably, potentially yes. Who knows? But then, we still couldn't get a handle on who was actually behind it all," replied Ray. "The trail for us ended there on both fronts until I discovered Asghar's identity in Paris a couple of months later. His details were passed around the various intelligence agencies, included the CIA," he added, casting a questioning glance at Ben Rutan. He saw no need to mention leaving the medallion in place of the letter. It was a personal sentiment. Ray felt he owed that much to the killer who had spared his life.

"It would appear this Asghar character had done the Jordanians a big favour!" chuckled the American.

"You'll be pleased to know that the letter – still sealed albeit a little weathered – has been returned to King Hussein. He was delighted and relieved to receive it. A diplomatic triumph, I may add," said the Minister. "I congratulate you again, Captain. A job well done."

Ray nodded in appreciation.

"Well then," started the Minister sitting up and stretching his lower back, "I think it's time we brought the good Captain up to speed."

"We believe, Ray, that…"

"Sorry to butt in again, Toby. Before we get too entangled in the matter," broke in the Minister. "To what extent are you *au fait* with the current state of Middle-Eastern politics and, more specifically our… that is, our sphere of influence and interests?" He directed the question at Ray.

"As you may recall, Sir, I headed the Middle East desk at Military Intelligence before my secondment to Oman. Since then, I have only maintained a peripheral curiosity. Nothing in-depth or specific," Ray responded cautiously.

In truth, his interest in the roller-coaster of the region's politics had largely disappeared after Leyla's death. However, he would occasionally feel pangs of guilt that he had not maintained contact with Baqar. He had deliberately stayed away and not visited during one of his furloughs while stationed in Oman – although it wasn't far! He had been wondering lately if it was high time to lay the ghost of Leyla's passing to rest. It wasn't that he didn't want to see him. It was to avoid bringing up the painful subject of Ray's love – Baqar's sister.

"Without wishing to bore anyone present, I think it a good idea to summarise. For the sake of understanding, as it were." Foster Braithwaite took a sip of his whisky before laying out the British Government's position and started by saying that its military commitment in the region was argued to be strategically unwarranted following the end of British rule in India '47. Central to the concerns lay in the investment and supply of oil, *ipso facto* the Suez Canal security.

"How can I put it delicately without embarrassing

ourselves in front of our American colleague? Following our postwar economy, the cost of the war weighed heavily on our treasury." He smiled awkwardly. "Accordingly, we have been unable to muster a requisite military response to challenge any serious threats against our concerns. As a consequence, we effectively opened the door for our American cousins to surpass us in influence in the region…, considering their economic and military power." He raised his glass towards the CIA agent in a show of acquiescence. Ben responded by lifting his with a wink and an apologetic smile.

Ray detected a deeper tone of regret in Sir Brathwaite's voice. The British Empire's fast erosion sat heavily with much of England's aristocracy – the ruling class's colonial self-consciousness. The idea of losing Britannic rule over a third of the world since the Second World War still caused discomfort among the privileged few. However, Sir Braithwaite continued his appraisal by stating that not all was lost. Britain's relationships with King Hussein of Jordan and the Sultan of Oman still remained strong. Their pro-British stance was regarded of great value to Britain. However, he did add that the Israelis could still be a little challenging at times.

"I should say," Sir Braithwaite carried on, "that we have successfully co-operated with our cousins on several occasions and directly collaborated with the odd project. With this in mind, we reached out to the CIA, and I am pleased to report that Agent Rutan has been tasked to work with us…. To provide whatever intelligence is required and assistance wherever possible… Hand in glove, so to speak." Ray continued listening intently to the Minister.

"Which leads me to the reason I have asked you to be here today. You were on leave on your return, and this has all occurred very much in the last forty-eight hours," the Minister singled out a still bemused Ray. "I have been charged with the creation of a specialised team or unit if you will. A unit that will operate outside the normal MI6 remit and with the CIA's direct assistance, whose influence and intelligence gathering virtues around the world – I have already extolled – would greatly enhance the unit's capabilities. It would also allow it to operate within MI5's domestic jurisdiction, given certain factors of international concerns. And that..., Captain Kazan, is where you come in." There followed an awkward silence while Ray took a moment to digest the information.

"Are you asking me to volunteer, Sir?" he said eventually, staring fixedly at the Minister.

"I... we were rather hoping you might accept the challenge without reservation, yes," he agreed with a reassuring smile. "There are few men with your qualifications." He hesitated momentarily before continuing. "I will not insult your intellect by trying to persuade you with implausible flattery, but we are all in agreement that you are the right man for the job. You possess a high level of initiative, are highly intuitive – as you have demonstrated on more than one occasion – are prepared to push limits and boundaries, have tactical skills, and experienced in military action. You also speak six languages... And I have been assured of your ability in personal, physical conflict."

"There is little that Toby's position aided by Agent Rutan's..."

"Call me, Ben. Please," interrupted the CIA agent.

"There is little that Toby's position, aided by... Ben's intelligence connections can't do. There's always *Interpol* to facilitate worldwide police cooperation. So why the need for such a unit?" Ray responded.

"You're right, of course, Ray. The idea...," Toby started.

[42]

"Sorry Toby, allow me," The Minister interjected again, clearing his throat loudly. "Sometimes, operations require a less formal approach – occasions that an unconventional and intuitive way serves best to achieve something. An indirect method, as it were. Take our involvement in Oman… Officially, we are not actively taking part in direct contact with the rebel force – supposedly only there to act as advisors – yet we are. However, the insurgency can only conceivably be quashed with our direct participation. You can attest to that. You've just spent two years operating on the frontline."

"I take your point, Sir… And I agree," said Ray. "Although, I have been considering returning to Oman for a second tour."

"We would very much like you on board, Ray," chimed in the Colonel. Ray cast a sceptical eye at his old commander.

"I take it you already have something in mind?"

"Tracking down this Alhalu outfit for a start," said Toby Gilmore.

Ray sat back with a fixed expression, absentmindedly twirling the polished-black band ring on his left hand's little finger. He sensed his life was going to take another sharp turn into the unknown – yet again. However, it would be a chance to settle an old score for Leyla's pointless death. Although the two were not directly connected to Ray, to him, they were inextricably linked. Had he not been engaged in the hunt for the mysterious organisation, he could have been there to protect her. And strangely, he also felt he owed it to Nadeem Asghar. An obligation to the man who chose to let him live, yet whose life he took. The enigmatic killer who only had to pull the trigger and end Ray's life but decided not to, and who himself became a target of the Alhalu – a loose end.

"I suppose I'm in!"

"Good, then without further delay, we can now discuss…"

The group was interrupted by a knock on the door.

"I'm sorry to disturb you, Sir Braithwaite. You did instruct me to notify you immediately your visitor arrived."

4   July 27th, 1973

London, England

Five pairs of curious eyes turned to watch as the unexpected visitor entered the room. Ray did a double-take. The fetching woman with coral-black hair tied back tightly in a bun, wearing a silky beige blouse under a black trouser suit with heels, was a picture of elegance. All five men instinctively leapt to their feet. Ray had only ever seen her dressed in unflattering, casual working clothes. This was not the same lady.

"Gentlemen, allow me to introduce Miss Gila Levenson."

"This is a surprise!" said Ray with a broad smile, once the formal introductions were over, and she took a seat on the settee between him and Colonel Madison. She gave him a cheeky grin.

"A pleasant one, I hope," she chuckled.

"I believe you are acquainted with your new partner," offered the Minister.

"Partner, Sir… I don't understand."

Sir Braithwaite turned to Gila.

"I assume you were put in the picture before travelling?"

"Yes, I was."

"Fully?

"Yes."

"Well, that leaves only you, Captain... and once again, my apologies. I am pleased to announce that Miss Levenson has been seconded to us... I believe you volunteered?"

"Yes, Sir."

"You could be far more effective with someone with Miss Levenson's experience partnering you," offered Toby Gilmore. "I trust you won't have any issues with our good fortune? Besides Miss Levenson's accepted skills and experience, her knowledge of the Mediterranean region would be of great benefit."

"I have no issues, Toby... But forgive me for my surprise. Yes, Gila is more than capable, and... she would be a pleasant alternative to the Scottish SAS character I worked with for the past two years," he smiled – referring to the brusque Sergeant James *Jock* Brody of the Special Air Services (SAS), his second in command in Oman.

"Good, then that's settled!" exclaimed the Minister.

"One point, though, Minister. Gila... uh, Miss Levenson is an Israeli citizen and could find travel inhibited..., restricted to certain countries. Forgive me for being blunt," said Ray.

"We have considered that. Miss Levenson will be provided British Citizenship and a diplomatic passport, as will you. No one need know her true nationality," Sir Braithwaite replied.

"My mother was born here before emigrating to Israel as a teenager," said Gila. "I'm half-British by birth."

"Well, your English is certainly good enough to pass," remarked Ray magnanimously.

"One other matter," the Minister said. "Please be careful not to overstep the boundaries of national proprieties and be sure to observe jurisdictions and protocols. We don't want you stepping on toes and risk

[46]

creating diplomatic embarrassments. You will mostly be operating covertly. If and when necessary, have either Toby or Agent Rutan pave the way with local authorities. Otherwise, it would be best you do not draw unwanted attention as you go about your business."

"Understood," responded Ray.

"Now, lady and gentlemen, if you will excuse me, I have a meeting with the PM. It wouldn't do to be late as I shall be discussing what has taken place here and in my administrative role pushing for an appropriate budget," said the Minister placing his empty glass on the table and standing up. "I'll leave you to cover the finer details between yourselves."

The group stood.

"Oh! I almost forgot. Ezra Brachfield would like to meet you – to thank you personally. He's staying at his Surrey estate over the weekend and asked if you would care to join him tomorrow afternoon. I suggest you take Miss Levenson along. Considering your suspicions, it might be a good place to start. Mary has the details. Good luck and good hunting," he added and left the room.

"Delighted to have you onboard, Ray… And you too, of course, Miss Levenson," Colonel Madison said before departing.

"I'll walk out with you," offered Toby Gilmore.

"I'm at a loose end, myself," said the CIA agent. "Look, I came across a quaint English pub last night. It's at the back. A couple of blocks up. Would you care to join me?"

"I'd love to," responded Gila. "Unfortunately, I've only just arrived and would like to sort myself out."

Ray glanced at his watch.

"I can make time," he said as they filed out into the outer office. The Minister's secretary handed Ray a typed note with the Brachfield's country address. Ray checked the detail, then turned to Gila and asked where she was staying.

"Same hotel, as you," she grinned suggestively. For a split second, he was taken by surprise.

How many more bombshells will I encounter before the day's over?

"Okay," he chuckled. "How about we meet in the hotel bar at eight."

The three made their way to the ground floor, then Ray and Ben left Gila and took the rear exit to the pub. The two men spoke little as they made their way to The Wellington across the busy Strand – a major thoroughfare in the City of Westminster, in Central London, and a stone's throw from the River Thames. The five-storey, traditional London pub with its neo-Gothic marble exterior – dating back to the turn of the 1900s – stood on the corner of Wellington Street and the Strand, next to the Lyceum Theatre. Ben led the way through the double-glass doors into a wood-panelled interior onto a polished, wooden floor under an ornate Edwardian ceiling.

"Drinks on me," said Ben as they approached the long wooden bar. A smiling bartender – leaning on a row of crafted beer taps – was already poised to take their order. Ray scanned the heavily stocked shelving behind the bar.

"I'll have a double *Stolichnaya*, no ice, and an orange juice chaser."

"And I'll have a pint of bitter." It always surprised Ray how foreign visitors took to English beer, even when served at room temperature. He, for one, had never acquired the taste.

"I'll grab us a seat," said Ray deciding on a table in front of the window at the rear of the pub.

He strolled over and sat on a chair with his back to the wall, stretched out his long legs, and watched as a large group entered, excitedly engulfing Ben at the bar. The venue was already beginning to fill. The daily ritual of many of London's white-collar class of corporate executives, stockbrokers, advertising account managers, bankers, public relation professionals, et al. congregating in their favourite watering hole at the end of a busy day was underway. A *couple* of drinks, a funny story, bitching about this person or that, complaining about the boss and impossible targets, and slapping backs for bagging a big deal. The format for the gatherings rarely changed. Once conversation stalled and strained nerves calmed, then it was ploughing a way through to the underground and home. Ray absent-mindedly observed the growing swarm talking and laughing amid the gurgling of foam spitting out of the row of beer taps attached to metal kegs below stairs.

That could never be a life for me, he thought, then turned his thoughts to the afternoon's events.

So it was that he was to come full circle. Hardly a year out of the Academy some thirty months earlier, and he had been thrust into a world of Middle East political intrigue and violence. Now he was to enter the same world again. Why had he volunteered so readily? Was it the excitement of the chase? Was it necessary to continue realising his potential and a desire to achieve personal fulfilment? Was it to get back on the trail where he had come so tantalisingly close to an answer – yet always stymied at every turn. Or was there still a savoury sourness within him stimulating a hunger – an appetite that could only be suppressed by sweetened bitterness? Time would tell.

He raised his eyebrows at the thought of Gila. She had popped into his head more than once since he had returned from Israel. Now they would be working closely together. He shrugged off the notion. They had a job to do. Temptations would have to be curbed. But what if…?

Ben placed a tumbler with the clear alcohol and a highball of orange juice on the table, distracting Ray's musings. Ray picked up the vodka, drowning half immediately.

"Hmm. I needed that... Thanks! ...Well, Ben," he said, sitting back and looking around the expansive and richly decorated pub. "Your definition of *quaint* isn't exactly how we Brits would describe this place!"

"We Texans do have a reputation for the theatrical..., but I assure you I don't own an oil well or wear a Stetson," he chuckled in return, then picked up the glass pint mug and took a sip of his chosen brew. He licked his lips and placed the beer on the table. "Although I am partial to a pair of soft leather boots!"

Ben had an easy way about him and spoke in a deeply modulated voice, giving away little of the iconic accented Texan twang so distinctive and easily identified. Slightly shorter than Ray – although he walked with a very slight limp that Ray noticed on the way to the pub – he was fair-haired, light-blue eyes behind a handsome, mid-thirties face radiating a quiet, uncompromising intelligence.

"I'm pleased we can spend a little time together," he said. "As we'll soon be co-operating closely with each other." Ray nodded in assent. "Incidentally, I had a word with your Colonel Madison about you earlier today."

"Oh!"

"He thinks very highly of you."

"He's a good man – a good Commanding Officer and Intelligence man."

"He'll be pleased you're on board..." Ben took another, longer sip of his beer before continuing. "I was curious to know why you volunteered for the Oman business... He mentioned something about a loss... Some tragedy you had suffered, which he suggested was behind your decision."

[50]

Ray hadn't spoken of Leyla for some time. It was a subject he hadn't volunteered since her death, other than with his father.

"Sorry, I didn't mean to pry… I was just curious," Ben apologised.

"It's no problem… Yes, I did lose someone very close to me. It was a hijack rescue that went wrong… At least for her."

"Were you two…?"

"…We were planning to get married. We had this wonderful notion of spending the rest of our lives together. We would have a big family, and I would have a glittering career in the Intelligence Corps." Ray picked up his orange juice. "She wanted six children." He smiled at the memory – more to himself – and gulped down some of the sweet liquid.

"Was she the reason?" Ray sighed deeply.

"Yes, she was… I was angry… I needed to vent my emotions. For a while after, I felt like I was punching a balloon. I was unable to connect… to vent my frustration. The secondment seemed a good way to achieve that… being face-to-face with an adversary – someone to hit back at." Ray suddenly found himself able to talk about Leyla. Something he hadn't been able or inclined to do.

"And now?"

"What…? Am I still angry?" Ben nodded. "A little…, perhaps."

"Anger's good provided it can be channelled for good."

"You sound a bit of a philosopher," Ray smiled at the agent's comment. They were briefly distracted by raucous laughter from a group standing at the bar in the middle of the bar – suggesting the *third* pint was already having an effect.

"And you, Ben? Married? Wife and kids?"

"Hmm! My story's similar to a few in my profession. Something which you may one day come to experience yourself."

"I'm all ears," Ray smiled at the man's quip, happy to move away from delving deeper into his story.

"Not much to tell… but at the risk of boring a new colleague. Let's say that until four years ago, I lived two lives."

Ben's story was no different from many in his situation. He had married his university sweetheart, bought a lovely home in the Washington suburbs, had two beautiful children, saw family and friends at weekends and over the holidays… The other side to him lived in the shady world where he chose to make a career. Increasingly extended stays away from home and dealing with people he wouldn't invite around for a Sunday afternoon BBQ. As time passed, he and his wife inevitably grew apart. The Agency was claiming too much of him.

"And so here I am, divorced and married to the *Agency*. I see my kids whenever I can. My daughter adores me – my son rarely speaks to me." He let out a deep sigh. He paused as more, louder laughter erupted behind him. "You know, it's not unusual for case officers to get married two or three times!" Ray hesitated. His eyes narrowed as he rested the glass on his lower lip – questioning.

"No! Not for me! Once is enough!" retorted Ben to Ray's unspoken query. "Tell me, how can two people who were so much in love turn out years later to despise the sight of each other?" He tried to smile, but it came out as a grimace, then he downed the remainder of his beer.

"Refill?" Ray smiled broadly to play down the serious direction the conversation was headed.

"Of course!"

Ray returned five minutes later.

"Tell me, Ben... I noticed you had a little difficulty walking on our way here."

"Oh! That! It was another nail in the coffin. It was while I was in Panama City... During a firefight with a drug cartel. The stupid thing was, I was only an observer but took a ricochet in the back of the left knee – shattered the kneecap. I spent the next six months in traction and physio." He sat back and rubbed his left knee. "I've had to say goodbye to fieldwork. I'm now mostly desk-bound, although I get out now and then. Remember that, Ray. I don't want to be stuck behind the desk given a chance."

The two men sat quietly, drinking their drinks, absorbed in their surroundings – reflecting.

"I'd be happy to stay on, but I need to retrieve my car and get over to the hotel. Can't keep the lady waiting!" Ray said eventually, and with a chuckle, added. "She can be extremely dangerous!"

5   July 28th, 1973

Surrey, England

The sudden sharp *brrring* of the desk phone startled him. He let it ring three times before slowly reaching for the handset.

"Hello? Ezra Brachfield."

"Your son has been returned safe and sound, as we agreed?" The voice spoke in a deep distorted pitch.

"Yes."

"Remember… we interceded at great risk to ourselves to make his safe return possible. The Israeli government would have never agreed to the extreme demands set by these people. You had no choice. The faction behind the abduction is highly political, motivated, and dangerous. They would have killed your son without a second thought… And as long as you keep to your side of our covenant, he will remain safe… You must bear that in mind." The disembodied voice was taut and matter-of-fact.

"I understand," answered the media magnate solemnly.

"Then, no more needs to be said. We will be in touch with instructions on how you will proceed in the next few days. Until then, speak to no one about this matter. We have eyes and ears everywhere." The line went dead, leaving a loud dial tone ringing in his ear.

Ezra Brachfield gave a deep sigh as he lowered the receiver, then slowly replaced it in its cradle. He should have been elated. His son was free at last – the loving boy he had cherished and watched grow from a child to a young man. And yet... he knew he was about to sell his soul. He knew the cost would be more than he had initially bargained for. However, Ezra reasoned he had acted with just intent. It would be a small price to pay for his son's life.

He was a man of mental resilience, never fearful of facing opposition or difficulties, of which he had endured many in his sixty years. He had developed a strong moral code from an early age, believing that he could make a difference by doing what was right and not easy. Ezra had faced hardship and uncertainty all his life but achieved success despite it all. Now he was to betray the very foundation that had given him the strength and courage that had carried him from a pitiful speck of a village in the southern Soviet Republic to riches.

He was born Ezra Bezkrovny in 1913, one year before a misguided Serbian student shot and killed Archduke Franz Ferdinand, sparking the First World War. The end of the war saw many changes. Earlier tolerance and willingness to accommodate the small Jewish village community became increasingly strained and under constant threat from the newborn Bolshevism gripping Russia since the revolution in 1917. After giving birth to baby Ezra, his mother – a sickly woman – died during those troubled years, leaving his father, a struggling tailor, to parent their only child alone.

Determined to provide a better life for his son, Elyakim Bezkrovny worked all the hours he could endure, scraping and saving every Ruble he could muster. Finally, in the summer of 1922, Elyakim sold his wretched cottage

[55]

and meagre furnishings to the village headman for a paltry amount, well below its market value.

"Be reasonable, Elya," the buyer had argued, justifying his exploitation, "these are unfortunate times. Money is tight. You are lucky I am still prepared to buy this... this poor excuse of a dwelling."

With a minimal amount of clothing and his prized portable sewing machine strapped to his back, Elyakim and his nine-year-old son set out on the treacherous journey for London, England.

The trek took a little over two years as they slowly but surely made their way through a ravaged and post-war Europe, hopeful yet fearful for the future. The young Ezra quickly adapted to their nomadic life, becoming increasingly resourceful and maturing beyond his years while his industrious father successfully sewed and stitched their way for food and lodging – leaving sympathetic well-wishers in their wake.

Their final destination led them to *Minsky Newsagent & Tobacconist*, in Finchley Road, Golders Green, London. Elyakim's second cousin Aaron Minsky and his wife, Hila, welcomed them with open arms. They shared a bedroom in the family's spacious two-storey apartment above the shop, and Elyakim soon acquired a position at a local tailor's. Ezra's third cousins were David – two months his senior – and Rachel. At two years younger than Ezra, the girl was a sweet child who took to him immediately. For six months, they settled into their new lives with Ezra attending a local secondary school... until tragedy struck.

The doctors believed the hardship and stress of the journey eventually took their toll on Ezra's father. A massive heart attack was no surprise. Elyakim Bezkrovny was put to rest in the *Hoop Lane Jewish Cemetery*, a distance of some four-and-a-half thousand miles from the village of his birth and his wife's gravesite.

[56]

The loss of his father devastated young Ezra. With tears flooding down his cheeks as he watched his father's coffin lowered into the ground, he swore that his father's sacrifice would not be in vain. He would dedicate himself to succeeding – to be his father's legacy. Wealth and prestige would be his goal.

As the years passed, Ezra left school to work full time for his uncle, quickly proving himself an indispensable business member. He took control of the newspaper deliveries, collating and marking the papers, magazines, and journals, then delivering them from a large canvas satchel slung over his shoulder. His infectious enthusiasm saw the concern triple the delivery side, adding a welcomed increase to the shop's revenue. He became fascinated by the written medium informing its readership of local, national, and international daily happenings. After dinner each evening, he would sit on his bed and avidly read through as many papers as he could – absorbing and learning. In contrast, David showed no interest in his father's business, preferring to further his education and pursue a literary career.

When Ezra turned eighteen, his uncle decided to open a second shop and asked if Ezra would take on the management, which he did without hesitation. Within a short time of opening, he had equalled the success of the original store. His ambition continued to gnaw at him, and on his twenty-first birthday, Ezra approached his uncle with the notion of creating a chain of shops. He pressed the advantages of volume buying, coupled with expanding the line of goods that could be sold across the counter.

His uncle initially resisted the idea until Ezra received surprising support from his Aunt. However, her motive for the venture was not the same as Ezra's. She had grown accustomed to the benefits of the second shop's additional profits, experiencing an increased social

[57]

standing within the community. A successful chain would certainly gain her more favour and the higher status she craved. To her, Ezra's proven commitment and success to date could be *the goose that laid the golden egg!*

So it was agreed that Ezra and his uncle would form an equal partnership on the understanding that Ezra would single-mindedly focus all his energy on managing the new enterprise. They would trade under a new name, *Brachfields.* Ezra believed the Englishness in the title would enable them to operate and expand without market bigotry and prejudice.

Over the ensuing years, he grew into a handsome young man. Oblivious to the flirtations from adoring females, he was entirely committed to expanding the corporation at every opportunity. Meanwhile, David continued his education, winning a Cambridge University scholarship to study literature and philosophy. Rachel blossomed into a beautiful young woman with suitors at every corner. Her heart, however, was always for one man who was too engrossed in business to notice – no matter how hard she tried. Eventually, with continual pressure from her parents, she relented and gave up on her secret dream, consenting to marry into a prosperous local family.

The wedding took place in the summer of 1939 and was a splendid affair with all the *right* people in attendance. It happened during the traditional *Mitzvah tantz* when the bride's family dances in front of the seated bride. Reluctant at first, Ezra was coaxed onto the dance floor to join in the ritual. It was then, for a moment, his eyes locked on hers. In that instant, Ezra knew he had made a desperate mistake. The realisation hit him like a cruel thunderbolt. He was in love with her, and it was too late. He had been blind to the truth and had let her slip through his fingers. Ezra threw himself into the business with an even greater determination. He would carry the burden of regret, sadness, and guilt for many years after.

In addition to the burgeoning *Brachfields* chain, Ezra had taken over a failing local newspaper. Introducing the ideas he had fostered over the years, he soon grew the readership and realised a small profit led to further purchases and mergers. By the time the Second World War broke following the invasion of Poland on 1st September 1939, Brachfields had owned and controlled several local, regional and national publications. The war years presented the enterprise with even more growth opportunities. David joined the war effort as a correspondent. Ezra immediately approached him to join him as his Editor in Chief to manage and oversee the content of the Brachfields group of publications. David quickly established a network of journalists feeding him with real-time stories from the war's battlefields. Following Ezra's blueprint, the group reported a mixture of timely frontline news with local and national feel-good stories capturing the nation's spirit. More takeovers and mergers took place over the six years, creating the most significant syndicated consortium nationwide by the war's end.

Meanwhile, Rachel's husband joined the Royal Air Force as a pilot officer. Tragically, his plane was shot down within ten minutes of his first engagement in July 1940 during the Battle of Britain. Sadly, he was killed outright like so many young and inexperienced hopefuls eager to participate in the campaign.

Ezra attended the funeral but remained distant from Rachel until they re-established their friendship after the war. Their relationship soon blossomed. Determined not to repeat the same mistake, Ezra proposed, and they married in 1949, following Ezra's decision to change his name from Deed Poll to Brachfield. Ariel was born two years later. Rachel and their newborn gave Ezra new meaning to his life until sorrow struck once again six years later. A hit and run ended her life in an instant.

Rachel's father also passed away during the same year following a long illness. Under the terms of the original partnership agreement, Ezra bought out the Minsky family's share of the business, leaving David cash-rich and still holding a prominent position on the board of directors. By the end of the 1960s, Brachfields owned and operated key publications and television stations across Europe and North America, making Ezra Brachfield one of England's richest men. A gentle knocking on the study door interrupted Ezra's reflective musings.

"Yes!" He smiled as Nicola peered around the door.

"So, this is where you've been hiding?" she said and entered his sanctum. He had become overly fond of his stepdaughter and doted on her as if she were his own child. Nikki, as he affectionately called her, adored Ezra in return. To her, he was the father she never knew who deserted Nicola's mother, Adele, shortly after her birth – never to be seen or heard of again.

Ezra was introduced to his new wife at a dinner party hosted by an old acquaintance. Content to remain a widower, he was nevertheless taken by the self-assured and captivating woman. And although she was twenty years his junior, the romance was brief, and the marriage – a lavish affair held at the prestigious Dorchester Hotel in London – took place six months before that fateful day when his son was cruelly abducted.

"We're all waiting for you, and you haven't even tied your cravat," she scolded him, noting the red paisley silk fabric hanging loosely around his neck. "Come on, *Papsy*, let me tie it for you." She walked around the large desk as he stood obediently. Ezra raised his chin as she loosely folded the necktie and gently tucked it inside his open-necked shirt.

"There!" she said as she stood back, admiring her work. "Now you look every bit the handsome gentleman you are," she added with a giggle. Nicola possessed a pleasing personality and an infectious enthusiasm people quickly warmed to.

"Thank you, Nikki," he said, taking her by the shoulders and gently kissing her on the forehead. "Give me a few more minutes, and I'll join you."

"Okay! But don't be long. It's a beautiful day, and I won't have you sitting here all on your own when you should be outside enjoying the sun... If you're not out in ten minutes, I'll be back to drag you out!" she smiled, gazing into his heavy eyes, then kissed him on the cheek before leaving him alone again.

6 July 28ᵗʰ, 1973

Surrey, England

The sun beat down from a cloudless, cocktail-blue afternoon sky as Ray and Gila sped along the A3 major road in Ray's dark-blue, soft-top *MGB GT* roadster – a gift from his parents on graduating from Sandhurst Officers' Academy and his prized possession. The forecasters had predicted the weather correctly. The weekend was turning out to be a glorious product of an English summer. The historic route developed as far back as the 1600s, headed sixty-seven miles in a near-straight, southwest direction linking the Capital with Portsmouth. Nicknamed *Pompey* by the resident navy and the city's football club. The town was the original home to the British Navy.

They had spent the previous four hours at Toby Gilmore's office establishing and agreeing on the unit's modus operandi with the other three and deliberating over the information gathered to date on the kidnapping.

Ray disengaged and engaged the clutch smoothly as he expertly worked the manual shift manoeuvring through the synchronised gearbox – optimising the six-cylinder engine's RPMs. He had missed driving the sports car and was pleased for the opportunity to take it for a decent run with the soft-top folded down.

He glanced over at Gila. The wind was blowing her hair freely around her head with the sun on her face. She caught Ray's gaze and smiled broadly. From an elegant cocktail dress the night before to smart casuals, she was still as appealing as she delighted in looking around through white-framed sunglasses at the slowly increasing rural scenery – the further they distanced from the City.

Forty-five minutes into their journey, they drove through the historic village of *Cobham* situated on the River Mole, then turned south off the main highway onto narrower, two-lane country roads. Before setting off, Ray had studied a map of Surrey – the shire bordering the counties of Hampshire, East and West Sussex, and Kent in addition to Greater London – and decided on the best route to the Brachfield country address. His photographic memory enabled him to wind along the country lanes without interruption.

"It's beautiful!" exclaimed Gila excitedly above the engine's throaty sound mingling with the sound of air swirling around the vehicle's windscreen. The picturesque, vivid-green rural scenery was in stark contrast to the desert landscape occupying half of Israel – the country of her birth. Ray decelerated, changing into third as they approached an ornamental road sign marking their entrance to the small village of *Albury*.

"The village's name comes from the Olde English *ald*, for old and *burh*, for fortification," Ray said, impressing Gila as they slowly passed through, but failed to add it was a piece of trivia he picked up while scanning through a travel guide at the hotel. A couple walking their dog stopped and waved as they drove by. Gila immediately reciprocated their friendly gesture and turned in her seat to wave back. Ray caught her excitement and smiled to himself. When they reached the far end of the village, the road took a sharp turn to the left, heading further south away from the historic county town of *Guildford*.

"The house will be on our right about a mile further along this road," said Ray, recalling the detail on the map.

A majestic style arched-gate attended by two able-looking security staff and two German Shepherds with forward-tilted ears announced the entrance to Eaton House.

"You can't blame Brachfield for the tight security," remarked Gila as they drove through under the alert and watchful eyes of the two dogs. The car's tyres crunched on a gravelled driveway as they wound their way through a gauntlet of leafy trees, eventually arriving in front of a grand, red-bricked Edwardian house covered in creeping ivy. Ray pulled up next to a white *Rolls-Royce Silver Shadow* and noted the two vehicles parked alongside – a blue *Mercedes-Benz 280* saloon and a red *Mercedes 350SL* sports model. As Ray and Gila climbed out of the MGB, a liveried butler appeared at the front door.

"Welcome, Miss, Sir!" he said as they approached. "The family is on the terrace… This way, please," and led the way along a carpeted hallway lined with textured wallpaper and adorned with paintings and artefacts. They emerged onto a stone-slabbed patio overlooking an extensive garden full of manicured shrubs and flowerbeds. Two men and women were sitting at an oval-shaped garden table under a large, green umbrella. The men immediately rose to welcome the visitors.

"Ezra Brachfield," announced a distinguished silver-haired man. "I'm delighted you could join us, Captain, so I could personally thank you for what you did for my son."

"I was just one of the team," responded Ray, wondering how many more times he would have to qualify his role in the rescue as he took the man's extended hand. The media magnate dismissed Ray's retort and stepped towards Gila.

"My associate, Gila Levenson."

"It's a pleasure," he smiled warmly as he bent over Gila's hand and motioned a kiss over the back of her hand. Ezra Brachfield was clearly a man who had not given up on the cultural values instilled long ago.

The other man was introduced as his brother-in-law, David Minsky. He was a well-dressed, athletic-looking man who stood an inch taller than his host with a well-modulated voice and whose appearance belied his sixty years. On the other hand, his wife appeared the opposite to her husband. She had the look of a prim and proper lady with her hair tied neatly in a bun – a sharp contrast to Adele Brachfield. She was a strikingly attractive, fair-haired woman – Ray reckoned to be in her early forties. It was easy to see why the media mogul had fallen for her and married the lady. As Ray and Gila took their seats, Ariel spotted them from the tennis court off to their right and waved.

"Would you be happy with a *Pimms*," asked Ezra Brachfield, referring to a large crystal jug full of a reddish-brown liquid and assorted chopped-fruit garnishes, "or would you prefer something stronger?".

"Pimms is fine for me," replied Ray casting a questioning glance at Gila, suspecting she was unfamiliar with the gin-based fruit cocktail.

"Looks interesting, thank you," said Gila.

Just as Ray and Gila had settled back in the cushioned seats with a glass of the British summertime drink, Ariel came bounding up the steps with a pretty young woman on his heels. Ariel introduced them to Nicola, his stepsister, insisting she was a *dynamite* hand at tennis and, now that they had arrived, was glad for the break.

"This is delicious!" declared Gila after taking a sip of the zesty cocktail, evoking polite smiles all around. The usual small-talk in the sun's outdoor warmth followed for a while before Ray opened up with their visit's real purpose.

"Now that you've had a chance to settle back into normal life," smiled Ray assuredly, "would you mind if I asked you a few questions about your time in captivity…" He caught Ezra Brachfield out the corner of his eye, wincing slightly. "If this is an inappropriate time or place, please say… Mr Brachfield?"

"No…, no… Please! Are you still pursuing the people behind the abduction? I thought I'd heard they had all been killed. No witnesses left."

"We have to be sure there wasn't more to your son's kidnapping than meets the eye," answered Ray. He had decided beforehand to suggest a deeper motive behind the abduction openly. Gila was watching the six intensely over the rim of her glass. "It's just routine," he continued. "You have to understand that this has not been regarded as a *run-of-the-mill* abduction. The demands were not just about money. Politics were very much at play. The additional demand for the release of four very dangerous individuals can't be ignored."

"Yes, yes, of course… I see. I'm sorry. Please. Ariel?" Ezra Brachfield picked up his glass and took a long sip.

"There's not much I can add to what I've already told you. I was hooded each time they moved me from one building to another. The only people I ever saw were the ones you encountered on the night of my rescue. My captors rarely spoke to me. Their English was limited, to say the least." Ray noted Nicola watching Ariel intently as he relayed his experience – her eyes blinking rapidly – clearly distressed at his recount. "Most of my contact was with the leader," he continued, "and that was minimal. I'm sorry, Captain Kazan, that's all I can give you." He apologised, sounding genuinely regretful. Ray had

[66]

expected as much and didn't push him further.

"Mr Brachfield! How about you?" Ray caught the mogul off guard.

"Me?" he responded, instantly placing his drink on the table in front of him. Ezra's heartbeat quickened. "I'm sorry... I don't know how I can shed any light on the affair!"

"Do you have any idea why Ariel was targeted? Anything that may have been related to your business? Anything at all you can think of? Any little could be of help." The media magnate lifted his sunglasses and scratched his nose.

"I'm sorry, Captain Kazan. I can't think of any reason... any reason at all, other than money," he assured Ray. "Believe me when I say, I racked my brain all the while Ariel was held. I kept blaming myself... I was at my wit's end. I did all I could. I can't think of anything specific... And as you are no doubt aware, contact with those people was being maintained by the Israeli Government."

"It's a puzzle, however." Ray paused. "How long before you travelled to Cyprus did you book the flight... and your hotel rooms?"

"A couple of weeks... Why?" answered Ariel.

"Who knew of your trip?"

"Of course, we all did," cut in Ariel's father. "The family, that is... And my secretary. She arranged the tickets and bookings."

"For both you and your friend... Michael, uhm...?"

"Winsham. Michael Winsham. Yes, Ann – that's dad's secretary – organised both," Ariel took over from his father. The Winsham lad and the secretary had been extensively interviewed by Toby Gilmore's office shortly after the abduction and had been wholly absolved of any part in the *snatch*.

[67]

"They were the only people who knew?"

"And David, of course… He's a senior member at the corporation and Ariel's uncle," added Brachfield senior. "The trip wasn't advertised. Just known among the few of us."

Ray decided to press further.

"The kidnapping was carefully orchestrated. Requiring advanced intelligence. Once in Cyprus, Ariel would have been watched, his movements and habits carefully studied before daring the timely snatch." All eyes were on Ray as he spoke other than Adele Brachfield, who was sipping her drink with eyes cast down. "Considering the motive behind the abduction, they would only have had the one attempt. It might also suggest they knew more about Ariel than just his travel plans." Ray noted Ezra Brachfield's jaw muscle twitch. He hesitated and glanced at each one in turn before smiling broadly and concluding,

"Anyway, if you happen to think of anything or anyone else that might have been privy to Ariel's plans, please let me know. You can leave a message at this number." Ray passed over a card to both men that simply read:

Captain R. Kazan and gave a contact telephone number.

Ezra Brachfield intuitively turned the card over in his hand.

"Of course… It goes without saying. I'll be happy to," he said and placed it in his shirt breast pocket.

They continued to make small talk about Ariel's return, Nicola's tennis skills, and as such chatter often does, turned to the weather, Pimms, the house, and the garden. Thirty minutes later, Ray glanced at his watch.

"I think we should be getting along. Thank you very much for your invitation and sorry for the questions." He smiled apologetically. "It's all part of the job."

"Not at all," responded Ezra Brachfield, "I'm sorry we couldn't be of more help. But thank you for coming…

[68]

And let me thank you again for bringing my son back to me," he said, reaching out his hand. Ray didn't bother correcting the man. The usual pleasantries over with Ariel offered to see them to their car in the company of an eager Nicola.

The two guards at the main gate saluted as he and Gila drove out of the estate and turned back onto the road into Albury. Midway through the village, Ray turned into the forecourt of one of the area's favoured haunts, the *William IV* – a rustic 16th-century pub.

"Come on!" he declared, switching off the car's engine. "Time for you to visit a typical English country pub."

Ray pushed open the old-style wooden door and stood back, allowing Gila to enter the spacious lounge. Deciding on the Public Bar, he went through a glass-panelled door and, ducking under the low oak beams in the dimly lit room, led them to a table by the single window.

"What would you like?" he asked as she took a seat at a rough-hewn wooden table.

"What are you having?"

"The usual… A double *Vod* with an orange juice chaser."

"Make it two," she responded.

It was just past 6 o'clock, and the place was empty.

"Still too early for our regulars," informed the landlord while preparing their order.

"I thought we'd kill two birds with one stone," Ray said, setting down the tray of drinks, then taking a seat with his back to the window. "We can stay for a meal before heading back to town. The place is apparently famous for its *Shepherd's Pie*."

"Have you been here before?"

"No… I read about the pub and the village in a Surrey Travel Guide back at the hotel," he confessed with a soft chuckle. "Anyway…, thoughts on our visit?"

"Nicola is definitely in love with Ariel," sniggered Gila cheekily.

"An interesting observation, however...?"

"Ariel couldn't add anything new. Adele Brachfield and the Minsky woman said little. The brother-in-law was very attentive to what was said, and Ezra Brachfield? I don't think he could help much either."

"I'm not so sure," remarked Ray thoughtfully, sparking a quizzical look from Gila.

"How do you mean?"

"It was when I asked him outright if he knew of any reason... businesswise... He scratched his nose," he said and took a sip of the vodka. Gila chuckled.

"Scratched his nose?"

Ray placed his glass on the table and leaned forward.

"Yes, quite a few times, in fact, as he talked... I may be clutching at straws, but I sense that he may have been hiding something."

"How do you figure that?

"Just something I noticed. Look..., when we're stressed, our blood flow increases. It's something we can't control. It happens spontaneously. Our noses contain an enormous amount of blood vessels, consequently receiving a lot of the extra blood... causing it to itch... The blood increase can also occur when we're uncomfortable... put on the spot." He picked up his glass of orange juice and arched his eyebrows. "His nose was definitely itching!"

"That's it...? You base your assumption on Ezra Brachfield's itching nose?" She laughed out loud. "Where'd you learn this incredible insight?"

"Military Intelligence," he answered. "Body language was one of the *must* courses I took. It's pretty useful info' when questioning or interrogating someone. Got pretty good at it too," he smiled a self-congratulatory smile.

[70]

"I think you're reaching, Ray, but okay..., I'm listening," she said, looking at him levelly, her face more serious and thoughtful.

"As I said, it's..." He was suddenly distracted by a vehicle pulling up sharply outside the window, causing him to lean back and look out over his shoulder. "Hold up!"

"What is it?"

"It's Adele Brachfield!" he said, surprised, watching her get out of the red Mercedes Sportscar. Ray caught the media mogul's wife pass by the bar door. He didn't move, prompting Gila to remain seated.

"I'll be back in a minute!" he said.

He hurried across the room and stood to the side of the door, looking through the glass panels as she passed by, and went directly to a wall-mounted pay-telephone next to the lounge bar. She appeared anxious as she picked up the handset, then deposited several coins into the slot. He couldn't hear what she was saying, but from her head movements could tell it was a serious conversation. He ducked back out of sight as she replaced the handset and hurried back to her car.

"That's interesting," he said, resuming his seat. "Why would she come out here when there's obviously a telephone at the house? I noticed one on a side-table halfway down the hall." He picked up the orange juice, took a sip, then put it back on the table.

"I need to make a phone call!" He got back up and went out to the payphone in the lounge.

"Is Toby Gilmore around?"

"I think he was just about to leave. I'll see if I can catch him. Who's on the line?"

"Ray Kazan." He pushed another coin into the slot. A short time later.

"Hi, Ray. What's up?"

"A couple of things. Can you trace the number rung from this public telephone five minutes ago?" Ray read out the number displayed on the rotary dial.

"Got it," responded Toby at the other end. "You said a couple of things?"

"Can you put a tail on Adele Brachfield?"

"Ezra Brachfield's wife?"

"Yes."

"Reason?"

"Can you do it? Currently, she's at their country address, Eaton House near Albury, Surrey. You should have the details on file. I'll fill you in on Monday."

"Okay, I'll get onto it straight away. Anything else?"

"Yes, there is," Ray had a sudden thought. "Can you get your people to go through Brachfield's operations?"

"Anything specific?"

"As his main interests are in media, concentrate on anything that may appear unusual, out of the ordinary. A stand or position against any entity that could be interpreted as embarrassing, threatening… whatever?"

"That's a bit vague, Ray."

"I appreciate that, but I've just got a feeling. I would suggest if there is anything, it would be political."

"Fair enough. I'll get the team onto it first thing Monday morning."

"Cheers, Toby. Talk to you then." Ray ended the call and replaced the handset.

"Okay," said an anxious Gila. "So what was all that about?" Ray explained his call to Toby Gilmore.

"Something else, Gila."

"Go on; I'm listening."

"Shaul Feuerman!"

"You mean the assistant director of *Shin Bet*?"

"The very same."

"What about him?"

[72]

"We need to do some digging… Find out how and why he got involved. What happened to the two-hundred *K* Ezra Brachfield put up for information on where they were holding Ariel? How was it disbursed, and who was behind it?" He leaned back in the chair. "I believe he may be a key to a door we need opening."

"You know that won't be easy. He's bound to find out if we start poking around."

"I'm not suggesting we do it," said Ray pulling his hand down his chin.

"Who then…? Avi?"

"No," he replied emphatically. "I don't think it should be anyone local."

"Then who?"

"I don't know!" He picked up the vodka and sat back – lips pursed.

"I think I know who could help!" Gila volunteered after a while, leaning towards him.

"Who?"

"The Israeli Ambassador."

"And how are we supposed to get his cooperation?"

"He's an old family friend, on my father's side," she replied with a self-satisfied grin. Ray gave a deep sigh, then downed the vodka emptying his glass.

"I think I'll have another one! You?"

7   July 30th, 1973

London, England

I t had begun to rain as they left for the appointment. It was still drizzling slightly as they got out of the black cab. The Israeli Embassy was situated in the exclusive tree-lined avenue in Kensington, central London, reputed to be one of the world's most expensive residential streets. They weren't kept waiting long before being shown into the Ambassador's richly decorated office overlooking the expansive Kensington Gardens – one of the city's Royal Parks.

"This is a pleasant surprise!" the Israeli Ambassador, Ethan Schulman, said from the middle of the room, stepping towards Gila. He placed his hands on her shoulders and, leaning forward, kissed her gently on both cheeks.

"Thank you for seeing us… I know you must be very busy," she said and hugged him.

"Nonsense! I was hoping you wouldn't leave it too long. Your mother called to say you would be coming over."

Bearded with specks of greyness, the Ambassador appeared more like an avuncular college professor with leather patches on his elbows than someone holding a prominent political position. Gila had mentioned that he had been her father's closest friend before his passing six years earlier and had basically been an uncle to her since childhood. He turned to Ray.

"I'm delighted to meet you, Captain Kazan. I've heard a lot about you since your success in securing the release of Ezra Brachfield's son."

"Your Excellency." Ray took his outstretched hand. "As I'm sure the Ambassador is aware, all praise is due to the local unit that was involved in Ariel's extraction." He found himself once again explaining his supportive role.

"Please!" The Ambassador indicated plush cushioned seating around a highly polished wooden coffee table. They took a seat each in one of the armchairs when a knock sounded on the door, and a man in a white jacket entered carrying a silver tray.

"I've taken the liberty of arranging tea and coffee. I wasn't sure which you'd prefer," said the Ambassador looking to Gila as the man laid the tray on the table.

"Coffee will be fine," she responded with a gleam in her eye.

"I'll have a coffee," Ray confirmed.

Ray and Gila sat quietly, looking around self-consciously while the servant poured out the drinks and set them down in front of them. The Ambassador thanked the man, dismissed him, picked up his cup and saucer, and sat back in his seat.

"I have to assume there is an ulterior purpose behind your visit besides catching up with your favourite uncle," he said with a kindly smile, directing the comment at Gila.

"I should tell you that I have been seconded to work with the British Government... with Ray, Captain Kazan. We're involved in..."

"I have been made aware of your assignment. There's no need to explain," he interjected.

"Can I ask how much you know of Ariel Brachfield's

kidnapping?" Ray took up the conversation.

"I happen to be a close friend of Ezra Brachfield's. Our relationship goes back several years. I was very much involved with Ezra and our Government back home – coordinating as it were – during that awful period. It was a difficult time for the family."

"Mr Ambassador," Ray decided to take the bull by the horns, "may we have your assurance that what we are about to discuss here with you remains in the strictest of confidence and only between the three of us?"

"You have me intrigued, Captain!" He leant forward and set aside his coffee on the table. "Of course, it goes without saying. You have my word."

"Are you familiar with the name Shaul Feuerman?"

"Yes…, I know who he is. I've met him three to four times… official engagements, that sort of thing. Why?"

Ray proceeded to give the diplomat an account of the Shin Bet's assistant director's role and involvement in the kidnapping saga and details of the extraction. All the while, the diplomat sat still and attentive.

"From your tone and what you've told me, I gather you have certain doubts as to the director's participation… and perhaps his motive," said the Ambassador, stroking his bearded chin thoughtfully.

"I didn't realise I was so obvious," smiled Ray.

"So, what is it you are asking?"

Ray leant back and looked to Gila as he took a sip of his coffee, prompting her to pick up the request.

"We are asking if you would be prepared to conduct… I mean, quietly look into the matter. Discreetly… behind the scenes. We wouldn't want to alert the director."

"Look into what precisely?" he said as he picked up the coffee jug and offered it to Gila. She declined with a gentle shake of the head.

"Why did he volunteer? How and from whom he

received Ariel Brachfield's location? And the two-hundred thousand paid over by Brachfield senior. What became of it, and who did it go to?" Ray added, taking over again and reaching out his cup for a top-up.

"You realise that what you're asking is highly irregular and unconventional..., contrary to norms."

"We understand..., but if my suspicions are founded, it could lead us closer to the people behind the kidnapping, and who knows what else we might be able to uncover... And should my / our misgivings be misplaced, then he would be none the wiser... No harm done!" Ray and Gila glanced at each other as a thoughtful quiet fell over the Ambassador. A sudden knock on the door interrupted the silence.

"There's a telephone call for Captain Kazan," announced the secretary from inside the doorway.

"You can take it at my desk, if you wish," offered the Ambassador.

"Ray, it's Toby. I've got the information on that telephone number you asked me to trace. Do you have a pen?" Ray wrote the information on a small notepad and thanked Toby before replacing the handset. He tore off the sheet and, as a second thought, removed the two underlying blanks, folded them, and placed them in his trouser pocket. He apologised for the interruption as he resumed his seat.

"I will do as you ask," agreed the diplomat. "For reasons, I shan't go into, but particularly for Gila... We, diplomats, are supposedly pragmatic and skilled negotiators, so I'll make sure I don't create a wake in my endeavours," he added, smiling broadly.

"Thank you, Sir," responded Ray. Gila nodded her head and smiled in relieved appreciation.

"There is one thing," said the Ambassador, immediately piquing Ray and Gila's interest. "I'm already able to provide you with some information without needing to dig… I met with Ezra before he transferred the funds – the reward for the location, that is."

"When was this?" Ray said.

"The same day and after Ariel was rescued. Late afternoon… about five o'clock. He called around, looking for assurance. Two-hundred thousand US Dollars is not a sum to be taken lightly."

"How was it paid?"

"A straight transfer to a Swiss account in Geneva. The *BBK Banque Privée,* if my memory serves me… I'll ask Ezra for the full details and pass them along."

"Do you know where the instructions came from?"

"No, I confess I didn't see the need. As far as we were concerned, it was merely a matter of following up on a pre-agreed arrangement."

"Any questions or queries from your Government?"

"Again, no. Everyone was relieved following the success of the rescue. As far as my Government was concerned, it was off the hook. It was no longer faced with the impossible demand for the release of the bombers. The affair was laid to rest as a personal matter with no further involvement by my Government." He gestured to the coffee pot. Both Ray and Gila declined. "By the way, how will I be able to reach you?"

Ray pulled out one of his scanty printed cards with his name and contact number and passed it over. The diplomat glanced at it, then placed it on the table.

"Your call shouldn't raise any eyebrows. You are a close friend of the family, after all," Ray assured him. "Your Excellency, please accept our thanks for seeing us and helping out with this matter. However, we need to be going… Another pressing task."

◆◆◆◆

The rain had abated when Ray and Gila arrived in the East End of London. The area's deep poverty, overcrowding, and associated social problems were well known and continued to be depressed less than thirty years after the War. They turned left past Aldgate East (Underground) Station into Commercial Street. Ray was looking around, bemused by the number of wall-mounted signs advertising factories, warehouses, shops, and office premises for sale, rent, and lease. The black cab driver slid open the glass, dividing-screen catching Ray's attention.

"The address is 'alfway down on the left, Guvna," he said over his shoulder.

Seconds later, they pulled up outside a three-storey brick building. The faded sign above the double-door entrance announced the establishment as *Link House – Business Centre*. Ray asked the driver to hold on.

"We shouldn't be too long," he assured the man.

"Righto!" responded the taxi driver.

Ray pushed the door open, and they entered a drab entrance hall with walls painted a dull grey.

"Here it is, Suite 25... Hmm, no name!" Ray said as he scanned the wall-mounted board listing the resident businesses. "You stay here. I'll nip up."

Ray climbed the stairs to the second floor and walked gingerly down a dimly lit, musty hall lined with dirt-ingrained carpet. The place appeared to be deserted – evidence of the address's popularity. He stopped at a door with an opaque, frosted-glass panel marked with the number 25. Thinking he heard movement on the other side of the door, he rapped sharply on the glass. Getting no response, he knocked a second time, then tried the handle. The door was unlocked. He called out a *hello* as he pushed open the door and stepped into a small office comprising a grey metal desk, chair, and a telephone.

A sudden, violent blow to the side of the neck sent Ray

to the ground, briefly losing consciousness. Disorientated and dizzy, he slowly rolled over onto his back a few seconds later. He placed his hand over his right ear and pressed his eyes shut tight to relieve the pain.

"Ray, Ray… are you okay?" Gila rushed into the room and knelt by his side.

"Ooh! Bugger… I didn't see that coming!" he exclaimed. Still feeling light-headed, he sat up with Gila's help, his back against the desk. "Whoever it was, knew his stuff," he said, rubbing his neck. "Caught me squarely on the *vagus* nerve," he shook his head. "How…, how did you know to come up?"

"I heard someone run heavy-footed and a door slam at the back."

"Next time, I'm going to send you in first. Whoever clouted me might not be inclined to hit a lady," he quipped, evoking a playful slap on the shoulder.

"Well, one thing we do know about him…, and I'm assuming it was a him," said Gila. "He's got to be pretty strong and about your height… unless he was standing on a chair by the door… And I don't see a chair."

Ray took a deep breath, exhaled heavily, slowly got off the floor and went to the back wall. He peered through the aluminium-framed window overlooking a narrow, back alleyway strewn with rubbish and a discarded sofa next to a rust-pitted dumpster.

"Whoever whacked me is long gone," he said, continuing to rub his neck.

"Used the fire escape," said Gila, looking through the dirty glass at a metal ladder attached to the building. Ray moved back to the desk and settled in the chair.

"Now, what has our Mrs Brachfield got to do with whoever was occupying this place?" he asked thoughtfully, drumming his fingers on the desk.

"Hopefully, we'll find out soon. Toby's already got a

couple of people following her every move," she said. "Do you think we should meet her again? Question her?"

Ray leant forward with his elbows on the desk and, clasping his hands together, rested his chin. He thought for a moment.

"No! Not yet. It's too early – no point alerting her. Let's wait and see what she does next. Who she contacts."

He looked at the telephone, took a handkerchief out of his jacket pocket, and wrapped it around the handset before removing it from the cradle.

"Well, at least it's still working!" he said and dialled. Two minutes later, Toby Gilmore appeared on the other end.

"Gila and I are at the address, and I have a sore head for our trouble... I'll explain later," he responded to Toby's query. "Can you get someone down to run the place for prints... although I have a feeling you won't find anything worthwhile? I don't imagine whoever's renting this sorry-state-for-an-office will be coming back. However, Gila and I will hold on and look around, just in case. We'll also try to locate the landlord. See what we learn from him." He ended the call and, sitting back, arched his eyebrows at a smiling Gila perched on the edge of the desk.

"One of us needs to go down and sort out the taxi," he said.

8 July 30th, 1973

Chateau de Fère, Loire Valley, France

The mood among the five men dressed in dinner jackets around an elegant table laid with silver cutlery, bone china, cut-glass crystal, and two solid-silver candelabras on an ornately laced tablecloth was one of extreme optimism.

"I must say, Jean-Marie, you have once again treated us to a splendid dinner," said the tanned, dark-haired man in his early-fifties, raising a glass of red wine to his aquiline nose. "And this Burgundy is quite delightful. Goes down a treat!" added the Englishman inserting his nose into the airspace of the glass, capturing the fresh and spicy, black fruit aroma.

Miles Hathaway was of *old* money – Dominic Hathaway's grandson who established the *Hathaway* empire in the early 1900s. As the only child, he had inherited the privately-owned enterprise when his father, William Hathaway, died suddenly eight years earlier. Miles was an ambitious and ruthless individual who, from those who knew his grandfather, said he had inherited his genes. He soon expanded the organisation beyond its core beef production business with numerous cattle ranches in South America and a chain of retail butchers throughout the UK into a conglomerate whose interests ranged from sugar, coffee, and refrigerated shipping.

"I was fortunate to obtain half-a-dozen cases of the 1962 *Richebourg Grand Cru* before it was too late," remarked the evening's host, Jean-Marie de Salignac, marquis d'Ambois, from his seat at the head of the table.

"Must have knocked you back a pretty penny," remarked the Englishman taking another sip of one of the most expensive wines on the market.

"It certainly complimented the *Beef Bourguignon*," offered Ludwig von der Marwitz with a pronounced German accent. "You must extend our compliments to your chef." The marquis turned to the liveried butler standing to the side.

"Henri, be sure to pass on the baron's kind words to Charles," he said, then motioned with his hand towards the half-eaten *chocolate mousse* in front of him. The butler immediately instructed the two young valets standing on either side of him, who moved quickly to remove the table's dessert plates.

"Now, gentlemen, I think it's time for the brandy. If you will, Henri?" said the host. "I'm sure our guests would rather pour their own," he suggested to the butler who carefully placed a crystal decanter on the table in deference to its worth.

"Ah! A *Louis XIII*. You remembered!" remarked the handsome, olive-skinned man with the black pencil moustache, who at forty-seven was the youngest member of the group. Fareed Al Safadi was a successful, self-made entrepreneur who had acquired sizeable property holdings throughout the Mediterranean region from his extremely profitable arms trade, though regarded by most western Governments as a dubious enterprise. The most reputably expensive cognac produced by *Rémy Martin* — known by aficionados the world over as the *King of Cognacs* — was the Lebanese businessman's favourite tipple.

"This is a rather extraordinary shape," observed the fifth diner – a well-spoken black man sitting on the host's right – turning the ornate decanter in his hands. The butler held an elegantly carved, wooden box steady as the marquis removed a *Corona* and a guillotine kept inside with the cigars.

"The decanter has a rather interesting history to it," the French aristocrat responded as he placed the head of the cigar into the hole, and in one quick chop, sliced off the cap. He gently rotated the tightly-rolled bundle of dried and fermented tobacco leaves while the butler flamed the end with a gold lighter. Once it had lit, he took a long draw then exhaled a thick plume of smoke.

"It goes back to the mid-1800s," he continued as the butler offered the cigar box to the African. "As the story goes, Paul-Emile Rémy – the grandson of the founder Rémy Martin –acquired a metal flask believed to have been recovered from the *Battle of Jarnac* site... Forgive me if I'm boring you, gentlemen?" he said, pulling again on the cigar.

"Not at all, my dear marquis. I would like to know more about this unique decanter. Please do continue," the African guest said with approving nods from the other three diners.

"The battle of Jarnac was, by all accounts, a remarkable encounter between the Catholic forces of Marshal Gaspard de Sauix, sieur de Tavannes, and the Huguenots, led by Jeanne d'Albret during the Wars of Religion... Anyway, I digress. So, he – that is, Paul-Emile Rémy, the grandson – decided a glass replica of the flask would make a fitting container for his superior cognac. The first decanters were made to honour the House's 150th anniversary."

"It's quite a spectacular form! It never fails to fascinate me," the German – his sharp angular features with a square jaw and high cheekbones belying his advancing years –remarked while helping himself to a cigar.

The marquis d'Ambois turned his attention to his Corona, slowly revolving it in his fingers before raising it to his lips and taking a long draw filling his mouth with the smoke. He exhaled slowly. The rich aroma of the finely aged blend had a calming effect on him.

"All the decanters are made here in France by three chosen crystal manufacturers," he concluded with evident pride in his voice. With that, the five men sat back in their chairs, quietly savouring the unique liquor and their cigars.

"Well, gentlemen, enough of French history… let us retire to the drawing-room. We have much to discuss and conclude," said the marquis rising. "Henri?"

The butler led into a plush room furnished with priceless antique furniture and various oil paintings of family portraits, horses, and landscapes. He set the brandy decanter on a table next to an open, Gothic-styled fireplace, then walked over to a sizeable panelled window overlooking the chateau's expansive moat and drew closed heavy velvet drapes.

"You might like to look through these,' the marquis said to the African, Abebe Adebowale, handing him a thick buff-coloured folder after the butler had left and closed the door behind him.

As Jean-Marie de Salignac leant against the side table, he cut an imposing figure at sixty-two years of age, watching his African guest as he slowly thumbed through the contents. He was every inch a French aristocrat, a *Noblesse Chevaleresque* (knightly nobility) – a lineage that stretched before the year 1400. One of France's privileged social class, the wealthy provincial aristocracy, who inherited their titles from time immemorial. He was an extremely rich man with a diverse portfolio ranging from vast tracts of vineyards, cosmetics, fashion houses,

[85]

agriculture, armaments, and banking. Standing a little over six feet, he was of slim build with a darker skin tone – reminiscent of a Mediterranean appearance – and piercing brown eyes.

"This is incredible... How did you manage to obtain these photographs? Surely, this couldn't have been him?" Abebe Adebowale uttered suddenly, gazing incredulously at grainy photographs of a man entering a bank building clearly identified as *CCB Banque Privée – Geneva.*

"A double... Well paid for his image!" responded the Englishman. "Enough of a likeness to fool your countrymen," he added.

"There's more. Please continue looking through the extent of *incriminating* evidence," said the marquis calmly, refilling his glass, then handed the decanter to the Lebanese.

"Twenty million US Dollars!" exclaimed the African, revealing a photocopy of a bank statement. "How?"

"No worries, we'll get the money back once the damage is done," said the marquis. "A simple matter of moving a few insignificant numbers... An erroneous entry easily rectified. I have a small interest in the bank," he added in assurance.

The African gasped at the next four photographs of the same man sitting naked on the end of a bed with a partially nude woman kneeling in front of him – her back to the camera.

"I'm not sure I want to know how you managed these?"

"The pictures were taken with a hidden camera in the same room he stayed in during his trip to Switzerland for the African Summit..., only taken a week later," grinned Fareed Al Safadi.

Abebe Adebowale chuckled to himself and shook his head as he skimmed through more fabricated and highly compromising photographs of the man involved in lewd, graphic activities. He closed the folder and, placing it on his lap, exhaled deeply.

"Am I glad you're on my side!" he grimaced. "So, what happens now?"

"In three days, the evidence of his *wrongdoing* will be handed over to a major news organisation. Four days should be enough for the news to explode around the world. A well-paid General Kanumba with loyal army officers is standing by – ready to act. We also have a small team of hand-picked professional mercenaries to support and ensure a smooth transition. You will be flown in on the same day as the arrest is made to take over as President with full media endorsement and favourable worldwide sanction." Jean-Marie de Salignac smiled assuredly at the African. "It would be wise for you to announce affirmative public programmes immediately. Getting the people on your side will be imperative to establish your worthiness and presidential longevity."

"Jean-Marie is absolutely correct," interjected Miles Hathaway. "We have invested a great deal of time and money in this venture – not to mention risk – for it to yield a short-term result. You must first win over the people before anything else. We would not want short-sightedness spoil this opportunity for all in this room."

"I assure you, gentlemen, I have no desire or intent to jeopardise this favourable circumstance, unlike so many of my continent's predecessors have been prone to do," responded the African, detecting a slight menace in the Englishman's voice.

"That's good to hear!" quipped Miles Hathaway. "Now, where's the decanter? I need a top-up!"

"You know, gentlemen," started the group's hopeful, sitting back and drawing on his cigar, "my family name, Adebowale, aptly translates to *return of the crown*." He broke

[87]

out in a hearty laugh.

"There is one final matter…, Mr President," said Miles Hathaway, emphasising the title with a conspiratorial smile as he passed the African another folder. "The documents are all in order. They only require your signature."

The four men sat back in their seats with their cigars and brandy, quietly observing the man who would in the very near future enable them even greater wealth – and with more wealth came even more power. It was a craving for added riches and economic dominance that had brought the men together in a bond of brotherhood six years earlier.

Abebe Adebowale scanned through the contract that would soon hand over exclusive mining rights for the precious minerals of the little-known country in central Africa to an organisation owned by the four heads of the obscure *Alhalu*. Fareed Al Safadi had once referred to the syndicate in Arabic as the Solution in jest. The four collaborators subsequently adopted the term as their code name.

"It all appears to be fine, and as we had agreed," confirmed the soon-to-be-President.

"Of course, we intend to spread the mining operations between various entities, seemingly unrelated on the surface. We wouldn't want to invite inquisitive eyes!" said the French aristocrat leaning forward in his seat. "Your percentage will, as we agreed, be banked every quarter into a Swiss bank in which I hold a majority interest through one of my myriad of investments. There will exist no direct link tying us together. However…, I strongly suggest you be careful with how you disburse the funds… We wouldn't want you suffering the same fate as the incumbent… That wouldn't do at all!" he added. He fixed his gaze squarely on Abebe Adebowale as he sat back and

[88]

pulled deeply on the Corona.

"Mr Hathaway, Sir," announced the butler from the doorway, distracting the group. "There is an international call for you."

The Englishman rose and excused himself. He followed the butler to the study, then sat in the leather chair behind a sizeable imposing desk. He picked up the receiver.

"Hello?"

"We had a situation earlier today," a deep voice with a hint of a Scottish brogue spoke at the other end of the line.

"I'm listening!" Miles Hathaway didn't care for surprises.

"I've been informed that the British Government is delving deeper into the kidnapping of Brachfield's son. Two agents met and questioned the father and son two days ago. A Captain Ray Kazan and Gila Levenson."

"What do you know of them?"

"According to my source, both have been recently attached to a special unit under Sir Foster Braithwaite, Minister for Domestic and Foreign Intelligence Services, and with a direct relationship with MI6 and the CIA. Kazan was with British Military Intelligence and recently completed a two-year frontline assignment in Oman. Levenson is on secondment from Israel. She was part of the unit that rescued young Brachfield. "

"A danger?"

"From what I learned, I would say both are more than capable... and resourceful."

"You would do well to keep tabs on them."

"It's already in hand."

"I suggest we keep this information to ourselves for the time being. Until we have something more concrete, I would rather my associates were kept in the dark. No need to broadcast."

"Understood."

"Have you been compromised?"

"Our temporary location was traced through the telephone number, but I immediately took care of that. Although…"

"Although what?"

"It was visited this afternoon… and from the description, I have to assume it was Kazan."

"Were you seen? Recognised?"

"No, I took care of him."

"Took care of him? How?"

"He should have a headache for a couple of hours."

"What about the location?"

"It's clean. As always, no contact with the landlord. We've never met. He's an Indian national whose primary concern for cash outweighed any curiosity. Gloves were always worn, and entry and exit were by the backdoor. The building is near empty. It's not a prime address."

"Can the telephone be traced back to you?"

"The telephone was set up in the landlord's name. The extra cash saw to that."

"I take it calls cannot be traced back to us?"

"No, absolutely not! All calls from the phone were limited to the one source."

"When will you establish a new site?"

"It's already in hand. I should be up and running by tomorrow."

"You were correct to exercise extreme caution. It does you credit. Remember, the slightest slip could jeopardise us."

"I assure you that whatever they think they have will only lead to a brick wall."

"I'm gratified to hear that. Make sure it stays that way." He paused for a moment. "There is another matter that needs your attention."

"Yes?"

"Our man in Israel... I'm not convinced he will act in accordance with instructions... He could act irrationally. The money is far too enticing... I'm concerned he might move too soon, exposing himself. It could lead to questions we would not want asked... It's a risk we would be wise to pre-empt."

"I understand. How much time do I have?"

"The sooner, the better."

"I will travel the day after tomorrow."

"I'll leave it to you – you know what to do... And keep me informed!" The line went dead.

♦ ♦ ♦ ♦

London, England:

The thickset man with the shaved head and grey goatee replaced the handset and picked up a half-full glass of a single malt whisky. He took a slow sip of the mature spirit with a hint of oak and maple syrup – his brow creased in thoughtful consideration. Formerly of the British SAS and retired detective inspector with the Serious and Organised Crime Command nicknamed the Heavy Mob or The Sweeney, Jack Frasier allowed himself the one extravagance.

In addition to the expensive *Balvenie* fifty-year-old Scotch, he lived a comfortable lifestyle financed through his moderately successful security firm identified as *J.F. Security Services Ltd*. It was an organisation that served only one paymaster, although its invoices reflected several domestic and international clients. Jack Frasier was a meticulous and thorough professional, who only employed men with similar experiences whom he knew, trusted, and like him had no qualms in dispassionately

[91]

carrying out tasks ordinary men would not contemplate.

His family ties were limited to his divorced daughter and her ten-year-old child – Melanie. His wife had passed away from cancer ten years earlier. He doted on his granddaughter and spent as much time as his busy schedule allowed. She, in turn, was a devoted child and eagerly awaited his visits.

There were a few things to arrange before he left for the Middle East, now added to by a nagging concern over the day's earlier intrusion. He would assemble his team and make the necessary overseas calls first thing in the morning. He would get Mary – his personal assistant since the business's inception and office-staff-of-one – to book his flight in the morning. There would be no need to bother her at home. Another two glasses of his excellent brew and some Jazz music by his favourite artists, *Billy Taylor* and *Dizzy Gillespie*, would round off the day nicely.

9 July 31st, 1973

London, England

The five were seated around a round table in a conference room on the tenth floor of *Century House* – a twenty-two storey office block housing the UK's foreign intelligence services. The prominent building on *Westminster Bridge Road* was once reported by one of the country's leading daily broadsheet newspapers to be: 'London's worst-kept secret, known only to every taxi driver, tourist guide and KGB agent.'

"So, what do we have, and what do we know?" Colonel John Madison said, taking the lead. "Ray?"

"Not a great deal, I'm afraid. Our only lucky break came in, catching Adele Brachfield, making the call from the pub. The address Toby got from tracing the number she called led us to the East End address. It's a pretty run-down place. Businesses rent out furnished office space monthly from a local landlord."

"Did you talk to him?" interjected Ben Rutan as he unscrewed the top of a plastic thermos coffee pot.

"We managed to track him down after Toby's team turned up to dust the place."

"We're running the prints they lifted, although they uncovered a few latent impressions strongly suggesting gloves were worn. We have to assume, whoever wore the gloves are the ones we would be interested in… but you never know, fortune may smile on us," added Toby Gilmore.

"The landlord?" pressed the Colonel.

"A local property owner – Indian. He was reticent to say much at first, then I threatened him with a *VAT* (value-added tax) audit. He confirmed he had only met the man once when he signed up. He couldn't remember what he looked like, only that he was of average height. Nothing distinguishing. He said it was a long time ago, and he even quipped that we Englishmen all looked alike to him." Ray caught Gila out the corner of his eye, chuckling to herself at the remark.

"He reluctantly admitted that an advance payment of six months' rent was paid in cash. A further three months was also paid in cash and left in a plain envelope in a landlord-designated, metal postbox fixed to the lobby wall. He had never seen anyone connected with the rented space since. Although he did add, he rarely attended the property... Which would account for its sorry state."

"I suppose it would be expecting too much if he still had the envelope?" Ben said.

"He laughed and muttered something under his breath I couldn't catch when I asked," said Ray. "Anyway, I doubt whether it would have revealed a fingerprint."

"So we know that whoever rented the office was most probably a Brit and that this landlord fellow is averse to paying ten per cent to the Inland Revenue!" cut in John Madison.

"What about the phone? A bill might point to someone," said Ben passing the coffee pot to Toby Gilmore.

"Milk?" Toby offered back.

"Black for me, thanks," he said, then blew gently onto the hot liquid.

"Unfortunately, no! The landlord arranged it in his name. Again for an added cash consideration," replied Ray.

"Then perhaps the calls made from the telephone should turn up something?" pressed the CIA agent.

"We have looked into the line's activity. Only incoming calls were received, and all from payphones," confirmed Toby Gilmore, "including the call from Adele Brachfield."

"Then how? That would imply someone had to sit by the telephone twenty-four-seven in case a call came in."

"I suspect there was an answering machine hooked up and removed before we got there. All outgoing calls would, I imagine, have been made from a call box," offered Ray. "All untraceable!"

"That would make sense," remarked Ben.

"Whoever we're dealing with appears to be quite meticulous," said the Colonel.

"What we can assume is that there's more than one person involved." All eyes turned to Gila. "Well, the person that gave Ray a headache," she started, ignoring a *do you have to mention that again* look from Ray, "must have been at least six feet tall and pretty strong. That would rule out someone of average height the landlord referred to."

Just then, there was a tap on the door, and Andrea – one of Toby's team – popped her head around the door, informing Gila there was a call for her from Israel. Gila immediately got up and left the room.

"How are you and Miss Levenson working out?" asked Colonel Madison, taking the opportunity while she was out of the room.

"She's self-assured and a confident person who knows who she is and what she's capable of. It's early days yet, but Gila's more than able in a tight spot. I've seen her in action. Granted, this is a little different from what she's used to, but she'll do just fine," Ray replied. He didn't add how she wasn't intimidated by the dominant male presence, contributing on an equal footing – and that she was definitely appealing! He was becoming more at ease with her as the days passed.

"So, what about the Brachfield woman?" continued the Colonel. Ray glanced across the table at Toby Gilmore.

"We have her under surveillance. Nothing out of the ordinary until yesterday evening." Toby's comment immediately had the other three sit back in their seats. "She visited the *Corinthia Hotel* in *Whitehall Place* at just past eight and went straight up to room 526 on the fifth floor. A bottle of *Dom Pérignon* champagne with two glasses was delivered to the room shortly after. She stayed for two and a half hours and then left."

"Okay, I'm hooked!" declared Ben.

"My man immediately made a discreet enquiry, only to find out the room was booked in the name of David Minsky…, Ezra Brachfield's stepbrother." Gila's return halted the conversation momentarily as she resumed her seat at the table.

"Hold on! Are you saying what I think you're saying?" Ray shook his head in disbelief.

"David Minsky walked through the lobby five minutes later," added Toby Gilmore.

"They're having an affair?"

"Who's having an affair?" asked a bemused Gila. Ray turned in his seat to face her.

"It would appear that our beautiful and devoted wife is having an *affaire du cœur* with her in-law!"

"How does that figure?" the American said. "No way can he be the guy who set up this office!"

"It would appear there is a further twist to this tale,"

Ray said, deep in thought, raising his cup to his lips.

"So, how can the two be connected? An affair between Adele Brachfield and her brother-in-law and whoever is behind the office rental?" John Madison threw the question onto the table.

"I think it's safe to assume – when we consider the time frame – whoever used the building could well be connected in some way to Ariel Brachfield's kidnapping. The office was rented three months before the kidnap took place. As for Mrs Brachfield...? That's yet to be determined," offered Ray.

"Could she be in league with the brother-in-law?" suggested the CIA officer.

"For what purpose? Money?" asked Toby Gilmore.

"It doesn't make sense. Why would they have also demanded the six PLO bombers' release if it was for money? Anyway, according to what we know of David Minsky, he holds a significant amount of shares in the Brachfield group and isn't exactly short of a penny or two," responded Ray.

"What possible connection could there be? What would they have been looking to gain... in fact, what did they gain?" said Ben Rutan.

"In the end... nothing!" chipped in the Colonel.

"That's another thing," started Ray scratching his chin. "It was a big operation! I can't see that she, or for that matter the stepbrother – assuming they were behind the kidnapping in the first place – could have pulled it off on their own," responded Ray.

"I agree," Gila chimed in. "An operation like that in my part of the world would have also required some significant local connections. Anyway, she didn't appear to be unnerved by our presence the other day. If their effort had failed so dramatically, we would have noticed something."

"Gila's right. We would have sensed something in her manner," said Ray. "But… to be sure, I think we should put a tail on Minsky as well as the wife."

"Hopefully, that might turn up something," pondered Ben.

"Did you find anything interesting with the Brachfield media organisation, as we discussed last Saturday?" asked Ray.

"No, nothing that stands out. All the group's reporting appears neutral – basic investigative journalism. Nothing unusual or out of the ordinary," responded Toby Gilmore. "At least nothing that we could see."

"Might be best to keep an eye open," suggested Ray.

"There might be a connection between Minsky and Shaul Feuerman," said Toby Gilmore. "That's still a possibility we've yet to determine."

"Yes, how about this Feuerman character?" asked Colonel Madison, directing his question at Ray and Gila. "You met with the Israeli Ambassador. How did that go?"

"The Ambassador has agreed to make behind-the-scene enquiries," Gila said, evoking a quizzical look from the Colonel. "Oh! I'm sorry, I forgot to mention… he's a close family friend." Gila turned to Ray. "By the way, that was Avi on the phone. They've identified the man the kidnap leader volunteered. He's based in Beirut."

"Well then! In the meantime, you two best get yourselves over to Lebanon and see where that leads us," said Colonel Madison and reached for the coffee pot.

"We'll keep watching Adele Brachfield, and I'll arrange for the Minsky tail and see what else comes up," said the MI6 officer.

"There's still something I'm having a problem with," said Ray shaking his head, catching the attention of the others. "The demands for Ariel Brachfield's release would have never been met in full. The reward was one thing.

Brachfield was more than prepared to pay, but the release of the bombers...? That was an impossible demand... It was known from the outset the Israeli Government was never going to cave in..., and whoever was behind the kidnap must have known that too. It doesn't make sense..." He paused briefly before adding, "We're missing something here. Something that could unlock a vital lead."

10 August 3rd, 1973

Beirut, Lebanon

R ay and Gila stepped out of the Baggage Claims Hall through the automated glass doors into a busy open area. Arrival Halls were much the same the world over, except it always appeared more hectic in Middle Eastern airports. In among the crowd to the back stood two men looking, searching the new arrivals' faces. One spotted the tall, tanned man with the dark-haired woman and nudged his partner. The other man nodded, then they slowly picked their way through the crowd.

Ray led Gila snaking through the mêlée of people pushing, shoving, and shouting as they swirled around. They emerged into the daylight and were immediately approached by eager hawkers touting their wares and services. Ignoring the onslaught, Ray hailed a taxi and shielded Gila onto the back seat, then placed their suitcases in the boot.

The drive from *Rafic International Airport* to the *Phoenicia Intercontinental* situated close to the city's central district took a little over twenty minutes. Half an hour later, Gila knocked on the inter-connecting door and entered Ray's bedroom.

"It's a fabulous view!" said Ray over his shoulder while standing at the large window overlooking the Corniche and the Mediterranean sea on the ninth floor.

"I'm sure it is," she replied as she moved to the easy chair and slumped down with her feet up on the padded rest. "I'll never get used to all the flying," she said and exhaled deeply.

"Drink?"

"I won't say no!"

"Vodka, whisky, or gin," he said, peering into the well-stocked refrigerator.

"I'll take a whisky," she replied, her eyes closed. "On the rocks."

The flight from London Heathrow had started badly with an hour's delay, then another two-hour stopover in Rome before boarding the flight into Lebanon. Ray prepared the drinks with the usual vodka for himself and handed Gila her whisky when there was a knock on the door. He immediately reached out his hand, staying Gila, then went to the door and peeked through the eyehole. Ray held the door open as a middle-aged man passed by.

"Sorry, I couldn't meet you at the airport," the man apologised.

"We've met before," remarked Ray as he closed the door and followed the man into the room. He had a remarkable memory for faces. "You picked me up in Syria three years back. My first trip here... Umm, Wilkinson, isn't it?"

"Peter Wilkinson, yes. I was transferred here for my sins," he smiled. "Nice to meet you again, Captain Kazan," he extended his hand.

"Ray," responded Ray. "Allow me? My associate Gila Levenson." The two exchanged greetings.

"Can I offer you a drink?" Ray asked the Embassy man.

"Love to..., but must dash. I am late for a meeting with the Ambassador. It wouldn't do to upset him," he replied.

"Anyway, I trust this is what London requested." He placed a canvas holdall on the bed.

Ray unzipped the bag, removed a leather shoulder holster with a Browning Hi-Power pistol, placed it beside the bag, and extracted a *Walther PPK*. The smaller, more concealable, and lighter variant of the *Walther PP* – made famous by *Ian Fleming's* fictional character, *James Bond* – with its shorter grip and aluminium-alloy frame was Gila's weapon of choice.

"Call me Bond, Jane Bond," she had joked the first time Ray had noticed the weapon on her. He viewed the pistol with sardonic amusement and replaced it in the bag.

"Looks fine, thanks," said Ray.

"Also, this." He handed Ray a buff-coloured A4 envelope. "That's your man," he said as Ray pulled out a black-and-white photograph. It was taken two days ago. Your Mr Gershen passed it over with the man's details on the back." Ray glanced at the image and turned the photograph to read the handwritten information before passing it to Gila.

"Well, as I said, I ought to be on my way," said Peter Wilkinson, handing Ray a card. "My number should you wish to contact me. Take care," he added and made his way to the door.

"Short and sweet!" remarked Gila as the door closed behind him. Ray glanced at his watch. He had converted to local time during the flight into Beirut – 6:35 pm.

"What say you we go out and get something to eat?" suggested Ray downing his vodka. "Best be prepared. You never know," he said and tossed over her pistol, canvas holster and silencer.

"Give me thirty minutes," she replied.

It took Ray twenty minutes to shower, clean his teeth, and put on the trousers of a lightweight suit and an open-necked shirt. He stood at the bed, drew the pistol from the holster, and then removed a box magazine from the holdall. He proceeded to go through the well-practised procedure – now second nature to him – first depressing the magazine's exposed round with his thumb to check the spring action. Satisfied, he slid the full clip into the grip and cocked the weapon engaging one of the thirteen *Parabellum* rounds into the chamber. Ray paused briefly, then decided he wouldn't carry a loaded gun and racked the slide to eject the chambered round. Before returning the slide, he visually inspected the chamber, then depressed the release and removed the magazine. He replaced the ejected shell into the spring-loaded magazine, pushed the clip back firmly into the grip, ensured the safety was on, then lay the pistol on the bed and picked up the holster.

Ray slipped the harness over his shoulders and adjusted the strap so that the holster was tucked horizontally and comfortably in his armpit under the left shoulder. He did the same with the spare magazine carrier under his right shoulder. Happy with the snug fit, he holstered the weapon, picked up his jacket, and put it on. He reached into the holdall and took out the suppressor Peter Wilkinson had remembered to include, then blew through the muzzle device before slipping it into his trouser pocket. Finally, he briefly looked at himself in the wall mirror to check for a give-away, telltale sign under the coat before knocking on the inter-connecting door.

They had decided against the hotel's restaurant and instead opted to walk along the *Corniche,* looking out for a place recommended by the hotel's concierge. A short distance from the hotel, they turned down *Rue Dar el-Mreisseh.*

"It seems strange," mused Gila.

"What's strange?" responded Ray. "It's a beautiful evening, and we're going to what I have been assured is a splendid restaurant… And you have me for company." She chuckled at his witty remark, then, putting her arm through the crook of his left arm, added in a hushed tone.

"No, I mean here in Lebanon. Out in the open. Not hiding in the shadows. I know we're here for a different reason, but for the moment, I feel like any other tourist." Ray stopped and turned to face her.

"I think I understand," he said with a smile gazing deep into her eyes. He held the look briefly before adding. "Well, let's pretend that we're just a couple of tourists out for dinner and enjoy the evening. We go to work tomorrow… And talking about dinner?" he said as he nodded to a sign lit up in a deep orange. "Here we are!"

He opened and held the door ajar while Gila entered the restaurant aptly named *Casablanca*. Ray paused momentarily and stole a glance back the way they had come. He possessed an uncanny sixth sense – an ability to perceive when something was out of the ordinary. It only took a look, a gesture, a sudden movement avoiding eye contact, a distance carefully maintained, out-of-place body language – the intuitive way a brain senses something of which consciousness is unaware. Two years of fighting a nearly invisible guerilla enemy in southern Oman's mountainous terrain heightened his senses. It paid for him to be cautious and not ignore such feelings.

The two men in the hotel lobby had immediately attracted his attention. However, he gave no sign to avoid alerting their interest. His excellent memory for faces also brought to mind both men standing back at the airport's exit as he placed their luggage in the boot. He caught them again out of the corner of his eye, then followed Gila into the restaurant. He decided to keep the detection to himself. He had promised Gila a pleasant evening. He wouldn't disclose his discovery until the morning, assuming nothing untoward would happen in the meantime. However, he would be on his guard and prepared for any surprise.

Ray had sipped on one glass of wine throughout the meal, ensuring his senses weren't impaired by overconsumption, and before leaving the restaurant, he excused himself. He removed the Browning and attached the silencer in the toilet cubicle, cocked the weapon, and slipped it into the right-hand side trouser pocket. The walk back to the hotel over two hours later was thankfully uneventful, although their two observers had emerged from the shadows but kept their distance.

They walked to their rooms in silence. When they reached Gila's door, she turned to him, and for a moment, they stared into each other's eyes – her heartbeat quickened.

"Thank you for a wonderful dinner." Her tone suggested there was more to say.

"You're welcome… fellow tourist," he answered and was about to move away when she reached over and kissed him delicately on the cheek. He hesitated, then briefly looked away before gazing back at her apologetically.

"Good night, partner," he said and crossed over to his door. They glanced at each other and smiled before entering their rooms. Ray walked over to the inter-connecting door, paused, then turned the latch – Leyla was still in his thoughts. He took off his jacket, slung it onto the bed, then removed the pistol from his trouser pocket and slid it under the pillow. Pouring himself a large measure of *Smirnoff*, he sank into the easy chair and put his feet up. The two-man scrutiny was very much on his mind. Who was behind it and why?

11   August 4th, 1973

Beirut, Lebanon

Gila found Ray sitting at a table at the far end of the dining room next to the windows overlooking the palm garden and swimming pool.

"Good morning!" He stood to greet her.

"I see chivalry is not dead," she remarked with a broad smile and took the chair opposite him. He sat back down and summoned the waiter.

"What's your poison?" he asked when a young, fresh-faced man hurried over to the table. Gila observed the teapot in front of Ray.

"Coffee would be nice," she said.

"Sleep well?"

"*Achla!*" she responded.

"Achla?"

"Great!" she translated. I'll have to teach you a few Hebrew words and phrases…, although not here," she added, glancing around furtively. A waiter came to the table and placed a plate of bacon and eggs in front of Ray.

"Same for you?" Ray inquired.

"Ooh, no! Looks a little too heavy for me," she chuckled. "Some Bran and fruit would be fine."

"By the way, we have company," Ray said as he finished his meal and pushed his plate away, then drew the cup and saucer towards him.

"Since when?" she asked, looking up from her bowl of fruit.

"Yesterday. The airport." He took a sip of his tea.

"How do you know?"

"I spotted them in the lobby before we went out for dinner and recalled seeing the same two standing back and observing us at the airport when we were getting into the cab... And then they followed us to the restaurant and back."

"Why didn't you say anything?"

"No point. You were enjoying the evening. Why spoil it," he smiled and picked up a piece of toast.

"Hmm, thanks. Any idea who they are... what they want? And more importantly, how did anyone know we were coming?"

"I called Toby last night. I managed to catch him at the office before he left for home. He assured me that besides the team, only one of his team, Andrea, knew of our travel arrangements."

"Then how?"

Ray paused, buttering the browned bread.

"That's the sixty-four-million dollar question. I puzzled over it before turning in. I can only assume that we've been on someone's radar since last Saturday."

"You mean since our visit to the Brachfields'?"

"May well have been from Adele Brachfield's call to the East End office... It would fit."

"That would link her closer to an involvement with the kidnapping."

"It would appear so, yes!" He took a bite of the toast.

"That would also imply the brother-in-law."

"Possibly... Then again, the two occurrences may just be coincidental... not related."

"But how would they have known...?"

"It wouldn't have taken much detective work. If we were followed to Heathrow, they could easily have found out from the *Check-In* using a viable excuse which flight we were on and put a call through to here."

"Have you seen anyone this morning?"

"Yes… I popped into the lobby before coming into breakfast… On the pretext of thanking the *Concierge* for his recommendation – the Casablanca."

"Do you think they know you're onto them?

"No, I made sure I was overheard, without overdoing it, when I thanked the guy. They were sitting apart this time, reading a newspaper."

"So, what now? Should we *talk* to them?" she smiled conspiratorially, arching her eyebrows.

"No! But I think we should determine who's behind the surveillance before we look into the chap Avi identified."

"Okay, how?"

"Did you bring a swimsuit with you?" Gila gave Ray a quizzical look.

"No, why…? Should I have had?" Ray chuckled at the innuendo.

"There's a Boutique just off reception. I'm sure you could find something appropriate. The sun is shining, and the poolside looks inviting. That should keep one of them occupied watching you, and the other will no doubt follow me. We won't give them time to arrange anything else."

"Useful having a female partner, isn't it?" she quipped. "What do you have in mind?"

"The *Souk El Tayeb* is only around the corner. What could be better than a crowded, busy place like a *bazaar* to turn the tables. A bit of misdirection!" He gave her a wink, then added, "Let the hunted become the hunter!"

◆◆◆◆

By the time Ray walked through the elaborately carved stone entrance, the Souk was already teeming with activity. He smiled to himself at the thought of the other minder getting the better end of the stick – keeping an eye on Gila in her new fetching black single-piece, sunning herself by the pool. He was about to get a rude awakening.

Ray took his time as he slowly weaved his way through the congested main artery leading to a maze of sunless alleys and passages brimming with stalls and shops selling a diverse selection of goods. A mixed smell of spices, cooking meat, fabrics, carpets, leather goods, and scents filled the air. Early morning shoppers eagerly attended by wide-smiling and bustling merchants were too absorbed to show interest in the Englishman.

The exotic marketplaces – embodying the *beating heart* of Middle-Eastern cities – never failed to fascinate Ray. Bazaars had always been a central feature of everyday life, typically positioning the lesser valued products on the outer edges leading into the main area where stores offering the more expensive items such as jewellery, gold, and silk carpets would be found. There were no price tags tied or stapled to goods in those ancient emporiums. The experienced shopper would ask a price only if they were prepared to buy..., then the haggling would start – typically from half the amount. Negotiations were never hurried, and the final price agreed that the buyer was ready to pay, and the merchant prepared to sell. Both sides to the bargain would walk away, satisfied with the deal. That could not always be said for the eager tourist unfamiliar with the age-old tradition.

Ray spotted his mark. A hawker, wearing a light-brown *kandora* (robe) and sitting cross-legged on top of a pile of rugs, smoking a cigarette. He approached the man and

[109]

immediately extended his hand, then gave a quick touch to his heart. The merchant showed little surprise at Ray's familiar greeting, sensing a sale in the offing. The display suggested more than a possible purchase to the man hidden from view and watching from a distance. To him, his quarry was making contact. Ray continued to make small talk with the seller before thanking him, extending his hand, then walking away, leaving a somewhat confused and disappointed merchant. Fifty yards or so later, he stepped behind a kaleidoscope of hanging lamps and looked back in time to catch his tail questioning the hapless merchant. He smiled to himself as he watched the poor hawker gesticulating his innocence, then pointing and shaking his finger skyward – in customary Arab fashion – unhappy at being judged for doing something wrong.

Ray stepped back further and out of sight as his stalker hurried past, looking perplexed, scanning the area in all directions – his eyes darting more wildly with each passing second. The ruse had worked. The *hunter* was about to become the *hunted*.

Showing apparent signs of frustration at losing his target, the man eventually turned and, with an occasional furtive glance over his shoulder, made his way back to the entrance. Ray waited until the man had moved a reasonable distance through the mêlée before following, hoping he would lead him to somewhere other than back to the hotel. The general rule is not to be seen when following someone – a caution Ray's minder could not have appreciated. Ray kept back as far as he dared, stopping now and again and stooping slightly to reduce his stature below the crowd's overall height. Remaining inconspicuous was more challenging for him. Fair-haired with blue eyes and at just over six feet, he stood out in the local crowd like a sore thumb.

On exiting the Souk, the man turned left down a back street leading away from the hotel. Ray peered around the corner of the building and waited until he turned another corner, then followed in long, hurried strides. He caught the man take another left turn before briskly going after him. The leap-frogging continued for four more streets before Ray lost sight of him down a deserted, narrow alleyway lined on both sides with a continuous row of buildings, extending down to a dead end. Thinking he had entered through one of the entrance doors, Ray cautiously moved down the passage, gently pushing on each door. He hadn't caught the sound of a metal door opening or closing.

He had moved along halfway when the man suddenly leapt out of an opening brandishing a switchblade knife and lunged it point-first at Ray's midriff. Ray instinctively moved his body to the inside and, at the same time, grabbed the attacker's right wrist. In the same movement, Ray thrust his right elbow into the man's throat. With no time to draw his pistol, Ray stayed close to neutralising the knife. The man was more muscular than noted from a distance, and the blow to his bull neck only briefly startled him. Increasing his grip on the man's wrist, Ray slammed his forehead into the bridge of the man's nose. Blood spurted, and he cursed in guttural Arabic, *el Sharmouta* – filling Ray's nostrils with a foul stench of the man's garlic breath.

The assailant continued to grip the knife as he leaned forward against Ray, struggling to free himself from the hold. He flared his left arm out, giving Ray enough time to counter his intention by squeezing his abdominal muscles tight as the man drove his left fist into his side. Ray momentarily relaxed his weight, then stepped back onto the ball of his right foot. He again leaned fleetingly into the man maintaining the momentum. He pulled back and, in the same motion, pivoted his hips and, using his full-body strength, wheeled him around – throwing him down onto one knee. Ray immediately struck out forcefully with his right foot at the man's jaw, causing him to arch his back and drop the knife… before collapsing at Ray's feet.

Ray took a moment to catch his breath, then drew out the Browning from his holster. He kicked the man's switchblade away, then knelt beside him and placed the muzzle against the man's neck. He glanced up and down. The alley was still empty. No one had been disturbed or curious enough to venture out. His concern was unnecessary. Residents kept themselves to themselves in that corner of the world, knowing it was best not to ask questions or mind anything other than their own business. The assailant started to move as Ray tapped his free hand around his jacket, then reached into the man's inside coat pocket.

"Uh-uh!" He pressed the weapon tighter, encouraging the man to remain still. "Who sent you?" he asked as he extracted a black leather wallet and placed it on the man's chest.

"*Ayreh Feek* (screw you)!" the man hissed.

"Come now," Ray responded calmly, continuing to speak in Arabic, "there's no need to be impolite. Now, who sent you?" he repeated as he unclasped the wallet with one hand and pulled out an identity card. The man didn't respond, glaring up at Ray.

"Ibrahim Haydar," Ray read out aloud the man's name off the ID – all Lebanese are obliged to carry by law. "Well, we know you're a Lebanese national, Ibrahim… Now let's start over… who are you working for?" his tone hardened.

"Screw you!"

Ibrahim Haydar cried out in pain as he recoiled from

the pistol blow to the side of the head.

"Who sent you?" Ray persisted calmly.

"I… I," the man's resistance was beginning to weaken. "I… can't say!"

"What's this?" Ray took out a visit card with a company name imprinted in bold: *Al-Shariff Construction SARL*. "Is this who sent you?"

"I'm already a dead man… you've seen to that! Failure is not something that's tolerated. You might as well shoot me!" There was palpable fear in the man's trembling voice. Ray paused for a moment gazing intently into the man's eyes, looking for every nuance of expression. He knew when someone was telling the truth, then raised and stood over the dejected assailant.

"I'll keep these for the time being," he said, referring to the man's ID and the card, then holstered the pistol. "You might want to disappear for a while if you fear for your safety," he added. "I suggest you advise your friend at the hotel to do the same." Ray backed up a couple of paces and kicked the knife further out of reach as he walked away.

Twenty-five minutes later, Ray stepped out onto the steps leading down to the Hotel's open-air swimming pool. He spotted Gila stretched out on a lounger on the opposite side of the pool, wearing a white, woven beach hat and reading a magazine. He hesitated for a moment – liking what he saw – before walking around the diving board towards her.

"I saw you coming down the steps," she said, raising her head and looking from under the wide brim and over a pair of black-framed sunglasses.

"I approve," he said with a broad grin.

She looks great in clothes and even better in a swimsuit.

"I'm so pleased," she responded in a silky tone, "seeing as you've had me staked out all morning like a choice piece of meat. So, what happened...? What did you find out?"

"I'll be back in a sec," he said as he spotted Haydar's partner sitting at the outside bar at the end of the pool. The man swivelled away on his barstool as Ray approached, too late to avoid eye contact. Ray climbed onto the seat next to him, propped an elbow on the counter, and then leaned towards the distinctly uncomfortable stalker.

"Here!" he started, handing over the other man's ID, "It's time you stopped ogling my alluring associate and left."

The surprised man feigned innocence until he recognised his colleague's photograph, then, with a quizzical look at Ray's smiling face, took the card, climbed off his seat, and hurried off.

"Can I get you something, Sir?" asked the barman as Ray watched the man climb up the steps and disappear into the building.

"What's the lady drinking?" Ray asked as he revolved himself, back to face the bar.

"Madamoiselle has been on a *Pimms Cup*," he replied, referring to the thirst-quenching, English summer drink Gila had tasted for the first time during the Brachfield visit.

"Then I'll take half a half-pint, and the lady will have another," he responded. "Can I make an outside call?" Ray asked, reaching for the telephone a short distance away.

"Certainly, Sir. Just dial 99 first," he replied and busied with the order while Ray dialled Peter Wilkinson's number.

"So, are you going to tell me? I saw you dismiss our minder," Gila said as Ray handed her the drink, then sat facing her at the foot of the lounger. He took a long sip

[114]

before recounting the morning's events.

"You'll have to work more on your surveillance skills!"

"It wasn't easy trying to blend in," he chuckled.

"Who did you ring?"

"Peter Wilkinson. I asked him to check out this outfit." He passed her the visit card he took off Haydar. "It's a limited liability company," he added, referring to the SARL title. "I think we should see what he comes up with before we approach our man. You never know how he may be connected to this company."

"Did he say how long it would take?"

"Mm-hmm." Ray took another sip of the Pimms. "He reckoned he'll have the information by this evening. He'll call when he's done."

"So, we sit tight until then?"

"Mm-hmm."

"Did you bring a swimsuit with you?" she asked, raising her eyebrows suggestively over her sunglasses.

12 August 4ᵗʰ, 1973

Tel Aviv, Israel

Shaul Feuerman stood in his fourth-floor office looking out over the recently completed *Yarkon Park* and opened to the public with its extensive lawns, botanical gardens, and large ponds. The *Yarkon River* glistened in the late afternoon sunlight as it wound its way through the expansive site. The city had grand plans for its new creation.

He looked at his watch and stepped away from the window. It was time to leave. He often came into the office on a Saturday – it wasn't necessary, but it was good to be seen, and thankfully, he also got him out of the marital home. He was an ambitious man who saw a position beyond the Shin Bet Assistant Director (Internal Security). He had set his sights on other more prestigious Government Departments and never missed an opportunity, scheming and manipulating his career path.

Taking on the Brachfield project was the most significant risk he had undertaken. It took little effort to obtain the lead role for a man skilled in saying the right things others wanted to hear and a master at taking advantage of weaker individuals to achieve his goals. Still, the clandestine approach offering the opportunity of succeeding combined with a readily available reward was too compelling to ignore.

He climbed into his four-year-old, Department-allocated vehicle and, leaning forward, slipped the key into the ignition. He hesitated, then sat back, reached into his inside jacket pocket, removed a pack of *Noblesse,* and pulled out a cigarette from the distinct green soft-pack. He struck a match and lit it, then took a long draw before exhaling the thick smoke into the roof – the vehicle's automatic lighter had ceased to produce a glowing heat a long while ago.

The temptation to buy the new series *Mercedes-Benz 280* grew stronger each time he sat behind the wheel of the nicotine polluted car – even though he was the main culprit in the continued build-up. He promised himself that no one would be allowed to smoke in *his* new Mercedes, including himself, as he exhaled more smoke onto the windshield covered in a thick film – no amount of cleaning could entirely remove. Only a brand new glass would do the trick.

What was the point of the two-hundred thousand US Dollars reward – together with a further quarter million for his role in the plot – sitting in the Swiss account if he couldn't spend just a small amount to buy his dream car? He had taken a considerable risk and had earned the right to enjoy a little luxury in his life. He ignored the voice in his head, reminding him what he had been instructed and not to access the account for at least two years, and then in only small quantities. It was to be considered a retirement benefit. However, he continually convinced himself that no one would question how he acquired the vehicle or where the money came from. Of course, there was his wife! How would he be able to convince her – to see reason? He would have to absorb a barrage of questions on where the sudden influx of funds had come from and then the arguments of how the money could have been spent on something more essential. She had been pressing for a bigger house since his promotion two years earlier. Perhaps a divorce would be the best thing – no need to share his good fortune.

No! His mind was made up; he would visit the showroom next Wednesday. There would be enough time to think up a plausible rationale for the windfall.

Shaul stubbed out the half-smoked cigarette in the crammed ashtray, turned the ignition, reversed out of the parking bay, and set off on the forty-five-minute drive home. As he passed through the gate and turned onto the main boulevard, he didn't notice the grey Toyota sedan pull away from the kerb behind him.

◆ ◆ ◆ ◆

"Hello, Jay Team. Target is on the move. Over." Jack Frasier insisted his team use the military format when relaying messages over the two-way radios. He was still a soldier at heart.

"Hello, Alpha. Bravo here. Understood. Target is on the move. Over," acknowledged Tim Grover, stationed some thirty-five minutes further along the route.

"Hello, Alpha. Charlie here. Understood. Target is on the move. Over," came the stock response from Sean Bridges sitting behind the wheel of a fully-laden, six-wheel tipper-truck – stolen the previous afternoon.

"Hello, Alpha. Delta here. Understood. Target is on the move. Over." Simon Dodge was positioned the furthest along the route.

"Hello, Alpha. Echo here. Understood. Target is on the move. Over." Ex-Company Sergeant Major John McIntyre looked at his watch and moved further into the tree line. Radio silence would be strictly adhered to unless an unforeseen event threatened to jeopardise or alter the job at hand.

His team was all ex-SAS, loyal, reliable, and thoroughly professional in carrying out their duties with callous indifference – no matter the task. The five had arrived in the country separately, leaving the UK with their valid passports and entering Israel with uncontested forgeries. They had wasted no time surveilling the mission's target and organising a plan of execution.

Jack Frasier kept enough distance to keep the other vehicle in sight. There was no need to concern himself. The man was a creature of habit, always sticking to the same route home. If he were to deviate, the operation would be cancelled immediately and attempted again on the Monday. Time, however, was not on their side. He was confident the team was ready and able to carry out the individual roles. The four were his favoured operatives who had never failed to deliver.

"Hello, Jay Team. Target passed Mark. Over." The message confirmed the vehicle had passed a predetermined landmark. The four were not expected to respond acknowledgements to that notification, other than in an emergency. Sean Bridges immediately turned the key, and the truck's engine sprang into a throaty roar. Ten minutes to go.

As the head of JF Security Services drove past, Tim Grover pulled away and followed for a short distance, then pulled into the middle of the road, jumped out, and immediately opened the bonnet of his car. Simon Dodge had already carried out the same manoeuvre to prevent interference from the opposite direction. His job was to simulate engine trouble and ensure no other vehicle could be in the action's vicinity. Traffic was generally light on that particular stretch of rural road – an important reason for its choice.

"Hello, Charlie. Countdown. Over."

[119]

Sean Bridges immediately gunned the engine keeping a sharp lookout for the target vehicle. Seconds later, the Government car came into view as it slowed into the sharp bend. On the count of predetermined seconds under his breath, Bridges released the clutch simultaneously as pressing down hard on the accelerator. The truck lurched forward, picking up speed as it hurtled down the wooded track. It was all a matter of timing. The critical phase had been practised several times the previous evening.

He rammed his right foot down hard on the truck's brake pedal just before impact, striking the vehicle dead-centre – directly between the front and rear doors above the rocker panel.

The force of the impact from the twenty-ton Mercedes-Benz truck's momentum catapulted the car off the road. It continued to roll viciously down the slope until it pounded to a stop against a tree. John McIntyre immediately sprang into action and ran to the vehicle. Shaul Feuerman's body hung limply through the smashed windshield, his face an unrecognisable bloody mess. The operative placed his fingers on the dead man's neck. Satisfied, he scrambled up the slope and jumped into the front seat of Frasier's car. Meanwhile, Bridges had backed the heavy-goods vehicle off the road, switched off the engine, and ran over, joining the other two.

"Go! Go! Go!" The brief message urged Grover and Dodge to leave immediately and in opposite directions. No one looked back as the car sped off. Mission successfully completed. The team would enjoy a generous bonus on their return to the UK. Shaul Feuerman would never know the irony of a Mercedes-Benz causing his death.

That same evening, Frasier and Bridges checked out of their hotel and made haste to catch the last flight out of

Tel Aviv. The destination was immaterial. McIntyre and Grover caught a taxi into Jordan to fly out of Amman, leaving Dodge to travel into Lebanon and disappear out of Beirut.

13 August 4th, 1973

Beirut, Lebanon

Peter Wilkinson joined Ray and Gila in the Hotel's plush dining room a little after eight that evening.

"Any luck getting the info?" asked Ray as he poured out a glass of white wine for the Embassy man.

"Yes," he replied, taking a seat and picking up the glass. "It wasn't easy being a Saturday, but I pulled in a couple of favours." He took a sip of the drink. "Mm, very nice…Here's to alcohol, the rose coloured glasses of life," he gushed, then removed a sheet of paper from his jacket.

"Al-Shariff Construction SARL is a limited liability company," he started, reading from his notes. "From what I've gathered, it's a medium-sized civil engineering enterprise involved in projects throughout the country, but mainly here in the north. They mostly carry out Government infrastructure contracts – roadways, underground work, maintenance, that sort of thing. Nothing too sophisticated. However, the business appears more profitable by about twenty-five per cent than the average company engaged in this industry."

"Connected?" Ray asked, knowing how things worked in the Middle East. Lebanon's underbelly was no different with its rampant corruption, nepotism, and cronyism.

"We have to assume so," scoffed Peter. "Now we

come to the interesting part. The board of three directors appears run-of-the-mill sorts except for the Managing Director, by the name of Khalil Shaheen."

"Isn't that…?" Gila started to say.

"Our man in the photo?" Ray finished. "It certainly is." He removed the photo Avi had provided from his pocket and placed it on the table. In his early forties, the image was of a stocky man with a thick black moustache and bushy eyebrows.

"He doesn't look much like the senior man of a successful company," quipped Gila.

"You should never judge a book by its cover," Ray jested. "But I have to agree with you… So that's it?"

"Oh, no! There's more. The company's shareholding is split between two other entities – a steel importer and concrete supplier."

"Nothing unusual there," Ray said. "Related industries."

"If I may continue… The ownership of these two businesses is further split between numerous sister companies engaged in a variety of products and services, all of which ultimately fall under a single entity – *Al Safadi Holdings*."

"Sounds all a bit complicated!" snorted Gila.

"I'm not a tax accountant, but I would suggest it's all about limiting tax liabilities. Avoidance, unlike evasion, is acceptable, even in this part of the world. Anyway, I was assured that it's all legit – nothing shady."

"Okay," cut in Ray. "So, who are the people behind this holding company?"

"It's not a case of who are they…, but who is *he*?"

"Okay, now you've got me intrigued," said Ray leaning forward onto his elbows. Gila followed suit.

"*He*… is Fareed Al Safadi. An extremely successful Lebanese businessman. Made his money mainly in the arms trade, and according to our sources, continues to do so." He pulled out a photograph and, placing it on the table, pushed it in front of them. "The arms dealings are not altogether the legitimate part of his organisation. A lot of grey areas where that's concerned!"

"Handsome!" remarked Gila looking at Al Safadi's black and white image.

"He's reputed to be one of the wealthiest men in the country... Came from humble beginnings... Made good," added Peter.

"I think we need to step back a second," Ray said, "and view this from the outside... This Khalil Shaheen could not have known before we arrived that he was a suspect in the kidnapping. His name was given up to Avi by the principal character in the abduction, and he didn't survive to pass anything along. As far as I'm also aware, Avi hasn't divulged the information to anyone other than us. That being the case..." He paused and leant back in his seat, tapping his index finger gently on the table. "I'm now convinced that whoever tipped Shaheen off, and I'm assuming he put the two clowns on our tails, is based in the UK."

"Which could imply a British involvement in Brachfield's kidnap," intervened Gila.

"It certainly appears to be the case," responded Ray. Peter Wilkinson sat quietly, sipping his wine while Ray and Gila continued to bounce the topic between them. "Which brings me to my misgivings about the kidnap demands... They were always too fantastic to have been met by the Israelis." He picked up Shaheen's photo and looked hard at the man. "I can't see how this man... is someone who would come up with such a grand and elaborate scheme?"

"Now, who's judging a book by its cover?" retorted Gila.

"Touché," chuckled Ray. "No, he's not the whip master in all this. He can't be!" He dropped Shaheen's picture back on the table and pointed to the other photo. "It stands to reason. This handsome face here," Ray returned Gila's earlier playful jibe, "as he owns the construction company and everything in between, we have to assume he holds sway over the board, the decision making, and particularly over our friend here." He referred to Khalil Shaheen. "I would have to say he could well be involved…, but to what degree?"

"Are you thinking what I think you're thinking?" chipped in Gila. "Alhalu?"

"Alhalu?" cut in a puzzled Peter Wilkinson.

"It's the handle of an outfit that's been behind a few questionable ventures and killings, to put it mildly, that may well have been connected with the kidnapping. Although at this point, it's pure conjecture."

"As I recall, wasn't he abducted in Cyprus?" asked Peter.

"Yes, why do you ask?"

"Interestingly enough, *Al Safadi Holdings* owns significant properties in the region… which includes Cyprus. It may just be a coincidence."

"Right now, these coincidences are adding up like two-and-two makes four," remarked Ray.

"Now would be a good time to look more closely at this Shaheen," suggested Gila.

"I agree. However, he will undoubtedly be on his guard, now I've pre-empted his involvement," said Ray.

"Maybe so, Ray. But he can't know that we have his name from the group that held the Brachfield boy… that we know he was behind the kidnapping."

"That's true," responded Ray after pausing briefly in thought. "The two goons watching us was no doubt by his order."

"That would imply that this handsome face," she smiled, "can't be acting alone…, if he's our man?"

"That would also suggest at least two heads making up the Alhalu. Assuming we're right, of course. I wouldn't expect this Al Safadi is someone who takes orders. No!" he picked up the photograph and studied the man's face again. "This man is a winner, and winners like him don't have bosses. No matter how pretty he looks, we also have to assume that he must be pretty ruthless if he's in the arms trade. It's not a business for the faint-hearted!"

"We could be looking at more than two," offered Gila leaning back in her seat. "There's also still the question of Feuerman."

"Let's hope the Ambassador can dig something up. If my suspicions about him are founded, it could well add another piece to the puzzle," remarked Ray rubbing his forehead. "I think we should pay a discreet visit to this construction outfit tomorrow… See what we can pick up."

"Now I'm hungry! How about you, Peter?" Gila said and picked up her menu.

"The lady's hungry," echoed Ray opening his menu.

14 August 5th, 1973

Beirut, Lebanon

The urgent sound of car horns filled the air as they made their way along the congested street. There appeared to be no order to the chaos with intermittent vehicles travelling in the wrong direction and overladen motorcycles zigzagging around all-too-frequent potholes. In the absence of pedestrian crossings, people walked through the traffic and haphazardly crossed wherever they spotted an opening.

"It's a beautiful country with an abundance of ancient ruins, glorious beaches, mountains, restaurants, and nightlife. It's sunny most days, and although it's hot and humid, particularly in the city in summer, it's still a lot cooler than the Gulf states." Peter talked over the steering wheel as he negotiated his vehicle through the free-for-all. Ray was sitting beside him and Gila in the back seat behind Ray.

"However, as you can imagine," he continued, gesturing to the outside of the vehicle, "life here can be pretty hectic – stressful, in fact. The electricity supply is generally unreliable, and in some areas running water is non-existent. Having said that, people are used to it. Of course, the well-to-do have it best. Money talks!"

After a while, they left the central district, and headed

north along a quieter road parallel to the coast. The Embassy man had volunteered his services as a driver during the previous evening's dinner.

"How else am I to repay you for this delicious meal," he had argued his offer. "Besides, I'm pretty familiar with the area, and I won't fleece you!" he chuckled.

Prepared for the unexpected and concerned for Peter's safety, Ray was hesitant at first but gave in to his insistence on the understanding that he would remain in the car at all times.

◆ ◆ ◆ ◆

Khalil Shaheen was sitting on the edge of a table – his large buttocks supporting his heavyset frame. He reached down and picked up a packet of *Dunhill*. He removed one of the filter-tipped cigarettes with a slow and deliberate movement, placed it between his lips, and returned the pack to the table. He fixed his gaze on the two wide-eyed men bound tightly to chairs for a few seconds before turning his attention to a box of matches next to the cigarettes. Again he went through a drawn-out act of removing a matchstick, then running the head along the box's striking surface. The Managing Director of Al-Shariff Construction held the lit match briefly before lighting the cigarette. He inhaled deeply, exhaled – blowing out the flame – then dropped the spent match onto the floor and replaced the matchbox. Drawing on the cigarette again, he then slowly blew out the smoke – all the while staring impassively at the two captives.

"So, you two pricks couldn't watch the Englishman and the woman without being seen and then getting caught?" he sneered contemptuously.

"I'm sorry, Effendi! He tricked me!" stammered a flustered Ibrahim Haydar – his wrists tied behind the chair's back and his feet to the chair's legs. Blood was dribbling from his nose down his face. "I thought he was making contact with the rug seller at the Souq! He spoke with him for a long time... They appeared to know one another... I thought I was doing the right thing."

"The right thing?" Shaheen scoffed. "He played you..., you idiot! I wouldn't be surprised if he had you pegged at the airport!" He shook his head. "What did you tell him after he so easily disarmed you. You pathetic excuse!" he spat out the words.

"Nothing... I swear to you Effendi. Nothing. I said nothing!" pleaded Ray's stalker. Khalil Shaheen stood up, shaking his head. He glanced at the grim and stoic faces – utterly without humour – of the three tough-looking men, standing in silence behind the detainees.

He was also angry with himself. He should have known better than charge the two pathetic clowns with the task. However, he didn't expect them to have been so easily discovered and, worse still – faced down. The man and woman were more adversarial than anticipated. The London contact failed to mention that! His main concern was to ensure the *boss* didn't find out about their, and by extension... his incompetence. He had to protect the organisation and the objective at all costs. Should he displease the boss, he would suffer a fate far worse than what he was about to inflict on the two hapless employees.

"I'm to believe you...?" he sneered. "You'll say anything to save your brawny ass. Now, what did you tell him exactly...? Because according to your failure of a fucking partner, he managed to take your ID!"

"Effendi, I swear to you... I said nothing... He had a gun to my head... What was I supposed to do?"

"You were supposed to die..., you snivelling shit!" he hissed loudly – his patience was growing thin. "Okay,' he continued, seeming to calm down, "perhaps I've been too gentle with you." He swallowed hard and gestured to one of the men as he propped himself back on the table.

The building's metal walls suddenly threw back the echo of a startling discharge. Still bound to his chair, the second man was propelled face forward onto the floor. Ibrahim Haydar gasped out loud as a thick red liquid seeped slowly around the dead man's head. His face turned ashen, and beads of sweat formed on his forehead. He looked up – abject fear in his eyes.

"I swear…, please…, I swear…! The only thing he took from me was my ID and a company card!" he blurted out, eventually finding his voice.

"Perhaps now, we'll get to the truth at last," sighed Shaheen. He stepped over to the cowering Haydar and bent over him, his mouth close to the frightened man's face. "So now he knows who you work for?" Haydar felt the man's foul smoker's breath on his cheek. He knew he was facing his last minutes and was desperately trying to fathom a way out.

"That's all he knows! There's no way he can connect us to anything… He has no idea!"

"Us?" Shaheen snorted loudly through flared nostrils. "There's no *us!*" He stepped back and cupped a hand over his forehead. The halfwit had conceivably opened a trail to the organisation, although he was still unsure how much the interfering Englishman knew.

"Did he mention anything at all?" he pressed.

"No, nothing… I swear. He just kept asking who I was working for."

"Now, think carefully before you answer," his threatening tone suggested a dire consequence for the terrified employee. "Did he mention the Brachfield kidnapping?"

"No, no, nothing at all… Just wanted to know who I

[130]

was working for. I said nothing… He pistol-whipped me, and I still didn't talk. On my mother's life… I swear." he continued to assert his claim.

"As I recall, you miserable shit… your mother died two years ago!" He spat out the words.

Ibrahim Haydar lowered his head onto his chest. He was a doomed man – about to pay the ultimate price. He should have taken the Englishman's advice. But then, to where would he have run? They had eyes and ears everywhere. Khalil Shaheen threw down his cigarette, then stubbed it out with a vicious twist of his shoe. He needed to think. He had to be sure before he silenced the second incompetent for good. Could one of the sacrificial lambs he had put in place to guard the Brachfield brat talked? He had made sure he remained well in the background – out of sight. Only the leader, Ibrahim, knew who he was. Could Ibrahim have talked before he was taken out? No one was to have survived – they were all expendable. It had been planned. The Palestinian refugee camps were rife with gullible young fanatics ready to take on a cause against the Jews and die in the process. So, if no one talked, what were they doing there, and why did the London contact warn him? His frustration was growing to a fever pitch, his temper rising. He wasn't going to get a conclusive answer from this man.

He moved to the table and picked up a pistol, cocked it, turned to face Haydar with cold eyes, and pointed the weapon. The two bullets – fired at point-blank range – slammed into the man's chest, throwing him backwards.

"Let's hope the sharks find them useful! Take them out in the boat and dump them!"

Just then, a sharp sound of metal connecting with concrete on the other side of the warehouse alerted the four men. Khalil Shaheen immediately snapped his head towards the clatter and gestured to two of his henchmen.

◆ ◆ ◆ ◆

Peter Wilkinson pulled the car over and stopped some distance from a high line of chain-link fencing topped with barbed wire.

"That's the place," he said as he put the vehicle in neutral and applied the handbrake. Ray peered through the windscreen at a large corrugated metal building inside the enclosure. A signboard in elaborate Arabic and English proudly announced the premises as Al-Shariff Construction SARL to the world.

"Okay?" Ray asked over his shoulder. Gila was already getting out of the vehicle. Ray opened the passenger door and, before exiting, turned to the Embassy man.

"Turn the car around, park it on the other side, keep it running and keep your head down," he instructed him. Peter nodded in acknowledgement. Ray and Gila glanced around before leaving the vehicle and gingerly headed towards the double gate.

"Hmm," muttered Ray as he noticed the loose fastening chain. "Looks like someone may be here." They stood back and looked in all directions to see if anyone was around, then Ray moved the barrier back without engaging the latch. He slid back the latch and pushed the unlocked gate wide enough for them to slip through.

"In case we need to beat a hasty retreat," he remarked.

They used the assortment of machinery and equipment parked in front of the building to shield their approach. Entrances into the building consisted of two large roller shutter doors, a loading bay between them, and two pedestrian doors at either end. Gila stood with her back to the wall looking out as Ray tried the handle at the nearest entrance. It was locked tight. The place was deathly quiet other than the muted sound of distant traffic. They quickly moved down towards the second door staying close to the building. Ray tried the handle. The door was unlocked. He sighed a sigh of relief, then, careful not to be heard, quietly turned the handle. A lingering smell of motor oil and grease greeted them as they silently entered the building.

Ray and Gila moved behind a backhoe digger perched on a hydraulic lift and listened for giveaway sounds. Satisfied, Ray nodded to an open exit, and they picked their way through an assortment of workshop equipment. A flatbed truck with an engine dangling from a hoist above its open bonnet gave them temporary cover. They edged into an expansive section of the building cluttered with more construction plant and equipment. The sudden reverberated sound of a gunshot further into the building stopped them in their tracks. They glanced at each other, then hurried towards a transparent dividing curtain.

Standing on either side, they peered between the hanging strips of plastic clouded with particles of dirt, grime, and grease. Ray immediately recognised the terrified form of Ibrahim Haydar. He shook his head at the thought the man had not heeded his advice, and his partner – Ray assumed was the prostrate body still strapped to a chair on the floor – had been the first to pay the price of failure. There was no mistaking the bulk of Khalil Shaheen standing over Ray's unfortunate stalker. They were some twenty metres away and able to catch Shaheen's questioning of the ill-fated employee.

Gila caught Ray's eye at the mention of the Brachfield kidnapping – a clear indication of Khalil Shaheen's involvement. They continued to listen and observe the interaction and Shaheen's mounting frustration from behind the plastic divide. There was no doubt in Ray's mind how it would end for Ibrahim Haydar when Khalil Shaheen suddenly picked up a pistol, and without hesitation, fired twice point-blank into the trussed-up

[133]

man's chest pitching him backwards.

Ray immediately indicated it was time to leave and stepped back with a nod of his head, accidentally catching a loose spanner lying on top of a tractor wheel. The loud clatter instantly alerted the four men as the hard, alloy steel struck the concrete floor.

Shit!

Without a second thought, Ray reached under his jacket for his pistol, cocked it, and pressed his back against the wall. Gila instinctively mimicked Ray's action. He inhaled deeply as the familiar rush of adrenaline started to fill his body. He glanced at Gila, knowing she was experiencing the same sensation. He was thinking on his feet – there would be no avoiding a confrontation.

They waited with bated breath.

Leading with his pistol arm, the first man cautiously pushed aside the curtain on Ray's side and stepped through. The second henchman followed. He cast his eyes around searching when he became aware of a presence directly behind him, too late to avoid Ray's pistol muzzle pressed into the back of his neck. Gila had simultaneously followed suit with the other man.

"Drop it!" Ray urged through gritted teeth and jabbed the barrel further to emphasise his *request*. The man hesitated for a moment before reluctantly dropping his weapon onto the floor. The second man needed less encouragement from Gila.

Grabbing the man by the coat collar and pressing the pistol into the small of his back, Ray steered him back through the curtain to a look of astonishment and consternation on Khalil Shaheen's face. It only took an instant for him to realise who were the man and woman.

"Well, well!" His eyes flashed angrily. "What do we have here?... The inquisitive Englishman and his Jew whore!"

"I suggest you place the pistol back on the table before you hurt someone else," demanded Ray with an insistent, steady glare.

"And what?" Shaheen responded, lifting the weapon and holding it as he weighed it in his hand. "You're going to shoot me?" he laughed mockingly.

"No one else needs to die here," Ray said, tightening his grasp on the henchman's collar.

"Oh! I see! You're threatening to shoot *him* if I don't comply... Is that it?" His tone became more aggressive. "Do you really think his life is any more valuable than this asshole's," he gestured at Haydar's sprawled body. Ray felt the man he was holding tense under his grip. "You could have done me a favour and killed this scum yourself instead of leaving it to me." A smile eased over his face. "No, my friend… You won't pull the trigger. You're not the type to kill someone in cold blood. If you were, you wouldn't have let this piece of worthless shit live!"

The exchange wasn't going to end well. Ray sensed Gila thought the same. He caught her in his peripheral vision edge behind her man – shielding herself further from the inevitable. She remained quiet – her eyes fixed on the third man. He was glowering back at her, his right arm hanging loosely by his side, clenching and unclenching the hold on his pistol.

Khalil Shaheen was getting agitated. It was not a good sign. His glare kept switching between Ray and Gila. Ray desperately weighed up their limited options. The killer was not about to give way. Ray could not see them walking away quietly from the impasse. He fast realised there could only be one outcome.

"As I said, there's no need for anyone else to get killed. It's up to you. All I want is information," Ray persisted as he carefully released the safety catch, unheard and unseen, as the *stand-off* continued. Shaheen remained rooted to the spot, scowling at Ray – challenging him. The third heavy was becoming more and more skittish, shuffling his feet and darting his gaze between Ray and Gila.

Ray's full attention was focused on Shaheen. He trusted Gila's was on the other man. When, and if the time came, there would be no hitting the replay button. The hair lifted on the back of his neck. He felt a prickling sensation on his scalp. A slow, twisted smile began to spread over Khalil Shaheen's face – his eyes narrowed. What happened next was over in a flash.

Ray's instincts kicked in a split second before Shaheen loosed off two rapid shots in his direction and ducked behind the table. Shifting to his right, Ray fired once at him as the first bullet hissed past his left ear. Shaheen's other shot caught the man Ray was holding square in the face, killing him instantly. Ray released the man's dead weight and dropped onto his right knee. He was in survival mode – disconnected, reacting instinctively, his mental focus sharpened. Without hesitation, he fired four more times in rapid succession at the crouched form behind the table. The big man slumped to the floor. Gila hadn't wavered. Immediately shoving her shield forward, she fired three consecutive shots at the third henchman's central mass. He managed to let off two random shots before gasping out in pain and pitching to the ground.

An eerie silence fell over the area as the firing ended abruptly. Ray and Gila stood stock-still, pointing their weapons at their downed targets, breathing heavily. The foul smell of blood hung in the stale stillness. They took a few moments to collect themselves.

"You okay?" Ray asked between breaths.

"Mm-hmm," she responded. "I'm good." She was breathing heavily. Ray stepped over the dead man lying at his feet and crouched beside the motionless figure of the second man.

"Looks like he's had it too!" he said as he rolled the man over. "Must have caught a stray from your chap." He moved over to Khalil Shaheen. Thick blood was seeping from his throat and chest. He wouldn't be answering any questions.

"I think it's time we disappeared," Ray said calmly.

"You've got a mess on your shoulder!" noted Gila pointing to his left shoulder as Ray made his way back to her. He glanced at a splatter of bloody tissue.

"That was close!" Shaheen's second bullet – travelling at high velocity from short-range – had ripped through the man's face, narrowly missing Ray's head. "Thank god it's not mine!" he declared, smiling nervous relief.

Getting hold of a nearby rag, he wiped off the messy deposit, dropped it next to the body on the floor, then gathered up both his and Gila's spent shells and put them into his jacket pocket. They wouldn't be leaving anything behind that could point to their presence.

When they returned to the workshop at the opposite end of the building, Ray picked up a cloth from a workbench and wiped the handles on both sides of the door before engaging the inside lock and closing it behind them. They kept a constant lookout as they made their way through the gate, then engaged the latch and briskly walked to the car. Thankfully, the area was deserted – not a soul in sight.

"Was that gunfire?" Peter appeared edgy as they climbed into the vehicle.

"Yes!" answered Ray curtly. "I suggest we get a move on but take it easy. Let's not attract any attention."

◆ ◆ ◆ ◆

"I have to make a couple of calls, and Gila and I need to decide on our next course of action," Ray said before

[137]

opening the passenger door. "Can we meet in the bar… say, at eight?"

"Fine by me," replied Peter. "See you then."

"I think I need to take a hot bath," said Gila when they arrived at Ray's bedroom door.

"You okay?" He guessed at what she might be feeling. She needed to be alone – to collect herself. Near-death experiences weren't easily brushed aside with a witty remark or gesture. Real-life was nothing like that depicted in movies.

"I'm fine. Just give me thirty minutes," she smiled encouragingly.

"Knock on the door when you're through," he said with a wink as he turned the key.

Ray took off his jacket, removed the recovered shells from the pocket, placed them on the dresser, and then inspected the bloody stain before tossing it on the bed. He would call housekeeping after his shower.

He sat on the edge of the bed, slipped off the shoulder holster, and then removed the pistol. Depressing the release, he expelled the magazine and racked the slide to eject the chambered round. After replacing the shell into the spring-loaded magazine, he smacked it against the palm of his right hand to align the rounds, then pushed the clip back firmly into the grip. Ensuring the safety was on, he returned the un-cocked pistol to the holster and draped it over the chair.

He reminded himself that only nine rounds remained in the magazine, should he need to use the weapon again before leaving the country. He made sure he flushed the eight brass shells down the toilet before stepping into the shower cubicle. The hot water felt invigorating as it cascaded over his head and down his back, running down his face and collecting in large droplets on his chin. As he leaned forward on both hands against the shower wall, he

[138]

couldn't prevent himself from reliving the morning's event, asking himself the obvious, what if?

What if he hadn't pre-empted Shaheen's sudden action. What if he hadn't been holding onto the man's collar? What if he'd moved to his left and not his right? The round that cleaved through the man's face narrowly missed his cheek! What if he'd been wounded, or worse still? He shuddered at the thought – so many *what-ifs*.

As so often was the case in such situations, luck had played a part in both of them surviving the ordeal. Fortunately, the same could not have been said for Khalil Shaheen and his three associates. The most troubling thought of all – running through his mind – was what if Gila hadn't acted decisively?

That was a close call!

He could not have possibly predicted with any certainty how she would have reacted when placed in such a circumstance. He needn't have been concerned. She had read the situation and acted instinctively, passing her trial-by-fire with flying colours. He smiled nervously at the thought. He still recalled how he had responded to the first stressful encounter with his life on the line and how it evoked a uniquely different rush from the feelings of exhilaration experienced in the many near-reality exercises he had been put through during the training with the SAS. There was no substitute for the real thing. He had been taken to the brink more than once and had already discovered what he was truly made of.

His introspection briefly turned to the man he killed. He had reacted with impunity, instantly dehumanising his target without a second thought. He felt neither anger nor hate each time he depressed the trigger. He was in a fight for his life. There was no question of morality. He shrugged off the feeling of self-admonishment.

Ray had already dressed in a fresh shirt and slacks and

was relaxed in the easy chair by the window with a large vodka in his hand when Gila knocked gently on the connecting door.

"It's open!"

Still looking a touch flushed from the hot bath, she came in and immediately went to the mini-bar. She took out a whisky, grabbed a fresh glass from the tray, hopped on the bed, and propped herself with her back against the headboard. Ray watched her with a quiet reserve.

"You okay?"

"Yes," she replied with a wide reassuring smile as she poured a *Johnnie Walker* from the miniature into her glass. "I'm fine!"

"Okay... So, what have we learned?" Ray kicked off. "We can safely assume from what we overheard that Khalil Shaheen was linked with the kidnapping." He paused momentarily. "However, I don't for one minute believe he was the mastermind behind the operation."

"You still believe that Fareed Al Safadi was the brains?"

"Absolutely, don't you? I can't see how this clown was capable of pulling off something that big. Let's face it – we watched him in action. Did he strike you as someone with the capacity to carry out something that complex?" Ray took a sip of the vodka and frowned. "There's another thing... Why would a Lebanese interest demand the release of PLO insurgents unless there was a significant Palestinian connection... and I haven't seen one. Not even a hint! It also doesn't make sense."

"It's beginning to be pretty clear that whoever was behind the plot didn't expect our Government to comply with their demand from the outset. There's also the London connection. He's... was part of a locally based enterprise. I doubt he would have had the international association," added Gila.

"I'm convinced he was just a cog in a wheel which I firmly believe is larger than appears for now... and that Al Safadi has to be our next line of inquiry."

"Well, we could always go and knock on his door and ask," chuckled Gila.

"Wouldn't that be nice," laughed Ray. "Top-up?" He got up and walked over to the mini-bar.

"Why not?" responded Gila. Ray took out two bottles, tossed her the whiskey, and sat back in the chair.

"There's not much we'll gain from hanging around here," he said.

"Where to next, then?"

"It has to be Cyprus," he replied without hesitation. "That's where Ariel was abducted... and Peter confirmed that Al Safadi had significant interests there. It could be just a coincidence, of course."

"But that's not what you're thinking?"

"No, it's not." Ray ran his open hand slowly down his face and gripped his chin, thinking. "I'll contact the Colonel and Toby later. We'll need a few essentials for our next port of call."

15 August 7th, 1973

Cyprus, Mediterranean

The six-seater speedboat swayed and pitched as it made its way across the sea, still choppy from a storm the night before. As the Cyprus coastline grew further away, the late afternoon was rapidly progressing towards evening.

Michael Darragh Doyle, known to family, close friends, and allies as Micky Da, or just Micky, gave a rueful grin as he watched an uncomfortable Liam O'Doherty struggle with the rolling motion of the boat. The man had a surprisingly weak stomach for a rough and tough paramilitary and had not looked forward to the trip.

"Sure, I wouldna have had the fecking fry up, had I known beforehand," he had complained, referring to the greasy meal of sausage, eggs, and chips he insisted on eating following their arrival earlier in the day.

"If you're gonna retch, do it over the side and not in the boat," Doyle ribbed his close friend and fellow volunteer of the *Irish Republican Army*, better known as the IRA. He was leaning back, relaxed with his arms outstretched loosely along the gunwale and looking towards the increasingly distinct shape in the distance. It had been a while since he had last felt so at ease. He closed his eyes, welcoming the occasional cooling spray of salty water on his face. The open expanse of water held no hidden threat as his thoughts were preoccupied with the thrum of the boat's engine mingled with the sound of waves buffeting the hull.

"Why'd he have to park the fecking thing so far out?" grumbled O'Doherty from the other side of the stern, interrupting Doyle's tranquil moment.

"It's a yacht, you uneducated eejit! It's not fecking parked…, it's at anchor," jibed Doyle. "If you're so curious, why don't you ask him when we get aboard?"

"Shite… It's still a long way out!" retorted O'Doherty, and clutched his stomach as the boat hit another swell. Doyle chuckled in amusement at his friend's discomfort.

Micky Doyle was a third-generation member of the IRA. His grandfather, Sheamus, rather than enlisting in the British Army, was one of the early volunteers during 1917 in what was then known as the *Irish Citizen Army*. His father, Michael – after whom he was named – joined in the struggle in 1932. His grandfather was killed in 1922 during the *Irish Civil War,* and his father was fatally wounded from a grenade in 1937. It was widely held that he deliberately shielded his comrades taking the full blast himself.

Doyle grew up believing the story but rarely talked about it. Besides his father, his hero was undoubtedly *Eamon de Valera*, who opposed the settlement granting dominion status to become Northern Ireland, preferring to carry on armed resistance. Continuing with his steadfast belief that Ireland should be completely rid of the British, Doyle had aligned with the *Provisionals* in 1969 – known more infamously as the *Provos* – following a factional split in the Sinn Féin political party. To him, violence – particularly terrorism – was the only recourse to achieve a united Ireland.

Determined that her only child should not follow in

his father's footsteps, Doyle's mother safeguarded him while nurturing him and encouraged his education leading to a degree in Business Studies from the prestigious *Queen's University Belfast*. Her dream of a violent-free future for her son sadly came to an abrupt end a year after graduation. She was caught in a firefight between a British patrol and an IRA sniper while returning home with her groceries. She was mortally wounded and died in hospital soon after. Arriving too late to comfort her, he swore that her death would not go unpunished. It was a British bullet that had killed her.

Doyle had grown into a ruddy-complexioned man standing six feet with dark-brown, wavy hair and piercing brown eyes. His long narrow nose sat above a square jaw. A permanent short boxed beard partially hid a scar down his left cheek. He kept himself fit and had a muscular build. He was not what women called handsome but had an appealing attraction to the fairer sex. A man of few words, he often gave the impression to outsiders of being unusually withdrawn and silent.

Forced to live further in the shadows since being directly implicated in the murder of a British soldier two years earlier, he had no attachments other than occasionally bedding a dissatisfied wife of an Ulster police constable. Doyle was one of several paramilitaries on the British authority's *Wanted List*. He knew he was living close to the edge and had once confided in O'Doherty that he likened himself to *Icarus* – flying too close to the sun.

"Icarus, who?" his friend had responded in ignorance.

Doyle's exceptional intellect and organisational skills were recognised early on, and he quickly rose through the ranks. Possessing a high mental capacity adhering to logic and reasoning gained him the trusted role of *Quartermaster General* – a position he had held for the past five years. His elevated responsibilities included the acquisition, concealed storage, and maintenance of the Provos' arms cache.

Liam O'Doherty was the opposite of his fellow paramilitary. A compact build and three inches shorter, he had mussed fair hair and darting eyes below bushy eyebrows. He maintained a permanent peppered stubble and a rascal's smile. Having played truant with indifferent parents for most of his teenage years, he developed a tough and scrappy street-smart compared to Doyle's educated upbringing.

They had become fast friends surviving more than one scrape along the way. Although likened to chalk-and-cheese, the two complemented each other and enjoyed occasional verbal sparring and playful banter.

◆◆◆◆

"The boat's nearing, Sir," declared the steward looking out over the top-deck gunwale at the stern of the yacht.

Fareed Al Safadi didn't respond and looked up at the sky in a lounge seat nursing a whisky. Unlike his mood, the clouds had all but disappeared, promising a pleasant Mediterranean evening. The news he had received that morning directly from Beirut's Chief Of Police – with whom he had a longstanding *relationship* – had unsettled him.

Insisting on a detailed account over the radio, he struggled to make sense of the described scene discovered in the early hours the previous day. His pragmatic approach to problems led him to deduce that Khalil Shaheen had been conducting an interrogation of sorts with two men on the company's payroll. He wasn't questioning why, for he had no aversion to Khalil's tactics – that's what he was hired for. There would have been an undisputed reason for his inquiry. The annoying question was, who had interrupted the activity and seemingly dispatched him and the other three so readily? The man would not be easily replaced. He had traits rarely found in others – essential attributes he required in his organisation. Then there was the more important question of why?

Following Beirut's contact, he had immediately got in touch with the other members of the syndicate. Perhaps they could shed some light on the event. The call he took half an hour earlier from Jack Frasier in London was even more disturbing. Were the British intelligence officer and the Jewish woman responsible for Shaheen's demise? What had they learned? Had they determined his involvement in the kidnapping? His innate logic convinced him there could be no other probable explanation. In his mind, their presence in Beirut pointed to one obvious answer. The nagging question was: had the Zuhuania project now been compromised?

"Sir?" The steward's voice cut into his troubling thoughts.

"Ah! Gentlemen!" Al Safadi immediately rose to greet his two guests. The matter would have to wait – there was business to attend to. "Welcome," he said, flashing a smile and extending his hand. "I trust you had an uneventful journey," he took each man's hand in turn, then indicated for them to take a seat at the table.

"Can I offer you a drink? I made sure we had some *Jameson*'s Irish single malt whisky onboard."

"Fine by me," responded O'Doherty, always eager and willing to partake.

"Thank you," said Doyle. To refuse would be inappropriate, but he would ensure he held onto the one glass. He needed a clear mind, and alcohol didn't aid in negotiations. His was a huge responsibility. The hard-earned millions he was about to divest his organisation was serious business. He had been charged with securing the best possible deal.

"This is some fecking boat!" remarked O'Doherty accepting a glass full of whisky from the steward.

"You have to excuse my ignorant colleague," cut in Doyle. "It's a first for both of us. It's a remarkable vessel."

"No, please. It's a Benneti. I'm rather proud of her. I took delivery of her in '71." He was always ready to talk about his pride and joy, given a chance. "She's referred to as a Classic Yacht with a length of a little over thirty metres, with a maximum speed of thirteen knots and cruises at ten knots."

"What's the difference between a *knot* and a mile?"

Doyle smiled at his friend's continued ignorance of maritime matters.

"A simple conversion is to multiply miles by one-point-one-five to give you speed in knots," replied Fareed Al Safadi.

"Seems an odd fecking term," smirked a bemused O'Doherty and took a sip of the smooth-blended drink.

"It's how a ship's speed was measured a few hundred years ago… Measuring the knots in a rope strung behind the ship and distance travelled," Doyle interjected, looking to end his friend's persistent questions. "But I'm also intrigued why you would anchor so far offshore," he said to their host.

"I enjoy the privacy," Al Safadi replied with a telling grin. "Sláinte," proclaimed the Lebanese, uttering the commonly used Irish toast and raising his glass. "I trust I pronounced it correctly," he added.

"Sláinte," responded O'Doherty without correcting him.

"Your health," repeated Doyle.

"To a successful conclusion to our business," said Al

Safadi with a wide smile.

"To an equitable transaction," countered a guarded Doyle. He was a man with a cause. The man sitting opposite was an opportunist. His organisation's need and the arms dealer's greed were the only reasons that had brought them together. They had met for the first time in Malaga, Spain, six months earlier. Doyle had not taken to the man finding him slick and full of himself but kept his feelings hidden.

"Never can trust a fecking Arab," he had commented to his superiors after committing to a badly needed arms deal.

"Now to the business at hand," declared Al Safadi beckoning over the steward and indicating for refills. "My ship is on route and due to dock late tomorrow afternoon. I propose you remain here until then. We have two very comfortable berths for you. You can inspect the shipment before loading it on board."

"We wouldn't want to put you out," responded a reluctant Doyle, preferring not to be too obliged to the Lebanese.

"I should remind you, gentlemen, that there is a significant British Army presence on the island. May I suggest it wouldn't do to expose yourself to possible recognition." Al Safadi was only too aware of Doyle's standing with the British. He was always careful when dealing with questionable clients and ensured he had whatever advanced intelligence he required to provide his business was safeguarded. J.F. Security Services had its uses. Besides, he had a reputation to maintain, and he wasn't about to compromise his investment.

Doyle smiled and nodded his agreement to the offer. The man was right – there was too much at stake. Personal prejudices should not impair his mission.

"There will be time enough later," added Al Safadi.

16 August 8th, 1973

Cyprus, Mediterranean

Gila slid into the passenger seat of the *Ford Escort* rental car.

"Where are we going?"

"*Akrotiri*," replied Ray while struggling with the seat's release lever. "Must have been a bloody midget!" he asserted, referring to the previous driver. He pushed back, eventually succeeding in adjusting the seat to accommodate his frame. "That's better! At least the steering wheel's on the correct side," he added and turned the key in the ignition.

"Why is it you British insist on driving on the left when the rest of the world drives on the right?" she quipped. "Is it your typical arrogance and the need to be different?"

"Now, now! Many countries drive correctly," he retorted as they pulled away from the hotel's forecourt. Ray had booked them into the *Amathus Beach Hotel* in *Limassol*, a city situated on the southern coast and adjacent to the territory of Akrotiri. It was the same hotel Ariel Brachfield, and his friend had stayed at. "Anyway," he continued, "I'll have you know that it was the ancient Romans who established the rule of *keep left*. It was natural for transport and animals to move to the left against oncoming traffic. And when you think of it... it makes a lot of sense."

"And how's that?" cut in Gila, continuing to tease him.

"If confronted by an attacking enemy… which side would you instinctively move to when drawing your sword?"

"I don't use a sword!" she retorted. "And what if I was lefthanded?" she realised she was heading into a trap. "How is it you know so much about it?"

"I knew you'd ask!" he chuckled, receiving a playful slap on his arm. "Anyway, the habit was carried on through the ages. All we're doing is honouring the age-old practice. It's what makes us Brits different… We like to adhere to tradition. Look at our monarchy, for example. One of the oldest in the world!"

"If I know my history, the Japanese have an older monarchy dating back over two-and-a-half-thousand years," she interjected.

"Granted," he responded. "I said one of the oldest."

"So, what is this Akratori?" she asked, giving up on the witty retorts.

"*Akrotiri,*" he replied, correcting her pronunciation. "it's one of our two British Sovereign Base Areas, or SBAs created when we gave the Republic its independence. It's essentially a military base and gives us a vital foothold in the region. It's quite something – comprising several village districts, with a couple of churches. Cypriots also own property in the territory, although it's administered by the Commander of British Forces, Cyprus. The place is like a little England – albeit with better weather! In the same way, the *Vatican* is in the middle of Rome. The other area is *Dhekelia*, further east along the coast past the port, *Larnaca.*"

"Have you been here before?"

"No, it's my first time."

"You seem to know quite a bit about the place."

"You forget, I was – technically still am – with Army Intelligence. I'm supposed to know these things," he grinned.

Gila leaned on her elbow against the open window, her head tilted towards the outside as she took in their surroundings. The warm onshore breeze swept over her face and bounced around inside before expelling through Ray's side of the vehicle. Twenty-five minutes later, they veered left at a sign for *Episkopi*, heading towards the Mediterranean Sea in the distance.

"Episkopi is the capital of both SBAs," Ray informed her.

"What's that?" She pointed to a square-shaped stone structure off to their left. Ray slowed the car.

"*Kolossi Castle*," he replied. "If my memory serves me, it's a fortified castle built sometime in the fifteenth century. It's quite a tourist attraction… and before you say anything, we've no time for sightseeing."

Eight kilometres further on, Ray turned right for *Episkopi Garrison*. He pulled up in front of a red-and-white boom barrier as a Military Police sergeant stepped out of the guard hut.

"Captain Ray Kazan and Miss Gila Levenson," he said, handing over his ID.

The MP took the ID, re-entered the hut, and, standing at the window, picked up a telephone. Thirty seconds later, he returned to the vehicle and passed back Ray's identification.

"You are expected, Sir. The HQ building. It's the large one opposite the parade ground. You can't miss it," he said and, taking a step back, saluted smartly. A single-striper standing by the barrier immediately pushed down on the counterweight, pivoting the pole upwards to clear their entrance into the garrison.

"I don't believe it!" Ray remarked as he pulled up in

front of the HQ building in a space designated for visitors.

"Don't believe what?" Ray didn't respond as he got out of the car. A uniformed officer was approaching the vehicle.

"George! How nice to see you!" Ray declared, grasping the man's hands in his. "This is a pleasant surprise!"

"Hi, Ray! We've been expecting you," he remarked with a beaming grin, then cast a curious eye at Gila.

"Let me introduce you… Gila Levenson… my associate," said Ray releasing the officer's hands and turning to Gila.

"Miss Levenson," 1st Lieutenant George Robertson bent slightly at the waist as he took her hand in his.

Ray, you lucky sod!

"George and I graduated from Sandhurst on the same day and were stationed together at Ashford," explained Ray.

"Until he was spirited away to the Middle East on some mysterious assignment," responded George. "He was always the adventurous type, never happy unless he was in the thick of things! Even volunteered for a spell training with the SAS," he smiled, directing his comments at Ray's alluring companion. "Unlike me – content to be a desk jockey!"

"How long?" Ray asked, moving the conversation away from him.

"Been here just under twelve months."

"We must catch up but first, did you speak with Colonel Madison?"

"I can't say I wasn't surprised to receive a call directly from the Colonel himself," he said as he started to lead them to the stepped access into the building.

"Welcome to my inner-sanctum," he said as he opened a door at the end of the ground floor corridor.

[152]

"Neat!" quipped Ray tartly as he entered. As expected, the office was sparsely furnished with typical military-grey, steel furniture. Ray smiled to himself as he and Gila sat on folding chairs in front of the desk.

The Army never changes. Long on demand and short on comfort!

"I'm sorry. I was unable to obtain a Walther PPK as requested. We're somewhat limited to specifics in our armoury. I trust the Browning will do? I know it's Ray's favourite pistol," George Robertson said, placing two shoulder-holstered weapons on the desk.

Gila reached forward and removed one of the weapons and immediately pressed the catch, smoothly released the magazine into her hand, checked it, cleared and made it safe, then finally set the safety. Ray watched George as he eyed Gila with impressed interest.

"It's fine, thank you," she said, replacing the weapon in the holster.

"I signed for both…" he started to say before Ray interjected.

"We'll return them before we leave. Thanks, George."

"Colonel Madison also requested a pair of binoculars and an ordnance survey map of the country," he added again, reaching into the desk drawer and placing the items between the holsters. "Finally, this lists the properties owned by Al Safadi Holdings and associated concerns." Ray glanced briefly at the sheet of paper before passing it to Gila.

"I should also inform you that the *Papillon Bleu* is currently anchored some way offshore from *Famagusta* – on the east side of the island."

"What's the Blue Butterfly?" asked Ray, translating the name from French.

"Fareed Al Safadi's yacht," replied the Intelligence officer catching Ray and Gila by surprise. "I don't suppose you can tell me what you're up to?"

[153]

"Sorry, George... can't say. Let's just say we're looking into someone of interest."

They covered the one-hundred-and-twenty kilometres in a little under two hours, arriving outside the fringe of the easternmost city of Famagusta just after midday. Ray pulled into a layby and reached for the map lying on the backseat.

Before setting out, Ray had spread the island's ordnance survey map out on the car's bonnet. Using the list the Intelligence officer had provided, he had marked the various Al Safadi properties' locations. All bar one were either commercial buildings or apartment blocks in either the capital, Nicosia or Famagusta. They were headed towards a warehouse complex further north of Famagusta. What had further aroused their particular attention was that it also included a private jetty.

"If we're right about Al Safadi, it's got to be from where they took Ariel Brachfield across to Lebanon. He said the trip in the van was pretty long, although he couldn't say exactly how long it took. He was, after all, blindfolded and scared out of his wits!" reminded Ray.

"Using a fishing boat also made sense. If Safadi's yacht had been used, it would have been an easier clue to follow," Gila had added.

"This road skirts the edge of the city and should get us to this point," Ray said, tracing the route with his index finger. "That's where we should locate the premises."

He refolded the map leaving the city and surrounding region exposed, passed it to Gila, and then pulled back onto the road. Twenty minutes later, they turned down a gravelled side-road and headed down an incline towards the coast and a cluster of large plain buildings.

"That'll do! Don't want to get too close," Ray remarked, bringing the vehicle to a stop alongside what appeared to be a row of empty premises. Once a bright white, the paintwork faded and peeling from a relentless sun. The windows grubby through lack of care, no longer permitting light into the interior. "Would you pass me the binoculars?" Gila unzipped a canvas bag lying at her feet, removed the pair, and handed it across.

"That must be it," said Gila leaning forward, squinting through the windscreen. A large sign proclaiming the site as *Invictus Imports & Exports* with an equally large warning notifying trespassers to stay out was affixed to metal perimeter fencing to the right of a double-gated entrance.

"Mm-hmm…," responded Ray – his elbows resting on the steering wheel with his fingers cupped around the outside edge of the lenses – creating a hood effect. He observed two men standing idly on the inside of the perimeter next to a metal-corrugated gatehouse. One was leaning towards the other, lighting his cigarette. Both were armed – *Kalashnikov AK-47* assault rifles slung over their shoulders. Other than the activity at the gate, the area appeared deserted.

"I think it's safe to assume they're not guarding food products!" he remarked as he lowered the binoculars and passed them to Gila. He stretched forward to view the row of buildings to their left. "The place seems abandoned otherwise," he observed. "Let's go around the back and see if we can get a closer look."

He shifted the gear stick into reverse and slowly backed up into a side alley. Noting a clear pathway behind him, he continued to the back of the building, stopped, removed the key from the ignition, and placed it under the driver's seat.

"In case either one of us needs to get behind the wheel, and we have to drive away in a hurry!" Ray said as he opened his door and climbed out of the vehicle.

Gila placed the bag on the car's boot, removed the two holsters, and passed one to Ray. He slipped the harness over his shoulders, adjusted the straps before removing the weapon, went through the usual checks, cocked the pistol, and replaced it in the holster. Gila was doing the same as he reached into the vehicle, removed two jackets off the backseat, handed over Gila's, and then put his on concealing the firearm. Gila nodded at Ray, and the two made their way gingerly along the strewn rear access staying close to the wall – occasionally peering through boarded windows at darkened and deserted interiors. They stopped at the last latched and padlocked door. A quick glance around, and Ray couldn't see anything suitable to break the lock.

"Nip down to the corner and keep an eye out!" he instructed Gila. She immediately hurried to the end of the building. He waited for a thumbs up, then balancing on his left leg, he drove his right heel with a forward momentum forcefully onto the locked side of the door. The screws holding the catch to the frame gave way releasing their grip on the entry.

"Nothing. No reaction," she took a breath on her return.

"There's something on the other side," Ray said and shouldered the door creating a gap wide enough for them to get through. He withdrew his pistol and entered first. Gila followed closely behind. Several wooden crates were haphazardly scattered around, obstructing the entrance. Ray pushed the door closed then stepped further into the building. Enough light was filtering in from the outside through cracks and spaces between the shuttering boards for them to get a clearer look once inside. A thick layer of dust on every surface confirmed the place had been empty for some time.

"I wouldn't be surprised if Safadi also owns these buildings. They give added security and privacy to whatever he's up to on the other side of the fence," Ray said, then pointed to a corner staircase to their left next to a lopsided forklift truck resting on the rim of its front wheels – both tyres deflated. He tested the first wooden rung to ensure stability before cautiously climbing to the first floor. A sprained ankle would be the last thing either would have wanted. The open floor was largely empty, with what appeared to be a partitioned office in one corner. A window, although thick with grime, conveniently overlooked the site.

"That's handy!" remarked Ray looking around for something to clean a portion of the glass for a clearer view. The two security guards were leaning against the fencing, still smoking – their backs to him. He found a piece of cloth and slowly rubbed an area of the dirt away, creating a circle in the bottom right of the window – large enough to give a wide enough field of vision into the enclosure opposite.

"Might as well be comfortable," remarked Gila, pushing a chair towards him she found in the office – its noisy castors in need of greasing.

"I'll need to get a look around after dark," he said as he sat on the chair and edged it closer to the window. "I'll take the first watch. Meanwhile, why don't you go and scout around," he added and lifted his feet onto the ledge. They were prepared for a possible vigil. Nothing had been planned. Although now convinced in their minds that Al Safadi was most certainly behind the kidnapping, they needed to discover something incriminating – anything that would point to his involvement. They were winging it – improvising, hoping!

Ray raised the binoculars and scanned the blue horizon. He could just make out what he assumed was Safadi's yacht moored in the distance. As he panned back across from the jetty, he caught sight of a dark-green, panelled van parked at the far end of the building – similar to the type described by Arial's holiday friend, Michael Winsham. The elevated position gave him an unobstructed view of the compound on the other side of the fence.

Coincidence? I think not!

Another indication they were more than likely at the location from which Brachfield was shipped over to Lebanon.

♦♦♦♦

Ray was lying with his eyes closed next to Gila on a bale of coloured rope.

"I think you'll want to see this," she said. He got up immediately, and she handed him the binoculars. The chair's swivelling castors made a squeaking sound as she pushed away from the window. Ray knelt down and peered into the compound.

"Where?"

"Out to sea. Straight ahead," she directed his gaze.

In the distance and slinking towards them head-on was a medium-sized ship.

"I can't tell for sure, but it looks like a fishing trawler," said Ray from behind the binoculars. The national flag denoting the ship's origin was fluttering in the onshore breeze at the ship's stern. "Looks like it's registered in Panama," added Ray, noting the distinct four-quarter, red-and-white rectangular pattern with a red and a blue star on each of the two white squares.

"It could be the one that Brachfield was on," opined Gila.

"Mm-hmm, you could be right," Ray responded, maintaining his watch on the inbound vessel.

Twenty-five minutes later, the boat pulled up alongside the jetty. Two crew members threw a ladder over the side, and two more clambered ashore and immediately set about tying both the stern and bow mooring lines to the dock's iron bollards.

"*Ash-Shujā*," Ray read off the vessel's name.

"It's Arabic for *Hydra*. It's the largest star constellation lying in the southern hemisphere," Gila said, sidling alongside Ray to get a better look.

"And also the multi-headed beast if I recall my Greek mythology. Didn't *Hercules* kill it during one of the twelve quests some king or other tasked him… I've forgotten the name." continued Ray. "What was the story?… Ah! Yes. If you cut off one head, two more grew back in its place."

"So the myth goes," interjected Gila. "He managed to kill it by cutting off the immortal head."

"I wonder if there's an irony there?" mused Ray thinking of the Alhalu… Hello, what's this?"

"What?" asked an inquisitive Gila.

"Here," he said, handing her the binoculars. "Look out towards the yacht."

"Looks like an inbound speedboat. I can make out about six on board."

"Maybe we'll get to see our Mr Fareed Al Safadi," smiled Ray, as he raised off his knee. "If we're to learn anything, I need to get over there."

"How do you intend to do that?"

"I can climb over there," he pointed to the far left-hand corner where the perimeter fence ended and was affixed to the building. "It appears to be in a blind spot, judging by the angle. Hopefully, the two characters at the gate won't be able to see me."

"Only one guy," she confirmed, looking towards the compound gate. "One of them is walking towards the boat."

"Okay! That's better! Only one to worry about."

"What about getting back?"

"It'll be dark soon," he answered, looking at his watch. "That'll be my cover."

"And if you run into trouble?"

"You'll just have to improvise, won't you?" He winked impishly. "Keep an eye out on that spot. I've got to be able to get in and out without them knowing."

"Then watch out for loose spanners!" she teased.

Ray held back at the corner of the building and looked around towards the gate. The remaining guard stood with his back to the entrance, appearing to be more interested in the jetty's growing activity – cigarette smoke curling up over his shoulder. Silently, cautiously and using whatever cover was available, Ray hastily crossed over the open area to the chain-link fence and momentarily pressed his back against the corner, listening.

Gila watched Ray intently with one eye on the gate, although unsure of what she might do without exposing herself, should he be spotted. He removed his jacket and, gripping it between his teeth, latched onto the top wall fixing with his left hand and the wire fencing with the other. Placing his left foot on the bottom bracket, he scaled effortlessly to the top of the railing and draped his coat over the barbed wire. In one fluid movement, he swung his right leg over, securing a temporary foothold against the wall, grabbed his jacket, and with knees bent to soften the impact, dropped to the ground. A cursory glance to his left, then he immediately darted to a side door. The man at the gate hadn't moved – the commotion around the ship had masked Ray's entry. From her vantage point, Gila exhaled a loud sigh of relief.

He tried the handle – it was unlocked. He gently pulled down, pushed the door ajar, and peered into the interior dull-grey light. He briefly looked up back at the window, assuming Gila was watching, and flashed a cocksure smile before stepping inside and quietly closing the door behind him.

She chuckled openly and shook her head at his boldness. She suddenly felt her face flush at the thought of his handsome and athletic build, his deep blue eyes and charming manner, and then she felt her insides quiver slightly – anxiety was creeping in. As much as Gila tried to resist, she felt an ever-growing sexual attraction to him. She couldn't deny the sense of euphoria when she was with him – the allure of his innate decency and intuitive way with her. His protective nature was never subduing or threatening her independence or inner strength intensified since her father died. She had always held out against getting too close towards her occasional flings, but Ray was different. He was difficult to oppose. She had already decided to give way to her emerging feelings and accept wherever they might take her.

Ray held at the door while putting his jacket back on and listened for ominous sounds before walking towards several wooden crates stacked in the expansive space's centre. He translated the stencilled black Cyrillic script: **ДЕТАПИ МАШИН** (Machine Parts).

Additional text warned HANDLE WITH CARE, and an arrow indicated the *right-side-up*. His curiosity aroused, he picked up a crowbar lying on top of one of the rectangular boxes. He paused briefly, listening out, then wedged the flattened curved-end into the seam at one end and slowly prised the nailed lid away from the body of the container. Moving further along, he re-wedged the jemmy to raise the cover further until he got a clear view of the contents. The eight *Kalashnikov AK47* automatic assault rifles racked firmly in place with two wooden spacer supports were not *Machine Parts*.

Well, this confirms he's an arms dealer!

Satisfied with what he saw, Ray secured the lid as quietly as he could, then turned his attention to a larger crate again with similar stencilled text. He again prised the cover using the crowbar to reveal a different consignment comprising *RPG-18* with *PG-18 High-Explosive Anti-Tank* (HEAT) rocket-propelled grenades – a familiar weapon from his stint fighting the Soviet equipped guerrillas in Oman.

Now, where's this nasty lot going?

Ray's thought was suddenly interrupted by voices outside. As quickly as he could, he fastened the lid and looked urgently around, then scurried for cover behind shelving to the side. He squeezed between a stockpile of packing cases just as the roller door engaged. Seconds later, the place was brightly lit from large ceiling lamps. He backed further into the shadows and drew his pistol.

He crouched between two stacked levels giving him a narrow but reasonable view to observe six men enter the warehouse. He was cornered with no way out other than through them. His heartbeat quickened, and he started to consider his options if he were to be discovered. Were they armed? If the two at the gate were any indication, then he had his answer. Would he be able to surprise them long enough to dash across to the side door? Could he hold them off long enough for Gila to respond? Would she be able to react quickly enough? He would have to be sparing with his ammunition.

"Well, gentlemen. Your shipment is all here and ready to be stowed aboard," announced Fareed Al Safadi coming into view. He cut a dashing figure in an all-white suit, black tie, and a white, broad-rimmed felt hat with a black band.

"I would like to take a look at what we're buying." The Irish accent caught Ray's immediate attention. He strained to make out the man whose back was turned to him.

"Of course, my dear Mr Doyle," responded the

[162]

Lebanese arms dealer.

Doyle?

Ray racked his brain. It had been some time since he had been privy to day-to-day Army Intelligence, but the name struck a chord.

"Has someone been tampering with these crates?" Al Safadi's question quickened Ray's heartbeat.

"It was most probably the guys who brought in the shipment," answered a heavily accented voice.

"From now on, you make sure all the boxes are securely fastened at all times." Al Safadi was clearly annoyed at the slip in security.

Lids were removed and hammered back in place for the next few minutes, giving Ray time to identify the second Irish participant. He would have to retain a clear mental picture of the two, he now realised, were members of the IRA. To him, Al Safadi had now crossed a line beyond the one of kidnapping a British citizen – he was arming a sworn terror enemy of the British people.

That alone should be enough to seal his fate!

"I trust you are satisfied?" said the Lebanese. "We shouldn't delay and get these crates aboard as soon as possible and get you underway." He gestured to one of his men, who immediately went to the open external door and waved.

"Shite! We're doing this under the very noses of the fecking Brits!" Scoffed O'Doherty at the fact the British Army was stationed on the island country.

"Let's not get too excited," responded Michael Doyle, "we still need to load this lot and get out to sea beyond Cyprus international waters."

"Fecking boat ride again!"

"Captain Farouk has confirmed the trip of some three-thousand nautical miles should take around fourteen days, weather permitting," confirmed Al Safadi evoking an incoherent grunt from O'Doherty. "I assure you, you will be happy with your quarters on board. And I've made sure there is an ample supply of Irish whisky for the trip. However, I apologise in advance for the pervasive odour of fish on board. It is a fishing vessel after all!" he chuckled loudly at his own jest. "My apologies, again. I didn't mean to be offensive."

"Not at all, Mr Safadi. We all have to endure hardships from time to time for our convictions," responded Doyle.

Doyle's comment was not lost on Ray. He had fought such believers who wouldn't accept the inevitable, yet he understood why they firmly held onto their political creeds. Eight crew members entered the warehouse and started busying themselves with the consignment. Ray was getting anxious. Until they left, he could not get back to Episkopi and report what he had witnessed. The ship would have to be tracked. It took another agonising hour before all the crates were removed and loaded on board the trawler.

"I take it I will be able to communicate with our people for transfer of the balance once I'm on board?" asked Doyle.

"Absolutely. The ship has bidirectional ship-to-shore and shore-to-ship radio communication," replied the Lebanese.

"Good. I will contact my people when we are well clear and underway. Say, in the morning?"

"That will be quite acceptable. And once I confirm receipt in my Swiss bank account. You have the details… I will provide an *all-clear* to Captain Farouk," he said as the three started towards the door on their way out of the building.

Ray breathed a heavy sigh of relief when the roller door closed, and the interior fell back into near darkness. Gila felt the same sensation as she watched the activity from behind the window on the second floor in the building opposite. She hadn't heard or seen any untoward action and assumed Ray was safe and would soon climb back over the fence. Her heart skipped a beat when she spotted him a few minutes later exit through the same door he had entered a long while ago. Ray looked to the entrance and noted the one guard had also moved further away – more interested in both vessels' departure than who might approach the gate at that hour. Repeating the climb in reverse, he made it to the back door without incident. Gila came out to meet him.

"We need to get to the Garrison as soon as possible. I'll explain once we get underway," he said and, taking her gently by the elbow, steered her back to the car.

17 August 9th, 1973

The Mediterranean

The British Royal Navy ship, *HMS Audacious* – powered by a combination of two *Rolls Royce Olympus* and two *Tyne* turbojet engines – cruised effortlessly at its maximum speed of twenty-six knots across the calm sea. The warship – one of the nine-strong *Type 21*-group *A*, Fighting vessels, commissioned in 1970 and designated a patrol frigate – fought under the proud motto, *Ludas Machabæus Fortis Erecti* – Valiant and Alert. The ship's impressive armament suite included a *Quadruple surface-to-air missile* (SAM) launcher and two *Triple torpedo* tubes to engage enemy submarines. The stern-based flight deck accommodated a *Westland Wasp* – a medium-lift navy helicopter.

"Distance and speed?"

"Approximately twenty miles and ten knots, Sir," the *Leading Rating* responded after checking the image on the radar screen – the ship's electronic navigation instrument. The picture was generated from a rotating antenna sweeping a narrow beam of microwaves around the boat over a distance of some fifty nautical miles.

"That puts it at just over seventeen nautical miles," confirmed Commander David Henderson lowering his binoculars. "We're gaining around sixteen knots on her, so at our current speed and bearing, we should intercept her in about fifty-five minutes," he added and looked at his watch. "That'll be around three... Assuming we're tracking the correct vessel!"

"I certainly hope so, Sir!" responded Ray, still holding his field glasses to his eyes. He was standing next to him on the bridge and deferred to the man's equivalent, senior army rank of Lieutenant-Colonel.

Standing an inch shorter than Ray and in his late thirties, the ship's captain was dressed in the sunnier-climes white uniform with dark hair under the white cap with a braided peak – proudly sporting the prestigious *Bullion* badge of Her Majesty's Navy. He had intelligent eyes under arched eyebrows, a patrician nose, and a prominent jaw – well-spoken and the manner of an experienced naval officer.

"She should come into view in about fifteen minutes," he continued, referring to the trawler in the female pronoun – a long-standing tradition in the navy relating to an ancient goddess guiding and protecting ships and crews. The high-powered binoculars would increase the visual distance of the naked eye by a factor of four. They would be able to see their target at twelve miles.

A flurry of frenetic activity followed when he and Gila reached the Episkopi Garrison around nine the previous evening. The first to return to the office was George Robertson, followed by the Command's Liaison officer, the Garrison Commander. Soon after, they were joined by the *Commander British Forces Cyprus* himself, Major-General Robert Buxton-Smythe. Urgent calls were made to the UK. Colonel John Madison, Toby Gilmore, and Ben Rutan were all contacted and aware of Ray and Gila's discovery. The decision to intercept the *Ash-Shujā* regardless of its Panama status was sanctioned by Sir Foster Braithwaite, Minister for Domestic and Foreign

Intelligence Services, following a late-night consultation with the British Foreign Secretary.

Two *Harrier Jump Jets* of the Royal Air Force – aptly named after the graceful and elegant birds of prey – took off from the Akrotiri air station. One searched on a northern route. The other followed a southerly direction towards *Sicily* and eastwards through the *Strait of Gibraltar* before swinging north to Ireland via the *Atlantic*. The target trawler was spotted mid-morning on the Levantine Sea's western edge, having taken the predictable northerly passage avoiding the Army's predominant presence on the southern part of the island.

Ray was directly tasked by the Minister to assume the lead and apprehend and take into custody the identified wanted IRA extremists, Michael Doyle and Liam O'Doherty. The arms shipment was to be confiscated or destroyed. Gila would not be involved in the operation lest it was found out later and cause embarrassment for the Israeli Government. She made her annoyance known at being excluded.

"Think of it... You get to lie on the beach and work on your tan," joked Ray in an attempt to console her frustration in being excluded. He got a shrug and pouted lips in return – a mock pretence of disappointment.

HMS Audacious was on patrol in the *Levantine Sea* south of Cyprus and ordered to pursue and apprehend the suspect vessel. Ray was immediately flown by helicopter to board the frigate.

◆◆◆◆

"Please join me on the bridge," sounded Captain Farouk's accented voice over the ship's onboard telephone system. Michael Doyle and Liam O'Doherty were sitting with a coffee in the dining cabin when the request came through.

"What's up?" asked an anxious Doyle. He had been restless since an unidentified jet plane's fly-by earlier in the day.

"We've been tracking a vessel on our radar approaching us on a direct course for the last twenty minutes."

"What could that mean?"

"I can only assume it's a naval ship… Judging by the size and speed, it could be a frigate or destroyer."

"Can we outrun it?" asked a naïve O'Doherty.

The Lebanese Captain smiled gracefully.

"No! It's impossible. It will be in sight in about twenty minutes, or maybe a little less. The sea is being kind today to our pursuers." An agitated Doyle looked around, desperately searching for a solution.

"Can they stop us and board us?"

"Why? For what reason? We are a fishing trawler going about our business and protected under the Law of the Sea Treaty and the High Seas Convention. Why would they apprehend us?"

"Could someone have found out about our trip? Tipped off the authorities?" chimed in an even more anxious O'Doherty.

"This is not my first such venture," responded the boat's Captain. "I have been doing this for many years. I have never before had a problem. Please relax. I just wanted to prepare you."

"The cargo?" interjected Doyle.

"The cargo is safe. They cannot board us. So they will not discover what we have below deck." Both Irishmen were not reassured. The whole adventure was completely new to them. Doyle felt nakedly exposed, stranded in the middle of an endless sea with no land in sight with the only place of doubtful refuge, a small cabin below deck stinking of fish.

"Shite, Mickey! I'm taking no fecking chances," said a troubled O'Doherty as they stepped outside the bridge, "It's gotta be the Brit navy. I don't fecking like it!"

"We don't know that yet!"

"Who the hell would be out here other than the fecking Brits, Mickey. I'm fecking arming myself!"

"Let's not get ahead of ourselves, Liam," responded a reluctant Doyle still unsettled by the revelation but sharing his friend's suspicion. "You heard what Farouk said."

"Do you believe him?"

"I don't know!" replied an increasingly exasperated Doyle.

"Do you trust him? After all, they've been paid in full. What's to stop him from handing us over?"

Doyle gave a deep sigh.

"That's not gonna happen... It wouldn't do Safadi's business any good if it got out that he had reneged on a deal just because the heat was on."

"Who's to fecking know, Micky?" Doyle's attempt at logical reasoning wasn't assuring his fellow IRA member.

"It's no good panicking! We still don't know who they are. It may just be a routine occurrence," he said, although he couldn't dismiss the feeling of impending trouble.

"I still don't fecking like it! I have a sixth sense of these things. You know I do, Mickey." Doyle couldn't deny his friend's uncanny nose for trouble. More than once, he had evaded capture through his intuition.

"Alright, alright! I take your point, Liam." He wasn't about to let the two of them become cornered animals if it came to it. There would be no glory in capture and spending the rest of his useful life in a British prison. "Let's get to the hold."

◆◆◆◆

"Right on time," remarked Commander Henderson looking through his binoculars. The silhouette was clearly visible on the distant horizon. "Get me, Chief Petty Officer Pedley," he instructed. Ray felt his breath momentarily bottle up in his chest.

This has to be the ship!

Now they were closing in, he refused to think otherwise. He continued to focus on the slowly enlarging form.

"Sir, you sent for me?" a matter-of-fact voice distracted Ray's concentration, and he lowered his field glasses.

"Is your team prepared?" asked the Commander.

"Yes, Sir," replied the forty-something thickset man with dark penetrating eyes and a full-set beard.

"This is Captain Kazan, Army Intelligence," he said, turning slightly towards Ray. The mariner momentarily hesitated as he cast a cursory glance over the tall, younger man dressed in a civilian pale-brown, lightweight suit and white open-necked shirt.

"Sir," he saluted Ray smartly – the tips of his fingers touching the peak of his cap, palm down.

"Chief Petty Officer!" responded Ray courteously, dutifully acknowledging the navy man with a slight bow of the head. The absence of a headdress precluded him from returning the salute.

"We will soon be coming up on our target vessel," said the Commander. "We have been sanctioned to board her with or without the ship Captain's permission or co-operation. Sidearms only… We don't want to display an overly threatening manner. However, before boarding, I suggest you instruct your team to chamber a round with safeties on. You should be prepared for possible armed confrontation."

"Sir?" queried the CPO.

"There is a strong belief that on board are two senior IRA members high on our Government's Wanted List... And who are also smuggling a large consignment of armaments headed for the Irish, or Britain's mainland." Commander Henderson caught the CPO cast a questioning glance at Ray.

"Captain Kazan will assume direct command once you've boarded. He will be the arresting officer should you apprehend the suspects. You will defer to his instructions until the situation is secured and you return to the Audacious."

"May I be so bold as to ask the Captain's previous experience in this sort of action." Ray smiled at the senior man's directness.

"I don't think you need concern yourself..."

"It's quite alright, Sir," intervened Ray. "I would have had the same reservations if I were in the Chief Petty Officer's shoes."

"Thank you, Sir," responded an apologetic CPO.

"Will you require a sidearm?" asked Henderson. Ray pulled back the left side of his jacket, revealing his shoulder holster and the Browning pistol.

"I guess not!" smiled the Captain of the Audacious.

Twenty minutes later, the frigate had caught up with the trawler and slowed to keep pace a short distance off its stern on the frigate's starboard side.

"Ash-Shujã, Ash-Shujã. This is HMS Audacious, HMS Audacious. Request working channel 8. Over."

No answer.

The wireless operator repeated the opening message three more times. No acknowledgements were forthcoming. He turned in his seat and faced the Commander.

"Keep going," instructed Commander Henderson. "It's nothing unusual," he said.

"Ash-Shujā, Ash-Shujā. This is HMS Audacious, HMS Audacious. Request working channel 8. Over."

"HMS Audacious, this is the Ash-Shujā. Go ahead. Over," came the eventual response.

The operator cleared his throat.

"Ash-Shujā. This is HMS Audacious. Please confirm your Master's name and nationality. Over."

Again, a deathly silence followed.

"Ash-Shujā. This is HMS Audacious. I repeat, please confirm your Master's name and nationality. Over."

"This is Captain Mohammed Farouk, Lebanese national and Master of the fishing vessel, Ash-Shujā. What can I do for you today? Over."

"Ash-Shujā. Please confirm the number and nationality of your crew. Over."

Ray shot Henderson a quizzical look.

"It's all part of a pre-boarding communication. We are bound by regulation. A convention we have to follow," he said with a tolerant grin.

Again a period of silence ensued before a reply.

"We have eight crewmen, all of Lebanese nationality. Over." Ray noted the man's seeming compliance.

"Ash-Shujā. Please state your last port-of-call and next port of call, including dates. Over." The wireless operator continued to use a formal radio language by referencing the ship's name each time he opened a message.

"Our last port was Famagusta last evening. We are on a fishing expedition. No next port of call has been decided. Over."

"Ash-Shujā. Say again the purpose of your voyage. Over."

"We are fishermen… We are out fishing. That is what we do for a living to put food on the tables for our families. Over." The responder appeared increasingly irritated.

[173]

"Ash-Shujā. Understood. Please confirm the total number of people on board. Over."

Captain Farouk hadn't expected the loaded question. The question was a game-changer. Does he lie and omit the two Irishman? To do so could open a can of worms! It was a question he would rather not answer. But answer, he would have to and without hesitation. Stalling a response could lead to greater suspicion. Something being withheld could open to possible complications.

"Repeat, please. Over."

"Ash-Shujā. Please confirm the total number of people on board. Over."

"We are nine. My crew of eight and me, the Master of this innocent fishing trawler, going about its business. Over." He had committed himself. He held his breath.

"Ash-Shujā. This is Commander Henderson, Captain of the British patrol frigate, HMS Audacious." The communication was about to move to a different level. "We believe you also have two members on board of the outlawed terrorist organisation known as the Irish Republican Army. Men wanted by my Government for crimes against the sovereign nation of Great Britain and Northern Ireland and its people. Over."

"You are mistaken, my dear Commander. We have no such people on board. Over." Farouk was resorting to polite flattery not lost on the two of them. Ray and he exchanged glances before he continued.

"Ash-Shujā. We are further reliably informed you are carrying contraband weaponry you intend to smuggle into our sovereign nation. Over."

"Again, you are mistaken, my dear Captain. We are doing no such thing. We are mere humble fishermen doing what we do best... fishing. Over."

"Ash-Shujā. If, as you say, this is so, we request your consent to board your vessel and confirm your assertions.

Over."

"My dear Captain," Captain Farouk carried on with the platitude, "as you may have noticed, we are flying the flag of Panama and are not obliged to grant your request. Over."

"Ash-Shujã. The two Irish nationals on board are Michael Doyle and Liam O'Doherty. This should indicate the accuracy of our intelligence. I will give you thirty minutes to comply with our request. I propose you consult with your owner for legal advice without delay. Over." He threw the switch immediately following his direct veiled message.

"Unfortunately, I have no choice other than making every endeavour to obtain the man's consent. I have to consider the safety and security needs of both my crew and his," he said as he leaned back against the bulwark and folded his arms across his chest. "I am obliged to undertake any action I deem fit to neutralise possible security threats once onboard the vessel. We've no idea as to potential crew hostility which could become apparent once and only when we board, escalating an already delicate situation."

"I fully understand," replied Ray.

"Pardon the pun…, but we are sailing in tricky waters!" he added, flashing a broad smile. "We also can't be sure the IRA fellows and the arms consignment haven't already been transferred to another vessel… Although, I'm pretty sure they couldn't have managed that in the time given to this point."

◆◆◆◆

"Papillon Bleu, Papillon Bleu. This is Ash-Shujã, Ash-Shujã. Request working channel 6. Over."

Captain Mohammed Farouk repeated the

communication three more times before a voice answered.

"Ash-Shujā, this Papillon Bleu. Channel 6 is open. How can we help you? Over."

"This is Captain Farouk. I require you to speak with Mr Fareed Al Safadi immediately. Do you understand? Over."

"Ash-Shujā. This is Papillon Bleu. Message understood. Stand by. Over."

The calm response was in contrast to Farouk's urgency. He let out a deep sigh casting his eyes back through the rear cabin windows at the looming form of the frigate off his starboard side. He started to drum his fingers nervously on the radar screen. After what seemed an age.

"Al Safadi here. Over."

"Sir. We have a problem," he exclaimed, ignoring radio communication protocol. "Over!"

A momentary silence followed.

"What sort of problem? Over."

"Sir, there is a British Navy frigate demanding to board the Ash-Shujā. They have given me thirty minutes to comply. Over." A longer silence followed before Al Safadi responded.

"They cannot force you to agree. You are travelling under a Panama flag and are under the exclusive jurisdiction of the Panama state and not the British Government. Over."

"I have already informed them, but they do not accept this. Over."

"They have no choice, Captain Farouk! Over."

Mohammed Farouk took a moment before he was prepared to inform his boss of the other news – the game-changer!

"They know of our Irish passengers! Over." He held

his breath, waiting on an explosive response.

"What do you mean... they know?"

"The Captain of the warship made it quite clear. They know they are on board and gave their names. How..., I can't say. Over."

"That's immaterial... They are bluffing... They can't board without your consent. Tell them to go to hell!"

Captain Farouk inhaled deeply.

"They also know of the consignment."

"What? How?"

The radio went silent, except for a dull static sound. Mohammed Farouk held tightly onto the handset with bated breath.

"What's the ship's name?"

"HMS Audacious. I repeat, HMS Audacious. Over."

"Stand by the radio. I will make direct contact. Await my instructions."

◆◆◆◆

Ray had taken a seat on a stool when a mess orderly entered carrying a tray of metal mugs.

"Begging your pardon, Sir. Cook thought you might need a cuppa," he said as he approached the Captain.

"Good old Cook! Always ready with a mug of tea in times of crisis," he chortled and picked two mugs off the tray and handed one to Ray. "Thank you, orderly." Just as Ray put the rim of the steaming brew to his lips, the radio burst into life.

"HMS Audacious, HMS Audacious. This is Papillon Bleu, Papillon Bleu. Requesting Channel 6. Over."

Henderson and Ray exchanged looks.

"That's Al Safadi's yacht! He's the trawler's owner," said Ray.

"Interesting," responded the Captain of the Audacious

– his eyes twinkled with curiosity. "Go ahead, reply," he instructed the wireless operator. The man adjusted a knob to the desired channel.

"Papillon Bleu, this is HMS Audacious. Channel 6, Out. Go ahead. Over."

"HMS Audacious. This is Fareed Al Safadi on the Papillon Bleu, Lebanese national and owner of the Ash-Shujā fishing vessel. I wish to speak to your Captain. Over."

David Henderson stepped over to the radio and took the microphone from the Leading Rating. He cleared his throat.

"Papillon Bleu. This is HMS Audacious. Commander David Henderson RN here. Over."

"Good afternoon, Commander Henderson. The Master of the Ash-Shujā has informed me of your illegal request to board his vessel. I wish to know on what grounds? Over."

"Papillon Bleu. This is HMS Audacious. I have made it quite clear to the Master that you are harbouring two wanted enemies of the British Government and carrying contraband weaponry with the attention of smuggling into the United Kingdom's sovereign territories. Over."

"Your claim is preposterous! You have no right, neither to threaten nor board my ship. It is a registered Panamanian vessel protected under that state's flag, and you have absolutely no jurisdiction! I repeat... you have no jurisdiction! Over." Al Safadi wasted no time in going on the offensive.

"Let us dispense with the communication protocol, Mr Al Safadi. I assure you, Sir, we have every right to board your vessel based on the indisputable intelligence in our possession. Over." He turned and smiled knowingly at Ray. "Cat and mouse!"

"I say again. You have no right... Absolutely no right

[178]

at all! If you attempt to board the Ash-Shujã, I will instruct the crew to resist by all means! Over!"

David Henderson clicked his tongue.

"That would be most unwise, Sir. You must be aware we possess far superior firepower and do not wish to harm anyone on board. However..., if in the act of boarding, your crew resist with force..., we will be compelled to react in a likewise manner. And I assure you..., we will prevail! Please do not underestimate our intention to board. Over."

"I must warn you in return that I will protest your action to the very highest authority of my country. You will not get away with your criminal intent. I repeat, you do not have my consent to board!"

"Mr Al Safadi, I gave your Master the courtesy of thirty minutes to comply with my request." He looked at his watch. "He has four minutes left before we commence boarding... with or without his or *your* consent. Over."

"You cannot..., you..." The line went dead.

"Well, I think we did our bit. I'll give it three more minutes; then it's time for action." Henderson picked up his mug. "Time enough for a few more sips," he added. Ray was taking a liking to the man commanding the frigate.

Three minutes later.

"Ash-Shujã, Ash-Shujã. This is HMS Audacious, HMS Audacious. Requesting Channel 8. Over."

The operator repeated the request three more times.

"HMS Audacious, this is the Ash-Shujã. Go ahead. Over."

"Ash-Shujã. This is HMS Audacious. Commander Henderson wishes to speak with your ship's Master, Captain Farouk. Over."

A short while later.

"Captain Farouk here! What can I do for you? Over."

[179]

"Ash-Shujã. I will ignore the usual protocol and speak directly. I have spoken with your vessel's owner, Mr Al Safadi and clarified our intention. You are requested to stop all engines, heave to, and be ready for us to board your vessel. Over."

"I do not accept your request! You have no legal right! I repeat, you have no legal jurisdiction! We are a Panama registered vessel flying under that state's flag. We do not, I repeat, we do not recognise your request! Over!"

Listening to the continued exchange started to sound like a broken record. However, Ray was only too aware of the need to follow a proper protocol. There was a lot at stake! The successful apprehension of the two IRA men and seizure of the arms cache he had witnessed would save countless lives – on both sides of the political divide.

"Captain Farouk, I once again ask you to stop your engines and heave to with immediate effect. If you do not comply, I assure you I will take measures to disable your vessel. Actions I do not think you would want if indeed you have nothing to hide. Our inspection of your vessel is merely to confirm your assertions. I should also warn you that any resistance by you or any member of your crew can only end badly for you. I implore you to reconsider your position. Over."

Mohammed Farouk uttered an expletive in Arabic and signed off.

"You don't by chance happen to speak the lingo? I didn't understand what the fellow said," Henderson turned to Ray, catching him with a ready smile on his face.

"With respect, Sir…, he told you to fuck off!"

"Did he now?" he remarked, suppressing a chuckle. "Ask the XO to report to the bridge," he instructed a crew member standing next to the onboard telephone. Lieutenant-Commander Phillip Snell entered.

"Phillip, we've had no luck in getting consent to board

[180]

and the vessel's Master — and I'm assuming Captain Kazan's translation was accurate — informed me that I should go and perform a sexual act on myself." The XO held back a snigger. "First things first, we'll back off away from her and fire a couple of salvos over her bow. Let's show them we mean business. If they continue to resist, we'll step it up a gear."

"Understood, Sir," responded the XO, and with a smart salute, left the bridge.

"Let the fun begin," muttered Henderson and backed up against the bulkhead.

18 August 9th, 1973

The Mediterranean

The splash from the first salvo was clearly audible from their position below the main deck. The second shot was closer still.

"What the feck are they gonna do next?" "They mean fecking business!" declared an ever flustered Liam O'Doherty, clutching a fully loaded AK47.

"Let me think, Liam!" responded an uneasy Doyle. He knew that Mohammed Farouk would only resist to a point. Would he risk the ship and his crew for the two Irishmen? Would he... if their roles were reversed? What would he lose if it came to it? He looked across at his increasingly fraught friend.

He understood that O'Doherty wouldn't want to go down without a fight. He was a scrapper and would be so to the end. O'Doherty had not enjoyed the nurtured years Doyle's mother gave him. His parenting was the hardship of the Belfast back streets, where he had to fight his way to adulthood each and every day – with his fists and anything else that was to hand. No! He would insist on fighting his way out. But hoping against all the odds, no matter, was a conviction Doyle couldn't completely share.

To surrender would betray O'Doherty's faith in him, yet rationale had to prevail. As much as his friend wouldn't want to submit even against such impossible odds, he had to rein in his desperate belief. At least with their capture, there was hope – hope that the bastard Brits would concede and leave Northern Ireland to a united Irish people and not a divided nation in the future. The trawler was still moving. It hadn't slowed.

So, Farouk's not ready to throw in the towel, thought Doyle.

"We'll wait down here, Liam. Keep hidden. Let's hope! Okay?"

"Okay, Mickey. Whatever you say, but I tell you now. I don't want to go down without a fecking fight!" His words were not what Doyle wanted to hear, but they were in it together.

♦♦♦♦

"Ash-Shujã. We again request you to stop all engines and heave to. Over."

The XO, Phillip Snell, returned to the bridge.

"What next, Sir?"

"I don't think that more salvos over the bow are going to change his mind." He paused and sighed, then acquiesced. "Two more, Phillip. Let's give them two more. One more chance to comply."

"Right'o, Sir."

The following salvos struck the water closer to the front of the trawler's bow. Still, the vessel ignored the warning and continued moving at the same speed.

"Still no change, Sir," confirmed the XO from the doorway.

"No, I'm afraid not!" Henderson walked over to the window. "Do you think you can take out their rudder and perhaps a propellor, or both? It looks like a two-prop job."

"I think our gunners can achieve that, Sir," the XO

confidently predicted. He held, waiting for the next order.

"Okay! Go ahead, Phillip. Make sure no-one's at aft."

"Of course, Sir." The XO smiled assuredly and disappeared once again.

"You might want to see this," said Henderson gesturing for Ray to join him at the window.

Shortly after, Ray watched as a strafing line of 20mm calibre rounds fired from the frigate's autocannon at a velocity of approximately 2,500 feet per second kicked up a series of water spikes as it homed in on the trawler's stern underside. Within seconds the vessel started to slow down from a direct impact on the propellors and rudders combined.

"Impressive," remarked Ray.

"Bloody good shooting, Phillip." His commanding officer congratulated the XO on his breathless return to the door of the bridge. "An extra shot of rum for the gunners tonight!"

"Now what, Sir?"

"Usual manoeuvre, Phillip. Have CPO Pedley and his team stand by the starboard gunwale. Captain Kazan will join them shortly."

Ray removed the pistol from his holster, chambered a round and re-holstered the weapon.

"Over to you, Captain, and good luck. Try not to get any of my men injured, or worse yet... killed."

"I'll do my best, Sir," he countered light-heartedly.

Ray climbed down the steps onto the main deck and approached the CPO. The team of twelve had already taken up on either side of their unit leader along the ship's gunwale. Two metres apart and facing the Ash-Shujã's mid-section, they stood with hands resting ominously on the exposed butts of their pistols. The frigate had approached within a few metres of the trawler. Ray took up a position beside the CPO as the Master of the disabled trawler emerged from the bridge, shaking his fists angrily and raging expletives at the line of uniformed personnel looking back with stoic resignation.

"Sir?" queried CPO Pedley.

"You can guess!" responded Ray. There was no need for him to translate the Captain's diatribe. All eight of the trawler's crew had already assembled on the deck, shuffling their feet and looking extremely nervous. From their look, Ray surmised it was their first such experience.

"I take it you've done this before?" said Ray.

"Yes, Sir. A couple of times," he asserted.

"Good! Then why don't you take the lead and get us onboard first?" Ray sensed the CPOs appreciation for his proposal.

"Very well, Sir," he replied. "One and twelve!" He barked out an order, and two of his unit – responding to their designated numbers in the boarding squad – immediately climbed over the gunwale and skillfully climbed down the netting hanging over the side of the frigate. Under the watchful eyes of the team's remaining members, the two jumped onto the main deck of the trawler and grabbed a rope each, thrown from the frigate by two others.

The Lebanese crew backed away cautiously from the activity. Meanwhile, Captain Farouk stood outside the bridge, gripping a railing, muttering to himself – anger in his eyes and the whites of his knuckles showing.

Commander David Henderson calmly watched the proceedings outside the bridge alongside his XO.

Several black rubber fenders (bumpers) – used to absorb the kinetic energy and avoid damaging either ship's hulls from the vessels berthing together – were hung over the side by other frigate crew members. The two lines were tied to cleats affixed to the trawler's gunwale securing the Ash-Shujā's mooring to HMS

[185]

Audacious. Once the ties were completed, unit members 1 and 12 turned their backs on the frigate and faced the trawler's assembled crew.

"2,4, 10 and 11, with me," called out the CPO. He climbed down the rope netting with his four men and went aboard the trawler. Once on the main deck, the four additional sailors surrounded the Lebanese crew and indicated to get down on their knees with their hands clasped behind their heads. Each man was then handcuffed and instructed to remain as they were. The remaining six members of the unit continued to hold their positions on the frigate.

"Okay! If you will, Sir." He called on Ray to join him, who thankfully managed to board the trawler without mishap.

"Thank you, CPO," he said, immediately taking charge and gesturing for the Captain to climb down the ladder.

"It's useless to continue with your protestations, Captain. We're now onboard your vessel and have assumed command," he said, surprising the Lebanese in his own language.

"You had no right!" countered the man lamely, his last fight weakened to near-total submission.

"Now, tell me where your two Irish guests are. We wish to avoid any bloodshed and require your complete co-operation," he continued, ignoring the man's feeble remark.

"Look what you've done to my ship!"

"Where are they?"

"Below, forward...They are armed," he conceded.

"Thank you. Now, if you will join your crew." Mohammed Farouk, spent of whatever bravado he had displayed previously, meekly turned and dropped to his knees with his hands behind his head.

"May I accompany you, Sir?" asked the CPO removing

[186]

his weapon in anticipation. Ray tried not to smile as he pulled out his *Browning* and led the way.

"Stay alert!" The unit leader instructed his team and followed Ray to the metal door accessing the ship's interior.

Ray stood to the left while the CPO pressed down on the handle and pulled the weathertight door open towards him. Holding his pistol against his chest, Ray carefully peered around into a short passageway. A set of stairs on his right led up to the bridge. He nodded at the CPO and, leading with his left leg, climbed over the raised bottom frame into the inside. He held momentarily, listening for a giveaway sound before descending eight steps onto the second deck.

Lowering his body slightly, he again peeked down the passageway, then crossed over into a recess opposite. Meanwhile, CPO Pedley followed his progress and remained at the foot of the stairs – his body pressed back and pistol at the ready. Ray nodded towards a closed door at the far end. The CPO nodded back in acknowledgement.

"Michael Doyle and Liam O'Doherty, this is Captain Kazan, British Army Intelligence. We have disabled the vessel and taken control. You are surrounded with no possible means of escape. Do you hear me?" Ray spoke loudly and deliberately. A moment later, a muffled reply sounded through the closed end door.

"Go feck yourself! If you want us, come, and fecking get us, you bastard Brits!" Standing on either side inside the closed-door – holding loaded AK47s – Doyle and O'Doherty exchanged glances. O'Doherty shook his head and whispered.

"Don't ask, Mickey Da."

"There is absolutely no point in you resisting. This can only end one way. Open the door, throw out your weapons, and come out with your arms raised. I'm sure you know the drill," pressed Ray.

"He's right, Liam. We're fucked. No point in denying it." Doyle urged his friend and compatriot. "There will be another day… Come on." He spoke softly.

O'Doherty eventually appeared resigned to Doyle's persistence and lowered his head. Taking that as his tacit agreement, Doyle called out.

"Okay! Okay! We're coming out!"

Ray and the CPO exchanged looks and held their breaths. They heard the door open, and before stepping out into the passageway, Ray peeked around the corner as O'Doherty came out closely followed by Doyle – still holding the assault rifles.

"Drop your weapons!" Ray called out as he ducked back. "Drop them now!" He released his safety.

What happened during the next short few seconds would haunt Doyle for the next twenty-eight years he would serve at Her Majesty's pleasure in the *Long Kesh Detention Centre* – infamously known later as the *Maze*.

With a sudden change of heart and on inherent impulse, O'Doherty raised the weapon and emptied the thirty-round magazine with a sustained wild barrage down the passage, splintering the wooden walling and narrowly missing both Ray and the CPO. Pressing his body back tightly, Ray waited for the familiar click of hammer on an empty chamber, then instinctively dropped onto his right knee and fired eight shots in rapid succession in the direction of the two men. Both IRA men slumped heavily to the ground – their weapons clattered onto the metal floor.

Ray immediately ran to them with the CPO close on his heels. Doyle was lying groaning on the immobile form of his friend. Blood was spreading outwards on the floor from the two men. He placed his fingers against

O'Doherty's neck. There was no pulse. CPO Pedley holstered his pistol and removed the assault rifles while Ray stepped over both men and pulled Doyle into a sitting position against the wall. Doyle had taken two of his rounds – one in the upper right thigh and the other further up, below his waist. He was bleeding profusely.

"We'll need a medic," said Ray over his shoulder while patting down Doyle searching for an additional weapon.

"You okay, Sir?" asked an impressed CPO.

"I'm fine… Medic?"

"Right away, Sir!" He hurried away.

◆ ◆ ◆ ◆

Fareed Al Safadi was in a fit, strutting back and forth in the plush lounge on board his luxury yacht, the Papillon Bleu. That sanctimonious bastard-Commander of the frigate had just extended him the courtesy – damn the man and all onboard his bloody HMS Audacious – the courtesy of informing him of the seizure of the Ash-Shujã.

How could they have known about Doyle and O'Doherty? How did they find about the consignment? It must have been that fool, Khalil Shaheen. That sadistic but occasionally useful idiot Shaheen. But then he knew nothing of the Irish contract. Could he have found out from someone else in the organisation? If so, then who? Did he have a security issue he was unaware of? Was that why he had been *questioning* the two men he had tied to chairs? But then they were only low-level employees. How would they have known? No! It couldn't have been him. Yet, he was killed, but by whom and why? Where could he get an answer to the puzzling questions?

The loss of the trawler would be bad enough. The failure to deliver both the IRA men and the paid-for consignment could have damaging consequences. And not just his reputation! Most of the people he dealt with were not the sort he'd invite to an evening at the opera. He would have to consider reimbursing the Irish Paramilitary Group. Maybe even extend additional monies to cover the capture of two of their operatives. The thought made him shudder. His usual cool manner under stress was being tested.

And what about that British intelligence officer and the Jewish woman Frasier had informed him about? That's the only possible connection that made the most sense. The British appeared to be behind both episodes. Deploying a British warship to intercept the Ash-Shujã would have had to have come from a high level. That thought alone caused him anxiety. This was not some lucky break..., surely? Perhaps the British authorities were already on the trail of the two IRA personnel? Maybe that's what led them to the weapon's cache? Maybe that's what they were really after?

The more he tried piecing the sparse bits of detail together, the more he was convinced that that's where the problem must have laid. He would have to contact Jack Frasier in London. The man would have to get out and do some digging. He would have to earn his money! Then there was the additional concern with the other members of the cartel. The Zuhuania project was already underway and about to unfold. There was too much riding on its success. Rocking the boat at this point may harm the massive investment the group had already disbursed? However, the rewards would far outweigh the loss of the trawler and its consequences. He would have to get on to his Government contacts and lay out a cover against possible recriminations. The British had little to no influence in the Middle East. He needn't concern himself.

He picked up the inboard telephone.

"How far out are we within Cyprus international waters?"

"About five nautical miles, Sir," answered the yacht's captain.

"Up anchor and take us out a further five and get me Mr Jack Frasier in London," he instructed and replaced the receiver. He picked up his untouched glass of brandy and slumped heavily into an armchair – frustrated, angry and still analysing.

◆◆◆◆

Two-and-a-half hours later, Ray was back on the bridge. Commander Henderson was sitting in his command chair, holding a mug of tea. Ray wondered how many times a day Cook would send up a cuppa of the sweet, milky beverage – a long-established staple of the British military since the morning of the *Battle of Waterloo* in 1815. And how many times would the Commander of the Audacious actually manage to finish a cup? Unlike the American forces who preferred a strong coffee, the Brits would counter with – *you can't beat a good cuppa tea!* The British Government's decision in 1942 to buy up all the available tea in the world (except from Japan) was the irrefutable indication of the importance and depth of the brew within the nation's fabric.

The British military really did run on tea!

"Overall a first-rate result," he started, acknowledging Ray's presence. "We have impounded the Ash-Shujā and have it in tow with our own skeleton crew on board, and Farouk and his men are currently enjoying our onboard hospitality. That fellow may have some useful intel to share back at Episkopi. This arms dealer chap, Al Safadi, could well have been involved in equipping the Provisionals for some time."

[191]

"I doubt whether there's much to be learned from the crew. They all looked pretty frightened. Just fisherman as he professed. However, from my experience with these people, our good Captain Farouk may not survive long enough to share any insight he may have. They're a pretty ruthless bunch if indeed Al Safadi is connected," added Ray.

"I suspect that curbing his involvement may well be top of your future agenda." Ray smiled to himself at the Commander's astuteness. "That remarkable array of armaments we seized will never see the light of day," he continued. "Never to be used to kill any of our boys in uniform or the poor innocents these fanatics are willing to sacrifice, and for what? A united Ireland! Overall, it went very well," he added with satisfaction at a well-executed operation.

"It was certainly a stroke of luck coming across the information," said Ray attempting modesty at his own contribution to the operation.

"Let's face it, Ray," the Commander had taken to referring to him by his first name – paying him a compliment afforded by people of higher rank for recognised calibre in a junior. "Life is a continual sequence of luck. Be that as it may, according to the Chief Petty Officer, your swift and decisive action was quite impressive. Killing O'Doherty couldn't be helped. He brought it upon himself. A death wish, it seemed." He smiled and nodded. "It would appear that you will be with us until we dock sometime early tomorrow morning. It's too late to send you back by helicopter. The XO has happily surrendered his cabin for the night."

"Sir, there's really no need for the XO..."

"Nonsense, it was his idea, and he was more than happy to do so. You're quite the hero on board. You should enjoy the moment. Anyway, I digress. I daresay you might want to shower before dinner. The Quarter Master will arrange a fresh shirt. You're cordially invited to join the XO and me for drinks and dinner in my private dining room for nine."

"That's very kind of you, Sir. It'll be my privilege," replied Ray. "I'd first like to see Doyle in the *Infirmary* beforehand, though."

"Doc has removed the bullets and patched him up. I believe he's awake – restrained but awake. Till nine then."

◆ ◆ ◆ ◆

The armed sailor at the entrance to the Infirmary saluted Ray and opened the door to let him in. Doyle was lying on his back with his head resting on two pillows. His left wrist was handcuffed to the bed's side-rail. A stand with a small bag of fluid – providing a steady drip of life-giving saline solution through a penetrated needle in his left arm – was positioned next to the rail. A monitor recording his vital signs was placed above his head. He looked pale, and his eyes were bloodshot – though Ray doubted it was from tears for his fallen comrade.

"How are you feeling?" asked Ray, approaching him on his right-hand side. Doyle looked up at Ray with coldness but didn't reply. "It needn't have come to this," Ray added, shaking his head. To Ray, the man was still a Brit – one of their own. Even if he did live under a delusion, to which Ray didn't subscribe. He understood that Doyle's was an ideological allegiance and just as strong in him as Ray's sworn duty was to the British military and the law.

Social injustices would be better tackled through the non-violent tactics and resistance advocated by the likes of *Mohandas Karamchand Gandhi* – known the world over as *Mahatma* (great soul). The little, underweight man whose strong beliefs yet simplicity of life led him to become India's spiritual leader. He was a radical thinker and activist that Ray admired. The man lying in bed was not of Mahatma's ilk!

Where does a person draw the line between radicalism and extremism? Opposing an idea and arguing openly without advocating violence was an acceptable course. People could co-exist and tolerate differences with that simple doctrine. Indiscriminate bombing of innocent civilians was unacceptable extremism which could only be defeated by locking those responsible from the rest of a peaceful society..., or putting them six feet below ground.

Deliberately taking the life of another human being who's incapable of defending himself – given no chance of an equal response – was an extreme act of cowardice to Ray.

"It still doesn't excuse what you did to my friend..., Englishman!" Doyle responded, spitting out the last word. Ray ignored the man's outburst. "You have no fecking idea! You believe that your cause is right, and ours isn't? What do you know or even care about our struggles? You kill from inside a uniform..., we kill from inside a deep belief."

Ray had no intention of assuming a higher righteous ground. He wasn't there to enter into a debate over differences in moral philosophies.

"If it'll make you feel any better, he's not going to be buried here at sea. He's being sent back to his family for a local burial... Whether you will be allowed to attend the funeral... is debatable, however." With that, he turned to leave.

"I thank you for that at least..., Englishman." Ray paused momentarily, then left the Infirmary without looking back.

♦ ♦ ♦ ♦

The hot shower had been refreshing and helped wash away any doubts over his earlier action. Standing at the sink – a towel wrapped around his waist – he was slowly coming to realise that the increasing *life-or-death* confrontations were having less of an effect on his psyche. Taking a life was coming easier with no forethought or anticipation. Was that such a bad thing? How would Leyla have viewed him if she were still alive? Would he always be the same person he was had she not been taken away from him…, and by such means?

He leaned closer towards the polished metal mirror riveted to the bulkhead and stared deep into his eyes. His world was changing fast – with new and even more challenging events ahead. Slowly he cleared his mind of such thoughts and glanced at his watch – 8:40 pm.

He reached for the shaving soap the XO had left him. It wouldn't do to turn up late to the senior officer's dinner invitation.

19 August 10th, 1973

Katkulu City, Zuhuania

Seething with anger and frustration, Obasi Bankole threw the newspaper onto the desk, pushed back his chair, and stood up.

"Lies!" he screamed at his personal assistant. "All lies, filthy lies! Why are they continuing with these inventions? This never happened! Where did they get such trumped-up stories? Where? If I find out who was behind this…, heads will roll!"

Two days earlier, the damning news broadcasts spread throughout the world by a major news organisation continued to be plastered over the morning's papers. Reports of condemnation were already filtering through from nations once considered friends. The President of the central African country – pronounced *Zoo..hwa..nee..ya* – thundered across his office to the window. The assistant took a step back. There was no reasoning with the President when he was in a temper – and this tantrum was at a level he had never before witnessed.

Thousands of protestors had taken to the streets, demonstrating their anger at the man who had always professed to be above reproach. Many were massing at the Presidential Palace railings carrying make-shift banners and placards calling on him to resign. Others were chanting the name Abebe Adebowale egged on by paid instigators. Posters emblazoned with a statesmanlike image of Adebowale had sprung up overnight across the whole city, declaring him the rightful replacement to the corrupt and depraved incumbent. Hostility towards the President had begun to grip the nation, and the threat of an unstoppable momentum was not lost on the man as he stood at the window, surveying the angry faces below. He told himself to remain composed. No good would come of over-reacting. However, he had to act and act quickly and decisively.

"Get me, General Olanwaju," he urged over his shoulder.

The p.a. hurried to the desk, picked up the handset and dialled. He listened nervously to the ring tone until a voice answered.

"General Olanwaju," he said crisply. "The President wishes to speak with him." A few tense minutes before, a deep voice spoke.

"Olanwaju here," said the head of the National Guard. The deputy passed the receiver to the President.

"General Olanwaju, I require you to mobilise the Guard immediately and quell these protests. This cannot be allowed to continue. These demonstrations must be stopped!" There was a pause on the other end.

"I'm afraid that will not be possible," the General spoke slowly and deliberately as he stared down the barrel of an AK47 submachine gun.

"Not possible? What do you mean..., not possible?" responded an increasingly agitated Obasi Bankole.

"As I said, Mr President... it will not be possible," he repeated and replaced the handset.

"The bastard cut me off!" he exploded and slammed the receiver down on the cradle.

"Get me the Chief of Police!"

[197]

"There's no answer!" the p.a. blurted out after redialling and holding several times.

"What do you mean, no answer? Does no one outside of this office realise what's happening?" He was beginning to feel cut off – the tide turning against him. The ingrates he had placed in lucrative positions were already backing off – rats deserting a sinking ship! He stomped back to the window. The crowds were growing and becoming more vocal. The door to his office suddenly burst open. General Kanumba, head of the Zuhuania People's Defence Force, entered the President's inner-sanctum with eight armed soldiers.

"What's... what's the meaning of this? How dare you...? How dare you burst into my office?"

"Obasi Bankole," announced the General ignoring the President's protestation. "You're under arrest."

"Arrest?" he responded angrily. "On what charge?"

"On the charge of high crimes and misdemeanours," answered the General.

"This is absurd! High crimes and misdemeanours? Are you mad? I'll have you shot for this gross misconduct!" The General turned to one of the soldiers, a young captain.

"Captain Zivai, handcuff the President." The officer moved towards the incumbent.

"This is outrageous!" retorted the President stepping back behind his desk. An ashen-faced p.a. stood trembling to the side. "This a set-up! This is not real. I tell you, somebody did this to me. This is all a mistake. You've got to believe me!" His earlier bravado and self-confidence began to wane as the reality of his situation rapidly dawned on him.

"You'll get an opportunity to tell your side of the story... I'm sure," said the military man ominously as the handcuffs were snapped onto Obasi Bankole's wrists.

◆◆◆◆

A beaming Abebe Adebowale stood in the open doorway of the *Learjet* aircraft with his arms outstretched, waving at the cheering crowd. This was his moment. This was the time when he would no longer be just the chieftain of the M'Buzi tribe but also the President of the country. It was a moment to remember, to savour. He continued to wave for a little while longer, then grinning from ear-to-ear, slowly descended the steps to be greeted by Generals Kanumba, Olanwaju, and several fawning government dignitaries.

The sycophants are already swarming like flies, he thought as he warmly shook their hands, smiling broadly.

He was led down a red carpet between two lines of fatigue-dressed soldiers proudly presenting arms. He stopped now and then to speak to a soldier – a warm gesture that was not lost on the huge waiting crowd held back by a police line, arms interlinked. He was the people's choice. Generous amounts of cash distributed into the right hands ensured he was. A loud cheer rose from the crowd as he approached a podium and a cluster of microphones. Every second of his arrival was captured by three television crews and reported by a host of journalists.

He adjusted one or two microphones as he waited patiently, then raised his arms, gesturing for them to quieten.

"You called me!" His voice thundered out from four large speakers trained at the people, triggering more cheering. He paused, waiting for the noise to subside. "And I have answered your call!" The crowd erupted. Again he waited, smiling broadly.

"Today marks a new dawn for our beloved country… I promise you… I will stamp out the corruption which has plagued the Government, been condemned by the world, and has become a blot on our country." More cheering and applause exploded from the gathering.

"I am ready to enact new policies. Policies that will benefit the people of Zuhuania and not the greedy few who are so quick to take advantage of their positions. My government will be a government for the people..." He beamed broadly as the gathered started to shout out his name in adulation.

♦ ♦ ♦ ♦

Grange Manor, Bedfordshire, England:

Miles Hathaway was comfortably seated in a leather armchair, gently swirling a crystal bowl in the palm of his hand, allowing his body heat to warm the cognac. He took a long draw on a cigar, then exhaled slowly, his eyes fixed on the television as he watched intently the cartel's protégé descend the aircraft steps. As the new President of the little known African country with its hidden mineral wealth spoke to the assembled crowd, a smile slowly crept across the businessman's face.

♦ ♦ ♦ ♦

Belgravia, London:

There was no such joy for Ezra Brachfield as he sat alone in his study, cradling his second full glass of whisky and watching the news coverage from the small African nation. He had a sour and bitter tang in his mouth as he took a sip of the alcohol. His thoughts were filled with guilt and self-loathing, but no amount of wishing could change what he had been compelled to do. He felt a sudden urge to confess, to share the burden, but knew he could not. Ezra closed his eyes and rubbed at the centre of his forehead as he recalled the heated argument with David. The latter had vehemently maintained that he was still the Editor in Chief and that the decision to publish the anonymously delivered information was still his to be made. David had argued that they would be going against the very principles the media group extolled of fairness and correctness in whatever they published, standing proudly behind every word.

"We cannot just accept this, no matter how accurate it may appear, without verifying its veracity and correctness," his stepbrother had asserted. Ezra had reminded him in no uncertain terms that he was the ultimate decision-maker and had overruled him. David had stormed out of his office, threatening to resign.

He averted his gaze as Abebe Adebowale started to speak, and downed the whisky, then reached across his desk for the glass decanter. He needed a refill. The drink wouldn't remove the sinking feeling in the pit of his stomach, but it might ease the guilt. His organisation was responsible, or rather *he* was instrumental in bringing down who he believed was an innocent man and possibly subjecting the country to a far worse future – a usurper who may well turn out to be a despot. The African continent had a history of such men. Only time would tell. He ground his teeth at the thought.

Ariel!

He did what he had to do to ensure his son's safe return and keep him safe. He had to keep telling himself that. He couldn't confide the real reason to David – he couldn't take the risk. It was his secret he daren't share. A *Breaking* announcement on the TV suddenly caused his jaw to drop.

"Earlier today and while in custody, Obasi Bankole took his own life. The weight of guilt and the embarrassment of an impending public trial was seemingly too much for him to bear. He leaves behind a wife of twenty-five years and three children."

20 August 13ᵗʰ, 1973

London, England

She always used the third and furthest elevator – her back conveniently turned away to the lobby to avoid recognition. However, she had half-a-dozen rehearsed and plausible stories in the event of running into an acquaintance and where the chance meeting at the *Corinthia Hotel* might embarrassingly pop up in a later conversation. She tapped her foot in frustration – she was running late.

Ezra had become withdrawn and less attentive than usual over the past few weeks, and she desperately needed David. Her sexual desires had never fluctuated over the years, even after giving birth to Nicola. If anything, they had become more heightened and rather than quell her high sex drive, she stubbornly held onto their *association*, knowing full well the huge risk she was taking. The fear of a divorce – and she knew it would come to that for Ezra would never forgive her betrayal – had been doubled since that catastrophic telephone call of a few months back. A call she had tried to forget but continued to loom over her like the *sword of Damocles*, still expecting her full co-operation without question when called upon.

David's was a childless marriage to a frigid woman. He compensated for his lack of a child he could nurture and

[203]

call his own, with a deep fondness for his nephew. As much as he needed her, and she desired him, he would also turn his back on her should he learn the horrid truth. Her life would have been easier if she had ended the affair after the discovery, but she was too weak. Weak in that respect, but cold and hard in her commitment to living her life on her terms.

Ezra was gentle and considerate during their intimacies when he was inclined to perform, whereas David displayed a hunger and passion lacking in his marriage, which she found intoxicating. She was bound to him completely and would not jeopardise her love for him – for she was in love with him.

Damn him!

She relished her new role as Ezra Brachfield's trophy wife and had no qualms about the tag she knew had abounded following their marriage. Yet, as so often happens, thankfully, the label dissolved over time. After all, she wasn't the only such youthful catch in the wealthy circle in which she was now happily established.

At last!

The bell announced the elevator's arrival, and the steel doors parted. She stepped inside and moved to the back. She was about to press the button for the fifth floor.

"Sorry!" urged a breathless male voice. With an outstretched arm to prevent the doors' closing, a man followed her inside.

"Fifth floor, Mrs Brachfield?" His sudden question caught her off guard.

"I beg your pardon… Do I know you?" Her flustered voice gave away her surprise at the man's intimate contact. He ignored her as he pressed the *Emergency Stop* button halting the lift's progress, then withdrew an Identification Card from his inside jacket pocket and held it out for her inspection.

"Brown, MI6," he said, then replaced the ID. "I didn't mean to startle you." His apology lacked sincerity. "Before you meet with uhm…, Mr Minsky," he continued without hesitation. "You should first meet with my superior."

Without waiting for her response, he released the STOP switch and depressed the fourth-floor button. Her face turned ashen as she stood back against the wall – lips and chin trembling.

A disarmed Adele Brachfield meekly followed the MI6 operative out of the lift and along the hallway to a door marked 426. The irony of the number coinciding by one-hundred to room 526 – her and David's reserved suite – didn't escape her. It confirmed she was about to be confronted by her worst nightmare. The man gently knocked on the door, opened a few seconds later by a bespectacled man in a brown, three-piece suit.

"Ah! Mrs Brachfield. Do come in," he said politely but firmly and stepped aside for her to enter the room. "Thank you, Brown," he added and closed the door leaving the subordinate outside.

"Please, have a seat," he said, leading her inside and gesturing to one of two easy chairs in front of the window. She dutifully did as proposed and, with an apprehensive demeanour, sat on the edge of the seat.

"Can I offer you a drink?" he asked over his shoulder, standing by the dresser and unscrewing the cap from a bottle of *Teachers* whisky. He either didn't catch or ignored the gentle shake of her head and unhurriedly poured out half measures into two glass tumblers. Using a pair of tongs, he added three ice cubes from a galvanized steel bucket, and picking up both glasses, turned around and walked over to her.

"Here," he said, holding out one of the goblets. "It'll help calm you," he added. She reluctantly accepted the drink and defensively cupped it tightly in her hands. He took the seat opposite and, smiling benignly, sipped his drink. She slowly raised her eyes and looked at him. His polite manner unnerved her.

"My name is Gilmore," he said eventually, leaning back in the chair and crossing his legs. "It must be pretty evident by now that we are aware of... how can I put it delicately...? Your assignations with your brother-in-law."

Adele Brachfield squirmed slightly.

"Now..., I'm not here in condemnation of your... infidelity," he carried on. "Rather, I am here to understand your possible collusion in the kidnapping of your nephew."

So that's it?

"My involvement with Ariel's kidnapping? What are you talking about? I wasn't involved. No, no, not at all...! How could you possibly have concocted such a ridiculous notion?" Her defensive nature kicked in. She had done nothing to have alerted the least bit of suspicion. This was obviously a ploy following on from the visit by the Kazan man and the Levenson woman.

He chuckled softly at her response and took another sip of the whisky.

"We followed up the call you made to the London number from the William IV pub at Albury in the late afternoon of the 28th, last month... And we've been monitoring your movements since. Quite discreetly, I should add." He paused, allowing her time to digest the revelation.

Her jaw dropped – *which* truth was about to come out? She may have no alternative other than to come clean. She would have to tread carefully – avoid walking into a trap!

"It's not what you think! Not at all! You have to believe me. I would do nothing to harm Ariel... He gave me no choice. You don't understand!" she blurted.

"Then, perhaps you would enlighten me," he interjected calmly and placed his glass on the coffee table, then resting his elbows on the arms of the chair clasped his hands together. "Take a drink first, then take your time and recount in detail what happened. Leave nothing out. No detail is too small."

She took a large gulp and smiled in submission.

"It umm... it started with a phone call three weeks before Ariel's abduction. I never meant... I mean, it wasn't..."

"Please, Mrs Brachfield. Don't digress. The facts, please."

"It was a man's voice – deep, distorted, menacing. He said he knew all about me and... and David... my brother-in-law. He gave me a number and threatened that unless I wanted my husband to find out, to call him back immediately... and from a public telephone." She paused. Gilmore gave the nod for her to continue.

"I was told in no uncertain terms that unless I did what I was told, then Ezra would receive photographs. I knew what he meant..., so I did as I was instructed."

"Did you ever meet this man?"

"No, never! All contact was by telephone."

"Please, continue."

"I was only to report on both my husband's and my stepson's movements, especially out of the country. Nothing more. Nothing that would harm either of them!"

"You informed him of your stepson's trip to Cyprus?"

"Yes, but I never intended... I didn't know... I couldn't know what was planned!" She started to rock back and forth.

"Now, if you don't mind...?" said the MI6 operative.

"After Ariel's abduction, I was to keep him posted."

"How, exactly?"

"I would call a number which most of the time was answered by a machine. Sometime later – could be hours later – he would call back. Other times he would call, and as soon as he heard my voice, he would just say Corinthia – the hotel's name. It would be the signal to call. Sometimes he would provide another number."

"Was it the same voice, each time?"

"I don't know."

"Can you describe his voice?"

"As I said, it was deep – distorted. I'm not very good at these sorts of things. I don't know."

"So what sort of information did he ask of you?"

"Just what was happening, being said, done at our end, progress the authorities were making, people we were talking to…, that sort of thing. He assured me that Ariel wouldn't be harmed and that he would be released in due course. I can't tell you how much I was worried! We all were, but there was nothing I could do!" She paused and averted he eyes gazing into her glass. "He said that if I didn't do as I was told or confess to my involvement, they would harm Ariel. I was frightened that if I had owned up, whoever was behind the kidnapping would carry out the threat and kill him!" She inhaled deeply.

"And, of course, you would have had to admit to your entanglement with your brother-in-law." Her eyes flashed a hint of anger at Gilmore's insensitive remark.

"You don't believe a word I've told you!"

"Oh! I believe you, Mrs Brachfield." He leaned towards her. "I can see that your indiscretions had led to you being used. A pawn, if you will, in a very high-stakes game that put your stepson's life in the hands of some very dangerous people."

"So, what now? Am I supposed to run to my husband and just confess all? What would that prove?" she countered – desperation in her voice.

[208]

"I didn't *invite* you here to judge you on your impropriety. No! What we..., what we're trying to fathom is why? What was to be gained?" There was no mistaking the directive in Toby Gilmore's tone.

"How? How am I supposed to help you? I've told you all I know."

Gilmore picked up his unfinished whisky and, leaning back again in his seat, paused while taking a sip – deep in thought.

"There is a way that you can help and maybe..., just maybe... get you out of trouble. Let me first caution you. You are to say nothing to anyone – anyone at all – about our meeting and what I'm about to direct you to do."

21 August 14th, 1973

London, England

Ben Rutan and Colonel John Madison were already seated at the table when Ray and Gila walked into the conference room on the tenth floor of *Century House*.

"Hail the return of the conquering hero!" greeted Ben.

"A bloody good result, Ray," added the Colonel. "Well done, my boy! The Minister asked that I pass along his compliments and meet with you sometime tomorrow. He sends his apologies."

"Thank you, Sir," answered Ray without wishing to delve too much into the events of the past few days. There would be time enough later.

"Have you contacted the Ambassador?" asked the Colonel before Gila took a seat. She hesitated.

"Not yet. We didn't get in until late yesterday evening," she replied.

"He called about fifteen minutes ago. Asked if you'd ring him back as soon as you came in." She glanced at Ray before leaving to use a telephone outside the room.

"You've had some fun since we last met!" chuckled the CIA agent passing Ray the ever-present coffee pot.

"It's certainly been an adventure!" responded Ray pouring out two cups. "As Gila mentioned, we only got in last night. No time to make a report."

"We'll hear all about it when you bring us up to speed later," chipped in John Madison. Toby Gilmore entered with one of his team, carrying a wad of newspapers, which were immediately placed in two separate piles in the middle of the table.

"Thank you, Andrea," he said, dismissing her.

"A lot's happened since you've been away, Ray," said Toby taking a chair on the opposite side of the table. Ray glanced over the two stacks but didn't respond. He knew he would be finding out soon enough once Gila returned. Just then, the door opened, and Gila stood at the entrance catching Ray's eye briefly before closing the door, and taking a seat next to him.

"By your expression," said Ray, pushing a cup towards her, "it's not good news!"

"No, it's not... Shaul Feuerman's dead! They found his body a couple of days ago. His car was discovered a few miles from his home. It appears he was run off the road. The truck involved was left parked on a dirt track opposite the point of impact. It was reported stolen a few days earlier."

"I'm guessing it would be too much to expect any clues as to who was behind it?" asked the CIA man.

"Nothing... No witnesses, no prints... nothing!" responded Gila.

"Hmm." Ray shook his head. "I've been down this road before!" He recalled the number of coincidental and convenient deaths from three years earlier. "I think we can now confidently assume he was part of the kidnapping saga."

"Tying up a loose end?" proposed Gila.

"That would also suggest that he was used for a purpose and was not a permanent member. If so...," Ray paused for a brief moment, "we have to consider his role in all this."

"Your suspicions about the man's involvement could be well-founded, Ray," John Madison said. "The question now is…, was it staged? Was he in place to make sure the kidnapping followed a particular plan, then conveniently provide the exact location for a successful rescue?"

"As I said earlier, a lot's been happening. Here, take a look at the headlines," Toby interjected, tapping one of the bundles of papers.

Ray dutifully picked up the top edition, read the headline, briefly scanned the feature, and then passed it to Gila. They continued to go through each paper dated since the eighth of the month, comprising differently-worded repeats of the same story.

"Okay?" said Ray as he passed Gila, the last of the stack.

"Now, take a look at a couple from this pile," said Toby.

Ray repeated the process with four editions before sitting back in his chair and looking questioningly at Toby.

"Do you see a difference between the two bundles?" Toby asked.

"Pretty obvious. It's all about a coup following high-level corruption in the African country, Zuhuania. Nothing new there," Ray scoffed. "Nothing mentioned in the second collection."

"The country's pronounced *Zoo..hwa..nee..ya*," offered the Colonel.

"*Zoo..hwa..nee..ya*," repeated Gila as if committing the name to memory.

"That's the thing," continued the Colonel, "all the newspapers with the story… belong to the Brachfield Media Group… The others do not."

"You suggested we keep an eye open for anything out of the ordinary, so we made discreet enquiries directly with a couple of the editors. It turns out the Brachfield organisation was running an exclusive... unavailable to the rest of the media world," Toby took over. "Only now have they been able to get out of the starting gate and run with the story, albeit a little after the Brachfield horse was already halfway down the track." He paused for a moment. "Something else was out of the ordinary... According to one of our sources, Ezra Brachfield and David Minsky had a falling out over how they would proceed."

"How come?" Ray's interest was growing.

"The stepbrother wasn't happy publishing without fact-checking the *confidential* information and photographs..., but was overruled by Ezra Brachfield."

"Why would that have been unusual?" asked Gila.

"The stepbrother's the Group's Editor-in-Chief... According to the editor we spoke with, it was the first time Ezra Brachfield had ever taken the final decision, without mutual agreement between the two."

"So, what's so special about this place?" said Ray.

"It's a pretty insignificant country in central Africa with a population of around ten million. However, it happens to hold some of the richest mineral resources, such as diamonds, copper, ilmenite, kaolin, manganese, to name but a few," said John Madison.

"It's starting to make some sense," mused Ray thoughtfully.

"That's what we figured," piped up Ben pre-empting Ray's thoughts. "I got our local assets to dig around and see what might surface. Turns out a couple of new boys had already managed to obtain exclusivity to mine uranium and kyanite from the new president – Abebe Adebowale. They certainly weren't going to let the grass grow under their feet!"

"Do we know anything about them?"

"Both enterprises are registered in Panama. I don't

know how much you know about the country, but it's like a *Fort Knox* to the outside world if you want to keep your business private and operations secret. The country's banking secrecy laws are designed to protect account holders' privacy, and there are no tax treaties with any other country and no exchange control laws. It's a veritable tax haven."

"I confess, I know little to nothing of Panama and what it offers to businesses," retorted Ray. "A dead end?"

"Ordinarily, yes. But the CIA can be useful now and then!" chuckled the CIA agent.

"Okay, I'll play along," remarked Ray smiling back. He was becoming fond of the man.

"Without going into how we obtained the information or the micro-detail. Let's just say it was a covert operation. We eventually traced one of the companies belonging to an Argentine outfit which through rather complex ownerships is owned by the Hathaway Corporation, owned and operated by a Miles Hathaway."

"Hathaway Corporation? I seem to have heard the name somewhere," said Ray.

"Are you suggesting that Ezra Brachfield's organisation and this Hathaway outfit colluded over this African coup?" asked Gila.

"We've considered that possibility but have ruled it out…"

"Because why kidnap your own son?" interjected Ray on John Madison's response.

"Unless you want a plausible cover for your involvement," chimed in Toby Gilmore.

"I can't see that," said Ray. He couldn't see how the doting father he had met would be a party to such a callous enterprise.

"Anything on the wife and her dalliance with her brother-in-law?" asked Gila impishly.

"As a matter of fact, yes. A great deal, "answered Toby Gilmore. "I met with her last night." He proceeded to recount his meeting with Adele Brachfield.

"It seems pretty logical to me that the kidnapping was behind the African coup. The two events must be tied together. And if that's the case, we need to get close to the Hathaway organisation," said Ray. "The question is, how?"

"While you two were away, we arrived at the same conclusion and have come up with a scheme," the Colonel responded. "How's your polo game, Ray?"

"Polo, Sir? I don't understand."

"According to your file, you captained the Sandhurst Polo Team during the last six months before you graduated," the Colonel informed the group.

"Polo? The sport of kings!" jibed an impressed Gila.

"Yes, I did. Played off a two handicap. Why the interest?"

"That's the way you're going to get into Miles Hathaway world… and hopefully lead us to more answers," replied Toby Gilmore. A tone of finality.

"Me? And how am I supposed to get into his world, as you put it?" mocked Ray.

"Let me explain," started Toby. "I know it's a hit and miss possibility, but with Adele Brachfield's collusion, it could well come off." Ray and Gila were all ears. "It so happens that this coming Sunday, Miles Hathaway's polo team, *Grange Manor,* are competing in the final for the *Grange Manor Cup* at the *Guards Polo Club* in *Windsor Park* – the trophy his father put up fifteen years ago."

"O…kay…" Ray said guardedly, "So?"

"The thing is, this will be the first time his team has made the final, and by all accounts, the man is desperate to win it. Call it family pride. The thing is, Polo is his passion. Spends millions on the sport!"

"By the way, they're referred to as Polo ponies, not horses," quipped Ray, correcting Toby.

"Whatever!" he took the jibe with a chuckle. "Anyway, if we can get you into his team, you will no doubt be invited to join him at his estate, *Grange Manor,* for Saturday practice. He insists on putting his team and *ponies,*" he emphasised Ray's correction, "through their paces the day before each match."

"How can that be possible? He would already have a team in place. I can't just turn up and say: Oy! Here I am! I haven't played for three years, but I'm available should you need to *boot* one of your own off and take me on instead!" His riposte evoked laughter around the table.

"No, of course, you're right. However, we've also discovered that if one of the players cannot play… for whatever reason, the rules strictly prohibit the inclusion of a member from a competing team. Which basically would rule out all polo players, and Hathaway's team would have to forfeit giving the match and his cherished family cup – he so desperately wants to win – to the other finalists."

"You've been busy while we've been away. And there's more to this," remarked Ray. "I agree that polo players don't grow on trees, and he would be hard-pressed to find a replacement at short notice. In fact, I'd say near impossible."

"Exactly what we were thinking," responded the Colonel.

"Then there's the question of the player's handicap and the effect on the team's overall handicap… What's the match going to be played as?"

"Played as? I don't follow," said Toby.

"Well, is the match a Low or Medium goal? I'm assuming it's not a High goal… if Miles Hathaway is on the team," Ray added.

"I'm sorry, I still don't follow."

"Do you know what the total handicap of the team is?"

"No, but I can tell you how it's made up," replied Toby.

"Okay. I'll figure it out. Who's in the team?" The lack of knowledge of the sport around the table was more than evident.

"Miles Hathaway is a 2; the English professional, Toby Jeffries is a 4; the American in the team, Ross Beauchamp is a 3, and the team captain is an Argentine by the name of Carlos Rocca. He's a 6."

"Okay, that makes a total of fifteen, which is at the max of a Medium goal team. So it's safe to assume they are playing a Medium goal match. That also makes sense for a prestigious cup," informed Ray. "So, what do you have in mind?"

"That's where Ben comes in," Toby took over. "Perhaps you would explain, Ben?"

"Other than the team handicapping business, we managed to deduce quite a bit about the sport. By removing my fellow citizen from the team, it would make sense for you to take his place as a *two* handicapper."

"And before you ask," intervened John Madison, "I had the office discreetly check on your handicap with the UK's governing body for polo – the Hurlingham Polo Association – and have been assured your two status still applies."

"Even though I haven't played for three years?"

"Come on, Ray. It'll be like riding a bike. Once you know, you never forget," chimed in a helpful Toby.

"Except these ponies aren't bicycles!" retorted Ray. "Be that as it may, how am I supposed to take Jeffries' place?"

"That's down to me," Ben resumed. "Being an American national, it won't come as a surprise when poor

Beauchamp lands in hospital with a stomach bug on Friday morning! The food here is awful! Not the good 'all stuff we get back home!" Ben chuckled out loud. "A little concoction in his breakfast coffee will lay him up for a few days. It won't be pleasant, but he's young. He'll survive!"

"A stomach bug?" Ray shook his head.

"And that's where Adele Brachfield comes in," chipped in Toby.

◆◆◆◆

"I'm intrigued," said Gila picking up a *papadum* and dipping it into a *mango chutney* dip. "How did you get into polo. From what I've learned today, it's not a sport you can just walk into like football, for example." She slipped the chunk into her mouth and licked her fingers.

"I'd be interested too," said Ben sitting on the opposite side of the table next to Gila. They had decided on an Indian restaurant not surprisingly named *Khyber Pass* on *St. Georges Road* – a short walk from Century House. Toby Gilmore declined due to a previously arranged family commitment, and the Colonel had to get back to barracks.

"There's not much to tell, really. I didn't ride until I was thirteen. I was what is referred to as a natural horseman. You know what I mean, Ben… You ride." Ben nodded as he crunched on a piece of the thin, crispy flatbread.

"Riding came easily to me. I enjoyed it – still would, particularly galloping. The sensation of speed with a powerful animal between your legs is a unique and exciting experience." Gila stifled a cough and started to choke.

"Very funny!" cracked Ray. "Anyway, it wasn't long before I joined the junior polo team and played at

[218]

Cirencester Park Polo Club. It's the nearest to where I lived. I didn't have a horse of my own. Couldn't afford to keep one. Depending on the number of *chukkers*…"

"Chukkers?"

"Matches typically comprise a minimum of four chukkers – that is, periods, seven minutes long. High profile matches are usually played over six such stages. I'm going to assume the Grange Manor Cup is a six-chukker match. A polo pony will cover as much as three miles during each spell on the field – especially if it's carrying an attacking player."

"That must be tiring for the horse…, sorry pony?" said Gila.

"That's the point. You change ponies for each chukker," said Ray. Gila raised her eyebrows in surprise.

"Wait a moment… That means there could be as many as six ponies per player! That would be a total of twenty-four ponies per match for the team!"

"Multiply that by the two," reminded Ben, spooning a generous portion of *meat madras* onto his plate. "Don't forget the other team."

"The point I was making! Various sponsors provided our rides. Wealthy families like the Hathaways, for example."

"Expensive sport!" chimed in Ben.

"It certainly is. Maintaining a stable of polo ponies, grooms, feed, transport to matches etc. Costs a pretty penny! It's a different world from the one we live in. It's a world of the very, very rich!"

"Well, if the plan works, we shall find out… Shan't we?" said Gila.

"Hmm," responded Ray, still unconvinced.

"What about kit?" asked Ben. "if the plan works, you can hardly walk in with all new shining boots and all! Might just give the game away!"

"I've considered that. I left my boots – two pairs, nicely broken in, of course, at the family home. Also pairs of jodhpurs – riding britches, kneepads and helmet. And just in case this crazy scheme was to come off, I was thinking of driving down tomorrow. What do you say, Gila? Care to join me?"

"Love to!" she said with a full mouth of *chicken curry* – happily warmed by his surprising offer. She swallowed the tasty morsel. "How's the game played?"

"How's it played?" repeated Ray. "Let me put it this way... You have a team of four players on highly spirited ponies – sprinting, stopping, turning on a sixpence and sprinting off again at a speed of thirty miles an hour, riding off the four players of the opposing team with a 52-inch long polo stick – usually made of bamboo – with a hardwood head of just under 10 inches so that you can hit a wooden ball around 3 inches in diameter through two goal posts set 8 yards apart."

"Sounds easy," chuckled Gila. "It also sounds dangerous."

"It can be. Two years before I got there, one of the players on a Sandhurst team came off a pony and broke his back. Confined to a wheelchair for the rest of his life! Yes, it can certainly be dangerous."

"It's a matter of horsemanship. The better you are, the better player you would make," chipped in Ben.

"That's true," agreed Ray.

"Priority is to stay on the animal at all costs," joked Ben.

"Toby said the match takes place on Sunday in front of a senior royal. Is there a dress code I should be aware of? For me, I mean?"

"It's pretty varied. Normally slacks or jeans. Skirts and sundresses – irrespective of the weather – are the norm. Smart and fashionable... And comfortable shoes."

"Comfortable shoes?" queried Gila.

"For treading-in during breaks between chukkers."

"Treading-in?"

"Spectators walk out onto the field and press back the divots the ponies kick up during each chukker – with their feet. Even the *Queen* does it when she's there. It's tradition!"

"Well, if it's good enough for the Queen of England, it's good enough for me!" Gila laughed a tinkling little laugh.

22 August 17th, 1973

London, England

The hotel bar was slowly filling as Ray, sitting on a padded stool with his feet resting on a brass foot rail, nursed a double vodka. His white shirt cuffs glowed a blue hue in the neon lighting over the bar. A pianist was softly playing a nondescript melody on a baby grand in the far corner. He glanced at his watch – 7:46 pm.

He smiled. She was running late.

A woman's prerogative.

"Top-up, Sir?" asked the bartender distracting Ray.

"No, thank you. I'll uhm…" His jaw dropped as he caught her reflection in the large mirror above the bar. He turned on his stool as she approached, looking glamorous with her shiny black hair cascading over a dark-red, off-the-shoulder dress accentuating her appealing curves and a golden laced shawl. Her perfectly formed ears were sporting a pair of beautifully crafted pearl earrings matching an iridescent pearl necklace.

"Sorry if I'm late," she said as she sidled up to him.

"You look stunning!" He gazed fixedly at her for a moment with an expression she found appealing.

"Why, thank you, kind Sir," she responded, then gestured to the barman. "I'll have a shot of Tequila. Hold the salt, and you better make it a double. You might also refill my friend's glass. He looks like he needs it!" she added, grinning cheekily.

"You look somewhat fetching yourself, Captain Kazan," she said as the bartender placed two glasses in front of them. "Black-tie suits you." He smiled and raised his drink in a toast.

"Thank you, Sam," said Ray to the barman with whom they had become acquainted during the on-and-off days spent at the hotel. The *Sam* was regarding the *Humphrey Bogart* line – believed to have been spoken by him but never was – in the iconic film *Casablanca*. His name, in fact, was Robert, but as Ray had said, *it wasn't sexy enough!*

"Will that cover it?" he asked the barman fifteen minutes later. He nodded his appreciation at the generous tip included and wished them a pleasant evening.

The twenty-minute ride in one of London's iconic black cabs through the heavy evening traffic took them into the heart of the city's affluent district of Belgravia.

"Impressive!" said Gila when they stepped out of the taxi in front of a palatial, three-storey Georgian building. A splendid portico heralded the double entrance doors manned by two heavy-set men in tuxedos. They were politely greeted, and the one holding a clipboard asked for their names, then ran his finger down a list.

"Yes, Captain Kazan," and glancing at Gila added, "and Miss Levenson. Please." He gestured to the door as his colleague pushed it open.

They stepped into a spacious hall with a bright, white-tiled floor illuminated by a massive chandelier. A spectacular, sweeping staircase rose to a balustraded balcony leading off to both sides. Two more *minders* were standing discreetly to the sides. Gila looked around in stunned wonder.

"Security looks tight," remarked Ray.

A middle-aged man in white tie and tails welcomed

them, then led them past an elegant flower arrangement in a large, cut-glass crystal vase set on a round marble table. The murmur of many voices greeted them as he opened a panelled door. The room with its high walls and vaulted ceiling was full of men in tailored tuxedos and women in assorted cocktail dresses bedecked in eye-catching jewellery. The gathering oozed wealth and social standing. A few heads turned to view the new arrivals as they entered.

It's not me that's caught their eye, smiled Ray inwardly.

A string quartet seated inside the door was playing a muted *Baroque* melody. A waiter in a white jacket and gloves magically appeared out of the crowd carrying a tray of champagne flutes. Others were circulating, offering canapés. Ray dutifully picked up two glasses and handed one to Gila. He had just sampled the bubbly when out of the group, a female voice caught their attention.

"Ah! There you are! I'm so pleased you were able to make it," announced Adele Brachfield. She appeared primed and waiting for their arrival.

A nice touch, thought Ray, for the pointed welcome.

"Come, we must find Ezra! He'll want to see you," she proclaimed excitedly, conferring the sort of attention one reserves for favoured guests.

Gila slipped her right hand through the crook of Ray's arm as they followed her. They had to perform as a couple if Gila was invited as his date for the weekend – an act he was warming to quickly. Heads turned as the attractive young couple passed through with an occasional nod to inquisitive looks.

Ray noted a faint look of apprehension on Ezra Brachfield's face as they approached him, standing with an authoritative looking, dark-haired man in his early fifties. Toby had shown them a photograph of Miles Hathaway in a recent edition of the *Horse and Hounds* – a weekly equestrian magazine of the UK – posing with his Grange Manor polo team.

"Miss Levenson, Captain Kazan, I'm delighted you could join us this evening," he said, appearing to collect himself. "Allow me to introduce you. Mr Miles Hathaway." The target of their visit extended his hand to Ray, then to Gila. "Captain Kazan was with the team that rescued Ariel…" He suddenly stopped himself. "I'm sorry, perhaps I shouldn't have…?"

"Nonsense, Ezra. I'm delighted to meet you and your… charming companion," he held onto Gila's hand while directing a hint of a smile at Ray. Like many men of power and wealth, Miles Hathaway appeared a roguish charmer with an eye for the ladies.

"From what I hear, Captain Kazan, you are to be congratulated. A well-executed rescue and Ariel's back with his family safe and sound,"

"I was only part of the team – invited along for the ride," answered Ray.

"I'm sure you are being modest," remarked Miles Hathaway with a broad smile on his face.

"Miles was just telling us his bad news," Adele Brachfield started. A look of exasperation crossed the billionaire's face.

"I'd rather not bother Captain Kazan and Miss Levenson with my dilemma."

"I'm sure Ray and Gila won't mind you saying, Miles."

Reverting to their first names was a nice touch – personalising their presence. People were more prone to open up in private company.

"Damned, damned inconvenient!" Hathaway stammered.

Ray cast a glance at Ezra. No emotion.

"It's the Manor Grange Cup," prompted Adele.

"First time my team's made the bloody final!" He took

up the invitation. "Damned, bloody inconvenient!" he repeated, then apologised for his language.

"Manor Grange Cup?" Ray inquired innocently. Sometimes – like pushing a stubborn, broken-down vehicle – a little extra effort is required to get it on its way.

"I just learned late this afternoon that one of my players has been hospitalised. Food poisoning! Bloody inconvenient! Out of action for at least a week, I'm told." Ben had done his bit.

"Is that a problem? asked Gila innocently – getting into the act – then took a sip of her champagne. Ray smiled inwardly at her seemingly innocent intervention.

We make a good tag team.

"Can't you just get someone else to take his place?" suggested Adele.

"The rules prohibit me from approaching the other teams' players, and there's no one else available at such short notice. My polo manager has been making frantic calls all afternoon. However, no bloody luck!"

"Ah! It's such a pity, Miles," said Ezra Brachfield. "Pity, you don't play polo, Captain Kazan."

"He does, actually," responded Gila without hesitation.

"I... I... haven't umm..."

"Don't be so modest," encouraged Gila. "He captained the Sandhurst polo team during his second year." Evidence of pride in her voice for *her man.*

"Is that so? Do you have a handicap?" asked an eager Miles Hathaway. He was about to take the bait. The media magnate had innocently and unwittingly opened the door – and not a hint of collaboration. It was now over to Ray.

"Well, yes... a 2, actually."

"That would be perfect! Ross Beauchamp is a 3... My hospitalised American! It would also mean we can take back the one-goal advantage. Is it current... your handicap?"

"I believe so..., but I haven't played for a couple of years... Overseas assignments. I'm bound to be more than a little rusty."

"What plans do you have for the weekend?" asked an excited Hathaway, seizing on a seeming gift-from-heaven – a possible answer to his predicament.

"Well... nothing in particular." He held himself back from showing over-eagerness.

"Well then, that's settled!" responded a man who rarely took *no* for an answer. "You must come and stay at Grange Manor. I'm holding a practice session tomorrow afternoon. It'll give you a chance to choose your ponies and shake off the rust! You could also spend some time in the cage to loosen your swing and sharpen your eye." Ray appeared hesitant.

"The thing is... I promised Gila..."

"Of course, I expect Miss Levenson..., Gila, to join us! I wouldn't have it any other way! I can promise you a wonderful two days. There would also be a financial consideration."

"No, sorry. I couldn't take any money."

"It sounds like great fun," Gila chimed in, encouraging Ray's agreement to participate.

Ray's only claim to acting fame was as a nine-year-old sitting cross-legged at the front of a stage wearing a red paper-mushroom cap on his head – and not one word of dialogue spoken. An embarrassing childhood experience best forgotten. It wouldn't have done to have overplayed his role.

"Looks as though you have yourself a full team."

Hook, line and sinker!

23 August 18th, 1973

Grange Manor, Beds, England

Ray and Gila left for the seventy-mile drive to Grange Manor in Bedfordshire shortly after ten in the morning. At the start of the journey, a sprinkling of rain forced Ray to put up the canvas top on the MGB.

Most of the trip was north-west on the *M1* motorway, eventually exiting on junction 13 in a northeast direction towards Bedford – the historic market and county town. Ten miles beyond the town outside the village of Kimberley, Ray turned left onto an unmarked single-lane access. The windscreen blades continued to wipe away intermittent droplets obscuring his vision. A mile further along, brought them to an impressive entrance flanked on both sides with huge concrete pillars supporting ornately patterned, wrought-iron gates.

Two small gatehouses were positioned on either side outside the property. It came as no surprise when a man in dark overalls – tucked into a pair of military-style boots – approached the vehicle from the driver's side. Another shorter, stouter man appeared on the left with two alert and fierce-looking Doberman pinschers – cropped ears and standing obediently erect with eyes fixed firmly on the car's occupants. Ray peered up at the sunless sky through the open door window while the security guard recorded their details.

"It's due to clear up shortly, Sir," he remarked politely after confirming Ray's business and stepped back into the keep's doorway. Two seconds later, the gates slowly opened. Ray nodded his thanks and gently accelerated through. The continued entrance into the grounds took them through a small wooded area, an expansive area of green fields, and an arched stone bridge across a narrow river. The Manor house came into view beyond a row of tall pine trees on their right.

"Wow! That's impressive!" exclaimed Gila. Only a charitable visitor could compare Brachfields' country residence to the magnificent manor building. Ray and Gila had just entered the world of the extremely wealthy.

The great two-storey house stood above an exposed basement level with a row of five projected and four inner bays with round-headed sash windows sitting under keyed arches. A colourful manicured garden adorned the front of the building. Two huge, elegantly square structures were positioned on both sides of the Manor House.

"What are those?" asked Gila.

"I should imagine they're the stable blocks," Ray said as he pulled up alongside a balustraded stone staircase leading up to the main porticoed entrance.

"Must have a few horses," she quipped.

"His passion is horses and polo," responded Ray matter-of-factly.

The rain had abated by the time they got out of the car. Two liveried staff hurried down the steps to carry their luggage into the house. A butler introduced himself as Peter greeted them outside the main door and ushered them into a magnificent wood-panelled hall.

"Mr Miles extends his apologies. He is currently away from the Manor but will be back to join his guests for lunch. Please, I will show you to your room," he said and led the way to the first floor and a door halfway down a heavily carpeted hallway adorned in a mixture of oil painted scenes and portraits and a variety of ornaments – antique and contemporary.

"I trust you will find this comfortable," he said as he stood to the side to let them enter a spacious bedroom boasting the main feature – a large four-poster bed. Ray hesitated momentarily. He had overlooked that he and Gila were visiting as an item.

"This will do just fine, thank you," cut in Gila with a smirk. The two valets followed and placed their bags on an upholstered wooden box at the end of the bed.

"Please make yourselves at home. The ensuite bathroom is through that door. Lunch will be served in the dining hall at half-past twelve." He smiled broadly. "Until then, should you need anything, anything at all, just pull on the cord," he added, pointing to a tasselled sash hanging right of the bed. With that, all three servants left the room, quietly closing the door behind them and leaving Ray and Gila standing in the middle of the room in awe of their surroundings.

"I'm sorry, I didn't foresee this," he grimaced.

"Don't be silly!" Gila responded with a cheeky grin. "I'm sure we'll manage." Looking around, she noticed the large wardrobe left of the door into the bathroom. "Might as well unpack my clothes. Give time for the creases to hang out," she said and, turning her suitcase around, slid back the locks and swung open the lid.

Ray picked up a smaller, black briefcase with a hardened polypropylene shell and carried it over to a traditional, vintage-looking writing desk next to the window. The stunning view from the room stretched over the front garden and beyond the steep-banked river far into the distance across expansive green fields. He placed his hands on the case and, leaning forward, paused to admire the scene. The clouds – as the security chap had predicted – had all but disappeared, leaving behind a blue sun-filled sky.

"I better check on Ben's toys," he said, as he removed a key from his trouser pocket and inserted it into one of the two locks on either side of the *Samsonite* brand name engraved under the handle. He sat on the chair and opened the lid to reveal a dark foam interior with a series of open sections. Two miniature tape recorders were set tightly in aligned cut-out compartments with an assortment of monitoring devices. Ben had referred to them as the best and most advanced *bugs* invented by *Uncle Sam*.

"We have our uses!" he had joked before instructing Ray and Gila how to employ the latest technology procured by the CIA. Ray casually glanced over the contents, happy they had met with no mishap since taking delivery the previous evening following the sting's success. He closed the lid and relocked the case. Gila closed the wardrobe, walked to the bed, clambered up and stretched her denim-clad limbs with her back against two large puffed-up pillows.

"You can sleep on the door-side," she mocked with a throaty chuckle patting the bedcover. "Don't forget, Ray. We're supposed to be a couple." She smiled a wide cheeky smile, then squirmed her back for a more comfortable posture against the bolsters.

Ray glanced at his watch. "I think we should go down and introduce ourselves to our fellow weekenders."

◆ ◆ ◆ ◆

Gila slipped her hand into Ray's before following the butler into the elegant room seemingly unmarked by the passing of time with its floor-to-vaulted-ceiling, oak-panelled walls. A large open stone fireplace occupied most of the opposite wall. A heavy twelve-seater-long table covered in a brilliant white tablecloth took centre stage. Running alongside was an equally heavily-carved wooden sideboard laden with silver dishes, platters and salvers. Appearing to keep a protective eye on the laid-out fare, two reserved liveried footmen stood chins up at either end, ready to spring into action.

"Captain Ray Kazan and Miss Gila Levenson!" The butler announced the new attendees and immediately walked over to the spread buffet, cast a confirming eye over the display, then took up an overseeing position at the far end of the table.

"Welcome! Welcome! At last, you have arrived to rescue the team from our *dulce de leche*," proclaimed an excited voice in a Spanish accent unique to the Argentine people. A handsome dark-haired man with chiselled good looks and sparkly dark eyes stood up from the middle of the table and approached Ray and Gila, extending his hand in welcome.

"Rocca, Carlos Rocca," he announced, flashing a winning smile and taking Gila's hand gently in his.

"Dulce de leche?" queried Ray.

"Don't mind, Carlos. He's been on tenterhooks since yesterday. He's been as desperate to play on Sunday as much as Miles. Perhaps, even more so." The attractive young blonde typified a well-bred English aristocracy with an upper-crust tone to match. Standing the same height as Gila, she projected the nurtured background of money, privilege and a *Cheltenham Ladies College* heritage and elocution. "Penelope Grant," she introduced herself. "It's a local expression," she continued. "It means a sticky situation." Carlos put an arm around Penelope's shoulder.

"She's my rock, inspiration and... interpreter," he chuckled.

"When he's in the country," she added. The hint of a handsome and flamboyant Latin-American *playing the field* was not lost on Ray and Gila.

"Ray, Gila," responded Ray.

"Jeffries, Terry." The hand extended around Carlos Rocca was from the Grange Manor's 4 handicapper. Terry was a talented English professional from a middle-class grammar school background. A pleasant and generally serious individual with a hawkish nose and defined cheekbones, whose playing ability spawned from his grandparent's land-owning generous benefaction.

"Don't forget me!" chirped the other young woman who made it immediately known she was attached to Terry Jeffries, taking him under the arm in a possessive move. "I'm Jane!"

Pleasantries were exchanged before the appointed Team Captain proposed Ray and Gila sample an Argentine delicacy Hathaway's chef specially prepared for the buffet. Jane took little time in attaching herself and sitting next to Gila.

"So, what does your father do?" she inquired earnestly as Gila was about to take a bite of honey ham.

Her immediate need to establish commonality through family background was in evidence. An accidental spillage of a vodka-and-lime at one of London's compelling discotheques six months earlier – leading to several increasingly inebriated dances with a suggestion of intimacy to end the evening – unexpectantly pitched a pleasant yet naïve police sergeant's daughter into rubbing shoulders with the *rich and famous*. A world – although intoxicating – in which she desperately tried for acceptance but found distant and generally intolerant of outsiders.

"He's dead," Gila answered with a smile and without fanfare.

[233]

"Oh!" she responded with apology in her voice. The meal continued in silence for a few minutes before the unannounced appearance of Miles Hathaway accompanied by an attractive fair-haired woman in her late forties.

"That's Susan, his mistress," whispered Jane conspiratorially, catching Gila's interest.

"My apologies, pressing away-business. However, I'm all yours now and eager to get our weekend underway. Peter, a bottle of *Dom Perignon* if you would. The 1962 I think," he proposed the most recent top vintage.

"I don't wish to celebrate early, but with Captain Kazan's, Ray's heaven-sent inclusion in the team, I believe the Cup is within our grasp."

◆ ◆ ◆ ◆

"How many ponies do you have?" Ray asked as Miles Hathaway led them through the first block between two rows of cubicles – a line of inquisitive heads leaning over the stable lower doors.

"Just over sixty. All thoroughbred Argentines. The majority are mares. We find them generally better built with softer temperaments, stamina and speed to gallop the distance. We also have a few gaucho... cutting ponies the grooms use when exercising or leading the playing ponies."

Gila stopped to stroke the head of a beautifully defined palomino standing obediently outside of its stable. A young female groom was busy braiding its white tail with a blue and gold ribbon. Gila ran her hand down its golden-brown mane and gave Ray a questioning gaze.

"The mane is always clipped," he responded to her unspoken query. "Otherwise, it would interfere with a player's rein hand, and before you ask, the tail is braided so it won't tangle with the mallet… stick." Miles Hathaway stopped and returned to the animal. He took its head in his hands and stroked his nose.

"This is *Canario* – one of my favourite gelded males. He's one of the mounts we've earmarked for you." The pony's soft whinnying and playful nudging of Hathaway's shoulder with his finely chiselled head displayed a happy recognition.

"He's a beautiful animal," said Ray. "I look forward to riding him. This afternoon's practice?"

"Yes, he's one of the one's Carlos and I have chosen for you. We were up early for breakfast going through Ross Beauchamp's mounts," he chuckled. "Seeing which would suit. He's as keen as me to win the cup!"

"I got that impression over lunch," smiled Ray.

"Ah! Jack!" exclaimed Hathaway.

Ray and Gila turned to see a tall sturdily-built man with a shaved head and goatee approach them. Dressed in a navy blazer, grey flannel trousers, white shirt and sporting a striped tie, he had the apparent bearing of a military man. The man Miles Hathaway introduced as Jack Frasier – his head of security – took Ray's hand in a vice-like grip.

"Pleased to meet you." He spoke in a distinctly Scottish brogue.

"And I you," responded Ray with deep eye contact, compensating the man's firm handshake with added pressure.

"I must get on!" he said, releasing Ray's hand, then nodded politely with a fixed smile at the two visitors. Ray subconsciously rubbed his neck as he briefly watched Frasier walk away. The three continued to stroll through the well-maintained and clean, stable block, occasionally stopping to stroke an animal and learn its pedigree. Miles Hathaway impressed Ray with his in-depth knowledge of each pony – able to offer the smallest of details without

[235]

hesitation.

"The second block holds pretty much the same that you've seen here, so I shan't bore you further. I know you wanted to get into a cage for a warm-up," Hathaway said at the far end, then summoned over an elderly male groom.

"Henry, would you please look after Captain Kazan. He wants to get into a cage for a bit. He'll need some sticks." He turned to Ray. "Anything else I can get you?"

"I would appreciate a glove. I seem to have forgotten to bring along a pair."

"We have dozens of gloves," he replied with a grin. "Would you also make sure the Captain has a couple of shirts for the afternoon? We'll decide on your position and relevant number over dinner this evening," he said to Ray. "We've arranged for the horses to be at the practice ground for three. Henry will let you know where you will find it over by the lake. It's a way out, so we tend to drive over. If you need a lift…?"

"We'll be fine," Roy cut in. "Gila's an excellent driver. Shouldn't do much damage to the car over such a short distance with little danger of other traffic," he ribbed her in the make-believe of a close relationship between the two and receiving a playful slap on the arm in return.

"Right you are!" he said and, with a broad encouraging smile, left Ray and Gila in Henry's willing hands.

♦♦♦♦

"What's so funny?" remarked Ray as he raised in the stirrups and started to swing his right arm in a pendulum motion finding the desired stick angle.

"You are… on that wooden horse!" she giggled from the outside of the netted practice cage.

"It's a pre-swing routine to relax the body and find my

timing," he responded, ignoring her jibe. "I haven't done this for a while, so don't give me any stick." She laughed out loudly, causing him to stop what he was doing and join in with her.

"Alright! Pardon the pun. This is serious. You're not helping."

Using the end of the mallet, Ray positioned a ball slightly forward of the offside front. Raising himself again, he swung the mallet through the air three times, picking up speed with each downswing before descending and sending the mallet's head through the stationary ball with a loud, sharp thwack – hardwood against hardwood. The ball's kinetic energy was immediately absorbed in the netting surround, then dropped with a light thud onto the angled side of the concrete flooring and rolled back into the well. Ray kept up the routine for around thirty minutes – altering between various swings and striking the ball at differing positions around the wooden replica. He gained confidence with each swing and impressed Gila looking on with encouragement.

"Just as well, I didn't have to keep fetching the balls for you," she said when he finally stepped out and closed the gate behind him.

"I'm as ready as I'll ever be!" he proclaimed as they walked back to the house.

24 August 18th, 1973

Grange Manor, Beds, England

Holding the reins loosely in his left hand, Ray placed his booted left foot into the near side stirrup and pulled himself onto the polo saddle's flat seat. He gently shifted his weight, adjusted his sitting and gathered in the double reins. The additional guide enabled him to signal his commands more accurately. Gila passed up one of six mallets of varying lengths – leaning in a neat row against the MGB's door – and placed a hand on his foot.

"Have fun," she said, "and don't fall off!"

"Be careful!" It was not to be all fun of games – she still had a job to do! He winked at her before turning the pony away.

His first mount, *Jade,* was a chestnut mare who, as soon as he settled, relaxed her ears, indicating she was happy with him on board. He pulled slightly on the reins testing her reaction. She immediately sensed an adventure and started to buck her head in anticipation. Ray again pulled back on the reins, reminding her who was in control. She radiated bridled energy and nobility, ready to take her master on a spirited ride. He trotted her out a short distance before putting her into a slow canter, rising up and down in the saddle in harmony with the mare's muscular movements. The familiar exhilaration was immediate as Ray held a comfortable position in the saddle and support in the stirrups – gripping with his knees and lower legs. The extreme agility, athleticism and ability to twist and turn on a sixpence was the sign of a well-trained polo pony. Jade displayed such prowess when Ray put her into a full burst onto the field – 300 yards by 160 in size. Carlos and Terry were already mounted and practising various swings, striking a ball as they galloped around on the mowed grass.

Ray caught sight of Carlos stop and hit a ball past him, then gestured with his stick for Ray to take on a shot at goal. Needing no encouragement, Ray immediately urged Jade into a full gallop, leaning forward to compensate for the momentum of the horses' motion. Placing his left hand firmly on Jade's neck for a third support, he pulled the mallet backwards and upwards, reaching its highest point. In the same motion, he pointed his left shoulder at the ball and, bending his right knee, rotated both in clockwise unison. The familiar fluid movement felt natural – muscle memory had kicked in. It felt good.

Keeping his eye firmly on the ball, Ray reversed the movement with a twist of the shoulders and hips in an anticlockwise motion, bringing the mallet down with as much momentum as he could muster. With his wrist at full extension, he connected the head of the mallet squarely with the ball, sending it in an arc towards the two lightweight posts set eight yards apart. Taking Jade on through the posts, he brought her to an abrupt halt as Carlos appeared by his side.

"Fantastic shot!" cried an excited Argentine. "Angles, Ray!" He was right in his observation. Ray's ball had sailed three yards past the righthand post – outside the goal! "It's all about angles!" he added before pulling sharply on the reins and galloping back up the field.

Ray shook his head and chuckled at his departing team

Captain. The angle at impact was crucial. He walked Jade over to the ball, and with a backhanded offside swing, struck the ball, sending it back into play.

"Oh! That's annoying!" remarked Gila just as Jane made a timely approach.

"What's annoying?" she asked, showing genuine concern. Penelope had appeared to be ignoring Jane, focusing her concentration fully on Carlos. Susan was leaning against Miles' Range Rover's bonnet, looking on as Miles was putting on his kneepads.

"I left my sunglasses in the bedroom," she replied, squinting into the cloudless sky. "Would you look after these while I pop back?"

Without waiting for a reply, Gila gathered up the remaining five mallets and passed them to Jane. With a quick *thank you*, she jumped into the MGB, reversed and took off back to the Manor, leaving Jane clutching the mallets, unsure of where to put them.

They assumed the house would be deserted other than low-level staff. Everyone would be at the practice ground, including Peter supervising drinks and snacks with two others. Gila parked in the front, unlocked the glove compartment, removed two items and her sunglasses, and skipped up the main entrance steps. The front doors were unlocked. The building was eerily quiet. She anticipated correctly that Miles' study — her target room — would be on the opposite end of the building to the lounge and dining room.

Slowly opening a door, she peered around the corner. Taking a firm grip on the doorknob, Gila swung the door open and stepped into a panelled study, richly decorated with fine, lush carpets and predictable antique furniture. The left wall was completely covered in book shelving packed with hard-bound books. A large walnut desk sat in front of the main window overlooking the garden. She turned and took a quick look outside before closing the heavy door.

She crossed the room to the desk and picked up the handset of a black, old-fashioned telephone with a decorative gold rotary dial. Following Ben's instructions, she unscrewed the microphone cap and lay a flat circular-shaped unit inside. Ray and Gila were told that the gadgets were the latest technology with an adequate range and would voice activate the two recorders. He also assured them of the high quality of transmissions. As she was refastening the cap, the sound of an approaching vehicle distracted her. She peered cautiously out of the window.

Jack Frasier had driven up in a Land Rover. She had seen him parked on the opposite side of the practice ground. Standing well back, she observed him get out of the vehicle and look over the MGB. He must have followed her. She had to act fast.

Satisfied that the transmitter didn't rattle and was firmly ensconced, she quickly wiped the handset with a handkerchief before replacing it in its cradle. She hurried to the door when she realised she still had the second bug in her pocket. Turning back, she pulled a tab off the other item exposing a sticky surface and pressed it against the underside of a coffee table in the middle of the room between two easy chairs.

With a final glance around, she quietly opened the door and slipped into the hallway. She heard the front door. Thinking fast, she remembered the back staircase she and Ray had accidentally discovered on their way to lunch. Moving swiftly and silently, she ran towards the door leading to the stairs in the opposite direction. Taking two treads at a time, Gila reached the first floor and ran to their bedroom. She opened the door, then immediately closed it firmly – ensuring that if anyone was around, they might hear her *leave* the room.

[241]

Gila took a deep breath, then slowly exhaled before calmly walking towards the main staircase. Jack Frasier was standing in the entrance hall as she skipped down the steps.

"Can't be without these," she said with a friendly smile as she put on her sunglasses and walked past. He stood aside and nodded slightly with a light smile in response. He turned and watched her open the front door and leave – closing it behind her. He remained looking around, still feeling disquieted. Did she really return for a pair of sunglasses... or did she have an ulterior motive? Was he being paranoid? He hadn't been comfortable since Miles had informed him of the surprise weekend guests. Realising that he was probably overreacting, he shrugged off his suspicion and decided to return to the practice ground.

Gila jumped into the sports car and, with a huge sigh of relief, turned on the ignition, then drove off without looking back.

Jane was still holding onto the mallets when Gila pulled up onto the same spot alongside her. Ray and the other three were already out on the field on their second mounts.

"Sorry about that!" apologised Gila, taking the sticks from a relieved Jane, then re-arranging them back against the door of the MGB. "How are they doing?" She gestured for Jane to prop herself against the car's bonnet next to her and view the lively equestrian activity.

"Just great!" she retorted excitedly in response to Gila's friendly approach.

They engaged in small talk while watching the men and walking out together to tread in each time the four rode back to change ponies. Gila squeezed Ray's hand during one divot replacement session – confirming the successful plant – and received a gentle *understood* squeeze

[242]

in return. Jack Frasier had returned to the practice ground and had again parked opposite, watching the action from inside the vehicle.

"You look smug!" Gila announced as Ray got off the final ride. He had ridden eight ponies in all and was breathless from the effort.

"It was great!" he confessed with a huge grin. They walked over – unconsciously holding hands – to a collection of upholstered garden chairs and a table set up next to Miles' transport.

"I trust a Pimm's will do after all that!" proposed a cheerful Miles Hathaway while wiping the sweat off the back of his neck with a hand towel. The other three exhausted team members slumped into the comfortable seats, letting their partners do the honours. Ray couldn't help but smile at Gila as she took a sip of her now favourite English summer tipple. He unbuckled his kneepads, dropped them onto the ground next to the chair, stretched out his legs and slowly let the cool refreshing drink relax him. He hadn't felt that good and abandoned from the reality he'd been living for the past three years.

"Penelope asked if she could ride back with us," said Gila after a while.

"Fine," he said – his eyes still closed.

Terry and Jane had already driven back in Terry's recent acquisition – a chocolate-coloured *Triumph GT6* hardtop. Miles and Susan were climbing into the Range Rover while Peter and his two staff were clearing up.

"I thought I'd take a walk down to the lake before setting back."

"Okay! I'll drive her over and come back for you," she said. Moments later, Ray heard her pull away and got out of the chair. He stretched his sore limbs as he slowly strolled across the corner of the polo field towards the lake. He planned to soak in a hot bath before dinner and relieve the sore muscles he hadn't used since his final year at Sandhurst.

Ray stood at the top of wide stone steps – lined on both sides with a low parapet leading down to the water's edge – and surveyed the expanse of calm water edging the woods on the opposite end. He took a seat with his feet planted on the last step and absentmindedly picked up a loose pebble. With a flick of the wrist, he tossed it into the water, creating an urgent ring of ripples. His thoughts turned back to late September 1970. He and Leyla were sitting under a leafy tree on a grassy bank of the *River Thames.*

Oh! I almost forgot," Leyla reached over the MGB's car door and retrieved her handbag from the passenger seat. "I got you something." She said and handed him a small, square, black box.

"What's this?" Ray opened it to reveal a polished-black band ring.

"I couldn't resist it… Do you like it?"

Ray removed the ring and instinctively slipped it onto the little finger of his left hand.

"It fits," he said, admiring it. "So now you've ringed me…, does that mean I'm your swan?" He giggled. She burst out laughing, recalling his earlier trivia about the Queen's swans.

"Now, you won't forget me while you're away from me."

"I could never and will never forget you," he said softly.

He was subconsciously twirling the ring when a hand touched him gently on the shoulder.

"I'm sorry!" Gila said and smiled ruefully. "I didn't mean to disturb you."

"Don't be silly," he responded and moved over, making room for her to sit beside him. They sat in silence, looking out over the lake.

"Isn't it beautiful?" she suddenly burst out, drawing Ray's attention to a blue butterfly nestled on a flower in the stone vase next to him.

Leyla raised her head slightly and saw a butterfly perched on her knee – its wings raised like hands in silent prayer. They continued to watch without disturbing the creature when it suddenly opened up at full stretch holding the pose and revealing a vibrant, sapphire-blue colouring.

"It's gorgeous," Leyla exclaimed as it flapped its wings and rose majestically into the air and flew away with a slow-motion of its impressive span.

"Every time I see a beautiful, blue butterfly, I will think of you," Ray said and leaned down and kissed her tenderly on the lips.

"You're such a romantic, Lieutenant Kazan."

Ray continued to watch the gentle creature when after a few moments, it opened its wings and lifted into the air, fluttered over to Gila and landed on her shin. Ray smiled as he watched Gila observe the beautiful creation, daring not to move a muscle lest she disturb it. She chuckled with delight when it suddenly flapped its wings and flew off across the lake.

Caught in that tranquil moment, they looked each other deep in the eye, then leaned closer – their lips seeking the others in anticipation. They held the embrace for a long while – neither wishing to break away.

"I think we've loads of time before dinner!" Ray said when they pulled away – a devilish twinkle in his eye. Gila leant in and kissed him again.

"More than enough time," she agreed – her soft breath warming his face.

♦ ♦ ♦ ♦

"What took us so long?" she asked – her head laid gently on his bare chest. He didn't reply and kissed her on the head.

He smiled innermost thoughts, recalling the surprising appearance of the butterfly. He was sure it was his cue to move on and surrender to the stirrings he felt for Gila.

"Ready for another round before that hot bath?"

"I thought you were too sore," she giggled as she pulled herself up and lay across him, then planted her lips hard onto his.

◆ ◆ ◆ ◆

The eight assembled in the lounge for cocktails before dinner. The men were attired in dinner jackets and the ladies in various styled and coloured cocktail dresses. Once again surprising Ray, Gila looked stunning in a glamorous black cocktail dress accentuating her sculpted figure. Her midnight-black hair pulled back tightly in a bun revealing her fine cheekbones and alluring almond-shaped eyes.

The bold bitter *Campari* concoction with vodka and a dash of Angostura Bitters expertly prepared by Peter – displaying a talent in addition to butlering the Hathaway household – was a delectable prelude to the evening. The group was treated to the chef's special starter. *Lobster* served with *pea purée* topped with a *Cilantro mayonnaise* sauce. Inevitably, the conversation soon turned to horses, polo, and the afternoon's practice leading to the final showdown the following day over the *Manor Grange Cup*.

"I was pleased to see you shake off the rust, Ray," remarked Miles breaking a bread roll into two.

"He sits well," chipped in Carlos.

"Sits well?" Gila was intrigued – wanting to know more.

[246]

"Before you can control the horse..." Carlos took up the response.

"You know you'll never hear the end of this conversation," warned Penelope with a chuckle. "Once Carlos starts... you won't be able to stop him. He lives and breathes horses and polo."

"Not at all the time, my darling!" chuckled Carlos.

"I thought you're only supposed to refer to them as a pony, not a horse," cut in Gila, joining Penelope in the jibing and evoking laughter from around the table, including Carlos. Unperturbed, he continued.

"Put it this way; a rider has to be able to sit well so the horse... *pony*... feels good with the rider it's carrying on its back. It's to do with posture and coordination. Both have to have an understanding... an agreement, if they are to move as one."

"I have to say all the ponies I rode were superb. It's difficult to choose one above the rest... although I admit Canario is most probably my favourite," Ray entered the conversation wanting to throw a compliment Miles' way. He was still undecided about the man and wanted to remain objective. He and Gila had listened to the scant recordings of a conversation between Miles and Carlos following the afternoon's practice after their bath. There was nothing spoken out of the ordinary. Gila ribbed Ray when they overheard a comment made by Carlos of how lucky Miles was to have accidentally bumped into him, saving their inclusion in the final and potentially returning the Cup to its rightful place at the family's ancestral home.

"As you know, Ray, it's a six-chukker match," Terry had finished his lobster and leaned forward to catch Ray's eye. "When would you want to ride him?" Ray considered the tactical question.

"It really depends on which number you chaps want me to take," he replied.

[247]

"We've given that some thought already," Miles said. "We know you've captained a team before. However, we believe you should take number 4."

"At the back?" Ray appeared surprised.

"We could see you're naturally an attacking player, and yes, we'll need to score goals. The *Diables Rouges*..."

"Diables Rouges?" Gila cut off Carlos.

"It's the name of the other team, Red Devils."

"I think I ought to explain," offered Miles. "It's because of me we have to take a different tack. It shouldn't come as a surprise, Ray... You saw me perform out there. I'm not a young fellow like you three. God..., I've been lucky to hold onto my 2 handicap, as it is." His humble statement elicited a *not true* look from Terry. Miles gave a quick smile in response as he leaned to one side while Peter topped up his wine. He waited for the butler to step back, then cleared his throat.

"I love the game, and, of course, I want to be out on the field – useless as I can be on most occasions."

"Now, now, darling, there's no need to put yourself down," interrupted Susan defensively.

"Let's face it. We'll have our work cut out tomorrow, ever since that old bugger, Vincent Plaskitt..." He caught Ray's quizzical look. "He's the owner of the team, and until this season, he's always played, but now he's stepped back, and his son runs Diables Rouge. They're a stronger team without him. No-one over thirty-five in that team."

"But still with the same team handicap," interjected Terry with a touch of contempt.

"He's made the final five times, winning the Cup on three occasions," continued Miles. "It would gall me no end..., if they walked away with it again this year," a hint of anger and frustration in his voice.

"It makes a lot of sense, Ray. We thought that if we put Terry in number 1, he'd be able to attack the goal whenever possible. Miles can sit in front of me as our number 2. I take my usual place as team Captain as 3..., and you... our number 4."

"Of course, I'll play in whichever position you want to put me in," confirmed Ray. "Glad to be part of the team!"

"We've seen you connect with the ball."

"Angles!" cut in Ray, making Carlos laugh.

"Yes, angles, my friend. You can certainly hit a long ball and will be able to feed from the back, coming in when opportunities present themselves."

"If I'm to play at the back, I'd like to use Jade for the third and leave the rascal, Canario for the final chukker... If you guys agree?"

"Absolutely. Makes sense to me," confirmed Carlos and raised his wine glass.

"I agree," chimed in an ecstatic Terry. Ray learned later from Carlos – over a glass of *Port* – that Terry had always coveted the number 1 position held by the hospitalised American, Ross Beauchamp.

"Thanks for understanding," Miles also raised in glass in anticipation of a toast.

"Looks as the team is all set for a victory!" piped up Jane. The poor girl was fated never to win over that group fully! There followed a slight embarrassing pause before Carlos baled her out.

"To the four amigos and the Cup!"

The buoyant and hopeful mood continued until just after ten when Susan excused herself and paved the way for Ray and Gila's eager exit.

25 August 19ᵗʰ, 1973

Great Windsor Park, England

The day promised to be sunny with a light breeze. Ray and Gila had skipped breakfast, preferring to remain – on Gila's insistence with little objection from Ray – in the four-poster until mid-morning.

They stood half-naked at the window watching the impressive procession of ten large horse transporters – sporting the Grange Manor livery of a blue/gold design – drive by from the rear of the stable blocks, over the stone bridge on the seventy-mile journey to *Windsor Great Park* in Berkshire. Miles' Polo Manager, James Driscoll, led the convoy, with two security in a similarly liveried *Range Rover*. A *Land Rover* followed in the rear with four more security – Ray learned were all ex-SAS and worked for a *J.F. Security Services Ltd*, the outfit run by Jack Frasier Miles used exclusively.

"That's some sight!" declared Gila from inside Ray's arms.

"Terry was telling me last night that they would have been up at four this morning. Miles is transporting an additional four ponies, just in case. We'll have three grooms apiece looking after our mounts." He continued to watch in awe at the spectacle. "Costs a pretty penny," he muttered.

"He's desperate to win that Cup," she mused. "Do you still think he was involved in the Ariel abduction?"

Gila was showing signs of warmth for the billionaire Ray couldn't allow himself to feel. Miles had shown himself to be a charming and generous host. However, he was also a successful businessman, prepared to challenge any obstacle that got in his way. A person couldn't build such wealth without being willing and prepared to cross the line. Ray could not afford to abandon his scepticism.

"Hmm…" Ray still couldn't help feeling a touch of guilt over their purpose. He was not duplicitous by nature, although he was learning fast.

"No idea. Time will tell. We're back tonight for the party he's throwing…, win or lose. Who knows what we might still learn between now and tomorrow morning."

"I know," she suggested slyly, whispering into his ear, then playfully took his earlobe between her teeth.

◆◆◆◆

They turned north-west into *Wick Road* off the *London Road* just after 1:30 pm, having stopped off for a light lunch at a country pub outside Bedford. The afternoon's programme was about to start with two low-goal matches of four chukkers each. The Grange Manor Cup's main event was scheduled for 3:00 pm.

Ray had elected to drive down in a sports jacket and jeans with his boots and kit in a bag sitting on the back seat. Gila chose to wear a fetching semi-formal, lightly patterned summer dress with a plain cream cotton jacket thrown over her shoulders. She had carefully stowed a matching wide-brimmed hat in the boot. The mile-long drive through the wooded section of the Park brought them to the official entrance to the *Guards Polo Club* ground. Upon presenting his Player's pass and Gila's

VVIP pass, he was directed to turn off the road across the grass where numerous transporters were parked, disgorging tens of ponies.

"There are Terry and Jane," Gila caught sight of them walking towards the car.

"You can park by our transporters," advised Terry. "You can't miss them. Bloody impressive as always. We're on our way for a drink in front of the clubhouse." Terry was already dressed in his jodhpurs and boots and proudly wearing his team shirt with the number 1 emblazoned in gold on the back.

"We'll save you a seat," chirped Jane happily as they walked off.

"He's keen!" chuckled Gila. She liked him.

Ray drove on a little further and was spotted by Miles' Polo manager, James Driscoll, who gestured for Ray to park alongside the team's Range Rover.

"I need to change," he said as he climbed out of the MGB.

"Use this trailer, Sir," he said. "It's the players' lounge."

Miles reached for his bag, then climbed the metal steps into an opulent carpeted cabin panelled from floor to ceiling in a light-brown wood veneer. A cushioned two-seater sofa, two matching easy chairs, a polished wooden coffee table and artwork pieces hanging on the wall offered the comfort of a five-star hotel lounge. Noticing a refrigerator in the corner, Ray gave a chortle as he sat in one of the easy chairs.

I bet that's well-stocked, he smiled. Miles Hathaway was a man who enjoyed a coveted lifestyle and was more than able to provide one. Fifteen minutes later, Ray emerged from the transporter booted and wearing his jacket over a fitted number 4 shirt. Gila was waiting by the car, looking a picture in her dress, hat and sunglasses.

"You look sexy!" quipped Gila as she took him under

the arm.

"Now, now. I have a match to play. No distractions, please," he replied and kissed her on the nose.

The place was a hive of activity as they made their way towards the clubhouse and the enclosure with several umbrella-covered garden tables overlooking the centre of the polo field. Ray spotted Jane vigorously waving from the middle of the cluster of tables. Ray and Gila meandered their way through as Carlos turned up with Penelope.

They took their seats around the table, having commandeered an additional two folding chairs from a nearby table to the disturbed annoyance of an elderly couple. A cheeky dazzling-white Argentine smile softened the blow with an accent to match.

"It's bloody mayhem in there," exclaimed Terry, struggling with a tray holding eight half-pint mugs of Pimm's.

"Sorry, ladies he said as he set the tray on the table. Couldn't be arsed! You'll have to drink out of these. Anyway, they've already run out of cocktail glasses."

Penelope helped herself.

"It's fine by me, Terry. We ladies can always handle a *mug*, don't you fear!" The pun was lost on Gila until Ray explained the homonym. Ten minutes later, Miles and Susan joined the group.

"Our team details have been handed over, and the committee have again confirmed Ray's handicap and validity as a member of Grange Manor," said a delighted Miles.

"That's a relief, seeing as I got all dressed up for the occasion," quipped Ray to chuckles from the others.

"And something for our team groupies," Miles added, at the same time as he pulled out a box from a white plastic bag, then handed it to Gila. He reached back in and gave two to Jane and Penelope and one to Susan.

"You're too generous!" declared Gila upon extracting an expensive compact pair of *Zeiss* binoculars.

"Ditto," remarked Penelope to Jane's simple but enthralled, *thank you*.

"Now, you'll be able to view our efforts on the field with more clarity," Miles chuckled with amusement. The man was making it more and more difficult for Ray to keep an objective opinion. A voice came over the public address system announcing the commencement of the first match. The ladies immediately raised their gifts to their eyes. After seven minutes of play, the first chukker over, they all got up and walked out onto the field to tread in.

"Each period is seven minutes long with a four-minute break in between and a ten-minute break at half-time," explained Ray as he and Gila were pressing in the loose divots.

"This is fun!" she exclaimed. "Now I realise the need for flat shoes."

The eight remained together at the table for the duration of the first match, clapping enthusiastically at times, encouraging the eight hopefuls dashing around the field. The four men swapped occasional critiques of the game — tactics, horsemanship, ponies, and cries of foul whenever a player crossed another's line. Once or twice, Ray caught Gila smiling at him, taking part in the banter.

"Shall we mount up?" suggested the Grange Manor team Captain with twenty minutes to go before the start of their match. The four women unanimously elected to join them and watch the game from the pony enclosure.

"We have our binoculars! We shan't miss any of the action," declared Penelope.

Ray sat on the passenger seat with his legs stretched out through the open door of the MGB while putting on his kneepads.

Gila stood looking on, holding his helmet and gloves. She couldn't recall the last time she was so happy. Ray had opened up so many possibilities. She was even contemplating leaving the unit – the dangerous and fraught world she had submitted to. It was time to move on – for all of them. Since their passionate kiss at the lake and Ray's mix of urgent and gentle lovemaking later in the bedroom convinced her, he felt the same way. However, it was still early days – hopeful, but no commitment forthcoming.

Ray's first chosen mount was a buckskin mare, Jewel, who, although not as fast as Jude, had a slightly more aggressive streak. He would need that if he were to protect their goal.

"Pass me the 53 inch…, the one with the blue handle," he prompted Gila backing up the mare. She was primed to go. All the ponies had sensed the occasion – tossing heads and twitching their ears, excited at their inclusion in the afternoon's proceedings. Gila had appointed herself as the *keeper of Ray's mallets* after one of the grooms carried over a selection he would choose from for each chukker. She was keen to be involved. The third match had just concluded, and the riders were returning to the enclosure. The four women followed the four members of the Grange Manor team as they walked their ponies to the edge of the field. Gila felt a sense of anticipation and nervous energy. She so wanted Ray to perform well – to prove his worth to the team. The announcer had already started an introduction to the main event:

"… *finalists for the first time. Miles Hathaway's Grange Manor is taking on the formidable opposition of the Plaskitt family's Diables Rouge, captained by Raymond Plaskitt – five-time finalists and three-time winners of the Cup. I should add, ladies and gentlemen, that today's match was close to cancellation due to the sudden illness and hospitalisation of one of the Grange Manor's team. However, Captain Kazan's fortuitous inclusion, an officer in the British Army, has enabled the six-chukker match to take place. As always, I wish to remind all spectators, including our visitors,"* the speaker was referring to the huge assembly of non-members parked and picnicking on the opposite side of the playing field, *"to join in with the treading-in, ensuring the continued safety of players and ponies alike."*

With a familiar, reassuring wink, Ray spurred Jewel forward, and the four players joined the other team and the referee for the traditional photograph in front of the Royal enclosure. The riders backed away and took their respective positions on the playing surface. The whistle blew, and the match kicked off in earnest.

Understandably and as anticipated, the first chukker was dominated by the opposition. Nervous and anxious energy prevailed throughout the first seven-minute session. Terry missed an open goal, Carlos was overly busy in the middle of the field, and Jewel took a ball accidentally in the head – thankfully saving a possible first goal for Diables Rouge.

"They're bloody over-aggressive with Miles!" bellowed Terry angrily on their return off the field. With only four minutes for remounts, no one went off to tread-in, preferring to remain with the team.

"Don't worry about me, Terry. You concentrate on scoring some damned goals," rebuked Miles. "Stop worrying about me!" he repeated as he climbed up onto his second pony. "Just get me some fucking goals!"

Ray was too preoccupied with his second pony, *Askari* and his stick selection, to witness a lapse in Miles' usual courteous manner.

The second chukker fared better until Raymond

Plaskitt sent a beauty of a shot over Ray's head. Grange Manor came off the field one goal down. The opposition was proving to be highly aggressive and skilled players. They would not be easily beaten. Ray was beginning to wonder if Miles was indeed a handicap too many for the team to handle. The third chukker was a vast improvement. Jade's exceptional performance allowed Ray to deny the other team a vital two-goal edge. Terry got the team's first goal, but a stumble and near dismount allowed the opposing team's number 2 to gain an advantage against Carlos and score their second. Ray was caught off position and was unable to intercede. Ray took Gila's hand for the ten-minute break and walked out onto the edge of the field to tread in.

"You're only one goal down," she said.

"I actually think we got a chance!" he remarked. "I really do! Miles has picked up his game and is playing well and not at all phased with the hostile attention he's been getting from the other team, especially their number 2."

"How are you doing?"

"Yeah, I'm fine. I'm enjoying it! Jade performed well. She's a great pony.' She tightened her grip on his hand. "We better get back," he said.

Grange Manor entered the field of play for the sixth and final chukker, a goal down. Halfway through the session, the extremely and talented Carlos saw off a strong challenge from the combined actions of Raymond Plaskitt and his number 2 – drawing gasps from the spectators. Then at full gallop, struck the wooden ball with deadly accuracy, sending it into a high arc from the middle of the field and through the opposition's goalposts. A huge cheer erupted from the crowd. Ray tapped *congrats* on Carlos' helmet as he passed to take up the rear position.

The game's direction was changed after each goal was scored, irrespective of which team did the scoring. Two minutes to go, and the match was all square. Whichever team got the next goal would surely win the Cup. Thirty-five seconds of play left, and Ray spotted an opportunity. To take it would mean exposing their goal to danger. Not to take it, would pass up a chance fast disappearing towards a tie, leaving the Cup in the hands of last year's winners – Diables Rouge. It was a split-second decision...

No going back!

Spurring Canario into a headlong charge at full gallop down the righthand side of the field – narrowly missing the inch-thick wooden board protecting the visitors' area – Ray collided heavily with James Plaskitt's mount, successfully riding him off his line. Clear to attack the bouncing ball, he raised and, leaning dangerously forward in the saddle, gripped hard with his lower legs and clasped what little of the animal's mane he could with his left hand. He marshalled all of his upper-body strength and swung the mallet up in a wide arc and then down and under Canario's neck. The mallet head caught the wooden projectile with maximum impact.

Sensing the possible outcome, the other three members instinctively moved at speed, pushing their mounts hard from the back through the middle of the field. The well-struck ball shot off – narrowly missing Diables Rouge's number 4 – and landed some fifty yards in front of the opposition's goal. Unable to turn about and face the oncoming riders without incurring a penalty, the number 4 could only watch as the skilled Argentine shot past with steely determination and struck the ball with a ferocious thwack...

Both teams left the field to a huge round of applause with a unanimous appreciation for an exciting final – undecided until the dying moments. All players dismounted in front of the Royal enclosure to continued enthusiastic ovation and handed over the reins to waiting grooms, who led the spent animals quietly away. Miles Hathaway's beaming face told its own story of what the win meant as he guided his three heroes to receive the Manor Grange Cup from a senior Royal personage. Dozens of flashbulbs were popping from an array of cameras as a sea of eager photographers jostled to capture the special moment – soon to appear in the *Horse and Hounds* and the glossy, quarterly *Polo Magazine,* among other publications. A magnanimous Raymond Plaskitt made a point of singling out Ray.

"Captain Kazan, that…," he started to say, extending his hand.

"Ray, please," Ray responded as Gila joined them.

"I would like to congratulate you on that most audacious and daring play. Incredible! Stroke of genius!" His natural complement was heartfelt. "If ever you would like a game, please don't hesitate to call!" he added, then, with a slight nod and polite bow, walked away to lick his wounds. The proud first-time recipient of his family's Cup wasted no time in commandeering the clubhouse and spoiling a growing crowd of friends, acquaintances and visitors to an endless supply of fifteen-year-old champagne he had previously arranged in the hope of a win. His generosity saw no bounds as he wallowed in the adulation with occasional cries of, *my boys did it!* and naming Carlos, Terry and the proclaimed hero of the hour, Captain Ray Kazan of her Majesty's forces.

"Man of the hour!" exclaimed a delighted Gila.

"You know what they say about the game?"

"No, what?"

"It's the strong animal attraction of polo that excites women," he chuckled as he steered the MGB off the grass.

26 August 19th, 1973

Grange Manor, Bedfordshire, England

By eight that evening, everyone had returned to the Manor and was preparing for the Winners' Party to commence in the great hall at nine – later than scheduled due to the protracted festivities at the Polo ground. Ray and Gila had been lying on the bed, shoes and socks off, reliving the afternoon's event when he climbed off and went to the Samsonite briefcase.

"We might as well see if there's anything. After all, we *are* technically on duty," he said as he placed the case on the writing desk and sat on the chair. Gila reluctantly joined him and leaned against the window sill, looking on as he opened the device. He immediately noticed a bigger portion of the tape had unreeled on the left recorder – connected to the table transmitting device.

"Looks like we got something here," he said, flipping the ON switch. He rewound the tape fully, then depressed the PLAY button. A crackling sound followed as the tape wound to the start of a conversation.

They listened intently without commenting on the whole exchange, then Ray switched off the recorder, got off the chair, stepped over to the window and stood next to Gila, staring out into the far distance. They remained in silence, absorbing the recorded conversation. After a while, he turned and leaned back against the sill and crossed his arms.

"Dr Jekyll and Mr bloody Hyde," he gave a derisive snort and chuckled scornfully. "A maverick who plays by his own rules!"

"We have a taped confession for the Feuerman murder," said a hopeful Gila.

"Words,' Ray responded with a sharp exhale. "Just words... easily manipulated to mean whatever you want... Wonders of the English language!"

"So, what do you suggest?"

"Well, for one, we'll need to remove the devices. Wouldn't want for them to be discovered... Especially now."

"Tonight?"

"Yes. I don't think we're going to learn much more of use."

He pushed off the sill and started to make his way to the bathroom.

"I need a shower!" He raised his eyebrows suggestively. "Fancy joining me?"

◆◆◆◆

The party's venue was already crowded with participants eagerly taking part in celebrating Manor Grange's great victory when Ray and Gila turned up. The impressive *High-Rise Silver Cup* proudly sitting on top of a *Rosewood* base had already found pride of place in an elegant cherry-wood glass cabinet in the main entrance. A pop group was busy blasting out a rendition of the latest chart-buster, and gyrating bodies had commandeered most of the hall's central area. Not surprisingly, Jane had been keeping an anxious eye out for them and took no time in making her way over – excited and somewhat flushed.

"We're over in the corner… away from the music!" she stammered above the high pitch of music resounding from two large speakers positioned on either side of the bandstand. Ray reckoned the copious amount of champagne flowing earlier at the Polo Club, and her unbounded enthusiasm not to miss out would soon tell on her. She had progressively endeared herself, and he smiled at her innocence, mouthing a *thank you* before dutifully following her. Carlos and Penelope held out an extra flute of champagne with huge *we won* grins on their faces. Terry was swaying loosely to the music and tapping his foot. His eyes had a strange sunken look suggesting he was slightly ahead of Jane's alcohol consumption. Miles Hathaway was standing next to Jack Frasier beamed broadly.

"We thought maybe you two might have had other plans!" Miles Hathaway's sexual jibe indicated he had reverted to his friendly and accommodating old self. Playing along, Ray chuckled conspiratorially in response.

"Congratulations on a game well played and especially the winning goal. I know how keen Mr Hathaway has been to win the prestigious family trophy." Ray noted Frasier's formal reference to Miles Hathaway – in sharp contrast to his manner adopted in the earlier recorded exchange.

"It was a team effort, Mr Frasier. It's a four-man team," he replied graciously as he was again subjected to the strength of the man's grip.

He was tiring from constantly having to explain his *assistance*. Carlos' brilliant move down the middle of the field and his vision and skill took advantage of Ray's fortunate ball placement that converted into the telling goal.

"Nonsense! My new friend made the win possible!" Carlos retorted gallantly and put his arm around Ray's shoulder. The strong odour of alcohol prevailed on his breath.

"Quite so," cut in Miles Hathaway. "Ray did win it for us," he said in a generous gesture, putting paid to further analysis.

"Oh! Damn!" exclaimed Gila catching everyone's attention. Jane had instantly put on a, *can I do anything to help?* face. Terry was continuing to wane and didn't react.

"Silly me, I left my camera in the room, and I so wanted to take a few pictures. Would you excuse me?"

Jane predictably offered to help.

"No, it's okay, I can manage," Gila excused Jane's offer placing a staying hand on her arm. "Anyway, I may end up having to carry you back as well!" she jibed. Gila was also beginning to warm to Jane and hoped she hadn't appeared uncharitable.

As Ray watched her disappear through the crowd, he sensed a pair of eyes glued on him from behind. He turned his attention back to the group and noted the hint of an embarrassed smile on Frasier's face. The sort of smile that suggests the man had just been caught measuring him up.

Ray raised his glass in a toast and took a sip of the champagne, averting prolonged eye contact with the Scot. The Grange Manor security chief returned the gesture. Miles Hathaway was giving no indication of his earlier belligerence evident during the recording. Perhaps it was a case of *no better an actor than in true ignorance.*

Gila returned breathless, apologetic and camera in hand – left conveniently behind a full vase of flowers on a table around the corner to disguise the time it would take for her to remove the two transmitters. Putting her arm around Ray's waist in a show of affection, she slipped the retrieved items into his jacket pocket. The heightened level of sound coming from the nearby speakers restricted conversation, for which Ray was quite happy. However, it didn't appear to deter Jane, who continued to engage Gila in a close-to-ear dialogue. The group was reduced to occasionally exchanging smiles each time eyes would meet until Miles Hathaway excused himself.

"Have to make a few calls before it gets too late," he announced in a raised voice, prompting Jack Frasier to follow his lead. "Please forgive and excuse me. See you at breakfast, if not before," he said before leaving with his head of security.

Ray and Gila eventually apologised around eleven, promising to join them for a final breakfast before the group went their separate ways.

27 August 19th, 1973

London, England

It was half-past-eleven when Jack Frasier reached his apartment in *Fulham* – a short walk from the River Thames' northern side. He poured himself a full measure of the fifty-year-old Scotch whisky, picked up the telephone, and, pulling on the chord, sat in the armchair. Disregarding Miles Hathaway's confidence, he had still been feeling uneasy during the drive back from Grange Manor. In hindsight, separately blackmailing Adele Brachfield with her affair was a stroke of genius. If that's all she told MI6, then her ignorance should have been convincing. However, running her parallel to his connection indicated a suspect source whose loyalty was also split. At best, she was duplicitous, and now MI6 was far too close to her. To him, Adele Brachfield was always a risky conduit. She was a liability – a threat. She needed immediate close scrutiny and neutralising before it was too late. He took a sip of the alcohol and put the glass on the adjacent coffee table, then, placing the telephone on his lap, dialled a number.

"Haaallo!" a voice answered after two rings.

"Bob, it's Jack… Sorry to be calling you so late."

"No probs! Just having a beer and watching the box. What's up?"

"I need a favour."

"Shoot!" Chief Inspector Bob Haskill was an officer with the *Sweeney* – Jack Frasier's old outfit at the Metropolitan Police.

"I need eyes and ears on an Adele Brachfield." There was a pause at the other end of the line.

"The socialite? The one married to the Media guy. Is that the one?"

"The very same."

"The kidnapped kid?"

"That's the one."

"As of when?"

"Asap."

"Okay. I'll get on the *dog and bone* as soon as we're through. We're talking a twenty-four-hour?"

"Yes. I need to know everything she does and where she's going. You know the drill." Haskill augmented his salary with six other like-minded colleagues through extra-curricular activities for J.F. Security Services. He wasn't a *bent* copper in the traditional sense – he was a *moonlighter* who happily meted out physical punishment and planted evidence where he believed it prudent and justified but drew the line at anything more permanent.

"The usual consideration plus bonus," added Frasier.

"Don't worry about that, me old mate. You've always been generous… Anything else I should be aware of?" he asked matter-of-factly.

"MI6 is sniffing around her, and I suggest it's close, so your boys will need to stay their distance and keep a sharp eye out."

"Understood. Contact number?"

"Flat or office. Should be okay. After all, we're old friends staying in touch," confirmed Frasier. "If not answered, just leave the usual message with your number, and I'll get back to you as soon as I can."

[266]

"Do you know where she is right now?"

"Sorry, can't say. No idea."

"No probs. Leave it to me."

"No info is too small, Bob. It's urgent!" affirmed Frasier.

"I understand, Jack. I'm onto it *tout suite*...Is that it?"

"Yeah, thanks." He replaced the receiver in the cradle, moved the telephone to the armrest, and took another sip. He wasn't finished.

He picked up the telephone again, placed it on his lap, and then dialled another number committed to memory. All the important ones were. It took a few rings before someone picked up the other end.

"Haaallo!" The loud voice compensated for the throbbing of background disco music.

"Is Simon Dodge in tonight?" Frasier also raised his voice to be heard above the noise.

"Yeah... he's around. Who wants 'im?"

"Jack! Tell him it's urgent. He'll talk to me." There was a momentary pause on the other end.

"Okay, I'll go get 'im!"

He held the receiver away from his ear while the irritating background noise persisted. He could imagine the scene of young kids gyrating with gay abandon.

"Dodge here!"

"Jack! Can you get to another phone and ring the flat?"

"Yeah, sure!"

"Quick as you can." Frasier clicked the cradle, and the line went dead.

Three minutes later.

"Okay, I'm calling from the office. What's up?"

"Can you get away?"

"Sure. How long?"

"No idea, but I need you ready to move at a moment's notice."

"What are we talking about?"

"Most probably terminal... I'll let you know."

"On my own?"

"No. I'm getting hold of Tim in the morning. A two-man team should do it."

"Okay. Where do you want us located?"

"North of the river. *Hammersmith* would be a safe bet."

"Okay, as soon as I settle in, I'll let you have the contact number."

"If it comes to it... it's got to be an accident. No witnesses. The usual. You'll need to acquire a vehicle. Clean. Got it?"

"Understood. Is that all?

"For now."

"Okay... I'll get onto it."

The line went dead, and Frasier lifted the phone onto the sideboard. He picked up his glass and sat back. Over the years, he had learned to read the signs... and the vibes he was getting regarding the Brachfield woman were not encouraging.

Then there was Captain Ray Kazan! He hadn't been comfortable being introduced to him, but Miles seemed fine and unworried about his presence. If the Captain had suspicions about Miles, he would almost certainly be in the frame. It would be interesting to see if his MI6 source would come up with anything useful.

However, he couldn't quite figure the young Captain. He was reading something... but couldn't make it out. He was aware of Ray's reputation and his two-year stint in the thick of things against the Guerilla insurgents – a man not to be taken lightly. Had he been instrumental in Shaheen's demise? Al Safadi was still bending his ear over that unexplained affair. If so, he had again proven to be an effective operative, considering how he dealt with the two IRA characters. He scoffed at the idea of their downfall.

He was no lover of the IRA and their ridiculous aspirations. The professional soldier still lingered within him, although his loyalties had changed.

No! He decided.

Captain bloody Kazan would have to be watched and perhaps, even be given a wide berth. He downed the remainder of the whisky. Looking into the empty glass, he rose and walked over to the bottle – next to the record player – for a refill.

He raised the clear Perspex lid of the player and removed an album from an overhead rack. He slowly extracted a Dizzy Gillespie LP and gently wiped it with a soft cloth before placing it on the turntable. Switching on the player, he lowered the needle gently onto the revolving *33 rpm* record, picked up his drink and sank back in the armchair.

It was too late to make the third call. It would have to wait till the morning.

28 August 20th, 1973

London, England

Ben and Toby were the first to arrive, followed ten minutes later by Colonel Madison. Satisfied they weren't being tailed or under surveillance, Ray had taken the opportunity of calling Toby Gilmore from a public telephone once they had cleared Bedford. Toby was to contact the other two for a meet in Ray's hotel room at midday. No one – absolutely no one – was to know of the called-for liaison and its location.

"I'm intrigued," said the Intelligence Colonel as he took a seat in one of the easy chairs. Ray and Gila had moved in an additional chair from her adjoining room, leaving the interconnecting door open – a conscious indicator that both were still leading separate professional lives. Toby took one of the other chairs while Ben opted for the bed, complaining of a nagging discomfort from his knee injury – humorously citing the English weather as the cause. Gila stood back with her arms folded, leaning against the window between the Colonel and Toby. Ray was positioned by the Samsonite case placed on the dresser – lid open.

"Okay?" Ray started after everyone had declined the offer of a coffee, preferring to get into the reason for the sudden get together and anticipating something of extreme importance.

"Thanks to Ben's equipment, we picked up a rather interesting conversation recorded early yesterday evening inside the study. The voices belong to Miles Hathaway and his head of security, a Jack Frasier of J.F. Security Services Ltd., based here in London." He depressed the START button. From Ray's position – reclined with his back against the inter-connecting door frame – he could view the other three men's faces.

"Come on in, Jack. You look a little rattled! Take a seat… Whisky? I have a bottle of Balvenie, your favourite tipple."

"Thanks," came the reply.

What followed sounded like someone pouring out two glasses of liquid, and with a soft splash, suggested ice cubes were added.

"Now, what's got you all excited? The transport there and back went without a hitch. Ponies are all back safe and well, and to cap off the day… I've won the bloody Cup!"

"You know what I mean! Your … so-called lucky replacement, Kazan," a voice with a pronounced Scottish accent continued.

"The bugger won me the Cup if I'm to be totally honest! …Not sure if Beauchamp would have taken that risky move!"

"You know who he is! So, why the hell did you allow him so close to you?"

The tape rolled on as a pause followed for a few seconds.

"I needed him!" came the emphatic reply. "The bastards at MI6, more specifically Mr Toby Gilmore, were most probably behind Beauchamp, ending up in bloody hospital!"

"How'd the fu…?" mouthed Toby Gilmore.

"How did you know that Beauchamp was going to end up with food poisoning?"

"I didn't… Adele Brachfield informed me that MI6 had collared her at the Corinthia. She was caught calling from her local pub the day our Captain and the girlfriend met with Ezra Brachfield. That's how they were able to track down the office the

[271]

day you had your run-in with Kazan. Anyway, it didn't take much to put two-and-two together when I later learned about Ross Beauchamp."

"How much did she tell them?"

"That's the beauty of it! She only admitted to her role with the blackmail over her affair with Minsky. Nothing about me."

"Can you be sure of that? She didn't contact me."

"She didn't need to... couldn't. MI6 was already onto her."

"Then her affair can well have turned out to be a lucky bloody break for us!" A relieved Jack Frasier's voice.

"You know how long I've been planning the Africa project. It was worth sleeping with that ambitious slut beforehand. She was a decent lay as it happens, and I needed someone close to Brachfield... and who better than our Adele? She did a good job getting Brachfield into her bed and the twenty-one-carat gold band on her finger."

"Who would have figured that randy bitch taking up with the brother-in-law so soon after getting hitched!" chuckled the Scotsman. There was a pause as glasses were refilled.

"In hindsight... a stroke of bloody luck. Gave me a second string to my bow — additional security. She was always a scheming little bitch. I couldn't trust her completely, so I came up with the idea of you... the cartel, putting a squeeze on her and reporting directly to me. I could then be sure that if she were looking over two shoulders, rather than just the one, she wouldn't do anything stupid... You were eventually in contact with Brachfield... It made sense. As it is, it's led MI6 to a dead end!"

"What about MI6?"

"Beware men with small minds in authority, Jack. You better contact your source and make sure we get the latest news from Century House."

Ray noted the look of consternation on Gilmore's face.

"And Kazan?"

"I couldn't do anything about that!" Miles Hathaway's tone hinted at aggression. "I had to go along with their petty little scheme. They had to be convinced their plan, and their control of her was

working! A case of friends close, enemies closer!" chuckled a calming Hathaway.

"That old Chinese chestnut of a proverb!" retorted Frasier.

"Yes, and you know how important making the final was to me. I wasn't about to lose out on a chance at the family Cup..." Again, a pause. "However, I still don't know to what extent Adele is colluding with MI6. Too bloody convenient Kazan and his bitch were invited to the charity event... I was being played."

"So, what do we do about that woman? She's already compromised and may well be open to give you up," said Frasier.

"You're right... Our Mrs Brachfield has outlived her usefulness. There's also the added problem that she's fallen for the brother-in-law, or at least she thinks she has. Love can be a very potent emotion, and who knows where that might lead her? She's a complicated woman! Can't have her running around loose."

"I'll get onto it."

Another momentary pause.

"Back to Kazan?"

"And what do you think he and the woman could have learned this weekend? Nothing! It's not like we're in a James Bond story, where – I the perceived villain – would have taken him into my confidence and outlined my devilish scheme for world domination!" scoffed Hathaway.

"And had a devilish and imaginative demise planned for him," chuckled Frasier playing along with the witticism. "However, it's a bit unsettling that they've linked you to the Kuhuania project so quickly. Put you on their radar."

"Let them suspect anything they wish. It's not going to go anywhere. I'm untouchable. You forget, Jack. It's not the Kings with the vision and will – it's the moneyed people behind the throne that wield the greatest power. I'm too well connected. Politicians are the easiest to corrupt and the quickest to protect their own... Top up?"

"Might as well make it a double. I think I'll need one before the night's out."

"By the way... had you met our Captain before I introduced you

yesterday?"

"Thanks," *Frasier was receiving the refill.* "Only that once when I chopped him on the neck. Solid bugger. Took quite a blow!"

Ray instinctively reacted to the painful memory. He reached for his neck, then rubbed the spot with the tip of his fingers.

"So, what about this Al Safadi fiasco? He's pretty pissed! Rang me again the other day complaining about inaction."

"It must have been Kazan. A lucky break from what I gather. It could only have stemmed from one of the kidnappers giving up Safadi's man. The damned Israeli unit Levenson was attached to. Ruthless lot!"

"But then, you took care of our potentially over-ambitious Feuerman. Another loose-end out of the way."

"Does the marquis know you sanctioned the hit?"

"Marquis? French?" John Madison interjected.

"Not yet. I'll bring him up to date when I see him next. Let him continue to think he's running the show. Meanwhile, he has his uses with the Swiss banking connection."

"And the Baron?"

"They're both aristocrats, full of their own self-importance. Let them enjoy their current flirtations. I will soon have a use for the Krauts' industry."

"What about Al Safadi, then?"

"We'll need to prevent him from doing anything rash. He's a pipsqueak — can be a bit hotheaded. You may have to fly over and convince him... Be careful, though! He can put an army together in no time. Disgruntled PLO youths are a dime a dozen out there. Let's face it... he did a good job with the abduction. That all turned out as planned."

"I can handle him."

"Don't forget he owes me. I'm the one that financed where he is today. But then again, he's an Arab — not to be trusted."

"That leaves Ezra Brachfield."

A long pause followed.

"I've invested a great deal in cultivating the man. You can't buy a man like Brachfield — too principled. A higher moral code than most of us. You have to play him intelligently from the side... Do you play chess?"

"Used to. Not anymore — I didn't get on with the game. Rather listen to good jazz with a whisky in my hand."

"He's on the hook now. I'm prepared for him to squirm from time to time, but he's definitely hooked. He'll develop a sore mouth, but he'll comply when required. His son means a lot to him. Family!" he scoffed. "A man's weakness!" A lengthy silence ensued.

"Look, Miles, you've been good to me... setting me up and all and helping out with the Met problem. You know I'll do whatever needs to be done — no issues there. Including my chaps. Loyal to the end! I've got your back, as the Yanks say."

"I know you have, Jack."

Ray hit the button, stopped the recording and stood by the machine. A mood of quiet concentration descended on the room. The look on Toby's face spoke volumes on hearing Frasier's reference to an internal MI6 source who was leaking information. No one would want to hear of such treachery within their own ranks. The lingering, pungent smell of betrayal following the discovery of the Cambridge Five treason was still hanging over Britain's security services. Unconnected officers like Toby were still carrying the shameful burden.

"Anyone want to listen to it again?"

"I've heard enough," responded John Madison. He stood up and crossed over to a drinks tray sitting on top of the minibar. No one spoke as he unscrewed the top.

"Toby? I think you need one," he said and poured out a half-measure, then handed it to the MI6 officer. "Ben?"

"Sure!"

"Miss Levenson?"

"No, thank you, I'll have a coffee."

"Same here," said Ray pushing off the door frame. Settled back in his chair with a whisky, the Colonel looked enquiringly at Toby.

"Three names have come to mind," the MI6 man started, "Two for sure and one maybe," a hint of underlying anger in his voice.

"Whoever it is will need to be flushed out..., and soon," chipped in Ben, adjusting the pillow and settling back again.

"I agree," Colonel Madison stated matter-of-factly. "From what we've just heard, I see we have two issues that would appear to be a priority. The first to identify the leak in your office, Toby. And I propose it should happen before he... or she makes contact with Frasier."

"Second is Adele Brachfield," snapped Toby. He knew he had been played and was showing it.

"No need to blame yourself, Toby... How were you to know? And if we just step back a moment and consider this as rational human beings..., let's consider an advantage we have been presented with. I... we've had more time to digest this stroke of luck," continued Ray. "Gila and I are pretty certain – judging by Hathaway's manner and attitude – he only knows what he implied on the tape, and right now... is sitting in the comfort of Grange Manor ignorant of we know."

"What are you proposing, Ray?" said Madison.

"First off, as you've said, Sir, we have to smoke out the leak. It won't be enough just to identify the individual. What if we set it up so that whoever it is that goes back to Frasier and informs him that Gila and I believe there's nothing there... no evidence... we may have got it wrong... the suspicion of his involvement in anything other than him desperately wanting to win the family Cup."

"You said two-fold," interjected an inquisitive Toby.

"The second is we now know that Adele Brachfield has led us up the garden path... Sorry Toby," he grimaced at the MI6 man. "We bring her in and threaten to charge her with conspiracy to affect the course of justice, or whatever fancy reason is more than feasible to detain her. I'm not a lawyer, but remember, Hathaway has the money and connections to ascertain whether that's fact or fiction."

"That, of course, will expose her," Gila shot Ray a disapproving look. Ray ignored the rebuke and continued.

"My chivalry towards the woman was thrown out the window a while ago," responded Ray with a smirk. "As far as I'm concerned, she's fair game. We use her as bait... What else do we have?"

"Ray's got a point," joined in Ben, getting off the bed. "Make it known she's prepared to flip. Tell all. Force the bastard's hand."

"It will certainly make her a target for this Frasier fellow and his mob," said the Colonel.

"Gila's already volunteered for that duty," said Ray. "She can provide Adele Brachfield with armed support."

"Women sticking together!" quipped Gila stepping away from the window for a coffee.

"It could be dangerous," Toby offered, getting a *do you mind* look from Gila.

"Are we talking about a safe house?" Ben asked.

"Not sure yet," responded Ray.

"Okay," chimed in Toby, "However, I have a problem... I can't see me putting together three times two operatives to shadow the possibles I've identified."

"I can help with that," interjected Madison. "We can work it out later, but we'll need to move fast as Ray proposed."

"I'm suggesting we meet at Century House tomorrow afternoon, say late afternoon. Will that give you enough time, Sir?"

"Yes, that should be okay. Toby can supply photo IDs of the three?"

"Yes, of course," confirmed Gilmore.

"Then, Toby must make sure the three will be around so that our *one* catches our intent," Ray continued.

"So, who of us, and when are we to confront Adele Brachfield?" Toby said.

"The three of us. You, Gila and me at the Corinthia. You can call her direct and arrange the meet, Toby. Even if she does manage to contact Miles Hathaway in the meantime. What can she tell him?"

"When for?"

"It would have to be before our meeting tomorrow afternoon. Say, eleven tomorrow morning."

"Okay, I can do that."

"There is one other thing we can get stuck into and get ahead of… the Feuerman killing," said Ray. "Having listened and met with Jack Frasier, I'm assuming the man is someone who keeps tight control on anything he's involved in."

"Meaning?" John Madison interjected.

"It's my guess he most probably took over his own team to deal with Shaul Feuerman. He wouldn't have used Al Safadi's assets… not inside Israel…, and I very much doubt he would have been able to use anyone locally. Toby, can you get a team onto the travel records… in and out of the country?"

Toby nodded *yes*.

"If you locate Frasier's travel times, you should be able to identify possible related individuals around the same time frame and travelling in the same directions and the same returning within a short time of each other," continued Ray. "From what we learned at Grange Manor, Frasier uses ex-SAS personnel. That should help you with further identification."

"As a precaution, you should conduct this particular enquiry outside of your unit at Century House. We wouldn't want the leak or anyone else to learn of this and also report on the activity," said Colonel Madison.

29   August 21st, 1973

London, England

Jack Frasier stepped into his outer office just after twelve and was greeted by his assistant, Mary, who handed over an opened post-selection.

"Just the usual," she said, anticipating his normal, *anything important?* look. "A Bob Haskill... your old buddy from the Met called a couple of times. Said he'll call again shortly."

"Cheers," Jack murmured as he entered his office.

"I'll take my lunch..., now you're in. Listen out for the phone," she called through the closed door. He heard the outer office door shut as he slumped into his office chair.

He scanned through the dozen or so papers – mostly bills – then dropped them onto the desk. Pressing his back against the chair and stretching his legs, he clasped his hands behind his head. He wasn't a man given to worrying but had a restless night nevertheless. He was a man used to controlling the situation, and Miles Hathaway's involvement with Adele Brachfield still left him uncomfortable. He was sure that Miles' side arrangement with that damned woman could lead to an even more damaging and irreversible scenario.

He had just come from Simon Dodge and Tim Grover, who were put up in a small hotel on *Shepherds Bush Road* and ready to move at a moment's notice. They had spent an hour going through possible game plans. The experienced operatives needed little direction.

"Just make sure one of you is ready to answer that phone!" he reminded them forcefully, referring to the public phone in the hall outside their room. The desk telephone suddenly rang, and he reached for the receiver.

"Frasier!"

"Bob here!"

"What have you got?"

"Okay! We picked up the Brachfield woman leaving the Belgravia address just after half-ten... Bit of money there!... Anyway, she drove to the Corinthia Hotel and went up to the fourth floor to room 426."

"Do you know who she was meeting... as if I didn't know."

"You know my boys are pretty sharp. They managed to get into the adjoining room – pretending maintenance. Being the police has its advantages! They caught most of the conversation through the interconnecting door... Useful things..., those stethoscopes."

"What did they learn?"

"Let me see... I've written it down. Hold on a tick. Ah! Here it is. People present other than the woman were a Toby Gilmore..."

"MI6," interjected Frasier.

"A woman called Gila," he continued, "and a Ray Kazan."

"Anyone else?"

"No, just the three.

"You sure your guys weren't spotted?"

"No way. You know how discreet my boys can be."

"Okay, what was said?"

"A lot of conversation about a Miles Hathaway, some sort of financial bigwig. They were talking her into turning

Queen's evidence against this Hathaway character. There was also some stuff about her brother-in-law… heh! The woman likes to spread it around. However, I digress… The pressure was on her to give up this Hathaway bloke for involvement in the Brachfield kid's kidnapping… Is that right, Jack? He was behind it?"

"It's best we leave that subject alone, Bob."

"Okay, mate. No skin off my nose. The thing is… and I think this is what you really wanted to know… She has agreed to come clean." Haskill sensed Frasier catch his breath. "Jack? You okay, mate?" Frasier found himself struggling to focus his mind on what he was hearing and what he had feared.

"Yes, I'm fine. Go on."

"Apparently, she agreed to speak up after she spoke…, confessed to her husband. At least about the Hathaway guy, and with their agreement not to bring her affair with the brother-in-law into the mix. He's due back from a business trip tonight."

"At the hotel?"

"No. no. She's driving down to their country place. Not sure where that is, though…"

"I know where it is," cut in Frasier.

"That's pretty much what my boys were able to pick up. The MI6 chap, Gilmore, and Kazan left at around twelve-thirty for a Century House meeting, leaving the two women together. They're planning to drive down late afternoon."

"Thanks, Bob. I appreciate it."

"No probs, mate. Do you want us to continue with the surveillance?"

"No, it's okay. I'll pick it up from here. Could your chaps stay at the hotel until my two take over?"

"I'll call them now. They'll be down in the lobby."

"Thanks again. We'll get together in the next few days

to square up… And again, thanks."

"As I said, no problem. No need to rush. Take your time with the readies… my trip to Spain can wait…" the policeman chuckled. Frasier replaced the receiver and inhaled sharply.

Gila was impressed with the comfort and the compelling power of the *Mercedes 350SL* sports car as Adele Brachfield confidently weaved her way through London's afternoon traffic. They had agreed to stop off at the Belgravia residence for Adele to collect some clothing for their onward drive to Eaton House. Gila's overnight bag was already stowed in the boot.

Adele had found the morning's broadside she'd endured humiliating – particularly in the presence and involvement of the young woman sitting in the passenger seat. What does anyone her age know about life – what would she have been prepared to do to achieve her social standing and quality of life? That they knew of her relationship with Miles was enough for her to have realised the game was finally up – at least in part. Threatening to arrest her as an accomplice in her stepson's kidnapping may have won them her agreement to co-operate, but their soft approach still allowed her to shape the outcome.

She would have to put her feelings and desire for David on hold – Ezra's *forgiveness* was her priority. She would have to play that card with care. He had become overly fond of Nikki – as he affectionately called her – doting on her as if she were his own child. He would think twice about jeopardising their relationship. Nikola was the ace up her sleeve.

Adele had suspected long ago that Miles was behind the scheme. The other voice – the Scottish brogue the caller couldn't disguise – assured her that Ariel wouldn't be harmed. She assumed he worked for Miles and trusted

[283]

that Ezra's precious son would come out of the whole ordeal unharmed. She pacified her occasional pang of guilt, telling herself *he's young. He'll get over it.* He was a spoilt rich kid that would only benefit from a dose of harsh reality. She knew only too well that life was tough – she had enough skeletons in her cupboard to attest to that. As for Miles' purpose? To what end, she didn't know – although this affair over the African country... *Zu-*something or other had angered David. Pillow-talk had its advantages. As far as she was aware, Ezra had never before overridden David's editorial position. It would help if she knew more. Her primary concern was to retain her marriage – her way of life. It was time for another *virtuous* performance.

The two women spoke little as they made their way southwest onto the *A3* highway out of London. Conversation was limited. They lived in different worlds.

◆ ◆ ◆ ◆

Surrey, England:
"There they are!" Tim Grover declared from behind the wheel of a dark-blue *Ford Capri 3000 GT* as they emerged from behind a large container truck. Dodge had acquired the car in the early hours of the morning. The vehicle's powerful *Essex V6 138hp* engine was more than capable of keeping pace with the red *Mercedes* sports car. The registration plates had been switched with those of a *Mini Cooper* Grover had *come by* before travelling up from the south coast.

"Okay, just keep your distance." Dodge didn't look up as he traced his finger down a folded map spread over his lap. "They will most probably take a left past Cobham village. It looks like the most direct route. If they do..., I think I've found just the spot."

[284]

Thirty minutes later, Adele slowed as she approached a sign warning of the road ahead narrowing on both sides followed a short distance with another caution, *Beware Sharp Bends Next Three-Miles*. The country road had been quiet and all but clear of traffic.

"What's that fool doing so close!" she exclaimed, looking into the rearview mirror. "Bloody idiot!"

Gila turned in her seat. A dark-blue car was gaining rapidly on them. The driver's expressionless faces and the bulky male passenger left Gila with no doubt about their intention.

"Put your foot down!" she shouted as she reached into her shoulder holster and extracted her *Walther PPK*, then wound down her window. Adele Brachfield tightened her grip on the steering wheel. Gila pulled on the weapon's short slide, chambering a round, then turned and knelt with her right knee on the seat. Leaning through the open side window, she held onto the full-length grip with both hands and took a deep breath. She was in fighting mode. Her adrenaline was kicking in fast. She waited until the Mercedes bore left, opening up a line of sight on the pursuing vehicle. She fired two bursts at the Capri's windscreen.

"Fuck!" shouted Grover and swerved to the right. A bullet glanced off the curved glass top left. The second pierced the windscreen, narrowly missing Dodge's left ear.

"Ram the bitch!" bellowed an angered Dodge as he ducked down. Grover instantly pressed down on the accelerator, lurching the car forward and catching the Mercedes' rear bumper. The sudden impact into the back of the slightly heavier sports car threw Gila's head against the upper part of the passenger door's frame. She winced at the sharp pain. At the same moment, a panicked Adele oversteered, bringing the Mercedes into a half-side-on

[285]

position with the Capri. Seeing her chance, Gila fired twice more, striking the windscreen above Grover's head. The cool-headed driver was not to be put off and again pressed down hard, ramming the other car on the nearside rear corner – demolishing the rear-light assembly. The impact spun the Mercedes further, simultaneously exposing the two ex-SAS operatives to Gila's direct aim. Wedging her upper body within the open window frame to steady her shooting, Gila saw another chance.

"Got you now, you bastards!" she cursed through gritted teeth, bringing the weapon in line with the driver's head.

The Mercedes' wheels suddenly slammed violently against the rock-hard earthside of the lane, throwing her arms wildly off target. Her shots disappeared harmlessly over the roof of the Capri. The kinetic momentum of the impact force launched the vehicle onto a stout, moss-covered tree trunk.

Adele screamed as she was thrown forward, smashing headfirst through the windscreen. The car's engine faltered, then sputtered into silence. A groggy Gila pressed down on the handle, pushed the door open and fell out onto the leaf-covered ground – still clutching the pistol. Flushed with anger, Grover threw the car into reverse and screeched backwards a few yards.

"Fucking bitch!" he swore under his breath as he re-engaged first-gear. Still disorientated and with a hand on the vehicle for support, Gila raised unsteadily and aimed at the assaulting vehicle. With a cruel determined curl of his lip, Grover launched the car at the struggling female. The solid metal grill caught her midriff. She fired a shot harmlessly into the air as she – like a limp rag doll – was propelled against the dry-stone wall.

Dodge immediately jumped out of the Capri and hurried to Adele Brachfield. She was their prime target.

Barely conscious, her breathing was shallow and laboured, and her head a mass of red. He quickly scoured around, and spotting a round stone – the size of a cricket ball – gathered it in his calloused hand. Without hesitation, he pulled back his arm, and with a powerful swing, struck Adele Brachfield a glancing blow on the back of the head. Satisfied, he hurled the stone in a high arc over the wall far out of sight.

"Let's get the fuck outta here!" he shouted as he jumped back in next to a heavily breathing Grover. The whole affair had taken less than ten minutes, and as luck would have it for the two killers – no passing traffic and no witnesses.

30 August 21ˢᵗ, 1973
London, England

Andrea Hutchins hurried north along *Pearman Street*. It wasn't her usual route to *Waterloo Station*, but the nearest telephone box was on the corner with *Waterloo Road*. She received the call early in the morning while feeding the cat. Any relevant information was to be relayed as soon as possible – he insisted on it. She spotted the iconic red kiosk and quickened her pace.

She flustered at the sudden unannounced mechanical voice asking her to leave a message. A bleeping sound alerted her. She immediately deposited three more coins.

"Oh! It's me," she nervously responded as if she were talking directly to someone on the other end. "You asked me to listen out for anything that might be relevant to you following… the weekend. From what I heard this afternoon, it appears that Mr Hathaway is no longer someone of interest." She gained confidence as she recounted what she had learned. "There was a lot of talk about winning a cup and how Captain Kazan and the woman, Gila, enjoyed the opportunity and the weekend. That's all that was said that's relevant." She paused. Was there anything else she should convey? "If I hear anything else tomorrow, I'll call again," she said finally and replaced the black bakelite receiver.

She pushed the heavy glass-panelled door open and stepped out onto the pavement. Taking a deep breath, she walked off in the direction of Waterloo Station and the *Northern Line* and to the comfort and sanctuary of her small flat in *Ashvale Road* – a short walk from *Tooting Broadway* underground station.

An hour later, an ashen-faced Andrea Hutchins was sitting shoulders curled forward at a small table inside one of the *interview* rooms in Century House. Trembling uncontrollably, she looked around the bare room with the stark white walls and two empty chairs on the opposite side of the table. A tape-recorder was ominously placed on the table in front of her. She glanced nervously at her reflection in the large mirror, knowing she was being watched – observed. She knew how these sessions were conducted. First, unnerve the subject. Was the cash she had enjoyed been worth what she was about to endure? She turned away with tearful eyes and, lowering her head, recalled that dreadful moment.

She had walked around fifty yards before the man stopped her and showed her his official ID, then escorted her back to the kiosk. Another man inside – leaning with his back against the side panel eyeing her all the while – was on the phone, engaged in a conversation she couldn't hear. An agonising five minutes later, he nodded and replaced the handset.

"You are to accompany us back to Century House," he had said matter-of-factly after exiting the phone box. No word was spoken as a timid Andrea Hutchins was shepherded back to MI6 headquarters between the two stoic men.

"I still can't bloody believe it!" muttered Toby Gilmore from the other side of the two-way mirror. "She's been with us forever!" Yet, he couldn't help feeling a touch of remorse for the woman.

"What will happen to her?" asked Ray leaning against the back wall, also feeling some sympathy for the shattered form on the other side of the glass. Toby sighed heavily.

"That's the thing… the service is still reeling from the revelations of the Cambridge Five. If the press were to get a hold of this titbit, it would be even more embarrassing. They wouldn't hold back… Not to mention questions in the House. Calls for more oversight."

He removed a handkerchief from his jacket pocket and pursed his lips while thoughtfully cleaning his glasses. "We'll get as much as we can from her," he laboured, "then make her sign whatever the legal boys draw up preventing her talking to the press, or anyone else for that matter, and then… and then… we'll let her go!"

The MI6 officer replaced his glasses, cast Ray a resigned grimace and went to the door.

◆◆◆◆

"She was about to spill everything."

"How do you know this?"

"Called in a favour from my boys at the Met and had her put under surveillance. They were in the next bloody room listening in on the proceedings with Gilmore, Kazan and the Levenson woman. She was going to make a written confession after she'd squared with her husband."

"When?"

"Late this afternoon on her way to their country estate. However, her supposed willingness to provide a confession contradicts what I learned from my MI6 source."

"Was I mentioned?"

"Yes. Apparently, you're not suspected of anything

other than wanting to win the family Cup."

"That's all you got?"

"Yes, that's all she said." Frasier couldn't avoid the Freudian slip subconsciously revealing that his MI6 mole was a woman. A point not lost on Hathaway.

"Okay, Jack. Any witnesses? Anything that might come back and bite us in the ass?"

"No, nothing. All clean. The stolen vehicle is now a metal pancake at a south London scrapyard. Totally untraceable."

"And your people?"

"Again, no trace... no connection. They have nothing, absolutely nothing to go on." Hathaway let a deep sigh on the other end of the phone.

"There is one other thing?"

"Oh! I don't like the sound of where this might be going."

"The Levenson woman was in the car with Adele Brachfield." There followed a long pause while Hathaway digested that particular news item.

"Couldn't be helped," he said after a while. "Collateral damage. Pity... she had a great ass. I assume she's also...?"

"Yes."

"Okay, then. There's more reason for you to vanish for a while. Go over and keep Al Safadi company as we discussed on Sunday. I want you to make sure he doesn't do anything rash over that IRA matter. He'll follow your advice. The African project has just kicked off, and I don't want him screwing it up."

"I'll leave in the morning. Mary can keep an eye on the office. Not much going on at the moment... What about you?"

"What about me? I'll carry on as usual. If it comes up, I'll put on my best act... feign shock and surprise at her unfortunate demise. Sad to see an old family friend go like that. Anyway, I've got a semi-final coming up on the 30th. We're on a roll." Frasier sensed Hathaway smile on the other end of the line. Besides the business, Polo was his addiction, and after Sunday's win, he was charged for more wins.

"If you need me, then you'll know where to find me. I could do with a bit of Mediterranean sunshine!" He replaced the receiver and took a sip of the Balvenie whiskey. The call had gone better than he anticipated, but then why shouldn't it have? He had covered both their hides. He picked up the telephone and dialled Mary's home number.

◆ ◆ ◆ ◆

Ray resisted the urge to rush in, walking at a measured pace – the clean and pure smell of antiseptic filled the air. Toby was at the main reception desk, looking anxious as if waiting for a bell to sound.

"What happened?" Ray had received the call just as he had returned to his hotel room. No details were given. Just that Gila had been involved in a car accident and was at *St Mary's Hospital* in *Paddington*.

"She's in ICU," replied Toby and led off towards the lift.

Ray audibly gasped at the sight of her surrounded by machinery, a tube strapped to her mouth, and an intravenous drip punctured into her arm. The steady beep of a heart monitor, the only sound in the room. The left side of her face was inflamed a reddish-blue and her eye swollen closed. She looked so helpless – vulnerable. Only a few hours earlier, he had left her, beautiful and full of confidence. He walked up to her and took her right hand in his and gently stroked it with his thumb – his thoughts

[292]

scrambled to understand, to reason what and why? Ray pretended not to hear Toby say:

"She's been hit pretty bad."

A gentle knock on the door caught their attention, and in came the Israeli Ambassador, Mr Schulman. He acknowledged Ray with a sad smile as he went over to the opposite side of her bed.

"Do we know what happened?" he asked.

Toby tactfully suggested that they talk outside the room. Ray and the Ambassador reluctantly followed Toby to a small lounge down the hall, where Ray introduced Toby to the family's close friend.

"Sir," Toby started addressing the Ambassador, "I'm not sure if… if you should be party to this discussion." The Ambassador shot him a stern look.

"That beautiful woman in there fighting for her life means more to me than just my best friend's daughter! I've known her all her life. Do you really believe the truth is going to shock me! Not only do I need to know what truly happened… I demand it!"

"My apologies," responded a chastened MI6 officer. "I'll speak frankly. It was not a hit-and-run… it was attempted murder."

"How sure are you?" Ray instinctively knew who was behind her attack but didn't want to be obvious in front of the Ambassador.

"Gila was under the wall some ten feet away from the vehicle, and her weapon had been discharged. Assuming she had a full clip, she fired off seven shots."

Atta girl, thought a saddened Ray.

"Her extensive internal injuries…"

"Means the bastards deliberately rammed her with their car! There's no other explanation." Ray's muscles quivered at the very thought of the callous act.

"That's what we concluded," responded a calm Toby.

[293]

He sensed Ray's anger building.

"Who would possibly do such a thing?" Ray and Toby exchanged glances. "Could this be anything to do with the Feuerman murder?"

"We have to assume that it's all part and parcel of the same organisation's doing," replied Ray. The Ambassador turned away momentarily as if pondering over a point.

"Gentlemen," he started, facing them again. "As you, no doubt, may be aware, I hold a great deal of influence with my government. I also have direct, authoritative access to an agency that is highly regarded in certain circles." He was alluding to Israel's notorious *Mossad*. "You can count on our full co-operation. Anything you require… anything at all. They will be ready to assist."

Just then, a breathless Ben entered the lounge.

"Sorry, I didn't get the call till I got to the hotel!"

Toby was about to bring Ben up to date when the attending doctor walked in.

"Would you prefer we discussed the lady's condition in a more private setting?" he said.

"Speak freely, please, Doctor," responded Ray.

The doctor proceeded to tell them that Gila had sustained significant internal injuries and that multiple broken ribs had severely damaged her lungs. They had managed to stem the internal bleeding and had to put her on life-sustaining treatment. She had further suffered some organ failure, in particular her kidneys. There was also the concern that an internal infection could become septic. Having said that, they were closely monitoring her and would keep them apprised as to her condition. The doctor gave a weak assured smile, then turned on his heel and left the four men to digest the news.

"What about Adele Brachfield?" asked Ray after some time.

"The morgue," replied Toby. "She was thrown

through the windscreen… Although, when one of our forensic boys examined her, he believed she had received a powerful blow to the back of the head inconsistent with the angle of her body."

"Finished her off!" opined Ben.

"Brachfield's been contacted. He's on his way up from the country. Just got back from a business trip abroad when we caught him," said Toby.

"If you gentlemen will excuse me. I need to call Gila's mother and see about getting her over as soon as possible," said the Ambassador and left.

"Gentlemen!" declared a voice from behind them. Sir Foster Braithwaite was standing in the doorway wearing a dinner jacket and a dark coat draped over his arm. "Your office, Toby, managed to reach me at a formal dinner function. I broke away as soon as I could." He came in and dropped his coat over the back of an easy chair.

"How is she?" There was genuine concern in his voice. Toby and Ben looked at Ray.

"It's not good, Sir. Extensive internal injuries. She's on life support. That's all we have."

"Adele Brachfield?"

"In the morgue," answered Toby.

"Has Ezra Brachfield been contacted?"

"He's on his way. Should be here in the hour," said Toby.

"Hm. I think I better handle this one," the Minister said, much to the relief of the other three. "Colonel Madison?"

"He's been informed but is stuck at *Oswestry*. He'll join us tomorrow." Again Toby brought everyone up to date.

"I'm going to go in and stay with Gila for a while," said Ray.

"I'll hang around for a bit too," offered Ben, echoed by Toby.

[295]

"Gentlemen, I suggest we meet in my office tomorrow afternoon," proposed the Minister. "Meanwhile, should there be any change... any change at all, please call me."

31 August 22nd, 1973

London, England

Ray knocked gently on the door and quietly entered Gila's room. The Ambassador was standing at the foot of the bed with his arm around a woman sobbing quietly into his shoulder. They exchanged nods and troubled smiles. He walked over to her bed and took her right hand in his, then began to gently stroke her wrist while looking hard into her beaten face.

Someone will pay for this, I promise you. He spoke with his thoughts. For the second time, he was about to lose someone he cared for. He knew it then as she lay there. He could feel the anger coursing through his entire body. This time he would be able to exact revenge – to make someone pay for wrecking her body, for taking her away from him. This time he would get closure, and he knew his targets precisely.

"The doctor's hold no hope... Her injuries are too extensive... There's nothing they can do..." The Ambassador's voice trembled as he spoke. "It's been agreed to shut off the life-support equipment." The sudden news made Ray catch an intake of breath. The Israeli diplomat observed the young Englishman and realised that his was more than an affection for a close colleague. "I'm sorry!"

A tear formed in Ray's eye as he averted his gaze – he didn't respond. He felt a tightness in his chest. He should have been prepared for the worst – not let her go off alone. He should have been with her, to protect her – unlike with Leyla. This… he could have avoided. He didn't want to leave her side, but he had to tear himself away. He had a lot to do. It was all planned.

"I'm so sorry!" he whispered.

Ray released Gila's hand and slowly leant over and held a kiss on her right cheek before taking a last look and turning to her mother and the Ambassador.

"Forgive me," he said, "I won't be able to be there when you put her to rest. I have to do something first. I'll visit when I've finished what needs to be done."

"I understand… She will understand… I'll make sure I tell her before…"

◆ ◆ ◆ ◆

Everyone was assembled in the Minister's office. Ray was viewed with sombre expressions when he arrived just after three. Sir Braithwaite took no time pouring out a whiskey and handing it to Ray as he took a seat next to his senior officer, Colonel John Madison. He took the glass and leant forward on his elbows – cradling the drink in his hands.

"They've decided to pull the plug," said Ray with sadness in his voice. "She's been kept on life support so her mother could say goodbye. She's with Gila now and the Ambassador." The group's expressions slowly changed to one of melancholy.

"This is such a tragedy. I can't imagine how you are feeling, Ray. I didn't know Gila well, but from I do know she was a beautiful and talented lady, and we shall miss her and her contribution," the Minister said, eventually breaking the moment. "So, Gentlemen, if you would. Let us raise our glasses to Gila. May she rest in peace."

"To Gila," they responded in unison.

"To Gila," muttered Ray again before swallowing the entire contents of his glass. They sat around awkwardly for a while. What does one say in such circumstances immediately after someone close has died? Stay strong; life goes on – empty words lost on a grieving soul. But life does go on, and Ray had a job to do... and needed permission.

"In my mind, there's no question as to who was behind Gila's *accident*," he suddenly uttered forcefully. "And there's only one way to resolve it."

"Toby has briefed me fully," said the Minister. "And it would certainly appear that Miles Hathaway is very much in the mix of things..."

"In the mix, Sir?" Ray interjected, raising his voice. "He's behind the whole bloody enterprise, and who knows how many bodies he's left in his wake?"

"Quite so, but he's a big fish, well connected financially and politically. As I recall, he turned down a peerage a couple of times. He's highly regarded within the upper echelons of government and the establishment. As I remember, I've only met him once at some charity do. He won't be easy if at all possible to bring to account."

"Bring to account?" Ray shot back forcefully. He could see where the Minister was leading to and was getting agitated. The Colonel placed a steadying hand on Ray's arm. "Bring to account? Sir...," Ray calmed down. "With all due respect... as I recall when you so eloquently put it, and I'll try to repeat verbatim... Quote, '*Sometimes, operations require a less formal approach. Sometimes an unconventional and intuitive way serves best to achieve something. An indirect method, if you will.*' Unquote. That's how you justified your reasoning that I should join the unit... How

[299]

far are you prepared to go to meet that sentiment? As the saying goes – if you pray for rain, be prepared to deal with the mud!"

The others didn't interrupt Ray. They knew he had every right to blow off steam and pursue his intent. There was more to his and Gila's relationship than they had earlier realised.

"You've certainly put me on the spot... You're right, of course, I did say that... One's words seem to carry a different weight when used at different times... and can return to haunt one."

"I think you should listen to Ray's plan, Minister," cut in Toby Gilmore.

"Very well..., I'm listening," Sir Braithwaite replied with a sigh.

"The projectile is totally feasible. I discussed Ray's requirement with our armoury expert this morning," said John Madison at the end of Ray's presentation.

"And you believe this can be done..., as you laid it out?"

"I'm the only one that knows the game, how it's played, when someone is about to take the strike, is at their most vulnerable. And yes..., I can make the shot!" affirmed Ray.

"If we're not prepared to cross the line..., then what are we doing here? I can understand your reasoning," the Minister said, acquiescing to the group.

"You don't drown falling into water. You drown by staying under," Ben offered with a wicked smile.

"It would be a case of poetic justice," mused the Colonel.

The Minister sat back staring into the brownish liquid in his glass, weighing and deliberating over the risk the plan would carry and what could be achieved. Never before had he been faced with such a decision – to be the executioner, the one to seal another man's fate. But then, he had volunteered to head the unit and be prepared to take whatever action was necessary. The team was looking for decisive action on his part. There was no escaping it.

"Very well…, you have my sanction, Gentlemen… Now, what about the French and German connection?" he said, eventually sitting forward.

"We've traced a few calls from Hathaway's phones to a Jean-Marie de Salignac, marquis d'Ambois and the German we believe to be a Ludwig von der Marwitz. We have nothing on them now. Then again, they would anyway fall outside our legal jurisdiction. We could offer their possible involvement to Interpol, but we might appear a little foolish considering the Cambridge Five's recent revelations. They most probably will suggest we were overreacting," said Toby.

"Yes, I agree. Let's keep that detail to ourselves for the time being," agreed the Minister.

"My team has also worked through the night and come up with four names that were – we believe – the team that travelled to Israel and killed Shaul Feuerman. All the dates leaving the UK and their independent returns coincide exactly. And all four are ex-SAS, as Ray suggested."

"Do we have enough to arrest them?"

"No, Sir," Ray said. "We've got a better idea. One that the Ambassador put forward… proposed. He's just as anxious for retribution as we are. Our thinking is that if we give the Israelis the names, they can deal with them in exchange for information on Jack Frasier's whereabouts."

"The security chap?" butted in the Minister.

"Yes. He left the country early this morning on a flight to Athens then onto Beirut. We rather he was out of the country, and I know who he'd be with. We've already sounded them out at the Israeli Embassy, and they are keen to sort out that particular problem for us – even though their man was perceived to have been a bad apple. They suggested it would be a good training exercise. Anyway, there's a quid-pro-quo opportunity for both sides!"

"It would appear you have everything planned. I can only wish you luck," said the Minister finally. "Now, who's for a refill? I most certainly am!"

32 September 30ᵗʰ, 1973

Great Windsor Park, Berkshire, England

Ray lay spreadeagled on the reinforced netting tightly strung between four stout branches in the crown of the selected tree's canopy. He rested the end of the wooden forestock inside the fork of two sturdy branches allowing himself enough gripping surface on the gunstock. He rested his cheek on the cheekpiece – a sculpted wooden addition fixed to the top of the shoulder stock – and brought his right eye level with the scope. He had a relatively wide field of fire in a south-westerly direction giving him an angled line-of-sight from his spot and stable shooting position.

The heavy rifle weighed in at a little over four kilograms – a sturdy weapon renowned worldwide since the Second World War and produced by the British company *Holland and Holland*. Reputed to be one of the finest sniper rifles ever made, the top-quality weapon sported the durable *no. 32 (Mark 2)* scope firing 303-calibre bullets from a box magazine of ten and highly regarded for its accuracy. One of the weapon's virtues was its ruggedness and ability to hold its *zero* – requiring infrequent readjustments – which Ray always kept at the traditional range-distance of a hundred yards. He slowly adjusted the sight to three-hundred-and-fifty – well within

[303]

its effective *field-of-fire* and the mid-yardage he had meticulously calculated. He had an unhindered line-of-sight down the playing field.

The tree's canopy he had chosen had grown slightly above two other trees between him and the far corner of the transporter's parking area, the pony's enclosure – a short distance beyond the maintenance yard. A golfer pinning his hopes on the oft-reasoned adage that a tree was ninety-per cent air was only fooling himself. The fallacy of such a myth would more often than not be quickly shattered when after taking the hoped-for-shot, he would find that a tree was actually… ninety-per cent wood and leaf. Ray couldn't afford the slightest obstruction that could affect the bullet's flight.

Slowly and with little movement of his body, he rotated the bolt handle anti-clockwise and drew it towards him, releasing one of the ten rounds into the chamber – although he had no intention of using more than just the one. Just as deliberately, he pushed the bolt forwards, turning it clockwise into a locked position. He was now ready for the shot.

The chamber held a specially designed bullet – the weight and design measured to overcome air resistance up to a distance of five hundred yards with a lower *ballistic coefficient*, yet maintained similar accuracy to a standard heavier projectile. The round was not intended to penetrate. The hardened plastic coating would splay upon impact and concuss rather than bury itself in the target – a critical factor for a successful outcome.

Leaving nothing to chance, Ray had spent countless hours at the Sennybridge Military Training area outside the village of Powys, Wales, testing the bullets and perfecting his tolerance of between four-hundred and six-hundred yards. Secrecy was paramount. By the time he was ready, Ray was able to adjust with the slightest of tweaks to the elevation – measuring a mere fraction of an inch – to ensure he would hit his mark with the lethal precision planned. The mental computation for the two-hundred-yard variable was firmly established in his subconscious.

Sunk deep in his camouflaged concealment, he panned the rifle slowly to read the clock above the clubhouse – amplified four times through the scope. Fifteen minutes to go before the six-chukker match was scheduled.

Fifty feet below him, the area had been roped off for routine tree surgery operations, warning inquisitive observers of potentially dangerous chemicals in use. Nothing unusual or out of the ordinary. Two of Toby Gilmore's men – alert eyes continually scanning the location – provided additional assurance, occasionally raking a small number of fallen leaves. The official start to the new autumn had already commenced following the passing of the equinox. The activity would appear completely normal to the casual onlooker – even though the piles were being aimlessly moved back and forth.

Ben was stationed on the other side of the playing field among the day-trippers – sitting on the spare-tyre fixed on top of the steel bonnet of a *Land Rover* – a pair of field binoculars, walkie-talkie, and a flask of black coffee by his side. The inclusion of a folded blanket under his rump helped soften his seat. All the other team members were also in position – primed and ready.

Frenetic bustle ensued in the pony enclosure below, following the announcement over the public address system to the start of the semi-final for the medium-goal, *Whittling Cup* – to be played over six chukkers. Ray shouldered the rifle comfortably in the crease of his right shoulder and waited. His rapt attention to the activity on the field and focused concentration was now paramount.

He eased his grip and slowed his breathing. The teams

[305]

had lined up with Grange Manor first attacking the west-side goal. He would have to wait until one of the teams scored and changed ends. The potential opportunity would come when *he* was riding towards the east goal. Ray could relax and continue to calm his breathing and hope.

The first chukker resulted in no goals for either side. Ray was impressed with Ross Beauchamp, the American, who appeared completely cured following his unfortunate spell in the *Chelsea and Westminster Hospital.* He played the best game surviving Grange Manor for the next chukker.

The second chukker saw the opposing team score two and Carlos one, with another impressive run through the middle of the field and sail a well-connected ball in a high arc between the posts. Miles Hathaway was continually played off the ball and denied the option Ray required. The third chukker was much the same as the previous two putting the opposing team ahead at four goals to three.

Ray grinned his approval at Hathaway's choice of mount for the fourth chukker after the ten-minute interval. Two minutes in, and Terry levelled the match, turning the Grange Manor team back in Ray's direction. Ray clenched his teeth, then relaxed his jaw and adjusted the stock slightly in his shoulder. This could be his chance, and he was ready.

He didn't have to wait long when all of a sudden Miles Hathaway broke away from a two-person challenge and was riding hard and fast at a loose ball – travelling down Ray's line and closing in on the optimum range. Ray took in a deep breath, then slowly exhaled as he tracked the man's head movement and direction of the galloping beast. His intimate understanding of the game and a player's natural motion when chasing down a ball for the inevitable strike allowed him to keep pace with his target. On he came with a singular determination to make the perfect strike. The rise out of the saddle, turn of the right shoulder (all polo players have to be right-handed) and pull of the arm back and up with a tight grip on the stick's handle came, then the downswing!

Ray calmly squeezed the trigger, depressing the hammer and igniting the gunpowder in the cartridge. The bullet travelling at a velocity of over two thousand feet per second slammed square onto the player's helmet above the peak.

It happened all of a sudden! The three challenging players instinctively pulled up their highly-charged ponies! Spectators recoiled and gasped in horror.

To describe the moment as it occurred was impossible. Various versions of the incident abounded among the knowledgeable of the game and mere open-mouthed spectators. Still, most recalled the tragic moment when the player suddenly disappeared off his mount into a heap below the chasing pack's legs and hooves.

It was widely held he must have lost his balance. After all, a player is at his most vulnerable when he's committed out of the saddle and reaching with the mallet. That could only be the explanation. He was an accomplished horseman and was mounted on his favourite pony. Though without his master, the palomino Canario continued to charge with a single purpose to the end of the field before being cornered by two grooms.

Ray looked on coldly at the justice he had meted out and laid the rifle aside. He had played his part. It was now for the others to do their bit and complete their tasks. As he climbed down the knotted rope – the weapon slung over his shoulder – he couldn't avoid a smug smile at the double-irony. The man would have met his fate doing what he loved most and on his favourite animal.

The St. John's ambulance crew were credited for their swift response – immediately driving across to the rescue and sweeping the fallen player into the ambulance, then speeding off to the nearest hospital. It was so important to have such professionals at hand!

The official bulletin confirmed Miles Hathaway was dead on arrival on reaching the *King Edward VII Hospital* in Windsor. The ambulance crew had tried to administer aid, but sadly to no avail. Results from the *post mortem* later confirmed the unfortunate man had died from traumatic injuries to the head caused by the heavy fall and the hoof of his own horse's trailing back leg.

However, a very groggy Miles Hathaway did come too for a few moments in the back of the ambulance.

"What happened?" he managed to utter.

"We haven't met. Allow me to introduce myself? Toby Gilmore, MI6." Sitting next to the stretcher, he gave the unfortunate patient a disarming smile as he took Miles Hathaway's right hand and proceeded to inject a needle under the index fingernail.

"Gila Levenson sends her best wishes," the MI6 officer added pleasantly as he laid the man's hand back on his chest.

Miles Hathaway – the leading figure in the organisation known to a few as the Alhalu – grimaced at the sharp pain.

Gila Levenson? I thought…

He desperately tried to make sense of what was happening. A feeling of nausea swept through him, and his vision became blurred. Toby Gilmore sat looking on impassively as the man finally succumbed to the toxic dose.

Meanwhile, the netting from the canopy was quickly removed, and the area around the tree re-opened. Two additional volunteers joined in the treading-in following the cancellation of the semi-final. With two small potentially incriminating metal particles, the bullet was located and removed close to the incident using a specially adapted detector cleverly housed within the end of a walking cane.

Calls to improve players' headgear followed the tragic accident of one of the Polo community's devoted and generous participants. An attempt to examine Hathaway's helmet proved fruitless, however. It was, unfortunately, never found.

Ray was pleased to learn later that Carlos, Terry and Ross had been snapped up shortly after by rival teams enabling them to continue their professional polo-playing careers without interruption.

33 October 1st, 1973

London, England

Miles Hathaway's tragic passing – resulting from a freak polo accident – was widely reported in the evening's papers. The Brachfield Media Group's announcement included a personal eulogy from a close friend and the head of the organisation, Mr Ezra Brachfield – himself recently widowed. The deceased was described as a successful entrepreneur with diverse business interests worldwide. A leader and visionary whose expertise and contribution would be sadly missed in Britain and the international community. Sir Foster Braithwaite and Ray visited Ezra Brachfield's Belgravia residence earlier that day and were shown into his study.

"Well, this is a pleasant surprise, Foster," the media mogul said as he came around from behind his desk. "I must say I was somewhat intrigued when I received the call from your office. It all sounded very mysterious."

"Thank you for taking time out in what must be a difficult and trying period for you and your family," the Minister opened.

"Yes, it is. However, life goes on, and we have to cope as best we can. Nicola has been the most affected losing her mother under such tragic circumstances." He smiled grimly.

"Please, gentlemen, do take a seat." He gestured to two leather curved-backed chairs in front of his desk.

"The thing is, Ezra, we're here to discuss a very sensitive matter, and..." the Minister started before Brachfield interjected.

"Before you do, may I suggest a..." he pointed to a silver tray with a whisky decanter and glasses on his desk. "I was about to indulge myself."

Both men politely declined. Their visit was not a social one. Ray observed Brachfield closely as he poured out a measure for himself. He detected a slight shakiness – a nervousness. The media mogul took a seat at his desk facing the visitors.

"It's about your son's kidnapping." Sir Braithwaite jumped straight in. Ezra Brachfield's posture stiffened. He hesitated and lowered his glass. "We were unable to approach you earlier. However, following Miles Hathaway's unfortunate accident, we can provide you with a fuller account."

"Miles Hathaway?" He furtively glanced at the two with unease. "How's his death anything to do with Ariel's abduction?"

"We believe we now know the true purpose behind your son's kidnapping... and the people involved." The Minister didn't directly respond to the magnate's question. Ray continued to watch Ezra Brachfield closely, peering intently at his face – looking for any giveaway intimations. "When I say, people... I mean the organisation." Ezra Brachfield kept a steady gaze at Foster Braithwaite. "It started to make sense when we reviewed your group's recent coverage of the Zuhuania scandal and investigated subsequent events. That is... who might benefit from a change in the hands at the wheel?" The Minister paused as Ezra Brachfield closed his eyes and took a deep breath. Ray gave the Minister a side glance.

[311]

"To put things into perspective," interjected Ray. "We believe that the people who kidnapped Ariel were the one and the same who provided the location... enabling his extraction."

"That doesn't make sense!" responded Brachfield. "Why would they abduct Ariel only to then provide the information for his rescue?

"That's the clever part," said Ray. "The people who orchestrated the abduction set impossible dictates on the Israeli Government... Demands that were so politically abrasive they knew couldn't be met. Once they felt the timing was right, they leaked Ariel's location through a credible source setting up a rescue, knowing full well the people holding him would be eliminated – leaving no one who could give away any meaningful information. They made sure the group holding Ariel knew nothing that would connect them."

"Then why go through such an elaborate scheme... And let's not forget they held Ariel for over three months. Why do that?"

"We have to assume that they wanted to keep their real intentions well-hidden – shielded. It was all part of an elaborate scheme to have you play along with the Zuhuania coup. To use your media empire to promulgate a positive spin on the take-over – to legitimise the incumbent's removal from office. Had that been the demand for Ariel's release from the outset, it would have been too obvious and opened up a trail easily followed. By being the kidnappers and then the informants, they could command events and the timetable. That would explain why Ariel was held for so long." Brachfield slumped back in his chair.

"They always kept complete control of the situation and acted when they were ready," chimed in the Minister.

"So what you're saying is that the ransom demand and

the release of the bombers was just a ploy to shield their true intent?"

"Precisely!" said the Minister.

"And I went along with it!" responded the media mogul. He let out a long low sigh, bowed his head, lowered his face into his hands, and gently rubbed his forehead. His heartbeat felt sluggish, and his face warm and tingling. He looked up, shame and regret written all over his face.

"Never in my life had I felt so helpless – so vulnerable. They said they would make sure Ariel was rescued, but if I didn't do as they instructed..." He swallowed hard. "You must understand that what I did wasn't easy. It went against all my principles. A moral code I had doggedly adhered to all my life. I did what I had to do to ensure the safety of my son... Surely you can understand that..., I had no choice. I had to do what I had to do... My intent was just."

"There's no question as to your position, Ezra. You should not blame yourself," pacified the Minister. "What you did was what any loving parent would do... And make no mistake, these people were ruthless individuals who would stop at nothing to protect themselves." He stopped short of mentioning Shaul Feuerman's killing.

"By also approaching you with a solution for his rescue, you might conclude they believed your gratitude would make you more compliant – a feeling of indebtedness on your part," suggested Ray.

"So what are you implying? That Miles was behind the kidnapping? Behind the whole affair?"

"That's correct, Ezra."

"No! I can't accept that. I've known Miles for years. He even introduced me to Adele – my wife." The Minister gave Ray a sideways glance. "He was also involved in a few charities with me..."

[313]

"The Hathaway organisation is already profiting from the country's change in leadership!" Ray's remark caught Brachfield short.

The media man hesitated, his face tight with emotion, unsure what to say. Could it be true? Could he have been behind such a callous scheme? He'd always known Miles – charming as he was – to be unashamedly ambitious in his business dealings, but to be so deceptive and cold-hearted? It seemed too incredible to believe, yet why would he doubt the Minister's revelation.

"Are you telling me that this nightmare is now over?"

"It is. However, there is more that you should know."

"More?" he said, clutching his hands.

"Yes, your wife, Adele. I don't wish to speak ill of the dead, but unfortunately, she was also involved."

"Involved? How?"

Ray and the minister discussed how far they should inform the media magnate about his wife's collaboration and her duplicity – her gameplays. Ray was keen to tell all – to leave nothing out. The Minister, however, wanted to show restraint, arguing that the man had suffered enough. The extent was left open.

"She was being blackmailed by Hathaway and was providing him information… starting with when Ariel was due to travel to Cyprus. After which, she kept him informed as to the lay of the land, so to speak," the Minister said.

Ezra's stomach suddenly felt heavy. His heartbeat quickened. A sudden coldness hit him at his very core. As much as he cared for her, he always sensed something was troubling deep inside the woman he thought was his soulmate – his confidante. He had been under no illusions when he proposed, and she eagerly accepted. However, he never anticipated betrayal.

"What umm… how could they have blackmailed her?

What did they have that they could do that?" He spoke falteringly. Ray glanced at the Minister, who looked to be grappling with the question.

"She had had an affair with Hathaway sometime before she met you, and he had threatened to leak it – to embarrass you. It would appear she was trying to protect you," said Ray. The minister shot Ray a *thank you* look.

"And finally, Ezra. It pains me to tell you that your wife was not in an accident... She was murdered by Hathaway's people, who before you ask... have and are being brought to book." The Minister's revelation hit Brachfield hard.

"Murdered...? You can't be serious?"

"I'm afraid so," responded the Minister.

"And Gila was killed protecting her," added Ray, unable to disguise a hint of contempt. He blamed Adele Brachfield and the games she played for Gila's death.

"But the news was that it was just a horrible accident," persisted Ezra Brachfield.

"That was our doing," replied the Minister. "National security and all that. We couldn't publicise the true nature... I'm sorry to have to share this with you at this later stage, but we had to keep the people behind the... accident... unaware and off guard. I hope you understand?"

"Yes, yes, I see," he muttered in response. His thoughts turned to Nikki. How would it affect her? Should he tell her what he'd just learned? She'd been through enough losing her mother!

"May I suggest you continue to regard your wife's death as an accident. It would serve to keep curious minds from the truth. Ignorance is bliss as it were," offered the Minister.

"I suppose you're right," said Ezra Brachfield, although his mind was elsewhere – racing.

"Again, I'm sorry we had to come to give you such shocking news. Unless you have any questions...," said the Minister. "I think we should leave you now. You can always reach me at my office should there be anything else I could help you with." A still troubled Ezra Brachfield came around the desk and extended a shaky hand.

"Thank you," he said, then watched the two men leave, closing the door silently behind them. He turned and walked around the desk and stared fixedly out of the bay window.

It was a while before he sat back in his chair – he had a lot to process. However, he had already decided that the Minister was right. There would be no point in pursuing the true nature of his wife's death. He had to protect both Ariel and particularly Nikki. She had been understandably devastated over the loss of her mother. To know the truth would be too awful to contemplate – his mind was made up.

Hathaway, the bastard! Well, he got his comeuppance!

Yet, a niggling question still preyed on his mind. He picked up his untouched glass of whisky and took a slow sip, then downed the remainder and reached for the decanter. Ezra Brachfield was no one's fool, and one disturbing aspect still haunted him – David's deep sense of loss displayed at Adele's funeral. As much as David tried to hide it, and even dealing with his own sorrow, Ezra noted it was more than a grieving brother-in-law would show. Was there more to his and Adele's relationship? Do his two surprise visitors know more than they were telling? He had always given Adele a free hand – never questioning where she'd been or who she was with – always trusting. However, he somehow didn't completely buy the story of Adele and Hathaway's relationship.

He poured himself a full glass, sat back in the chair,

and recollected the day of the funeral and David's manner. He also recalled the wife's offhand way towards her husband. On an impulse, he picked up the receiver and inserted his index fingertip into the hole marked zero and rotated the dial.

He watched as the dial slowly returned to its starting position, then placed his finger into the hole marked two – the second number in a London code. He hesitated momentarily, then removed his finger. Ezra Brachfield held onto the receiver for a long while before returning it to its cradle.

34 October 1st, 1973

Chepstow, England

He patted his left breast pocket, checking he hadn't forgotten the small leather case, then pulled firmly on the metal grip, engaging the night latch and closing the front door. He glanced at his watch, then looked up at the murky sky. He shivered slightly and pulled the collar together of his hip-length parka before walking away from the small terraced cottage at the far end of *Cwy Court*.

Seventy-five paces took him to the intersection with *Bridge Street*. Turning left and climbing the gentle slope for a further two-hundred-and-eighty strides brought him to the Three Tuns' front door – a sixteenth-century pub with low oak-beamed ceilings and period features. He looked at his watch before entering – 7:30 pm. Retired *Company Sergeant Major* John McIntyre was a creature of simple habits. Monday night was *darts night* – an occasion he never missed unless away on assignment for J.F. Security Services Ltd.

He had bought the small two-bedroomed house shortly after moving to the lower part of Chepstow – a historic market town nestled on the River Wye banks and bordering the shires of Monmouth and Gloucester – nine years earlier. In his early fifties and a devoted bachelor, he lived modestly on a military pension, augmented by an additional income as a part-time civilian lecturer at the *Army Apprentice College, Beachley Camp*. The generous compensation received for his questionable services rendered to J.F.S.S. was deposited directly into an untraceable Spanish bank account. The one luxury he granted himself was an annual two-week break in a well-appointed apartment overlooking a sandy cove outside *Nerja* on the *Costa del Sol* – a property he owned outright but *rented* to himself. He planned to retire on his sixtieth birthday and disappear permanently to the sun, where he would live out his days in comfort and financial wellbeing. He hadn't wasted money on a vehicle, preferring instead to ride around on a second-hand five-speed bicycle he had bought at a local market.

"On time, as always, John," greeted the ruddy-faced man behind the bar. "Usual?"

Morgan, the proprietor, turned to an open wooden barrel without waiting for a response and ladled out a full measure of *scrumpy* into a half-pint glass mug – a strong rough cider made from unselected apples and a speciality of the house – then placed it on the counter. John McIntyre acknowledged the barman's serving with a nod as he joined five others at a table against the back wall and behind the *oche* – the line behind which dart throwers stand. He removed the darts case, took off his parka and hung it on a peg next to the table. Monday evenings were always practice nights for the *Three Tuns Darts* team, of which he was a passionate and committed member.

The pub generally enjoyed unrestricted local use until Saturday evenings when cadets from the military college would descend upon the town looking to spend what was left of their meagre weekly wage of five-to-six guineas and monopolise the dartboard. The purchase of *Blanco* for whitening belts, a tin of *Brasso* to keep metals gleaming, black boot polish and essential toiletries took priority.

Remnants of senior cadets could still be found around town on a Sunday afternoon – usually nursing a single jug of scrumpy bought with the scant remains of earlier filled wallets. He was busily chatting with his fellow team members while focusing on fitting the flights to his dart shafts, ready for a full evening in honing his skills for a match that coming Wednesday against a rival pub from *Newport* in Wales. No one took notice of the nondescript man in a plain brown sports jacket and grey slacks as he approached the bar.

"A packet of twenty *Woodbines*, please," he said, smiling and pointing to the selection of packets on a shelf behind the counter. While the landlord was reaching for the cigarettes, a single capsule of a lethal concoction of *anthracyclines* slipped into the mug of cider and quickly dissolved in the harsh liquid. The man thanked the proprietor and handed over a five-pound note as he took the pack.

"How was the pie?" asked Morgan as he returned the man's change.

"Excellent! As good as last Monday," he replied with a satisfied grin. "I shall make it a point to come in for a repeat next time I'm in the area," he added, then returned to his table and an unfinished pint of *Guinness* and the *Daily Mail.*

"When would you like your pie?" asked the proprietor when McIntyre walked over for his first sip of the local brew.

"I'll throw a few darts first, Morgan," he replied and returned to the group clutching the drink.

By nine-thirty, more regulars had arrived, adding to the positive atmosphere generated by a bout of high scoring. Morgan was clearing the team's empty glasses.

"I'll have a refill, Morgan!" said McIntyre holding his last dart and about to try for a third treble-twenty to the enthusiastic encouragement of his teammates and spectators. He was throwing as accurately as he had ever thrown.

"You can do it, John!"

"We'll slaughter them on Wednesday!"

"Nothing will prevent us from making the final if you keep this up!"

"Fingers crossed, John. Go for it!"

With a smug smile on his face – the ex-professional soldier and collaborator in several murders for the organisation calling itself the Alhalu – slowly raised his arm, balancing the projectile lightly between his thumb and three fingers. A deafening silence descended on the room as he shifted his stance slightly, lining up diagonally with the board. Briefly glancing down, he checked that his leading foot was behind the throw line. He brought the dart up level with his eyes and focused on the narrow space between the two metal wires – already gripping the sharp points of his first two darts.

Suddenly and without warning, he dropped the dart and grabbed his chest – taking sharp panicky intakes of breath. The group reacted in horror. One of the women screamed. Two of his teammates reached out as he started to sag and gently lowered him to the floor. He couldn't make sense of what was happening! His chest was on fire. He couldn't breathe. He tried to focus – bewildered. Anxious faces towering over him were a blur, and concerned voices an inaudible muffle. He was losing consciousness! With one final gasp…, John McIntyre finally yielded to a massive heart attack.

In the commotion that followed, the man in the sports jacket calmly folded his newspaper, tucked it under his arm and without looking back, quietly and unobtrusively left the pub.

[321]

35 October 3rd, 1973

Bierton Village, Buckinghamshire

The animal curled his upper lip and snorted as Sean Bridges scratched his forehead, then patted him gently on the jaw. The two had formed a close relationship over the eighteen months since *Escritor* had been retired from an equine career as a medium-goal polo pony. During Bridges' spell as security at Miles Hathaway's Manor Grange stables, he had formed a fondness for the chestnut gelding, often visiting him with a treat or two.

When the animal started to show signs of flinching when mounted, it was decided that his playing days were coming to an end. The fear was that the animal would develop a hammock back – as many ponies often did – and was relegated to a low-goal ride. However, it soon became evident the problem would quickly worsen and rendered the horse surplus to requirements, prompting Bridges to offer to take him and give him a home.

With the Polo Manager's blessing and the Broadhurst's permission to use their backfield, he rented a Land Rover with a horsebox and transported the animal to *Bierton*, a village in a farming parish a mile northeast of the market town, *Aylesbury*, in *Buckinghamshire*.

John and Jane Broadhurst were an elderly childless couple and the owners of *Maple Farm*. A farm in name

[322]

only, the property comprised a Tudor longhouse with a thatched roof – well overdue for renewal – and a brick-and-timber walling buckled over time and sited end-on to the adjacent main road. The property's entrance was over a side track and through a weathered timber gate facing a rundown open L-shaped stable. A chance meeting two years earlier saw Sean Bridges move out of a dim room with an annoying resident mouse into two small but comfortable rooms on the first floor above the kitchen and adjoining tack-room at Maple Farm.

Between assignments for Jack Frasier, Sean worked as needed with a printing company next door and in his leisure time with regular visits to the King's Head pub across the road.

"What you be 'avin, me duck?" would herald many an evening drinking and playing the famous English pub game, *shove ha'penny*. A game in which players attempt to *shove* (slide) an old English half-penny in between scoring lines, and one which locals would always fair far better than visitors.

With a final stroke of the animal's nose, Sean walked back to the house for lunch.

"Working this afternoon?" asked John chewing on a morsel of beef.

"Outwork deliveries," replied Sean.

"You mind and don't go carrying too many of those boxes all at once now," intervened Jane adding two more potatoes onto Sean's plate. He smiled at her kindly, concerned remark.

The shared fondness between the three was beginning to give Sean deep feelings of guilt, particularly when returning from a morally questionable assignment for J.F.S.S. He always gave the least detail and avoided talking too much about where he'd been, which was accepted and not pursued over time. However, the last excursion to

[323]

Israel left him conflicted. He increasingly felt that he was letting the Broadhursts down – deceiving them and preying on their good intentions.

His mother was the last person for whom he cared, and she had passed away when he was seventeen, just before he joined the *Royal Fusiliers* as a junior soldier. His father had run off with a *tart* – as his mother always referred to the bleached blond barmaid – before his tenth birthday. He was seriously considering speaking to Jack about being excused further such contracts, although he knew he was in as deep as the rest of them, which might pose a problem.

"We're all in this together," Jack had reminded the hardcore more than once. "We either swim together or sink together!"

"Must be off! Chris said they'd be ready for me by two," he said, pushing his empty plate forward and getting up.

"Thanks a bunch for a super lunch, Jane."

"You always say that!" Chuckled Jane. "Now, get off and don't be late for tea."

He left the house by the tack-room door and stopped to look towards the field. Escritor was at the gate and, on seeing Sean, bucked his head, turned and galloped away excitedly up the narrow pasture. Sean chuckled to himself, then turned and walked down to the pedestrian gate.

"Quite a load today!" he noted, looking into the back of the *Bedford* box van piled to the ceiling with cartons full of colourfully printed album covers.

"We've had to put the glues in the cab. As you can see, there's no room here," said Chris Payne, Managing Director of *Payne Printers Ltd.*

The company had recently been taking on projects that required an assembly after printing referred to as *outwork*, gainfully employing an eager community of house-bound ladies looking to augment their husbands' wages, or in some cases, for extra cash for themselves. Sean had garnered several such willing helpers over the previous few months – in and around a council house estate outside the village – adding to the company's span of operations, fortunes and his pocket.

"Don't forget the shove ha'penny match tonight at eight!" shouted out one of the workers from inside an open window. Sean waved his acknowledgement, climbed into the cab and turned the key in the ignition.

"*Come in, David. We're a go. Over.*"

"*Understood, Bunim. Over.*"

"*Come in, Michael. Stand by. This may take some time. Over.*"

"*Understood, Bunim. No movement here. It's all clear. Waiting for your instruction. Over.*"

The man with the radio call sign, *Bunim*, placed the short wave radio on the passenger seat and slowly pulled away from the layby and followed the van. The three-man team stationed along the anticipated route were in for a long wait, but then they were accustomed to long periods of surveillance.

Most of his workers were in that afternoon accepting more than usual due to the ten per cent increase offered for the work to be completed by the end of the week. Sean meticulously maintained a record of the name, address and amount of flattened sleeves and glue he had left with them. The job simply entailed folding each printed soft cardboard sheet three times and glueing in place the final fold. They would receive the princely sum of two pence for each completed album sleeve on collection for their effort.

Sean's penultimate visit was to his favourite mother and daughter team residing in the estate's furthest house.

"We was wonderin' when you might be round, me darling," said the younger of the two females in her late forties as she opened the front door. "Well, what is it this time? Record sleeves again?"

"I'm afraid so," replied Sean apologetically, although he knew the task was their favourite.

"What you got left, then?"

"I've held back twenty cartons for you. You should be able to knock them out without breaking a sweat." He always enjoyed a lighthearted banter with the ladies.

"Okay, let's get them in and have that tea," she said, stepping back and placing a metal stop to the bottom of the door to hold it open.

"Come in, David. Tea break. Over."

"Understood. Over."

"Come in, Michael. It's the tea break. Stand by. Over."

"Understood. Still okay here. Awaiting your instruction. Over."

Twenty minutes later, Sean Bridges left the Woods' home and climbed into the Bedford van for his final port of call – a wheelchair-bound man in his early twenties living with his elderly mother in a small isolated farmhouse two miles further on. Sean had grown fond of him, whose only wish was to do something useful with his time. The outwork may not have been much, but it meant a lot to the disabled young man. Sean always paid him double the rate without him knowing – making up the difference out of his pocket.

"Come in, David. Action. Over."

"Understood. Over."

The message was repeated and confirmed by Michael.

Sean glanced at his watch. He was running late and stepped on the accelerator. The one-way lane was essentially a private road leading to the farmhouse and always clear of other vehicles. No one visited the Hardies.

He saw the big lorry parked across the ninety-degree bend too late and instinctively turned the steering wheel sharply to his left. The van ploughed through the flimsy

[326]

wire fencing, running the railway embankment's length. The vehicle's continued momentum carried it over the edge, landing hard onto its nose and flipping onto its back across the railway track – fifty feet below.

The team member identified as David over the radio – waiting a short distance from the planned spot – immediately ran to the van. Sean Bridges was lying crumpled awkwardly on his back on the inside of the roof. He was breathing heavily, blinking rapidly and trying to speak, when an obscure shape appeared at the smashed side window. From the angle of his right leg and neck, it seemed he was suffering several broken bones. The man, David, reached in and, without hesitation, went for Sean's head, clasping it in his right hand and turning it towards him. A weak smile crossed Sean's lips at the consoling touch. He recoiled at a sudden sharp pain inside the soft tissue deep behind his right ear. The man slowly released his head and withdrew the left hand, holding a syringe. Sean Bridges' breathing progressively slowed.

The third member of the team threw down a rope to David. He quickly scrambled up the embankment and jumped into the truck. Michael joined him moments later. The whole affair took less than five minutes.

Sean Bridges' body was discovered later that evening. Two stolen vehicles – a blue *Ford Escort* and a *Bedford Three-Ton* truck were recovered undamaged two days later – miles away from the incident.

36 October 4th, 1973

Pevensey Bay, East Sussex

Tim Grover reached over and pulled the curtain aside. It was 7:00 am, and dawn was breaking. He pulled back the duvet and swung his legs out, planting his right foot heavily onto an upturned beer bottle cap.

"Fuu…ck!" he cried out, then caught his big toe kicking over three empty bottles with a clatter in the narrow space between the bed and the caravan's outer wall. He plopped back onto the bed and vigorously rubbed the soft tissue of his bare sole where the serrated outer ring had left an impression. He ignored the incoherent guttural remark from the form lying next to him – totally covered to the top of a blond head – and gingerly stood up. Tim pushed away two more empties with his foot before crossing over naked to the small dresser. Everything was space-saving and cramped in the two-berth van, but it was his home, and he liked it that way.

He removed a pair of fresh swimming trunks from the top drawer and a tee-shirt – green and discoloured from seeing the inside of countless laundromat machines – and pulled on both items. Running his hands through his hair, he gave a huge yawn, stretched his arms above his head and stepped into the combination kitchen hall. He ignited

[328]

a flame under a metal kettle and sat on one of the two facing bench seats on either side of a small table.

He gave an involuntary shiver in the cold crisp interior air. Autumn had already made its mark on the caravan site a short distance from *Pevensey Castle* – built after the *Duke of Normandy's* army landed in 1066, heralding the *country's Norman conquest*. Although small, the unkempt site commanded a seafront position, enabling the absentee landlord to receive a *not to be scoffed at* annual rental. The eight permanent mobile homes were set out in an *L* facing the *English Channel* five miles northeast of the coastal town of *Eastbourne*. Although the park was officially closed for the winter, he was allowed to remain for a reduced monthly consideration provided he maintained an eye on the place.

The kettle started to whistle. He got up, made a strong black coffee, and resumed his seat by the double window overlooking the parking area. The only vehicle was his mustard two-door 1972 *Vauxhall Firenza*. He looked up at the white sky – it didn't look promising. It would be anything but a rough day. Nevertheless, it wouldn't stop him from taking his morning swim.

Since leaving the SAS (Special Air Service) as a lance corporal, Tim Grover was essentially a restless soul who lived for each mission. He missed the adrenaline rush, making up between tasks with a mix of booze, sex and physical endurance – pushing his body to limits the average man couldn't stomach. Each morning when at the caravan, he would swim the two miles from shore and back again irrespective of the weather, then push himself through a ten-mile jog in the afternoon. His obsession stemmed from years as an abused orphan driven from pillar-to-post by uncaring patrons until he was old enough to run to a family of his choosing – the army.

He didn't equate the army discipline to that meted out

in the variety of orphanages he had the *pleasure* of passing through. In fact, he found that he relished it. He would have stayed with the unit if not for the strict maximum number of duties before retiring as a well-trained and dangerous operative. He looked into his empty mug.

"Time for my swim," he grunted, and took the cup to the sink, swilled out the inside under the tap before placing it on the draining board.

He walked back into the bedroom and took a towel off a pile placed on the dresser, and glanced at the barely visible partner for the night – her name still a mystery. Jane, Janice or Jessabelle? It didn't matter; she wasn't the best he'd had or the worst. There might be a repeat performance that afternoon if she was still around. At thirty-eight and with rugged looks, he possessed enough charm to succeed in a string of conquests. The generous rewards he'd earn from Jack's various assignments helped, although barely lasted until the next mission.

Throwing the towel over his shoulder, he opened the door and stepped down onto the rough grass in his bare feet. He pulled his arms back, stretched and started to make his way to the shingled beach.

"Good morning!" A middle-aged man wearing a windcheater and steel-rimmed spectacles – walking in the same direction near the parked Firenza – surprised Tim.

"Morning," he replied.

"Sorry! I didn't mean to startle you. I'm staying over the road with the wife. I thought I'd get out for a bit of fresh air. Not like you, though..." He referred to Tim's scanty attire.

"Just off for a morning swim," Tim said as the man approached.

"That's brave of you!" The man responded. "Say, are you staying around here?"

"That's my place," replied Tim pointing over his

[330]

shoulder to the caravan.

"Ah! What luck! We've been... that is, the wife and me... have been considering bringing our van – it's a 1970 *Jubilee*, four-berther... too big to keep at home. We live outside of *Watford*. Anyway, I'm dragging this on a bit, sorry!"

Tim started to jog on the spot lightly. The cold was beginning to bite, and he wanted to get into the water.

"We were wondering... um... if there was anyone around to talk about renting a permanent spot in the area," the man continued, seemingly oblivious to Tim's growing discomfort. "Can't seem to find anyone. Would you happen to um...?"

"I tell you what, let me get this swim over with, and when I get back, I'll get you a number," Tim said and was about to move away.

"That's jolly decent of you," he said and, stepping forward, reached out his hand. "Richard, Richard Blemshaw." Tim instinctively took the man's hand and jumped back in shock.

"Shiiit!"

"I'm so sorry!" The man immediately apologised. "It must be this damned nylon jacket. I shocked the milkman earlier today. It must be the nylon! I'm so sorry!"

Tim felt as though he'd been stabbed by a needle.

"It's okay. No harm done," he responded vigorously, shaking off the sudden sharp pain from his hand and fingers. "I'll get that number for you after the swim," he confirmed, and without waiting, continued onto the beach and hurried down over the shingle to the water's edge. He threw the towel over a breaker post and dived into the cold dark-green water.

The man watched Tim submerge before re-emerging, and with strong, purposeful strokes, swim away from the beach. He reached into his jacket pocket and removed a

[331]

small metal box — no bigger than a snuffbox. Holding it tightly in his right hand, he flipped the hinged lid open with his thumb, then, with two fingers of his other hand, carefully slid a metal ring with a sharp protruding point off the second finger and placed it in the box. He closed the lid and dropped the box back into his jacket pocket. He walked over to a wooden-railed fencing section and, propping back against the structure, continued to watch Tim Grover's effort with a stoic facial expression.

As he ploughed his way through the cold Channel water, Tim felt the familiar sensation of prickling skin and the muscles in his upper back constrict, making him pull harder through the salty water. He had reached the halfway point when he suddenly developed an agonising cramp in both legs. The pain quickly spread through his body, his shoulders and down his arms to the tips of his fingers. He couldn't understand what was happening and started to panic. Try as he could, he couldn't keep his head out of the water and kept slipping under. The more he struggled, the more he went under until he yielded to the inevitable and disappeared from view.

The man glanced at his watch. It normally took sixty seconds for a fit and healthy man to drown. He gave it four minutes before pushing off the fence and walking away.

Tim Grover's body was washed ashore ten miles south of Eastbourne. The post-mortem ruled his demise as an unfortunate death by misadventure.

37 October 5th, 1973

Amman, Jordan

Ray hesitated momentarily at the wrought-iron gate and cast an uneasy eye over the despairing rows of gravestones before entering the cemetery. The temporary plot he had stood at – the day after her burial – had been replaced with a beautifully maintained grey granite-lined flowerbed of vibrant colours with a headstone to match. The epitaph bathed in light from a bright midday sun simply read:

LEYLA EL KORDY
A beautiful and loving daughter and sister
Taken from us too early

"I'm sorry I haven't been to see you." He spoke quietly, softly. "A lot's happened since… I would have so much to tell you if only you…" He paused. He wanted to share his feelings and thoughts with her. Slowly, he went down onto one knee and raised his right hand about to make the sign of the cross when he stopped himself. He wasn't about to kneel in deference to a cruel higher authority. He no longer held the vestiges of a nurtured religious belief. That obligation had long gone. He was kneeling to get closer to her – entombed six feet below and out of his reach.

"So much hurt and anger. I'm sorry, I'm not the same man you fell in love with. What's happened since you… has changed me. I'm not sure if you'd approve…" He sighed softly. "I will never remove this as I promised at the river," he said, twirling the band ring with his thumb. "Do you remember the afternoon you gave it to me… your swan?" He stopped speaking and stared hard into the flowers trying to picture her face. Her image had been fading away faster over the last few weeks. How he wished he'd had a photograph of her… Perhaps it was for the better.

"I saw the butterfly…, down by the lake… Thank you for that…" He paused again. He felt his eyes moisten, then quickly cleared his throat. "I'm not sure if I'll ever be able to visit again… It's not a goodbye. I have to move on… have moved on. I know you would understand. I have to let go… as you have… Please understand." He raised the single-stemmed red rose to his lips, placed a lingering kiss on its soft petals, laid it gently among the blooms and slowly pulled himself up.

"Mother comes every Sunday to tend to her," spoke a familiar voice behind him. Ray turned to face a bearded officer of the Jordanian Army, standing a few feet respectfully behind – his braided-peak cap tucked under his left arm.

"It's beautiful," responded Ray.

"Mother and father would want to see you," the officer continued.

"I would like that," Ray answered and walked over to him. They grabbed each other in a strong wholehearted embrace.

"It's so good to see," enthused Captain Baqar El Kordy breaking away and grasping Ray's elbows in both hands. "I've missed you," he added, all smiles and grins.

[334]

"And before you ask, I've transferred your bag and dismissed the taxi." Ray took a long last look at the grave.

"I have a lot to tell you," Ray said as the two old friends slowly walked away.

◆◆◆◆

"I'll leave you two to catch up," offered Baqar's father, gently pushing the half-full bottle of *Baczewski* vodka towards Ray. It was his gift that had been gathering dust in the drink's cabinet for his Christmas visit three years' earlier – eagerly anticipated by the family but sadly never happened following Leyla's tragic death during the recapture of a hijacked airliner – and one her father was determined would not go back in storage. Dinner was a lavish array of local dishes specially prepared by Baqar's mother and her longstanding maid, Aisha. The four had also agreed over the sumptuous meal that they should all move on and remember Leyla in their own way – privately and with a glad heart.

"I gather the King is somewhat miffed at the Israel Government," said Ray unscrewing the top on the vodka bottle and refilling both glasses. "The agreed withdrawal of troops from Israeli-occupied Egyptian held territory with no proposition for Jordan."

"In truth, the Israelis were put out by us sending tanks supporting the Syrian confrontation in the *Golan Heights*. Even though the King refused to take part with our troops, it still put the Israeli's nose out of joint." Ray was somewhat taken aback by Baqar's frank admission suggesting he didn't support the decision to commit tanks – what could only be interpreted as a symbolic gesture – to assist Syria.

"Last month's surprise attack on Israel by both Egypt and Syria didn't end well. Pity, you guys got involved."

"The situation here continues to be fluid," Baqar responded with a deep sigh and gulped down the fiery alcohol in one. "We're piggies in the middle. Our future relations with our immediate neighbours, the Israelis, cannot continue to be problematic. As much as our esteemed Majesty hopes, I can't see the Israeli Government ever agreeing to return the *West Bank*. It's gone, and we have to live with it. And as long as our more radical neighbours continue to bloody the Jews' noses, we will be drawn into taking sides. Sides, we don't wish to be obliged into taking."

"Well, at least you've managed to resolve the PLO issue."

"Yeah, it's Lebanon's problem now. Their leader, Yasir Arafät, is a complex character, and from all our intelligence, a smart cookie not to be underestimated. It'll be interesting to see how much latitude the Lebanese will give the organisation, although we do see a storm brewing." Baqar took the bottle, refilled his glass, and raised it in a toast.

"To the *Odd Couple!*"

"The Odd Couple!" Ray responded with a throaty laugh. "I'd almost forgotten that label," he said, stifling a cough.

They sat back in their upholstered chairs and looked up into the clear night's sky – silent and reflective. The outdoor verandah at the El Kordy home was like a mini replica of the gardens of Babylon with a diverse variety of potted indigenous trees and plants – a pleasant and relaxing locale.

"We can't let this go to waste!" declared Baqar eventually and reached for the near-empty bottle. "So, what about you? I heard you were at the frontline down in Oman... That couldn't have been easy?"

"It was certainly an adventure," responded Ray with a

grin accepting his refill. He proceeded to give an account to a stunned Baqar of his chance shooting of their elusive killer, Nadeem Asghar, then leading to his role within the unit headed by Sir Foster Braithwaite.

"So, you're on the trail of that outfit we were chasing?" said an excited Baqar. They had always been hampered and left without closure.

"More than that. We dealt with the main man a few days back, a Miles Hathaway. It appears he was the head of this *Alhalu* cartel. There still remains a French and German connection, but unfortunately, nothing can positively link. We intend to keep digging. Meanwhile, I'm here to resolve the Lebanese element. A Fareed Al Safadi..."

"The arms dealer?" interjected Baqar.

"The very same. You know him?"

"He's under our radar. Been supplying arms to the PLO and we believe finances a radical splinter group that's still operating in the country."

"We believe he's also a senior element and currently sheltering the cartel's security chief, Jack Frasier. Man has killed for the group. Most probably was pulling strings way back over the King's letter fiasco."

"By the way, the King was certainly relieved when the letter was returned untouched. Your name did come up in its retrieval. My uncle let me know."

"How is Brigadier-General El Kordy?"

"Major-General now," responded Baqar proudly.

"I'm not surprised," offered Ray, "and, by the way, congratulations on your Captaincy, my friend."

"Connections help here."

"Don't be silly," replied Ray. "You'll make an excellent Captain... then Major... then who knows?" He added to their joint amusement loosened by the nearly completed bottle of Baczewski.

[337]

"Any idea why this organisation was after the letter specifically?"

"Not entirely. Unfortunately, we couldn't give Hathaway a chance to explain himself. He was too well connected and extremely wealthy. It was decided to take him out without alerting him beforehand if he did a runner. Foster Braithwaite…"

"Your Minister?"

"Yes. He's currently following up officially with the King's office, but it would appear that it's most probably arms-related. Back then, our government agreed to provide a substantial loan package for you guys. We're assuming the cartel simply wanted in. With everything going on in the region at the time, it was a perfect way to disguise their involvement. Once the letter was to secured, they would have been holding a pretty useful bit of coercive bargaining power directly with the King's office."

"As it was, Nadeem Asghar screwed up that particular plan!" opined Baqar.

"Exactly! It would appear that they were exercising extreme caution in keeping themselves well hidden. Quite prepared to cover their asses and remove any loose ends. As you and I were only too aware… Totally underestimated Asghar, though."

"You sound as if you admired the guy?"

Ray didn't immediately respond to Baqar's insightful remark, letting himself be distracted by an inviting bluish reflection in the limpid vodka. Yes, perhaps he had begun to understand the man – why he had turned into a cold-blooded killer. Ray had learned about the man, his roots, and a fortuitous act of compassion that rescued him from a desperate childhood. How would a man react to losing his loved ones from a cruel, vicious, uncompromising act with no one accountable? How would he – how had he?

[338]

Ray recalled one of Nadeem's poignant dying remarks:

"We are no different... you and me. We both kill."

"Maybe so, but I'm no killer," Ray had responded.

"Because you kill from... behind a uniform?"

Does a line really exist? A line which depending on which side one stands, defines a person as simply... an assassin or executioner? Does wearing a uniform make the difference? Until Ray took the shot five days earlier, he believed it did – and still did. However, it was a nagging question for which there was no simple answer. Nadeem Asghar's words occasionally continued to prick Ray's conscience. Perhaps the two were inextricably linked – even in death.

Baqar was closely observing his old friend brood over his glass and realised how he had changed, but then they had both experienced what soldiers in times of war do. They were no longer the *odd couple* – two officer cadets playing war games, learning to kill a wooden cut-out on the firing range, theorising leadership and engaged in endless bouts of kit cleaning, drills and inspections. They had been through their *baptism of fire* together and survived to take on new challenges. Yes, they had both changed – there was no way back.

"I shan't lie to you, Baqar," Ray pulled himself up in his chair and exhaled loudly. "Asghar could have killed me in the alley that night. Let's face it. I was the aggressor..., yet he chose not to take me out. I think about that sometimes."

"That's destiny, Ray. As we say in this part of the world, *it was written.*"

"Maybe so," he paused. "That day... in the cave, when I asked him why he didn't shoot... He simply said, *it seemed the right thing to do.*"

"A killer with a conscience? I don't think so!" Baqar replied, his disdain for the man palpable.

"I'll never know!" Ray said, dismissing the subject. He was only too aware that Baqar's perspective was moulded differently, considering the violent political environment in which he lived.

"You said you're here to resolve the Al Safadi connection?"

"Our intelligence puts him holed up in a villa in northern Lebanon, outside a place called *Aabdeh*. Got himself quite an army. Local thugs and an assortment of Palestinian fighters. I'm crossing over into Israel tomorrow. I'm looking to put a team together with Avi Gershen's help in the next two or three days... He also has a vested interest in Al Safadi's demise."

"To take them out?"

"Yes."

"If I can get permission to go along, will you count me in?"

"That's the second reason why I'm here," Ray grinned, raising his glass.

38 October 6th, 1973

Brixton, London

Saturday evenings were understandably the busiest. Eager patrons – money in pockets and ready to dance and party the night away – were already lining up six-deep outside the roped area. The live-music venue known locally as, *The Dive* – on *Rushford Road* just off *Coldharbour Lane* – was popular with its multicultural community.

For the first time, people meeting Simon Dodge would be forgiven if they didn't identify his name with the powerfully built man. Standing at six feet two – naturally bronzed and with a permanently shaved head – he was the older at thirty-six of two unions of Miles Dodge and Mavis Walsh. His dark features were inherited from his two-thirds Jamaican and one-third Irish mother. Even though twenty-two years old and refusing to mature – constantly getting into trouble with the local male population – he nevertheless doted on his younger sister, Jannette. He blamed his father – who was serving a final two years of sixteen years for attempted armed robbery in the local *HM Prison Brixton* – for the damage caused to the family fabric. Although he contributed generously to the household – a three-bedroom apartment he still shared with his mother and sister – his mother was a proud woman and continued to work all the hours allowed as an office cleaner for a contract cleaning company.

The fourth and most dangerous of Jack Frasier's inner circle of ex-SAS operatives, Simon Dodge was slow to temper – preferring to talk his way out of a potentially violent solution rather than resorting to his iron-fists. However, when called upon, he would dispense swift and convincing justice. As the club's head-bouncer, he was responsible for keeping order and a happy but unthreatened patronage. There was never trouble from the over-excited assemblies when he stood at the door. Occasionally, drinks beforehand brought out the bravado in a young, naïve hopeful. However, such an act was quickly dispelled when confronted by the big man. One didn't pick a fight with Simon Dodge.

He looked at his watch and nodded to two of his associates standing on either side of the double entrance doors. With his calm and steadying presence, entry into the premises was peaceful and orderly. He waited for a while before going in and down the stairwell into the lower ground floor. A live rock group was shouting unintelligible dialogue into a microphone backed by a strong throbbing rhythm from four instrumentalists. It wasn't his kind of music.

Dodge made his way to the corner at the far-left end of the bar, where the speakers thankfully failed to make as loud an impression as elsewhere in the club.

"Give me a sparkly water, would you?" The young female bartender smiled brightly and passed him his usual *Perrier*. He held the bottle for a moment before twisting off the top and gulping down half the contents, then returned the cap and placed the bottle on the bar.

"You look like you're floating elsewhere tonight," observed the young woman. She had fantasised about him taking her to bed since she took the job three months earlier, but he showed no interest – always friendly but no more. He didn't respond to her remark as he stared across the sea of gyrating bodies. Something wasn't sitting right with him. A nagging feeling he couldn't dismiss. It was unusual for Jack not to have called since the car wreck. Contact had just died with no explanation.

It was agreed at the outset of their collaboration and fully understood that he..., that is, none of the four would ever make direct contact with Jack Frasier unless instructed beforehand. They would have to observe an absolute minimum of interaction between the five. Neither he nor his other three associates knew anything of each-others personal details or circumstances – only coming together just before an assignment for briefing, planning and execution. Then it was *adios* till the next time.

Connections could be discovered and lead to trails that would be easily followed. It was an indispensable rule that had worked well over the past five years and one that Jack had never deviated from – insisting on its strict adherence.

Sharing and deliberating over the questionable jobs undertaken for J.F. Security Services served no purpose. Once completed, the jobs were best forgotten, and each member moved on with their private life. They were well-compensated for their dispassionate professionalism.

He believed that all was normal until he caught the news item about Miles Hathaway killed while playing polo the previous weekend. He wasn't one for keeping up with the news, but he knew enough that Jack had a business relationship with the man. Had that anything to do with it? He picked up the Perrier and was about to remove the cap.

"Trouble brewing!" informed one of his fellow employees, indicating with his head to the other end of the long crowded bar. Dodge let out a *here we go* sigh, re-screwed the loose cap, replaced the bottle on the counter, and then followed, gently shouldering his way through the fast-growing throng.

"You fucking whore! Bitch!"

The man being held back by his shoulders by two bouncers was screaming at a very attractive dark-haired woman, also being restrained by a third member of Dodge's team. She kicked out savagely, missing her assailant, instead catching one of the men controlling her target in the calf.

"Bastard yourself! You're just a waste of fucking space. You don't know how to treat a lady, you arsehole!" She was giving as good as she was getting. Little attention was given to the quarrel other than a small amused cluster in the immediate vicinity.

"Okay, now! Enough. We don't want any trouble here!" Dodge had to raise his voice due to the proximity of the band's speakers. The appearance of the big man quietened the two combatants momentarily. Then the woman screamed at the man again, evoking more verbal diatribe. Another wild kick failed to connect with anyone.

"Whore!"

"Pig!"

"Go on, mate... don't let her talk to you like that!" A couple of drunk male witnesses were offering suggestions.

"Kick him again, luv!" proposed a female observer.

"Scratch his eyes out! Don't let him call you names. Stick up for yo'self," yet another woman offered.

"I said, that'll be enough, now!" Dodge exclaimed and grabbed the man in a painful vice-like grip by his left elbow, immediately curbing his tirade.

"It's time for you to leave," he declared, and repeating a similar hold on the now quietened woman's right elbow, steered them away to the back of the club and through the stockroom to the rear fire exit. The back way out was always his way of dispensing with undesirables. Taking

[344]

troublemakers out of the front of the premises would give the wrong image.

"Want any help?" chuckled one of the crew.

Dodge shot him a, *do I look as though I need your help* look.

The three stepped out into the narrow back alleyway. One single wall lamp above the door illuminated a small area of the darkened space. Dodge released his hold on the woman and turned to the man.

"I suggest you two go home, and unless you're gonna behave next time… don't bother coming back," he said with a determined stare.

"What the…?" A sharp kick on his ankle made him turn back to the woman.

Suddenly, a strong hand covered his mouth, jerking his head rearward, and at the same time, he felt a sharp pang in his upper back. The assailant's powerful plunge of the thin narrow blade penetrated the right kidney under Dodge's ribs, followed immediately by two more thrusts with a twisting and jerking motion. The man stepped back, and Dodge dropped to his knees. The woman, meanwhile, had taken a covering position with her back against the exit door.

Dodge looked up at the woman – confusion and surprise across his face – then at the man standing in front of him holding the instrument of death. Neither the man nor the woman spoke. Slowly Dodge lost focus and pitched forward, slamming hard onto the stone surface.

After a cursory glance at both ends of the alley, the two conspirators walked calmly away in the direction of Coldharbour Lane.

39 October 6th, 1973

Tel Aviv, Israel

Avi Gershen's apartment was as Ray remembered when he last visited one day short of three years earlier. The bulky furnishings were functional and not stylish, reflecting a masculine choice denied a feminine touch. The tiled floor was bare except for a circular, patterned rug lying under a coffee table between a soft-cushioned leather sofa taking up most of the left-hand wall and two upholstered easy chairs. A medium-sized television sat on a small table under a plain-curtained window. A dark, open cabinet held a few books and a small selection of framed photographs next to an equally robust, wooden sideboard. A large oil painting of a mountain scene hung on the wall opposite the seating area – the only wall decoration in sight. The surprisingly neat and tidy surroundings enjoyed a measured degree of comfort without frills.

Dzorah, Simeon, Dalfon and Rani were already at the flat when Ray and Baqar arrived. Avi and Terach had met them at the border crossing and driven them to Avi's place in a newer and more comfortable Bedford snub-nosed van to the one Ray had been subjected to the first time he had joined the unit. Greetings were exchanged between Ray and the others. Then Ray caught them unawares.

"Lady and gentlemen, I'd like you to meet my very close and dear friend, Captain Baqar El Kordy of the Jordanian Army – Military Intelligence and National Security." There followed an awkward silence. Ray stood back and watched the group's collective surprise with amusement.

"Well, I'll be fucked!" Chortled Rani stepping forward and extending his hand to Baqar. "If you're a friend of Ray's, then you're also a friend of ours. Welcome!" His response prompted a similar reaction by the others steering Baqar further into the abode. Ray gave Avi a knowing wink. His Israeli friend returned a calming smile at the unprecedented meeting and acceptance of a sworn *foe* in their midst. They were to take on a common adversary, and maybe Baqar's involvement would mark a step – albeit a small symbolic one for the moment – towards reconciliation between two reluctant war-faring neighbours.

"I see Mrs Andelman is still looking after you?" Ray quipped, looking around at the tidiness as Avi led him to the kitchenette.

"You remembered," he laughed out. "And she's also cooked up a *Cholent* for us." He reached for a bottle of red-label Stolichnaya and two stemless glasses set on the counter. The others had already established that Baqar was a Christian and more than happy to try a *Maccabee* – a locally brewed beer – with them. Ray smiled at Dzorah, who appeared over-attentive towards the handsome Arab officer.

"Here," Avi said, passing Ray a full glass of the clear vodka. "I think we have a private toast first to Gila. When I last spoke with her over the phone a week before... When she mentioned you, my friend... there was something in her voice... Nah?" Ray tilted his head as if to say, *what?* "You can be honest with me," he added conspiratorially and quiet enough not to be overheard by the others.

"Yes, I confess. There was something between us," Ray replied softly and with a brief sad smile. "That's why that bastard's mine!" he added with clenched teeth.

"Okay, listen up!" Avi turned to face the rest over the kitchen counter. "We're here for two reasons. The first is to hold a wake for a dear departed…"

"Murdered!" interjected Dzorah.

"Yes… For one of our own, Gila. You should also know that Ray has removed the responsible son of a bitch… and our brothers in the Mossad have taken care of the others."

"Good on you, Ray," and, "he had it coming," remarks chimed in.

"As I was saying," Avi continued unabated, "we're here to celebrate Gila's life… not her death. We will eat, and we will drink, and we will remember."

"Hear! Hear!"

"Then, we will sit and discuss our mission planned for tomorrow evening." He concluded, "now come around, grab a bowl of Mrs Andelman's delicious stew and take a crust of her homemade bread. There's loads of beer, whisky and vodka." Ray stepped aside as the group made their way around into the kitchenette.

"Avi," he said, taking him by the arm and gently guiding him away. "Would you mind driving me to the cemetery?"

"Now?"

"Yes. Would you mind, before we start? I'd rather go tonight. Tomorrow we'll need to be focused."

"Sure, let's go," then to the others.

"Ray and I are nipping out for an hour. Look after our Jordanian guest," he added with a chuckle.

[348]

◆◆◆◆

Once again, Ray found himself standing at a grey-granite headstone gently illuminated by pale moonlight. He could not read the inscription etched in *Hebrew* under a hexagram depicting the *Star of David*. It was enough to know she was there, and he could visit. He had had a job to do before he could say his farewell. Avi had led him to the grave, then walked back to the car, leaving him alone.

"I'm sorry, I couldn't come earlier. I'm sure you'd understand...I had to do something first." He spoke in a whisper. "At least you can rest in peace knowing the people responsible for you being here have paid the ultimate price. There's one more who will also soon pay for what he did to you." He weighed the smooth pebble in his hand Avi had picked up for him as they walked through the cemetery.

"Avi says I should leave this for you. He said it's to ward off evil spirits as well as symbolising a memory." He leaned forward and carefully placed the stone among a row of others on top of the headstone. "I will always regret not having had more time together, but I won't ever forget you." He stepped back and looked up into the moonlit sky, and sighed.

How many more times am I to lose someone I care for?

He smiled a mournful smile, putting on his best effort to quell the anger within him. Ray stood for a long while staring hard at the headstone, picturing her face and remembering their too short intimacy, before turning and slowly walking away.

40 October 7th, 1973

Aabdeh, Northern Lebanon

The eight passengers were wearing headphones to shield against the uncomfortable loudness – close to a hundred *decibels* from the main rotor spinning four overhead blades driven by the *Sikorsky*'s powerful piston engine. They sat on either side, holding onto a buffeting rubber boat. The aircraft's side doors were left partially ajar to accommodate the sixteen-foot length of the ten-man craft. The resultant overhangs of almost five feet added to the noise level inside the cabin. The increased drag from the six-foot-wide inflatable side-up stowage further reduced the speed of the most recognisable helicopter – its distinctive hump once likened to a flying banana. The boat's weighty outboard engine was tied and ready to be winched down for a speedy attachment.

From embarkation to the planned drop-off beyond Lebanon's northern-most, Tripoli, the flight was estimated to take around ninety minutes. To avoid both being spotted from the shore and catching the aircraft's sound – which at night could be heard as far as eight miles distance – the two pilots took the extra precaution of swinging out twelve miles from the coastline. The evening's waning moon illuminated the water's surface allowing the experienced pilots – sitting in the cockpit

[350]

high above their passengers – to navigate their way without the benefit of still primitive night vision devices. Flying at night was always fraught with danger and left to the most experienced pilots.

Ray was seated with his back to the front of the aircraft to the right of Dalfon, who was to be the first to shimmy down onto the boat. Baqar was the third in, sitting next to Dzorah. Terach – sitting opposite Dalfon and out of view – would be the second man on board. Avi was next to him, with Rani and Simeon. Rapid deployment off the helicopter would be in alternate order practised several times earlier in the day. Stealth and speed were paramount.

The eight were dressed appropriately in black overalls tucked into rubber-soled boots. Balaclavas would be worn for the night's incursion. They would also benefit from the latest USA produced *Night Vision Goggles*. The spooky-looking indispensable gadgets amplified ambient light with the two protruding tubes strapped to the head. The image-intensifier tubes gave the wearer a clear circular view in a green hue.

Weapons were restricted to knives and suppressed sidearms with ample addition of three spare magazines except for the team's sniper, Simeon. He carried his trusty *L42A1* sniper rifle – a 303 British Lee-Enfield conversion. Besides his favoured Browning pistol securely fastened in his shoulder holster, Ray also carried Gila's Walther PPK. Other than two two-way radio devices and a length of rope, they would be travelling light and unhindered by bulky weaponry.

The pilot's voice – speaking in Hebrew – came over the headphone, followed by a sensation of weightlessness felt by the passengers as the helicopter banked right. Five minutes later, the craft started to descend, eventually hovering some six feet above a calm water's surface.

The rubber inflatable was immediately man-handled out onto the water instantly, followed by a nimble Dalfon rappelling down a rope, then Terach. The two-hundred-and-five pound outboard engine was carefully lowered using an overhead winch and mounted by the two men onto the stern wooden transom board. Ray followed next, with Avi immediately behind him. Once the remaining four members were on board, the team was away within ten minutes. Ray and Avi took up the forward position side-by-side as the vessel skimmed across the water at thirty knots towards shore – six miles on. The well-fabricated craft provided extra cushioning for its occupants through two additional chambers beneath the gunwale called *speed skags*.

Upon completing the mission, they would retrace their steps and return as they arrived, waiting out the helicopter's pick-up planned for four the following morning. Ray glanced at his watch.

The luminous dial read – 9:05 pm.

The darkened silhouette of the rocky shoreline rapidly came into view. Ray raised his arm, and Terach immediately cut off the engine. They silently drifted forward, straining to hear for any unwelcome activity. It was calm and tranquil – the only sound a gentle brushing of water against the rubber hull. Ray raised his arm again and was passed a long-handled wooden paddle. With decisive coordinated strokes, the team proceeded to row towards land. Twenty minutes later, Rani and Dalfon jumped out on either side of the craft, grabbed hold of the length of rope fastened to the gunwale, then pulled it onto a small stretch of sandy beach. The remaining six clambered out and deployed, kneeling around the boat.

Ray raised his arm again, and the eight picked up the craft by the rope fastening, hurried to a large rocky outcrop and set it down gently out of view. It was agreed that Ray would lead the mission.

"It's your idea, after all," Avi had reasoned in agreement.

The Israeli Mossad provided the intelligence for the objective location, layout and security strength in return for the details of the four ex-SAS members behind Shaul Feuerman's murder – brokered by Ethan Schulman, the Israeli Ambassador. A favour-for-a-favour.

Ray checked his watch again – 9:21 pm.

He removed a circular metal box from a top pocket and flipped open the lid revealing a prismatic compass. Orientating the instrument to line up the luminous needle with north, he cast his eyes in a northeast direction, picked out a distant landmark, and then pointed out the blackened shape to the rest of the team. They would be leap-frogging their way from geographic feature to feature in the semi-darkness. There was sufficient ambient light to proceed without the night vision goggles.

With Ray in the lead, the team moved off in single file, leaving Terach behind to watch the inflatable. Even though the danger of the craft being unearthed was unlikely, Ray considered it too risky. They were too far north in a hostile region just eight miles south of the Syrian border –exposed and vulnerable to chance its discovery. Terach had lost the toss and reluctantly accepted the responsibility to remain behind and miss out on the *bloody action!*

The narrow coastal strip wedged in between the Mediterranean Sea and the mountainous terrain stretching from the north to the south of the country – locally called the *Sahil* – was at its widest north of Tripoli. Fareed Al Safadi's villa compound was at the prominent Mount Lebanon's foothills – a cedar studded mountain range rising in parts to over eight thousand feet. The near five-mile trek would take around one-and-a-half hours across the unfamiliar landscape and in the dark.

"Keep a steady pace and be careful as you climb over the uneven ground, and be mindful when stepping on branches or anything else that might break under your weight. Watch out for loose stones and rocks... We don't need anyone spraining an ankle. Finally, absolute silence, no talking. Sound does carry, and we don't want to attract unwanted attention." Ray had instructed the team only to receive an immediate peppering of jibes from the highly-trained unit.

"Ray thinks he's back in the Oman mountains, and we're members of his ramshackle outfit!" laughed Simeon out loud, evoking a hearty response from the group and a chuckle from Ray.

"My apologies, lady and gentlemen, for overlooking your extraordinary skills in *urban* encounters. My Omani chaps were part-man and part-mountain goat, and still, I needed to remind them," countered Ray, gently enforcing the need for care on the team.

"Touché!" chipped in Avi.

The humour among the eight disguised the underlying gritty determination to exact payment for Gila's murder and the sickening manner in which she had been killed.

The trek's initial phase took them over an area of sedimentary beach rock before reaching the main north-to-south highway. As anticipated, the road was deserted other than a heavily decorated truck heading north – the loud *jingling* of the traditional chains hanging off its bumpers breaking into the stillness of the night.

Once over the main road, they made their way through olive groves and fruit orchards, staying well clear of possible local contact – most of which was already behind locked doors for the night. The team had maintained a steady pace on reaching the edge of the arable district and proceeded up a gentle slope meandering through tall pine trees and sparse patches of undergrowth.

Ray would momentarily halt the team at intervals as he rechecked the compass to direct the next leg, always moving northeast. A half-hour or so later, the incline increased, slowing their progress and making the hike more challenging. The use of hands was occasionally required to negotiate a route over precipitous parts of rocky terrain, careful to avoid hazardous roots and jagged rocks.

The six continued to follow their resolute guide ever upwards — no recognisable trail insight. Nature hadn't etched a convenient route. After a particularly steep stretch, they came to a level expanse alongside a gravelled roadway.

"This must be it," whispered Ray, crouching behind a tree, as Avi and Baqar joined him. "The compound can't be far."

Ray removed the Browning from his holster and a silencer from his trouser pocket, prompting the others to do the same. Only too aware of how far sound travels at night, Ray used his clothing to muffle the metallic sound as he cocked the weapon and chambered a round leaving the safety engaged. He watched the others fuss over their guns. The break allowed everyone to catch their breaths before continuing armed and ready for action. Ray caught Baqar watching him and gave him an assured nod. Baqar smiled back awkwardly — slight nervousness apparent.

The *hooting* of an owl resonating through the night air momentarily distracted Ray's line of thought. It always fascinated him how sound travelled farther at night — something to do with the refraction of sound waves.

I should have paid more attention in Science class!

He closed his eyes for a moment indulging in the distinctive aroma of leaf and soil. All around, the forest was shrouded in silence. Even the birds were quiet. He imagined them perched on branches high above, beaks open, eyes closed and breathing gently in unison with him, replenishing muscles with much-needed oxygen for the morning's breakfast hunt.

The arrival of fragmented clouds diminished the moonlight beaming through the trees requiring the seven to put on the night vision devices strapped to their belts.

"Okay," Ray touched Avi on the shoulder.

Giving the track a wide berth, they moved quietly and cautiously through the trees, making sure that each step they took wouldn't alert unwanted attention. A few steps on Rani's foot caught a root, and as he stumbled, he grabbed onto a stout branch holding on tightly while he regained his balance. The team paused, listening, hearts pounding. The woodland seemed ominously quiet, just the gentle sound of a gentle breeze brushing through the leaves. Ray held his breath, straining his ears.

Nothing! No movement!

Fifteen minutes later, Ray caught the pungent smell of cigarettes and raised his arm, halting the team's progress. Turning to Avi, he indicated for him to follow, leaving the rest behind. The track had led to an open expanse in front of high-walled premises lit with two bright pillar mounted lights. Two four-wheeled drive vehicles were parked facing each other in front of a double-gated entrance denying immediate access. Ray had anticipated using a commandeered vehicle for an easier and quicker return to the boat.

Avi tapped Ray on the shoulder and put up two fingers confirming the two shadowy figures leaning and smoking against the right-hand car – predictable Kalashnikov submachine guns slung over their shoulders. The building was equally well lit up and positioned some distance beyond the gates accessed by a straight driveway lined with palm trees.

"First things first," whispered Ray as the group crouched around him. "There are two at the front." Simeon tapped the Enfield. "No, too risky. It'll need to be silent – in close. We don't know who and how many are on the other side of the gate," Ray responded.

"Knives?" said Avi.

"Knives," agreed Ray.

"Dalfon, you take the left and Rani, you'll need to back-track and cross over the road unseen before coming in from the right. Simeon, some pretty decent trees should give you a good position with a line of sight down the property's left. The palms on either side of the drive prevent full field of vision, but as the external door into the generator room is accessed from the left of the house... our approach should be covered." Dalfon removed the length of rope looped over his shoulder and handed it to Dzorah.

Without a further word, Rani immediately made his way back as Ray, Avi, and Baqar returned to Ray and Avi's earlier position on the edge of the clearing. Dalfon, Simeon and Dzorah moved off to the left. There was no need for further discussion. Each member knew what they had to do.

Rani made sure he had covered a sufficient distance before crossing over into the tree-line opposite. He took his time, carefully avoiding a sound as he neared the extreme right edge of the wall some hundred metres along from the entrance and well out of sight of the two hostiles by the vehicles.

Ray had decided to go in before midnight, counting on both Frasier and Al Safadi to be up still and catch the security off guard. According to the Mossad, the compound had around twenty combatants on site – most of whom were young untrained Palestinians welcome for the hard-to-come-by cash. The odds didn't faze Ray's well-trained and experienced unit. Unbeknown to the hapless crew, the Israelis included one of their own with a fuel delivery three days earlier. The property was too far out from the nearest grid and was reliant on a generator for its electricity supply – a factor that would play a pivotal role in the assault.

Dying men didn't always go down quietly. When Ray was laying out the incursion plan, he enlightened the group of the old 5 Ps British Army maxim – proper planning prevents piss-poor performance! Having intelligence beforehand eliminated the need to keep a sentry alive for time-absorbing and possible noisy interrogation.

Ray watched as Rani got into position, removed the night vision device, strapped it back on his belt, then unsheathed a stiletto-style commando knife and gripped it in his right hand. Dalfon was already prepared at the opposite end of the perimeter wall. With their backs tight against the concrete wall, the two stepped around and slowly sidled their way to the edge of the illuminated patch in front of the gate. It seemed like an age before they coordinated a silent move across to the cars. The two guards continued to chatter away, unaware of the two killers now close by. Rani and Dalfon held back, waiting for their opportunity, when one of the guards suddenly pushed off the vehicle, inadvertently releasing the weapon's grip on his shoulder and sent it clattering onto the gravelled ground. The other man laughed at his colleague's clumsiness exposing his back at the same time to Dalfon.

Both Israelis sprang out in cat-like fashion, gripped the men's mouths from behind and in one fluid movement drove the sharp, steel-hardened blades upwards into the hearts of the unsuspecting sentries. They slowly moved back, collapsing the bodies and placing them into a sitting position with their backs against the cars' front wheels. Taking a wide return, Dalfon hurried back to the gate and peered through the railings. Two men were walking the grounds some distance away, seemingly oblivious to the goings-on outside. He returned to Rani, lighting two cigarettes he'd taken off one of the guards.

"Place these in their mouths," he said with a big grin. "Should anyone look through from the other side of the gate, they'll see the smoke and assume our boys are alive and kicking!"

Ray joined the two operatives by the vehicles while Avi and Baqar hurried over to Simeon, who was already climbing up a tree with one end of the rope tied to his belt. He climbed onto a large horizontal branch some five metres above the ground. Leaning against the hard bark of the thick trunk, he planted his feet firmly against a bough growing up into a web of limbs and offshoots into the sky above. He pulled up the rope and curled it around the branch, then rested the heavy, hammer-forged barrel of his *L42A1* bolt-action rifle on a sturdy limb convenient for his need. Satisfied with the field of fire his position gave him, he gave a *thumbs up* to the three below.

Slowly and with little movement of his body, Simeon rotated the bolt handle anti-clockwise and drew it towards him, releasing one of the five rounds into the chamber. Just as deliberately, he pushed the bolt forwards, turning it clockwise into a locked position. Camouflaged within the full leaf of the tree, he nestled down comfortably, satisfied with his concealment. He was now ready for a kill.

"Did they have a two-way?" asked Ray, referring to communication with the compound.

"No, nothing," replied Rani.

"Okay, then, Dalfon, you won't need to stay here. The three of us will sweep up the right-hand side."

With his back to the wall and interlocking his hands on one knee, Rani took Ray's right foot and hoisted him up the perimeter wall – at the far right-hand corner. Ray pulled up and held himself on his elbows while he peered into the grounds. Thankfully no spikes or other lethal deterrents were running along the top of the wall. He glimpsed over both shoulders, then using his elbows at the same time lifting his right leg, he raised himself and stretched out flat along the top of the wall. He strained to hear for any signs of movement near his position. An owl sounded somewhere in the distance. Night crickets were chirping intermittently, calling for female contact.

Good, no dogs!

An illuminated, gravel driveway led onto a forecourt in front of an imposing square-shaped two-storey house. The generous-sized property was extensively lawned and landscaped with a variety of manicured trees, bushes and assorted plants. He motioned for Dalfon to join him, then lying on their stomachs and facing each other, Ray and Dalfon reached down and pulled Rani up until he managed a grip with both hands.

Ray dropped silently onto the hardened grassy area below and, remaining in the shadows, paused momentarily, then gestured for the other two to come down. At this point, Avi, Baqar and Dzorah were also inside the grounds and about to make their way to the generator room.

Ray felt the familiar sense of adrenaline coursing through his body as he removed the pistol from his holster and released the safety – his heartbeat quickened. With Ray taking the lead, the three – using the foliage as cover – moved gingerly towards the house.

They had covered half the distance when the air was again thick with smoke from the pervasive stench of cigarettes. Ray had never taken up the habit and couldn't understand the insatiable reliance on nicotine in the region. In that instance, the unpleasantness was a warning. The three moved back into the darkness of the foliage as a man stepped out from the bushes fiddling with the buttoned flies of his trousers. A cigarette was dangling from his mouth – his rifle hung by the strap off his left wrist. Ray tapped Dalfon on the arm. He wasted no time pocketing his pistol and drawing out his knife. He stepped around Ray, grabbed the man under the chin from behind, and jerked his head back. He plunged the blade into the back and upwards into the heart with one swift practised movement.

"My gut's on fire. I don't know what was in that fuckin' curry we...!" Another man emerging from the undergrowth – suddenly confronted by a dark form holding onto his colleague – cut short his complaint. A mere gun for hire and untrained, he hesitated, unsure of what he was seeing. It was enough for Ray. Two bullets dead centre chest threw him backwards onto the grass. The two bodies were quickly pulled into the underbrush and out of sight.

Meanwhile, Avi, Baqar and Dzorah were also using the darkened area of foliage running the full inside length of the perimeter wall on their approach to the house. They had managed to cover half the distance when a figure appeared at the door to the generator room. They remained frozen to the spot as they watched him pull a chair away from the wall to the left of the entrance and sit down with his rifle lain across his knees.

Avi could see no way of approaching near enough to be sure of a kill shot without being seen. Certain that Simeon watched their every move, Avi slowly raised his arm and pointed. Simeon was indeed watching and smiled a cool smile as he panned the rifle around to the seated guard. Three seconds later, a 7.62mm calibre bullet passed cleanly through the man's chest and the chair's top rail, striking the concrete wall behind. The dead man's rifle slid onto the ground as he slumped back spread-eagled.

Keeping his eye fixed on the scope, Simeon immediately chambered a second round in time to catch another man appear around the corner of the building. Whether he had been disturbed or just happened to come around would never be known as a second copper-alloy bullet slammed into his chest, killing him instantly. The three waited briefly, listening before they hurried over to the two men and immediately dragged them unceremoniously into the bushes and out of view.

Avi tried the door while Baqar and Dzorah kept a sharp lookout. It was unlocked. At that moment, Ray joined him with Rani.

"Okay, the front's secured, Dalfon's watching the door," Ray said. "How many did you take care of?"

"Two," replied Avi, casting a glance over his shoulder at the undergrowth.

"That's six, leaving around fourteen." Ray looked at his watch – 11:04 pm. "The ground floor is pretty well lit up, so I'm assuming our boys are still up."

"I suggest there maybe three or four inside, not counting household staff, and the rest must be in the quarters behind the garage," said Avi.

"Okay, they're our priority. We'll need to neutralise them before going in." He turned to Rani. "It's over to you. Make sure you first secure the internal door. Our friends," he was referring to the Mossad, "confirmed it could be bolted from the inside. When we're ready, I'll press the walkie-talkie button twice. That's when you shut down the generator. Three, you switch it back on."

"Understood. Don't worry," responded a confident Rani.

"Dzorah, you remain outside. Make sure no one tries

to enter. It might be an idea to get inside the brush. Stay hidden, okay?"

She nodded and immediately backed up.

Ray eyed the remainder of the team.

"Are we ready, gentlemen?"

41 October 7th, 1973

Aabdeh, Northern Lebanon

Fareed Al Safadi put the glass on the mantelpiece and, using a guillotine, placed the head of the *Corona* into the hole and, in one quick chop, sliced off the cap. Biting the end off with his teeth – as was so often depicted in Hollywood films – would tear and unravel the wrapper giving the smoker an uncomfortable mouthful of tobacco. Such a habit was not worthy of a serious cigar smoker. He leaned over and took a piece of wood, alight at one end, and lit up. He inhaled deeply, then exhaled a thick plume of smoke into the air and threw the firewood back onto the fire.

Clenching the cigar between his teeth, he picked up his glass, returned to the coffee table and replaced the guillotine in the ornate wooden cigar box before sitting back in the armchair. He downed the remnants of his drink, then reached over for the distinctive crystal decanter – shaped in the form of a flask – and removed the top.

"You know, Jack, you could have a very good life here," he said as he poured out a full measure of a Louis XIII cognac. "Perhaps it's time you had a change. After all, you're not getting any younger." He replaced the top loosely and pushed the decanter towards Jack Frasier –

[364]

his house guest since he abruptly left the UK.

"I don't doubt that, Fareed, but what would I do here?"

"I need a good, dependable and experienced man at my side. That fool Shaheen did well enough, but he lacked style. Too rough around the edges…, if you know what I mean? It still baffles me how the hell he managed to get himself killed. I can only assume it was linked to the IRA fiasco," he muttered. "Never mind, we move on. What's that famous saying of *Omar Khayyam*'s…, something about *the moving finger writes and moves on once it has written.*"

"Arabic would be a problem," Frasier countered. "We Scots have enough bloody trouble with our own language, let alone learning a second one," he quipped.

"We have enough people here who could act as your interpreter until you grasp the language. It's not difficult," persisted Al Safadi.

The idea of staying put was growing on him since learning of Miles Hathaway's demise. He was certain his death was no accident. It just didn't smell right. And yet, would they have dared to take him out, or was it just a freak accident? How could they have achieved it anyway? He came off his horse as he was playing a ball. He'd seen enough games to know it was impossible to contrive. Had he been drugged? That was the only explanation…, yet drugs weren't that precise in timing. All that nonsense when administered, *it only takes ten seconds*… was a lot of rubbish. Every person's constitution was different – reaction times and severity varied. No, he concluded, he wasn't drugged before the game. So how was it done?

Miles Hathaway was an important man; questions would be asked. Although it was ruled an accidental death – case closed. It surely wouldn't have led them to take such drastic action? However, it was all too convenient, and it could explain why he had been unable to get hold of Simon Dodge. He had also disappeared – as had the other three! There was also the question of how little they knew and could connect him. He was lucky. He managed to get away before meeting a similar fate and had already made mental provisions to close down the business and sell the apartment. Mary could sort it all out. He would provide her with a *power of attorney* – she would benefit financially. He would see to that. It was only material assets, nothing of sentimental value. But then there was Melanie. He would miss her as he knew she would miss him. He would write her a letter explaining why he could not see her. Not being with her and seeing her grow up would be the most difficult burden to bear.

"It's certainly tempting, Fareed," he said, stretching out his legs and settling back in the chair with a full glass of the cognac. He concentrated his thoughts on the fire – watching the dancing flames and listening to the hissing and crackling as the logs burned.

"I spoke with the marquis earlier today. His people are working on the Africa project," said Al Safadi after a while.

"How do you mean?"

"Protocols had been agreed and put in place in the event one of the principals were to… how should I put it… unable to continue their participation."

"You mean if they were dead?" Frasier spoke succinctly.

"Of course, Miles' unexpected passing is regrettable…"

"Regrettable! How easy it is to dismiss the man with a simple adjective," mused Frasier.

"Now, now, my friend. I know how much he meant to you… as he did to me. I haven't forgotten how he helped me with my business… got me started. But as I said earlier, we have to move on, protect our interests."

"You said protocols."

"Yes. Contracts are being revised, re-routed and re-distributed among the surviving members of the cartel."

"You're going to become an even wealthier man, Fareed." He spoke with a hint of sarcasm ignored by the thick-skinned Lebanese businessman.

"It'll make up for the loss I incurred over the IRA debacle. And don't forget, I've agreed to reimburse the organisation as you advised. The additional..." He was cut short as the room plunged into darkness.

"What the...?" Frasier reacted.

"It happens. The clowns most probably forgot to top up the tank," responded Al Safadi.

"What if...?"

"Calm yourself, my friend. I have enough security to take care of the foolish aspirations of one or two ambitious infiltrators. We are perfectly safe here. Far away from possible threats. Now come, I can see well enough from the fire to top up our glasses." Frasier leant forward, offering his empty glass.

"Well, I suppose I'll have to take you up on your offer," said the director of the soon to be dissolved J.F. Security Services, sitting back with a refill.

"Then that's settled," Al Safadi responded with a big grin and raised his glass in the semi-darkness as a toast to their new association. Just then, the power came back on, bathing the room in bright light.

"What did I tell you!" exclaimed Al Safadi and took a long draw on his cigar.

The door suddenly burst open, and three figures clad head-to-toe in black entered the room, pointing their pistols at the two startled occupants.

"What...? Who...? Who are you?" A pasty-faced Fareed Al Safadi rose quickly from his chair and backed away from the intruders. Frasier started to move, then remained seated with a blank expression – showing no emotion. He instinctively knew what was happening.

"I demand to know what…?" Al Safadi didn't finish as he grunted and staggered back from the bullet's impact. He looked down, dazed at a deep scarlet rapidly seeping through his starched white shirt. A coldness hit him for a brief moment as he grasped the reality, then his knees gave way, and he slumped to the floor.

Avi lowered his pistol.

"He was talking too much!"

Ray removed his balaclava as he walked over and sat in the empty chair recently vacated opposite Frasier. Avi and Baqar followed suit and remained standing behind Ray.

"It had to be you!" Frasier spoke in a quiet voice. Part of him had already resigned to his impending fate.

"Allow me to introduce you to Mr Avi Gershen of Israeli Special Forces." Fareed Al Safadi's executioner gave Frasier a mock salute. "And Captain Baqar El Kordy of the Jordanian Army's Military Intelligence and National Security," Ray said as he slowly unscrewed the silencer from the Browning pistol while maintaining a fixed stare at the Scotsman.

"I don't need to tell you." Ray gently blew into the suppressor before pocketing it, then continued. "I'm sure you're aware that your employer is no longer around, having met with an unfortunate accident while playing his favourite sport." Ray holstered his pistol while Frasier shifted uncomfortably. His brows bumped together in a scowl.

"You expect me to talk?"

Ray ignored him.

"Your band of four accomplices has also been taken care of… by our Israeli friends, I should add… For their part in killing Shaul Feuerman." He removed Gila's Walther PPK from his pocket. "They also paid the price

[368]

for killing my partner."

"I uh…, it couldn't be helped. She was not the target… It was unfortunate." Ray frowned at the indifferent remark. Then in an unexpected act of defiant bravado, "Your eyes betray you, Captain Kazan." He had nothing to lose and would have his say. "It would appear Miss Levenson was more than just your associate!"

Ray calmly slid the bolt back – engaging a round in the chamber – and levelled the pistol at the man.

"Yes, she was," he replied coolly.

The first round thumped into Jack Frasier's chest, followed by a second between the eyes, causing a gaping hole instantly filled with blood.

THE STORY CONTINUES

COLD DECEIT

J.J. Kaminski

For an excerpt, turn the page

1 July 4ᵗʰ, 1975
Southern Oregon, USA

The dark-brown *Ford Bronco* manoeuvred its way up the stony incline guided by a line of red-and-white tape strung between metal rods embedded in coarse, grassy soil. The off-roader eventually crossed the crest of a ridge bringing into view the extent of overwhelming destruction and carnage spread out wide over the rugged, rocky terrain. With a gentle touch on the driver's arm, the passenger indicated that he stop the vehicle.

The young man behind the wheel audibly gasped in horror. The second occupant surveyed the tragic scene in stoic silence. An unsettled while later, the tall, lanky man in his late forties with an expressionless lined face opened the passenger door and climbed out of the vehicle. He slowly ran his fingers through his wiry hair as his trained eyes took stock of the scattered sight through gold-rimmed spectacles. Leaning back against the Bronco, he removed a packet of *Marlboro Gold* from his jacket pocket and opened the flip-top. He pulled out a cigarette, lit it with a butane lighter, and then pondered briefly before replacing the packet and lighter. He drew in deeply, feeling the familiar warmth in his lungs, then, with a resigned shake of his head, exhaled a thick-blue cloud of smoke.

[1]

"I'll walk from here!" He turned to the driver and closed the passenger door. The driver didn't respond – gripping tightly onto the steering wheel – staring incredulously at the haunting sight.

Henry Grover took in a long breath, then exhaled heavily, and with lips pressed tightly in a grimace, made his way to a white canvas tent erected on the east side of the fragments-strewn area. There was no escaping the lingering smell of smouldering flesh, decomposing human remains, metal still hot to the touch, the toxic stench of aviation fuel and melted plastic. The day's warmth had aided the congealing of blood spread over the debris and around the area. He tended to smoke more at crash sites. It helped mask the unpleasantness.

A Lead Investigator with the *National Transportation Safety Board* – the U.S. Government's independent agency responsible for civil transportation accident investigations – Henry Grover would never be able to erase the memory of the three crash sites he had been involved with during his eight-year tenure since formation of the agency. Even the carnage he had witnessed during a two-year posting to Korea as a young fighter pilot had not prepared him for his first assignment. Had he grown immune to the horrors over his tenure?

No! He didn't believe he would ever succeed in shaking off the troubling reminders of his vocation. He had considered a new line of work more than once, only to be persuaded to remain with the agency. He had a talent: a skill for recreating the disasters and forming a clear image of what had happened. He was needed, and there had to be closure. Too many conflicting concerns were pushing for an answer. Angry grieving families, aviation authorities, politicians with self-interest agendas, insurance companies, not to mention the airline's fear over the potential costs. Who was to blame? More often than not, it was either a case of human error or a part failure from fatigue.

Halfway across, something caught his eye. He bent down and plucked a white teddy bear from under a scorched seat cushion. In stark contrast to its surroundings, the toy was surprisingly pristine with the maker's label attached, suggesting it had been purchased at the airport before departure. The investigator paused and glanced around before shrugging off the notion of spotting its less fortunate owner. It didn't pay to become emotionally involved. He would have to take comfort in the thought that he was the proud father of two healthy teenage daughters. Clutching the bear, he continued towards the operation's temporary onsite centre.

The wreckage stretched over a wide area just north of *I5*, the *Pacific Highway* about 18 miles north of *Medford* – a city in southern Oregon, USA. To the west and just over two miles lay a small farming community ironically named *Independence*, whose population numbered a mere 301 recorded in the 1970 census. The aircraft narrowly missed the *Meadow's* farm and ploughed into the elevated rocky landscape known locally as *Sky Creek*.

"What have we got?" he said as his slightly unkempt *go-team* deputy approached – the senior leading the first group onsite and coordinating the initial field investigation. In his early forties, John Martinez was a second-generation Hispanic American balding and a little on the heavy side – for which he jokingly blamed his wife's cooking.

"*Crimson Air* domestic Flight CM822 – carrying 131 passengers and six crew – flew out from Dallas, Texas at local time 11:30 hours. Scheduled ETA at Portland Oregon International Airport at 1340 hours. You need to allow for the two-hour time difference from Texas being ahead. A total distance of 1,620 miles and an estimated

[3]

flight time of a little over four hours," replied Martinez. Grover could always count on his meticulous-for-details deputy having the facts at his fingertips.

Grover glanced at his watch – 6:56 pm.

Almost five-and-a-half hours ago, he had been nursing a cup of sweet black coffee at his desk in the Washington HQ when the call came in. A fast taxi ride, one hour by helicopter, a flight in a recently commissioned *Learjet 35* into a private airfield outside Medford, and the final leg in the waiting Bronco had brought the Lead Investigator to his fourth assignment – and by what he was already observing, potentially the most devastating.

"We're about 230 miles distance from the airport, so it's safe to assume the aircraft was still some way away when it encountered the problem. It would have been at its cruising height and not have commenced its descent," continued the deputy. "We arrived just over two hours ago. By then, the fires had been by-and-large, doused by the firefighters out of Medford, but not before causing pretty awful and extensive damage…, as you can imagine. The plane was scheduled for a return flight after an hour's stopover, so, unfortunately, the plane's fuel tanks were over half full. Most of the spillage came from the left-wing when it split in two on impact with the tree-line." He gestured in the direction with his head.

Henry Grover cast an eye towards the woodland. What was once a vibrant summer brown and spreading green canopy was now a collection of lifeless posts of charcoal and scorched earth.

"The fire brigade took some time to find a way up here and eventually managed to bring it under control… But by then, there was significant damage," he confirmed. "The fire spread rapidly, taking out quite a tract of the vegetation. You can't see it all from here. As for the plane? The cockpit came to rest wedged in the trees. It suffered the most from the ensuing firestorm." The senior investigator would be acquainting himself soon enough with the full extent of the damage.

"Have you been in contact with air traffic control, Portland?"

"We've set up a field phone and have established a connection through the local exchange. The senior traffic controller, Dick Brock, is on standby and expecting your call."

"Okay," he nodded and sighed loudly, then continued to walk onto the tent – Martinez by his side.

Henry Grover paused at the entrance and turned to survey the flurry of activity around the site. The passengers and crew's removal appeared to be well underway, with several technical specialists also inspecting, taking photos, and recording information – trained eyes looking for any evidential detail. The source is where the team would find clues to how and why, not just in the lab.

"Who's heading the recovery effort? I see there are a few people other than us out there."

"An independent crew out of LA. They came up by helicopter and got straight to it. A guy called Gus Jefferson is running the show."

"Yes, I know him," responded Grover. "He's got a good reputation. A good team!" The job of collecting, tagging and bagging the bodies, body parts, and personal effects was a gruesome task.

"They are being assembled and stored in an empty warehouse in Medford. The city council has been very cooperative," added the deputy.

Clearing away the bodies and human remains took priority. Once the site had been dehumanised, it would be a matter of gathering every scrap and performing meticulous and detached forensic work.

[5]

"Black Boxes?" He asked about the flight data and cockpit voice recorders usually stowed in the aircraft's tail. The bright-orange shoebox-sized units were known by the misnomer - black box.

"Nothing yet. Still looking. It appears the tail took the brunt, and the remnants are spread out pretty wide. Hopefully, we'll locate them soon."

In her late twenties, a woman sitting at a portable, folding table with a pair of horn-rimmed glasses perched on the end of her nose looked up as Grover set foot in the onsite H.Q.

"Hi, boss! Glad you could make it!" she said with a grin.

"Thanks, Jean! I see you've already got stuck into it!" responded Grover, smiling warmly. Jean Davis was one of his able-bodied team members, meticulous and dogged in her work, and with whom Grover had worked for the past four years. She gave an approving smile and turned her attention back to the table.

"What security do we have?"

"Oregon's state police was on the scene soon after the local sheriff's office and immediately took charge. One or two of the local boys couldn't stop puking."

"It's understandable," muttered the senior investigator under his breath. "Who could ever get used to this?" he added as he raised his leg and bent his knee, then stubbed out the cigarette butt on the leather sole of his shoe. He looked around, then tossed the spent cigarette into a nearby metal bin. At that moment, a gritty and tough-looking man in his early-forties wearing the dark/light blue combination uniform of the Oregon State Police and sporting the traditional *smokey bear* hat entered the tent.

"Ah! Captain!" acknowledged Martinez. "There you are. Let me introduce Henry Grover, our Senior Investigator."

[6]

"Captain Dave Moore, Oregon State Police," the policeman said as he shook the Lead Investigator's hand.

"Pleased to meet you," responded Grover. "Tell me, how many troopers do you have onsite?"

"At the moment…, ten," he replied.

"How are they bearing up? It can't be easy for the first-timers," suggested Grover.

"I admit it's the first time for me too… A bit gruesome, to be sure, but we have a job to do, and my boys will handle it. It's not that we're in the thick of it… only providing peripheral control and security."

"I suggest you organise more people. I'm afraid the word's already out, and we'll soon be having to cope with sightseers. We can't have anyone contaminating the site. Unfortunately, from our experience, souvenir-hunters tend to materialise out of nowhere and could unwittingly walk away with a vital piece of evidence." Although most citizens were considerate from Grover's experience, there were always ignorant eager individuals to contend with. "You'll also have to be prepared to work through the night. There's a lot to do."

"I understand. I'll get straight onto it." He immediately excused himself and left the tent, barking instructions into his walkie-talkie.

"We'll need to get the place lit up before it gets dark… What time is sunset?"

"Around nine," replied Martinez. "The equipment is already on route out of Portland with four generators and enough fuel to keep us going for a while."

"It looks like a wide area," remarked the senior man.

"I made sure to arrange excess. Don't worry. The place will be flooded with light."

"What's the weather forecast?"

"Dry, thankfully," replied Martinez with a sigh of relief. A rainfall would greatly hinder an investigation and

[7]

potentially contaminate vital evidence – not to mention the added unpleasantness in working conditions.

"Okay, good. Can you connect me with air traffic control?" Martinez busied himself with the radio.

"He's on the line," confirmed the deputy after a while and held out the receiver. Realising he was still holding the bear, Grover propped it against the radio and accepted the handset. The toy would remain there until the owner could be identified – a further reminder of the importance of finding the answer.

"Hello, Henry Grover, NTSB here!" he said.

"Good afternoon. Dick Brock, senior air traffic controller. I was on duty during the incident with the Crimson aircraft," replied a gravelly voice on the other end of the phone.

"What can you tell me?"

"The *Mayday* distress call came in at just after 1300 hours. The aircraft was approximately 325 miles out. We had taken over the flight five minutes earlier as it crossed into the state over the northwest corner of Nevada... The pilot insisted a huge explosion rocked the plane and threw it out of control... That is, whatever caused the problem. It would appear they lost power from two of the three tail-mounted engines."

"Is there anything else you can tell me?"

"Not a great deal. As you can imagine, the usual spate of back-and-forths with a final, *we're going down*. It was all a bit short – only some five minutes from receiving the Mayday to radio silence. It's created quite a shock here!"

"Do you have a copy recording we could have?"

"Yes. Would you like for me to get it over to you at the site?"

"I'd appreciate it if you would. Thanks!"

"It's an extremely sad event. We're all pretty shaken up over here... First time..."

And hopefully, the last, thought a woeful Grover.

"Anyway... please don't hesitate to call again should you have any more questions... I shan't be leaving for a while!"

"I won't... and thank you."

The deputy raised an eyebrow.

"Did I catch him say something about an explosion?"

"Let's not yet jump to any conclusions, John," responded Grover, as he replaced the receiver in its cradle, then reached into his jacket for the packet of *Marlboro Gold*.

"First things first, I need to inspect the site!"